FAERIE TALE

also by Raymond E. Feist

DAUGHTER OF THE EMPIRE (with Janny Wurts)

A DARKNESS AT SETHANON

SILVERTHORN

MAGICIAN

RAYMOND E. FEIST
FAERIE TALE

Doubleday

NEW YORK

1988

Library of Congress Cataloging-in-Publication Data
Feist, Raymond E.
Faerie tale.
I. Title.
PS3556.E446F3   1987   813'.54   87-10113
ISBN 0-385-23623-9

One of life's truly rarest treasures is friendship. I count myself exceedingly fortunate in this regard. My friends have given of themselves above and beyond the call, in far too many ways to recount, but, most important, in love, support, and acceptance. I shall never be their equal in generosity.

But as a humble token of appreciation, this book is dedicated to:

The Original Thursday Nighters:
Steve A., Jon, Anita, Alan, Tim, Rich, Dave,
Ethan, Jeff, Lorri, Steve B., and Bob
(and April, for I can't seem to
remember a time when she wasn't there)

back when April & Steve's house was Steve & Jon's apartment and we all sweated finals, experimental results, orals, dissertation defenses, finding jobs, the triumphs and the failures, the pain, the love, and the growing . . . together.

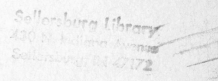

ACKNOWLEDGMENTS

My deep appreciation to:

April and Steve Abrams, Richard Freese, Ethan Munson, Richard Spahl, Adrian Zackheim, Jim Moser, Lou Aronica, Pat LoBrutto, and Janny Wurts for helping me realize a rather odd idea.

Raymond E. Feist
April 1987
San Diego, California

FAERIE TALE

PROLOGUE
MAY

Barney Doyle sat at his cluttered workbench, attempting to fix Olaf Andersen's ancient power mower for the fourth time in seven years. He had the cylinder head off and was judging the propriety of pronouncing last rites on the machine—he expected the good fathers over at St. Catherine's wouldn't approve. The head was cracked—which was why Olaf couldn't get it started—and the cylinder walls were almost paper-thin from wear and a previous rebore. The best thing Andersen could do would be to invest in one of those new Toro grass cutters, with all the fancy bells and whistles, and put this old machine out to rust. Barney knew Olaf would raise Cain about having to buy a new one, but that was Olaf's lookout. Barney also knew getting a dime out of Andersen for making such a judgment would be close to a miracle. It would be to the benefit of all parties concerned if Barney could coax one last summer's labor from the nearly terminal machine. Barney absently took a sharpener to the blades while he pondered. He could take one more crack at it. An oversized cylinder ring might do the trick—and he could weld the small crack; he'd get back most of the compression. But if he didn't pull it off, he'd lose both the time and the money spent on parts. No, he decided at last, better tell Andersen to make plans for a funeral.

A hot, damp gust of wind rattled the half-open window. Barney absently pulled the sticky shirt away from his chest. Meggie McCorly, he thought absently, a smile coming to his lined face. She had been a vision of beauty in simple cotton, the taut fabric stretched across ripe, swaying hips and ample breasts as she walked home from school each day. For a moment he was struck by a rush of memories so vivid he felt an echo of lust rising in his old loins. Barney took out a handkerchief and wiped his brow. He savored the spring scents, the hot muggy night smells, so much like those that blew through the orchards and across the fields of County Wexford. Barney thought of the night he and Meggie had fled from the dance, from the crowded, stuffy hall, slipping away unnoticed as the town celebrated Paddy O'Shea and Mary McMannah's wedding. The sultry memories caused Barney to dab again at his forehead as a stirring visited his groin. Chuckling to himself, Barney thought, There's some life yet in this old boyo.

Barney stayed lost in memories of half-forgotten passions for long minutes, then discovered he was still running the sharpener over a blade on Andersen's mower and had brought the edge to a silvery gleam. He set the sharpener down, wondering what had come over him. He hadn't thought of Meggie McCorly since he'd immigrated to America, back in '38. Last he'd heard, she'd married one of the Cammack lads over in Enniscorthy. He couldn't remember which one, and that made him feel sad.

Barney caught a flicker of movement through the small window of his work shed. He put down the sharpener and went to peer out into the evening's fading light. Not making out what it was that had caught his attention, Barney moved back toward his workbench. Just as his field of vision left the window, he again glimpsed something from the corner of his eye. Barney opened the door to his work shed and took a single step outside. Then he stopped.

Old images, half-remembered tales, and songs from his boyhood rushed forward to overwhelm him as he slowly stepped backward into his shed. Feelings of joy and terror so beautiful they brought tears to his eyes flowed through Barney, breaking past every rational barrier. The implements of society left for his ministrations, broken toasters, the mower, the blender with the burned-out motor, his little television for the baseball games, all were vanquished in an instant as a heritage so ancient it predated man's society appeared just outside Barney's shed. Not taking his eyes from what he beheld beyond the door, he retreated slowly, half stumbling, until his back was against the workbench. Reaching up and back, Barney pulled a dusty bottle off the shelf. Twenty-two years before, when he had taken the pledge, Barney had placed the bottle of Jameson's whiskey atop the shelf as a reminder and a challenge. In twenty-two years he had come to ignore the presence of the bottle, had come to shut out its siren call, until it had become simply another feature of the little shed where he worked.

Slowly he pulled the cork, breaking the brittle paper of the old federal tax stamp. Without moving his head, without taking his gaze from the door, Barney lifted the bottle to the side of his mouth and began to drink.

ERL KING HILL

door to the hallway. Bad Luck bolted down the hall toward the front door. She followed and opened it for him, and as he dashed outside, she shouted, "Go find the boys!"

Turning, she spied the family's large, smoky tomcat preening himself on the stairs. Philip had named the cat Hemingway, but everyone else called him Ernie. Feeling set upon, Gloria reached over, picked him up, and deposited him outside. "You too!" she snapped, slamming the door behind him.

Ernie was a scarred veteran of such family eruptions and took it all with an unassailable dignity attained only by British ambassadors, Episcopal bishops, and tomcats. He glanced about the porch, decided upon a sunny patch, turned about twice, and settled down for a nap.

Gloria returned to the kitchen, calling for her husband. Ignoring Bad Luck's mess for the moment, she left the kitchen and walked past the service porch. She cast a suspicious sidelong glance at the ancient washer and dryer. She had already decided a visit to the mall was in order, for she knew with dread certainty those machines were just waiting to devour any clothing she might be foolish enough to place inside. New machines would take only a few days to deliver, she hoped. She paused a moment as she regarded the faded, torn sofa that occupied the large back porch, and silently added some appropriate porch furniture to her Sears list.

Opening the screen door, she left the porch and walked down the steps to the "backyard," a large bare patch of earth defined by the house, a stand of old apple trees off to the left, the dilapidated garage to the right, and the equally run-down barn a good fifty yards away. Over near the barn she caught sight of her husband, speaking to his daughter. He still looked like an Ivy League professor, she thought, with his greying hair receding upward slowly, his brown eyes intense. But he had a smile to melt your heart, one that made him look like a little boy. Then Gloria noticed that her stepdaughter, Gabrielle, was in the midst of a rare but intense pout, and debated turning around and leaving them alone. She knew that Phil had just informed Gabbie she couldn't have her horse for the summer.

Gabbie stood with arms crossed tight against her chest, weight shifted to her left leg, a pose typical of teenage girls that Gloria and other actresses over twenty-five had to dislocate joints to imitate. For a moment Gloria was caught in open admiration of her stepdaughter. When Gloria and Phil had married, his career was in high gear, and Gabbie had been with her maternal grandmother, attending a private school in Arizona, seeing her father and his new wife only at Christmas, at Easter, and for two weeks in the summer. Since her grandmother had died, Gabbie had come to live with them. Gloria liked Gabbie, but they had never been able to communicate easily, and these days Gloria saw a beautiful young woman taking the place of a moody young girl. Gloria felt an unexpected stab of guilt and worry that she and Gabbie might never get closer. She put aside her momentary uneasiness and approached them.

Phil said, "Look, honey, it will only take a week or two more, then the barn will be fixed and we can see about leasing some horses. Then you and the boys can go riding whenever you want."

Gabbie tossed her long dark hair, and her brown eyes narrowed. Gloria was struck by Gabbie's resemblance to her mother, Corinne. "I still don't see why we can't ship Bumper out from home, Father." She said "Father" in that polysyllabic way young girls have of communicating hopelessness over ever being understood. "You let the boys bring that retarded dog and you brought Ernie. Look, if it's the money, I'll pay for it. Why do we have to rent some stupid farmer's horses when Bumper's back in California with no one to ride him?"

Gloria decided to take a hand and entered the conversation as she closed on them. "You know it's not money. Ned Barlow called and said he had a jumper panic aboard a flight last week, and they had to put him down before he could endanger the crew and riders, and he almost lost a second horse as well. The insurance company's shut him down until he resolves that mess. And it's a week into June and Ned also said it would be four or five weeks before he could get a reliable driver and good trailer to bring Bumper here, then nearly a week to move him, with all the stops he'd have to make. By the time he got here, it would be almost time for you to head back to UCLA. You'd have to ship him right back so he'd be there to ride when you're at school. Want me to go on? Look, Gabbie, Ned'll see Bump's worked and cared for. He'll be fine and ready for you when you get back."

"Oooh," answered Gabbie, a raw sound of pure aggravation, "I don't know why you had to drag me out here to this *farm!* I could have spent the summer with Ducky Summers. Her parents said it was all right."

"Stop whining," Phil snapped, his expression showing at once he regretted his tone. Like her mother, Gabbie instinctively knew how to nettle him with hardly an effort. The difference was that Gabbie rarely did, while Corinne had with regularity. "Look, honey, I'm sorry. But I don't like Ducky and her fancy friends. They're kids with too much money and time on their hands, and not an ounce of common sense in the whole lot. And Ducky's mom and dad are off somewhere in Eu-

JUNE

1

"Stop it, you two!"

Gloria Hastings stood with hands on hips, delivering the Look. Sean and Patrick stopped their bickering over who was entitled to the base-ball bat. Their large blue eyes regarded their mother for a moment before, as one, they judged it close to the point of no return where her patience was concerned. They reached an accord with their peculiar, silent communication. Sean conceded custody of the bat to Patrick and led the escape outside.

"Don't wander too far off!" Gloria shouted after them. She listened to the sounds of eight-year-olds dashing down the ancient front steps and for a moment considered the almost preternatural bond between her boys. The old stories of twins and their empathic link had seemed folktales to her before giving birth, but now she conceded that there was something there out of the ordinary, a closeness beyond what was expected of siblings.

Putting aside her musing, she looked at the mess the movers had left and considered, not for the first time, the wisdom of all this. She wandered aimlessly among the opened crates of personal belongings and felt nearly overwhelmed by the simple demands of sorting out the hundreds of small things they had brought with them from California. Just deciding where each item should go seemed a Sisyphean task.

She glanced around the room, as if expecting it to have somehow changed since her last inspection. Deep-grained hardwood floors, freshly polished—which would need polishing again as soon as the crates and boxes were hauled outside—hinted at a style of living alien to Gloria. She regarded the huge fireplace with its ancient hand-carved façade as something from another planet, a stark contrast to the rough brick and stone ranch-house-style hearths of her California childhood. The stairs in the hallway, with their polished maple banisters, and the sliding doors to the den and dining room were relics of another era, conjuring up images of William Powell as Clarence Day or Clifton Webb in *Cheaper by the Dozen.* This house called for—no, demanded, she amended—high starched collars in an age of designer jeans. Gloria absently brushed back an errant strand of blond hair attempting an escape from under the red kerchief tied about her head, and fought back a nearly overwhelming homesickness. Casting about for a place to start in the seemingly endless mess, she threw her hands up in resignation. "This is not what Oscar winners are supposed to be doing! Phil!"

When no answer was forthcoming, she left the large living room and shouted her husband's name up the stairs. Again no reply. She walked back along the narrow hallway to the kitchen and pushed open the swinging door. The old house presented its kitchen to the east, with hinged windows over the sink and drainboard admitting the morning light. It would be hot in the mornings, come July, but it would be a pleasant place to sit in the evenings, with the windows and large door to the screened-in back porch left open, admitting the evening breeze. At least, she hoped so. Southern California days might be blast-furnace-hot at times, but it was dry heat and the evenings were impossibly beautiful. God, she wished to herself, what I'd give for an honest patio, and about half this humidity. Fighting off a sudden bout of regret over the move, she pulled her sticky blouse away from herself and let some air cool her while she hollered for her husband again.

An answering scrabbling sound under the table made her jump, and she turned and uttered her favorite oath, "Goddamnitall!" Beneath the kitchen table crouched Bad Luck, the family's black Labrador retriever, a guilty expression on his visage as he hunkered down before a ten-pound bag of Ken-L-Ration he had plundered. Crunchy kernels rolled around the floor. "You!" she commanded. "Out!"

Bad Luck knew the rules of the game as well as the boys and at once bolted from under the table. He skidded about the floor looking for a way out, suddenly confounded by discovering himself in new territory. Having arrived only the day before, he hadn't yet learned the local escape routes. He turned first one way, then another, his tail half wagging, half lowered between his legs, until Gloria held open the swinging rope." He cast a knowing glance at his wife. "I doubt they have a hint who's sleeping at their house these days."

"Look, I know Ducky's an airhead and has a new boyfriend every twenty minutes, but I can take care of myself."

"I know you can, hon," answered Phil, "but until you've graduated, you'll have to put up with a father's prerogatives." He reached out and touched her cheek. "All too soon some young guy's going to steal you away, Gabbie. We've never had a lot of time together. I thought we could make it a family summer."

Gabbie sighed in resignation and allowed her father a slight hug, but it was clear she wasn't pleased. Gloria decided to change the subject. "I could use a hand, you guys. The moving elves are out on strike and those boxes aren't going to unload themselves."

Phil smiled at his wife and nodded as Gabbie gave out a beleaguered sound and plodded toward the house. When she was up the steps to the porch, Phil said, "I'm probably selling her short, but I had visions of having to fly back to bail her out of jail on a drug bust."

"Or to arrange for her first abortion?" queried Gloria.

"That too, I suppose. I mean, she's old enough."

Gloria shrugged. "For several years, sport. I hadn't when I was her age, but I was raised with the fear of God put in me by the nuns at St. Genevieve's."

"Well, I just hope she has some sense about it. I expect it's too late for a father-daughter talk."

"From the way she fills her jeans, I'd say it was about six or seven years too late. Besides, it's none of our business, unless she asks for advice."

Phil laughed, a not altogether comfortable sound. "Yes, I'd guess so."

"Sympathies, old son. Instant parent of teenager was tough. But you've done a good job the last two years."

"It's no easier for you," he countered.

She grinned up at him. "Bets? I'm not her mother, and I remember what it was to be a teenage girl. Look, Gabbie's not going to be the only one around here throwing temper tantrums if I don't get some help with those boxes. After combative twins, that clown in a dog suit, and a smug alley cat, it comes down to you, me, and Miss Equestrian of Encino."

Phil's face clouded over a little. His dark brown eyes showed a flicker of concern as he said, "Having second thoughts about the move?"

Gloria hesitated, wondering if she should share her doubts with

Phil. She decided the homesickness would pass once they settled in and made new friends, so she said, "No, not really. Just about unpacking." She changed the subject. "I had a call from Tommy about an hour ago."

"And what does Superagent allow? Another movie offer?" he asked jokingly.

"No." She poked him in the ribs. Tommy Raymond had been her agent when Gloria worked off-Broadway and in Hollywood. She had quit acting when she and Phil married, but over the years Tommy had stayed in touch, and she counted him among her few close friends in the business. "He called to say Janet White is opening a play on Broadway in the fall. They're reviving *Long Day's Journey.*"

"Getting the itch again?"

She smiled. "Not since the last play I was in bombed in Hartford." Phil laughed. She had never caught on in New York or Hollywood, where she and Phil had met. Phil had taken to calling her "the Oscar winner," and it had become a family joke. She didn't regret her choice, as she had little desire for fame, but she did occasionally miss the theater, the challenge of the work and the camaraderie of other actors. "Anyway, we're invited to the opening."

"Rented tux and all, I suppose."

She laughed. "I suppose. Assuming Janet can survive the out-of-town run." Tugging on her husband's arm, she said, "Come along, handsome. Give me a hand, and once we get things under control, you can run out to McDonald's or the Colonel's for dinner, and when the kids are in bed, I'll scrub your back, then show you a few things I didn't learn from the good sisters of St. Genevieve's."

Kissing her cheek, Phil said, "Just as I suspected. Scratch a good Irish-Catholic schoolgirl and underneath you'll find a dirty old woman."

"Complaints?"

"Never," he said as he kissed her on the neck. Giving him a hug, Gloria put her arm through his and they walked toward the old house that was their new home.

2

Sean and Patrick marched along the little stream, wending their way among the rocks as they followed the tiny rivulets of water. The gully deepened and Sean, the more cautious of the two, said, "We'd better go up there." He pointed to where the bank began to rise on the right.

Just then Bad Luck came galloping down the creek bed, red tongue lolling and tail wagging a furious greeting. He circled around the boys, then began sniffing at the ground.

"Why?" asked Patrick, contemptuous of anything resembling caution.

" 'Cause we could get caught down there," Sean answered, pointing to where the gully dropped rapidly into a dell, his voice sounding thin and frail over the water's merry gurgle. "Besides, Mom said not to go too far."

"That's dumb; she always says stuff like that," was Patrick's answer as he tugged on Bad Luck's ear and set off to follow the water. His catcher's mitt hung by a thong from his belt and his Angels cap sat upon his head at an aggressive angle. He carried his Louisville Slugger over his shoulder as a soldier carries his rifle. Sean hesitated a moment, then set out after his brother, struggling to keep his beat-up old Padres cap on his head. Twins they might be, but Sean just didn't seem to have Patrick's natural confidence, and his timidity seemed to rob him of grace, causing him to slip often on the loose gravel and rocks.

Sean stumbled and landed hard on his rear. He pulled himself upright, all his anger at the tumble directed at his brother. He dusted himself off and began to negotiate the steep drop of the gully. He half scrambled, half slid down the incline, his baseball glove and ball held tightly in his left hand. Reaching the bottom, he could see no sign of Patrick. The gully made a sharp bend, vanishing off to the right. "Patrick?" Sean yelled.

"Over here," came the reply. Sean hurried along, rounding the bend to halt next to his brother.

In one of those moments the boys shared, they communicated without words. Silently they voiced agreement, *This is a scary place.*

Before them squatted an ancient grey stone bridge, spanning the gully so a trail barely more than a path could continue uninterrupted as it rambled through the woods. The very stones seemed beaten and battered as if they had resisted being placed in this arrangement and had yielded only to brutish force. Each stone was covered in some sort of black-green moss, evidence of the presence of some evil so pernicious it infected the very rocks around it with foul ooze. Overgrown with brush on both sides above the high-water line on the banks, the opening under the bridge yawned at the boys like a deep, black maw. Nothing could be seen in the darkness under the span except the smaller circle of light on the other side. It was as if illumination stopped on one side of the bridge and began again only after having passed beyond its boundaries.

The boys knew the darkness was a lair. Something waited in the gloom under the bridge. Something evil.

Bad Luck tensed and began to growl, his hackles coming up. Patrick reached down and grabbed his collar as he was about to charge under the bridge. "No!" he shouted as the dog pulled him along, and Bad Luck stopped, though he whined to be let loose.

"We better get back," said Sean. "It'll be dinner soon."

"Yeah, dinner," agreed Patrick, finding it difficult to drag his eyes from the blackness under the bridge. Step by step they backed away, Bad Luck reluctantly obeying Patrick's command to come with them, whining with his tail between his legs, then barking.

"Hey!" came a shout from behind, and both boys jumped at the sound, their chests constricting with fright. Patrick hung on to Bad Luck's collar and the Labrador snarled and spun around to protect the boys, pulling Patrick off balance.

Patrick stumbled forward and Sean fell upon the dog's neck, helping to hold him back from attacking the man who had come up behind them.

The man held out his hands to show he meant no harm. Bad Luck struggled to be free. "Stop it," shouted Sean and the dog backed away, growling at the stranger.

Both boys looked the man over. He was young, though not recognized as such by the boys, for anyone over the age of eighteen was a grown-up.

The stranger examined the two boys. Both had curly brown hair protruding from under baseball caps, deep-set large blue eyes, and round faces. Had they been girls, they would have been considered pretty. When older, they would likely be counted handsome. The stranger smiled, and said, "Sorry to have scared you boys and your dog. It's my own damn fault. I shouldn't have shouted. I should've known the dog'd be jumpy." He spoke with a soft, musical voice, different from what the boys were used to hearing.

Seeing no immediate threat to the boys, Bad Luck stopped his growling and reserved judgment on this stranger. The boys exchanged glances.

"Look, I'm sorry I startled you guys, okay?"

The boys nodded as one. Patrick said, "What did you mean about Bad Luck being jumpy, mister?"

The man laughed, and the boys relaxed. "Bad Luck, huh?"

Hearing his name, the dog gave a tentative wag of his tail. The man slowly reached out and let the Labrador sniff his hand, then patted him on the head. After a moment the tail wagging became emphatic. "Going to be friends, right, boy?" said the man. Leaning forward, with hands on knees, he said, "Who are you guys? I didn't know there were any big leaguers around here."

Sean grinned at the reference to their caps and equipment. "We just moved here from California. We live on a farm."

"Philip Hastings your father?" Both brothers nodded. "I heard he'd be moving in at the Old Kessler Place. I didn't know he was here already. Well, I guess I'd better introduce myself. I'm Jack Cole." He held out his hand, not in the manner of a grown-up making fun of kids but as if they were just like anyone else he'd met. The boys said their names in turn, shook hands, and silently judged Jack Cole an acceptable human being, even if he was old.

"What'd you mean about Bad Luck being jumpy?" Patrick repeated.

"There's this bull raccoon that's been hanging around this part of the woods for the last month, and likely as not that's what your dog smelled under the bridge. If so, it's a good thing he didn't get loose. That coon has torn up most of the cats and half the dogs in the area."

The boys looked unconvinced. Jack Cole laughed. "Look, take my word for it. This isn't some little critter from a cartoon show. This coon is almost as big as your hound and he's old, tough, and mean. And this is his turf, clear?"

The boys exchanged glances and nodded. Jack faced back up the gully. "This isn't a good place to play, anyway. We get some pretty sudden showers in the hills near the lake, and if we get a big one, this gully could flood pretty fast. I mean, it can hit you without warning. I'd stay clear of this creek in future, okay?" They nodded. "Come on, I'll walk back to your house with you. Must be close to your dinnertime. Besides, I'd like to meet your dad."

The boys tugged at Bad Luck's collar and began to hike back up the gully. As they rounded the corner, Sean cast a backward look toward the bridge and for an instant felt as if he was being watched by someone . . . or something . . . deep within the gloom beneath the rocky arch.

3

Gloria regarded the grotesque carvings cut into the roof lintel over the front porch and shook her head in dismay. She gazed at the odd-looking creatures who squatted below the eaves of the roof and muttered, "Just what every girl dreams of, living in Notre Dame." Upon first seeing the house, she had inquired into her husband's mental health, only partially joking. It was all the good things he saw, sturdy turn-of-the-century construction, hardwoods used throughout and every joint dovetailed and pegged, with nails only an afterthought. It was made of materials a modern builder could only dream of: ash, oak, and spruce now rockhard with age, marble and slate, teak floors, and copper wires and pipes throughout. But Phil couldn't see that it was also a living exercise in gracelessness, a testimony to Herman Kessler's father's knowing what he liked without the benefit of taste. The first Kessler had built an architectural hodgepodge. A gazebo, stripped from some antebellum plantation and shipped north to this gentleman's farm, sat off to the left of the house, under the sightless gaze of Gothic windows. Regency furniture clashed headlong with Colonial, while a stuffed tiger's head hung upon the wall of what was going to be Phil's study, looking balefully down upon the ugliest Persian rug Gloria had ever seen. All in all, Gloria decided it would be a good year's work fixing up Old Man Kessler's place.

She entered the house and moved quickly toward the back door, expecting to have to shout for the boys for ten minutes before they'd put in an appearance. But just as she was about to open the screen door Patrick's voice cut through the late afternoon air. "Maaa!"

She pushed open the door, a half-smile on her lips as she watched her twins approach from the woods behind the house. Bad Luck loped alongside the boys and a young man walked behind. He was dressed in jeans and a flannel shirt, with the sleeves rolled up, and practical-looking boots.

When the boys were within shouting distance, Patrick yelled, "This is Jack, Mom. What's for dinner?"

Gloria glanced at her watch and realized it was getting on toward five. "Hamburgers or chicken. Whatever your father brings back from town. Hello, Jack."

"Hello, Mrs. Hastings," answered the young man with a grin and a decidedly southern lilt to his voice.

"How did you manage to cross paths with Heckle and Jeckle here?"

"I noticed the boys were wandering down a gully. Spring floods can come quickly if you don't know the signs." Seeing a tightening around Gloria's eyes, he quickly added, "Nothing to fret about, Mrs. Hastings. There's been no rain in the hills for a couple of weeks, so there's no chance of a flash flood. But it's not a good place for the boys to play. Thought I'd mention it to them." Gloria fixed a disapproving eye upon her boys, who decided it was time to vanish into the house in a clatter of sneaker-clad feet on the porch steps, punctuated by a slamming screen door.

Looking briefly heavenward, Gloria turned her attention to Jack. "Thanks, Mr. . . ."

"Cole, Jack Cole. And it's no trouble, ma'am. I hope you don't mind my being in your woods?"

"My woods?" asked Gloria.

"Your family's, I mean. Your property line runs back a half mile beyond the creek bridge."

"A half mile. We own property for a half mile from the house?"

"More than that. The bridge is almost a quarter mile from here, ma'am."

"Gloria."

For a moment he looked embarrassed, then he said, "Excuse my discomfort, ma'am, but I haven't met a lot of actresses."

Gloria laughed. "God! What are you? A fan, out here in the wilderness, after all these years?"

"Well, I've never seen you onstage, ma'am, but I've read about your husband, and they mentioned your career in passing."

"Fame, so fleeting," Gloria said with mock sorrow. "Anyway, just the fact you knew of my humble career calls for a drink, assuming the refrigerator is still working and you'd like a beer?"

"With deep appreciation," he answered with a smile. "I'd been hoping to meet you and your husband."

"Then come inside and I'll scare up a beer for you. Phil should be back with the food shortly."

Leading the young man into the kitchen, Gloria pulled the kerchief from her head, letting her ash-blond hair fall freely. Suddenly she was aware of a desire to primp, feeling both amused and alarmed by it. She hadn't been in front of the cameras since before the twins were born, and had lost a lot of the automatic checking of appearance that was almost second nature to young actresses in the film jungles. Now this young man, little older than Gabbie from his appearance, made her wish for a mirror and a washcloth. Feeling suddenly silly, she told herself she wasn't going to apologize for her appearance. Still, he was handsome in a way Gloria liked: unselfconscious, dark good looks, athletic but not overly muscular. Gloria smiled inwardly in anticipation of Gabbie's reaction to the young man. He really was cute. Turning toward Jack, she said, "We're still uncrating around here."

Jack looked concerned. "I'm sorry if this is an inopportune time, ma'am. I can visit another day."

She shook her head as she opened the refrigerator. "No, I just mean pardon the mess." She handed him a beer. "And it's 'Gloria,' not 'ma'am.' "

Jack's eyebrows went up as he regarded the white bottle. "Royal Holland Brand," he said approvingly.

"Phil is that rarest of all birds, a well-paid writer. He buys it by the case."

Jack sipped the beer and made an expression of satisfaction. "I can imagine, considering the success of his films. Still, I've often wondered why he hasn't written another book."

"You've read one of Phil's books?" Gloria asked, suddenly interested in the young man.

"All of them. And all the short stories he's published. They should be put in an anthology."

"You've read all three of Phil's books," she said, sitting down.

"Four," Jack corrected. "He wrote that romance paperback under the name Abigail Cook."

"God! You've done your homework."

Jack smiled, a boyish grin on a man's face. "That's exactly what it is, homework. I'm a graduate student up at Fredonia State—"

Conversation was interrupted by an explosion through the door in the form of the twins and Bad Luck. "Dad's here!" yelled Patrick, with Sean echoing his cry.

"Hold it down to a dull roar, kids," commanded Gloria. As expected, she was ignored. The unpacking was a constant pain for Gloria, but the boys thought food from the local fast-food emporiums two nights running a treat.

Phil came through the hall door carrying two barrels of the Colonel's best. Setting them down, he kissed Gloria on the cheek and said, "Hello! What is this? Cheating on me already?"

Gloria ignored the remark. "Phil, this is Jack Cole, a neighbor. He's a fan of yours."

Phil extended his hand and they shook. "Not many people pay attention to who writes a movie, Jack."

"He's read your books, Phil. All of them."

Phil looked flattered and said, "Well then, Jack, there are fewer people still who've read my . . . Did Gloria say all of them?"

Jack grinned. "Even *Winds of Dark Passion* by Abigail Cook."

"Well, I'll be go to hell. Look, why don't you join us for supper. We've both original and extra crispy, and there's another bottle of beer where that one came from."

Jack appeared about to beg off when Gabbie entered the kitchen carrying paper bags filled with rolls, potatoes, and other accompaniments for the chicken. She was on the verge of some comment when she caught sight of Jack. For a brief moment the two young people stood facing each other in an obviously appraising fashion, and equally obviously both approving of what they saw. Jack's face slowly relaxed into his biggest smile so far as Gloria said, "Jack Cole, this is Gabrielle."

Jack and Gabbie exchanged nods, while Phil ordered the twins to wash up. Gloria fought off the urge to giggle. Gabbie absently touched her collar, her cheek, and a strand of dark hair, and Gloria knew she was dying for a mirror, comb, and clean blouse. And Jack seemed suddenly unable to sit comfortably. Gloria glanced from Jack to Gabbie and said, "Right, one more for dinner."

4

Dinner was relaxed. Phil and Gloria, Jack and Gabbie sat around the kitchen table while the twins ate sitting on a crate before the television in the parlor. Jack had spoken little, for his questions had coaxed Phil into explaining the family's move from California.

"So then," said Phil, "with *Star Pirates* and *Star Pirates II* being such tremendous hits, and with me getting an honest piece of the box office, as well as a creator's royalty on *Pirates III, IV,* and however many more they can grind out, I have what I like to call 'go to hell' money."

" 'Go to hell money'?" asked Jack.

Gabbie said, "Dad means that he got enough money to tell every producer in Hollywood to go to hell." Gabbie had managed to find a mirror, comb, washcloth, and clean blouse and had barely taken her eyes off Jack throughout the evening.

"That's it. Now I can go back to what I did first, and best: write novels."

Jack Cole finished eating and sat back from the table. "You'll get no arguments from me. Still, most of your films were pretty good. The *Pirates* films had darn good writing compared to most others in the genre; I liked that sly humor a lot—made those characters seem real. And the plots made sense—well, sort of."

"Thank you, but even so, film's more of a director's medium. Even with an editor's input, a book's a single person's product. And it's been too many years since I've been able to write without story editors, directors, producers, other writers, even actors, all screaming for changes in the script. In films the writing's done by committee. You've never lived until you've been through a story conference." There was a half-serious, half-mocking tone to his voice. "Torquemada would have loved them. Some idiot from a multinational conglomerate who needs to have every line of *Dick and Jane* explained to him is telling you how to rewrite scenes, so the chairman of the board's wife won't be offended. Or some agent is demanding changes in a beautifully thought out script because the character's actions *might* be bad for the star's image. There are agents who would have demanded a rewrite of Shakespeare—have Othello divorce Desdemona because his client's fans wouldn't accept him as a wife murderer. Or the studio wants a little more skin showing on the actress so they can get a PG-13 rather than a G, 'cause they think teenagers won't go to a G. It's a regular *Alice Through the Looking Glass* out there."

"Is it really that bad?" Jack asked.

Gabbie rose and began gathering up the paper plates and napkins. "If the volume of Dad's yelling is any indication, it's that bad."

Phil looked wounded. "I don't yell."

Gloria said, "Yes you do. Several times I thought you'd smash the phone slamming it down after speaking to someone at the studio." She turned to Jack. "You've been doing most of the listening, Jack. We haven't given you a chance to tell us anything about yourself."

Jack grinned as Gabbie replaced his empty bottle of beer with a fresh one, indicating he should stay a little longer. "Not too much to tell, really. I'm just a good old boy from Durham, North Carolina, who got a B.A. in English from UNC and wandered up north to study at SUNY Fredonia. I had my choice of a couple of different grad programs, including a tempting one in San Diego, but I wanted Agatha Grant as an adviser, so I pulled some strings and got her, and here I am."

Phil's eyes widened. "Aggie Grant! She's an old family friend! She was also my adviser when I got my M.A. in modern lit. at Cornell. She's at Fredonia?"

"Emeritus. She retired last year. That's what I meant by pulling strings. I'm her last grad student. I'm after a doctorate in literature. In a few more months I'll be taking orals to see if I get to continue, and an M.A. in passing. I'm doing my work on novelists who became film writers, on how work in films affects a writer's work in print. I'm looking at writers who did both, like Fitzgerald, Runyon, William Goldman, Faulkner, and Clavell. And of course yourself. Though mostly I'm working on Fitzgerald. When I figure out the thrust of my dissertation, I'll probably concentrate on him."

Phil smiled. "You put me in some fine company, Jack."

"It's all pretty technical and probably pretty boring." He looked embarrassed. "When the local papers printed the word you'd bought this place, I thought I might impose and get an interview with you."

Phil said, "Well, I'll help if I can. But I don't have much in common with Fitzgerald. I don't drink as much; I'm not having an affair with another writer; and my wife's not crazy . . . most of the time."

"Thanks," said Gloria, dryly.

"I was going to call Aggie, and take a weekend and drive up to Ithaca. I had no idea she'd moved. First chance I have, I'll get up to Fredonia and see her. God, it's been years."

"Actually, you don't have to go to Fredonia. She lives on the other side of the woods now, right at the edge of Pittsville. That's part of the deal. I double as something of a groundskeeper, general factotum, and occasional cook, though she prefers to putter in the kitchen most of the time. She only runs up to the university when she has to, commencements, a colloquium, guest lecture, the occasional alumni function, that sort of thing."

"Tell Aggie I'll be over in the next day or two."

"She's at NYU for the next two weeks. She's editing a collection of papers for a symposium in Brussels. But she should be back right after. She wouldn't miss the Fourth of July celebration in Pittsville."

"Well then, as soon as she returns, have her give us a call."

"She'll be glad to know you're back home. She'll whip up something special for the occasion, I expect." Jack finished his beer and rose. "Well, I want to thank you all—for the hospitality and the dinner. It's truly been a pleasure." The last was not too subtly directed at Gabbie.

"I hope we'll be seeing you soon, Jack," said Gloria.

"If it's not an imposition. I hike this area when I'm thinking around a problem in my thesis, or sometimes I go riding through the woods."

"Riding?" asked Gloria, a calculating expression crossing her face. Jack's presence had lightened Gabbie's mood for the first time since they'd arrived, and Gloria was anxious to keep her diverted from any black furies.

"There's a farm a couple of miles down the highway where they raise horses. Mr. Laudermilch's a friend of Aggie's, so I can borrow one sometimes. Do you ride?"

"Infrequently," answered Phil, "but Gabbie here rides every chance she gets."

"Oh?"

"Bumper—that's my horse—he's a champion Blanket Appaloosa. Best gymkhana horse in Southern California, and one of the best cross-country horses at Highridge Stables."

"Never ridden an Appaloosa; they tend to be a little thick-skinned, I understand. But I guess they're good working stock. Champion, huh? Pretty expensive, I guess."

"Well, he's a good one. . . ." Gabbie shrugged, indicating money was not an issue. Gloria and Phil smiled.

Jack said, "Back home I had a Tennessee Walker. Perhaps you'd care to go riding some afternoon, after you're settled in?"

"Sure, anytime."

"I'm going down to visit my folks in Durham, day after tomorrow. I'll be there two weeks. When I get back?"

Gabbie shrugged. "Okay."

"Well then. As I said, it's been a pleasure. I do look forward to the next time."

Phil rose and shook Jack's hand. "Don't be a stranger," offered Gloria as Jack left through the back door. Returning to her husband's side, she said, "So, Gabbie. Things don't seem quite so bad, do they?"

Gabbie sighed. "Oh, he's definitely a hunk; Ducky Summers would say, 'He's got buns worth dying for.' But how am I going to keep from losing my lunch when he shows up with some retard rockhead, cold-blood farm horse? Ugh!"

Gloria smiled. "Let's unpack another crate, then I'll chase the boys to bed."

Gabbie nodded resigned agreement, and Phil led her out of the kitchen. Gloria followed, but as she started to leave the kitchen she was struck by a sudden feeling of being watched, as if unfriendly eyes had fastened upon her. She turned abruptly and for an instant thought she saw something at one of the windows. Moving her head, she saw flickering changes in the light of the kitchen bulb as it reflected off imperfections in the glass. With a slight sense of uneasiness, Gloria left the kitchen.

5

Sean tried to settle deeply into the bunk bed. The smells were new to him. Old feather pillows had been dug out of a closet when it was discovered the boy's familiar ones hadn't been where they were expected to be, and despite the clean pillowcases, they had an ancient, musty odor. And the house made strange sounds. Creaks and groans could be faintly heard; odd chitters and whispers made by creatures of darkness had Sean burrowing deeply below the heavy comforter, peeking out over the edge, afraid to relax his vigil for an instant.

"Patrick?" he whispered, to be answered by his brother's deep breathing. Patrick didn't share Sean's fear of the dark. The first night Patrick had tried to bully his brother out of the top bunk—they had both wanted the novel experience of sleeping that high off the ground —but Mom had prevented a fight and Sean had picked the number closer to the one she had been thinking. Now Sean wondered at the whim of chance that put him in the top bed. Everything looked weird from up high.

The moon's glow came through the window, and the light level rose and fell as clouds crawled slowly across the sky, alternately plunging the room into deep gloom and lightening to what seemed almost daylight. The dancing shadows had an odd pattern Sean had come to recognize.

Outside, an old elm tree rose beside the bedroom, its branches swaying gently in the breeze. When the moon was not obscured, the tree shadows became more distinct, making their own display. The thick leaves rustled in the night wind, casting fluttering shadows that shifted and moved around the room, shapes of ebon and grey that capered in mad abandon, filling the night with menace.

Sean watched the play of shadows with a thrill of danger that was almost delicious, a sweaty-palm-and-neck-hairs-standing sort of feeling. Then something changed. In the blackest part of the gloom, deep in the far corner, something moved. Sean felt his chest tighten as cold gripped his stomach. Moving in the wrong rhythm, against the flow of greys and blacks, it was coming toward the boys' bunk beds.

"Patrick," Sean repeated loudly. His brother stirred and made a sleepy sound as the shape began to slither along the floor. It would move a beat, weaving its way across the carpet, then pause, and Sean strained his eyes to see it, for when it was still, it would vanish. For long, agonizing moments he couldn't see any hint of motion, then just when he finally relaxed, thinking it gone or an illusion, it would stir again. The maddeningly indistinct shape approached the bed slowly, at last disappearing below the foot of the bunks, out of Sean's view.

"Patrick!" Sean said, scooting backward to the corner of the bunk farthest from the creeping shadow. Then he heard a sound of claws upon wood, as something climbed the old bedpost. Sean held his breath. Two clawlike shapes, dark and terrible in their deformity, appeared beyond the end of the bunks, as if reaching up blindly for something, followed an instant later by a misshapen mask of terror and hate, a black, twisted visage with impossible eyes, black opal irises surrounded by a yellow that seemed to glow in the gloom. Sean screamed.

Suddenly Patrick was awake and shouting and an instant later Gloria was standing in the door turning on the lights.

Phil was a moment behind, and Gabbie's voice came through the door of her room. "What's going on?"

Gloria reached up and hugged Sean. "What is it, honey?"

"Something . . ." began Sean. Unable to continue, he pointed. Phil made a display of investigating the room while Gloria calmed the frightened boy. Gabbie stuck her head in the room and said, "What's going on?" She wore the oversized UCLA T-shirt she used as a nightgown.

With a mixture of contempt and relief in his voice, Patrick said, "Sean's had a nightmare."

His brother's tone of disdain caused Sean to react. "It wasn't a dream! There was something in the room!"

"Well," said Phil, "whatever it was, it's gone."

"Honey, it was just a bad dream."

"It was not," said Sean, halfway between frustrated tears at not being believed and a fervent hope they were right.

"You just go back to sleep and I'll stay here until you do. Okay?"

Sean seemed unconvinced, but said, " 'Kay." He settled in and began to accept the idea he had been dreaming. With his mother nearby and the light on, the black face seemed a nightmare design, not a thing of solid existence.

"Broth-er," said Patrick in disgust. He rolled over and made a display of needing no such reassurance.

Gabbie's grumbling followed her back into her own room as Phil flipped off the light. Gloria remained, standing patiently next to Sean's bunk until he fell asleep.

Outside the boys' bedroom window, something dark and alien slithered down the drainpipe and swung onto the nearest tree branch. It leaped and spun from branch to branch as it descended, dropping the last ten feet to the ground. It moved with an unnaturally quick, rolling gait, a stooped-over apelike shape. It paused near the gazebo, looking back over its shoulder with opalescent dark eyes toward the boys' window. Another movement, in the woods, caused it to duck down, as if fearing discovery. Bright twinkling lights flashed for an instant, darting between boles, and vanished from view. The dark creature hesitated, waiting until the lights were gone, then scampered off toward the woods, making odd whispering sounds.

6

The house became a home, slowly, with resistance, but soon the odd corners had been explored and the ancient odors had become commonplace. The idiosyncrasies of the house—the strange little storage area beneath the stairs next to the cellar door, the odd shed in the back, the way the pipes upstairs rattled—all these things became familiar. Gloria considered her family: Gabbie wasn't happy but had ceased brooding, and the twins shared their secret world, seemingly content wherever their family was. Gloria had been most concerned over their reaction to the move, but they had shown the least difficulty in adapting. The most positive aspect of the move had been in Phil's attitude. He was writing every day and seemed transported. He refused to show Gloria any of his work so far, saying he felt superstitious. She knew that was so much bullshit, for she had talked out story ideas into the night with him before. She knew he was simply afraid she wouldn't like what he was writing and the bubble would burst. All in good time, she thought, all in good time.

Seventeen days after Jack Cole's visit, a note was delivered by the mailman. It was addressed to "Philip Hastings and Family." Gloria opened it while Phil scanned a letter from his literary agent. ". . . look forward to presenting your newest work. Several publishers already have expressed interest . . ." Phil read aloud.

"Read this," Gloria instructed as she handed him the note.

He scanned the envelope and frowned. One of his pet quirks was about Gloria's opening letters addressed to him, something she loved to do. "It said, 'and Family.' That's me," she said with mock challenge in her tone.

Phil sighed. "Defeated before I begin." He read aloud. " 'Mrs. Agatha Grant invites Mr. Philip Hastings and family to dinner, Sunday, June 24. Cocktails at 5 P.M. Regrets only.' "

"What does that mean?"

"It means R.S.V.P. only if you can't come, you California barbarian."

Gloria playfully kicked her husband. "Barbarian! Who was it who called the town 'La Jawl-lah' the first time he propositioned me?"

"I did?"

"You most certainly did. It was at Harv Moran's house, at the wrap party for *Bridesdale.* You came sliding up to me while my date was over getting drinks—Robbie Tedesco, that was who I was with. You and I had just met at the studio the day before and you said, 'I've got an invitation to spend the weekend at a friend's beach house in *La Jawl-lah.* Do you think you could get away for a couple of days?" She spoke the lines with a deep voice, mimicking his speech patterns.

Phil looked only mildly embarrassed. "I remember. I still can't believe I did that. I had never asked a near stranger to spend the weekend with me before." Then he smiled. "Well, you did come with me."

Gloria laughed. "I did, didn't I? I guess I just figured someone was going to grab up this eastern square and it might as well be me." She playfully grabbed a handful of his greying hair and pulled his head down, kissing him quickly. "And La Jolla was beautiful."

"So were you . . . as you still are," he said, kissing her deeply. He felt her respond. Playfully nipping at her neck, he whispered, "We haven't pulled a nooner in years, kiddo."

Then the phone rang, and Gabbie shouted from upstairs, "I'll get it!"

Instantly they heard the sound of the screen door slamming as the boys tromped into the kitchen. "Maaa!" shouted Patrick.

"What's for lunch?" inquired Sean in counterpoint.

Passion fled. Leaning against her husband, Gloria shook her head. "Such are the prices of parenthood." With a quick kiss, she said, "Hold that last thought for tonight, lover."

Gabbie came running partway down the stairs, holding the phone at the limit of the cord's ability to stretch. "It's Jack. He's back. We're going riding this afternoon, then getting a bite and a movie. So I won't be home for dinner. Okay?"

Phil said, "Sure," as the boys came marching in from the kitchen. Gabbie dashed back up the stairs.

"Mom," said Patrick. "What's for lunch?"

"We're hungry," agreed Sean.

Gloria shrugged regretfully toward her husband. Putting her hands on her sons' shoulders, she turned them around and said, "With me, troops." Suddenly she was gone, heading for the kitchen to feed her small brood. Phil could still smell her clean scent in the hall air and felt the deep stirrings that contact with her always brought quickly into existence. With a sigh of regret at the moment's being gone, he returned to reading the mail as he walked back toward his study.

7

Gabbie stood in mute and pleasant surprise. At last she said, "All right!" slowly drawing out the exclamation.

Jack smiled as he motioned for her to come take the reins of the bay mare he had led. It was a beautiful, well-cared-for animal. Gabby took the reins. "They're terrific."

"Mr. Laudermilch raises Thoroughbreds and warm-blood crosses. He's a friend of Aggie's and I've helped out around his farm, so he lets me borrow one every so often. He used to race Thoroughbreds, but now he's into jumpers."

Gabbie admired the animals, noting the curve of the neck and the way the tail rose up, and the slightly forward-facing ears. "These have some Arabian in them," she declared, as she took the reins from Jack.

Jack nodded with a grin. "And quarter horse. These don't compete. They're what Mr. Laudermilch calls 'riding-around stock.' Yours is called My Dandelion and this is John Adams."

She hugged the mare's neck and patted it. "Hi, baby," she crooned. "We're going to be buddies, aren't we?" She quickly mounted. Settling into the unusual position of the English saddle, she said, "God, this feels weird."

Jack said, "I'm sorry. I thought you rode English."

Gabbie shook her head as she spurred her mount forward. "Nope, cowgirl. I've ridden English before. It's just been a long time." She waved at her foot. "Acme cowboy boots. I'll pick up some proper breeches and high top boots in town. My knees will be a little bruised tomorrow, is all."

They rode out toward the woods, Gabbie letting Jack take the lead. "Watch out for low branches," he said over his shoulder. "These paths aren't cleared like riding trails."

She nodded and studied his face as he turned back toward the path. She smiled to herself at the way his back moved as he reined his horse. Definitely a fox, she thought to herself, then wondered if there was a girlfriend back at the college.

The trail widened and she moved up beside him, saying, "These woods are pretty. I'm more used to the hills around the Valley."

"Valley?"

"San Fernando Valley." She made a face. "Ya know, fer sher, like a Valley girl, totally tubular, man. I mean, like bitchin', barf out, and all that shit." She looked irritated at the notion. "I grew up in Arizona. That image grosses me out." Suddenly she laughed at the slip and was joined by Jack. "L.A.'s just reclaimed desert. Turn off the garden hose and all the green goes away. It's all chaparral—scrub, you know—on the hills north of the valley. Some stands of trees around streams. A lot of eucalyptus—nothing like these woods. It's mostly hot and dry, and real dusty. But I'm used to it."

He smiled, and she decided she liked the way his mouth turned up. "I've never been west of the Mississippi, myself. Thought I'd get out to Los Angeles once a few years back, but I broke my leg sailing and that shot the whole summer."

"How'd you manage that?"

"Fell off the boat and hit a patch of hard water."

For a moment she paused in consideration, for he had answered with a straight face, then she groaned. "You bullshitter. You're as bad as my dad."

"I take that as a compliment," he answered with a grin. "Actually, some fool who thought he could sail put the boat around in a jibe without warning any of us, and I caught the boom and got knocked overboard. Smashed my leg all up. I spent the next day and a half with a paddle for a splint while we headed back to Tampa. Spent nine weeks in a cast, then six more in a walking cast. The surgeon was great, but my leg's not a hundred percent. When it gets cold, I limp a little. And I can't run worth spit. So I walk a lot."

They rode in silence for a while, enjoying the warm spring day in the woods. Suddenly there was an awkward moment, as each waited for the other to speak. At last Jack said, "What are you studying?"

Gabbie shrugged. "I haven't decided. I'm only a few units into my sophomore year, really. I'm sort of hung up between psychology and lit."

"I don't know much about psych." She looked at him quizzically. "I mean, what you would do when you graduated. But either means grad school if you want to use them."

She shrugged again. "Like I said, I'm barely a sophomore. I've got a while." She was quiet for a long time, then blurted, "What I'd like to do is write."

He nodded. "Considering your parents, that's not surprising."

What was surprising, thought Gabbie, was that she had said that. She had never told anyone, not even Jill Moran, her best friend. "That's the trouble, I guess. Everyone will expect it to be brilliant. What if it's no good?"

Jack looked at her with a serious expression on his face. "Then it'll be no good."

She reined in, trying to read his mood. He looked away, thoughtfully, his profile lit from behind by the sun shining through the trees. "I tried to write for a long time before I gave up. A historical novel, *Durham County*. About my neck of the woods at the turn of the century. There were parts of it that I thought were fine." He paused. "It was pretty awful. It was difficult admitting it at the end, because enough of my friends kept encouraging me that I thought it was good for a long time. I don't know. You just have to do it, I guess."

She sighed as she patted the horse's neck. Her dark hair fell down, hiding her face, as she said, "Still, you don't have two writers for parents. My mother's won a Pulitzer and my father was nominated for an Oscar. All I've managed is some dumb poetry."

He nodded, then turned his mount and began riding along the trail. After a long silence he said, "I still think you just have to do it."

"Maybe you're right," she answered. "Look, did you keep any of the stuff your friends told you was great?"

With an embarrassed smile, he said, "All of it. The whole damn half novel."

"I'll make you a deal. You let me see yours and I'll let you see mine." Jack laughed hard at the school-yard phrase and shook his head. "What's the matter? 'Fraid?"

"No," Jack barely managed to croak as he continued to laugh uncontrollably.

"Scaredy-cat," Gabbie mimicked, plunging Jack into deeper hilarity.

Jack finally said, "Okay, I give up. I'll let you read my stuff . . . maybe."

"Maybe!"

The argument continued as they crested a small rise and vanished behind it. From deep within the woods a pair of light blue eyes watched their passing. A figure emerged from the underbrush, a lithe, youthful figure who moved lightly on bare feet to the top of the path. From behind a bole he watched Gabbie as she moved down the trail. His eyes caressed her young back, drinking in the sight of her long dark hair, her slender waist, and the rounded buttocks as she held a good seat on the horse's back. The youth's laughter was high-pitched and musical. It was an alien sound, childlike and ancient, holding a hint of savage songs, primitive revelries, and music-filled hot nights. His curly red-brown hair surrounded a face conceived by Michelangelo or a Pre-Raphaelite painter. "Pretty," the young man said to the tree, patting the ancient bark as if it understood. "Very pretty." Then, nearby, a bird sounded a call, and the youth looked up. His voice shrilled with inhuman tones, a whistling whisper, as if a mockingbird imitated the call. The little bird darted about, seeking the intruder in its territory. The youth shrieked in glee at the harmless jest, as the bird continued to search for the trespasser. Then the youth sighed as he considered the beautiful girl who had passed.

High above, among the leaves, a thing of blackness clung tenaciously to the underside of a branch. It had watched the two riders with as much interest as the youth. But its thoughts were neither merry nor playful. An urgent need arose within, halfway between lust and hunger. Beauty affected it as much as the youth. But its desires were different, for, while lust was the youth's driving motivation, to the black thing under the tree branch beauty was only a beginning, a point of departure. And only the destruction of beauty allowed one to understand it. The fullness of Gabbie's beauty could be realized only by a slow journey through pain and anguish, torment and hopelessness, ending with blood and death. And if the pain was artful, as the master had taught, such torment could be made to last for ages.

As it contemplated its alien dark thoughts, musing on the simple wonder of suffering, the black thing realized a truth. Whatever pleasure the girl's destruction could produce would be nothing compared to the elation that could result from the destruction of the two boys. Such wonderful children, still innocent, still pure. They were the prize. Lingering terror and pain given to such as they would . . . The creature shuddered in dark anticipation at the image, then stilled itself, lest the one below take notice and make the black thing feel just such pain in turn. The youth stood another moment, one hand upon the tree, the other absently clutching at his groin as he held the image of the lovely human girl who had ridden past. Then, with a move like a spinning dance, the man-boy leaped back into the green vegetation, vanishing from mortal sight, leaving the small clearing empty save for the reverberations of impish laughter.

The black thing waited motionless after the youth vanished into the woods, for despite his youthful appearance, he was one to be feared, one who could cause great harm. When it was satisfied he was gone, and not playing one of his cruel tricks, it sprang with a powerful leap away from the tree. Its movements through the branches were alien, the articulation of its joints nothing of this world, as it hurried on its own errand of dark purpose.

8

"What's your mother doing?" asked Jack.

"I don't know. Last I heard she was off someplace in Central or South America, writing about another civil war or revolution." Gabbie sighed. "I don't hear from her a lot, maybe three letters in the last five years. She and my dad split up when I was less than five. That's when she got caught up doing the book on the fall of Saigon."

"I read it. It was brilliant."

Gabbie nodded. "Mom is a brilliant writer. But as a mother she's a totally lost cause."

"Look, if you'd rather not talk about it . . ."

"That's okay. Most of it's public record. Mom tried writing a couple of novels before she and my father moved to California. Neither of my folks made much money from writing, but Mom hated Dad's getting critical notice while she was getting rejection slips. Dad said she never showed much resentment, but it had to be one of the first strains on their marriage. Then Dad got the offer to adapt his second book, *All the Fine Promises,* and they moved to Hollywood. Dad wrote screenplays and made some solid money, and Mom had me. Then she got politically active in the antiwar movement, like, in '68, right after the Tet Offensive. She wrote articles and pamphlets and then a publisher asked her to do a book, you know, *Why We Resist.*

"It was pretty good, if a little heavy on polemics."

Gabbie steered her horse around a fallen dead tree surrounded by brush. "Well, she might have written bad fiction, but her nonfiction was dynamite. She got her critical notice. And a lot of money. Things were never very good for them, but that's when trouble really began and it got worse, fast. She'd get so involved in writing about the antiwar movement, then later the end of the war, that she'd leave him hanging all the time. Poor Dad, he'd have some studio dinner to go to or something and she'd not come home, or she'd show up in a flannel shirt and jeans at a formal reception, that sort of stuff. She became pretty radical. I was too young to remember any of it, but from what my grandmother told me, both of them acted pretty badly. But most folks say the breakup was Mom's fault. She can get real bitchy and she's stubborn. Even her own mother put most of the blame on her.

"Anyway, Dad came home one night and found her packing. She'd just gotten special permission from the Swiss Government to take a Red Cross flight to Vietnam, to cover the fall of Saigon. But she had to leave that night. Things hadn't been going well and Dad told her not to bother coming back if she left. So she didn't."

Jack nodded. "I don't mean to judge, but it seemed a pretty special opportunity for your mother, I mean with Saigon about to fall, and all." He left unsaid the implication that her father had been unreasonable in his demand his wife remain at home.

"Ya. But I was in the hospital with meningitis at the time. I almost died, they tell me." Gabbie looked thoughtful for a while. "I can hardly remember what she looks like, except for pictures of her, and that's not the same. Anyway, she became the radicals' darling, and by the time the war was over she'd become a pretty well-respected political writer. Now she's the grande dame of the Left, the spokesperson for populist causes all over the world. The only journalist allowed to interview Colonel Zamora when the rebels held him captive, and all that junk. You know all the rest."

"Must have been rough."

"I guess. I never knew it any different. Dad had put in pretty rugged hours at the studio and travel on location and the rest, so he left me with my grandmother. Anyway, she raised me until I was about twelve, then I went to private school in Arizona. My father wanted me to come live with him when he married Gloria, but my grandmother wouldn't allow it. I don't know, but I think he tried to get me back and she threatened him." She fixed Jack with a narrow gaze. "The Larkers are an old family with old money, I mean, serious old money. Like Learjets and international corporations. And lawyers, maybe dozens all on retainer, and political clout, lots of it. I think Grandma Larker owned a couple of judges in Phoenix. Anyway, she could blow away any court action Dad could bring, even if he had some money by most people's standards. So I stayed with her. Grandma was a little to the right of Attila the Hun, you know? *Nig-grows*, bleeding hearts, and 'Communist outside agitators'? She thought Reagan was a liberal, Goldwater soft on communism, and the Birchers a terrific bunch of guys and gals. So even . if she considered Mom a Commie flake, Grandma didn't want me living with 'that writer,' as she called Dad. She blamed Dad for Mom becoming a Commie flake, I guess. Anyway, Grandma Larker died two years ago, and I went to live with Dad. I lived with the family my last year in high school and my first year at UCLA. That's it."

Jack nodded, and Gabbie was surprised at what appeared to be genuine concern in his expression. She felt troubled by that, somehow as if she was under inspection. She felt suddenly self-conscious at what she was certain was babbling. Urging her horse forward, she said, "What about you?"

Jack caught up with the walking horse, and said, "Not much. Old North Carolina family. A many-greats-grandfather who chose raising horses instead of tobacco. Unfortunately, he bred slow racehorses, so all his neighbors got rich while he barely avoided bankruptcy. My family never had a lot of money, but we've got loads of genteel history"—he laughed—"and slow horses. We're big on tradition. No brothers or sisters. My father does research—physics—and teaches at UNC, which is why I went there as an undergraduate. My mother's an old-fashioned housewife. My upbringing was pretty normal, I'm afraid."

Gabbie sighed. "That sounds wonderful." Then, with a lightening tone, she said, "Come on, let's put on some speed." She made to kick My Dandelion.

Before she could, Jack shouted, "No!"

The tone of his voice caused Gabbie to jump, and she swung around to face him, color rising in her cheeks. She felt caught between embarrassment and anger. She didn't like his tone.

"Sorry to yell," he said, "but there's a nasty bit of a turn in the trail ahead and a deadfall, then you hit the bridge, and that's tricky. Like I said, this isn't a riding trail."

"Sorry." Gabbie turned forward, lapsing into silence. Something awkward had come between them and neither seemed sure of how to repair the damage.

Finally Jack said, "Look, I'm really sorry."

Petulantly Gabbie responded, "I said I was sorry."

With a fierce expression, Jack raised his voice slightly. "Well, I'm sorrier than you are."

Gabbie made a face and shouted, "Ya! Well, I'm sorrier than you'll ever be!"

They both continued the mock argument for a moment, then rode past the deadfall and discovered the bridge. Gabbie's horse shied and attempted to turn around. "Hey!" She put her leg to My Dandelion as the mare attempted to jig sideways. As the horse began to toss her head, Gabbie took firm rein and said, "Stop that!" The horse obeyed. Looking at Jack, Gabbie said, "What?"

"That's the Troll Bridge."

She groaned at the pun. *"That's* retarded."

"Well, that's what the kids call it. I don't think there's a troll waiting under it for billy goats, but for some reason the horses don't like to cross." To demonstrate the point, he had to use a firm rein and some vigorous kicks to get John Adams across the bridge. Gabbie followed suit and found My Dandelion reluctant to step upon the ancient stones, until Gabbie put her heels hard into her horse's sides. But as soon as the mare was halfway across, she nearly bolted forward, as if anxious to be off.

"That's pretty weird."

Jack nodded. "I don't know. Horses can be pretty funny. Maybe they smell something. Anyway, these woods are supposed to be haunted—"

"Haunted!" interrupted Gabbie, with a note of derision.

"I didn't say I believed, but some pretty strange things have gone on around here."

She rode forward, saying, "Like what?"

"Lights in the woods, you know? Like fox fire, but there's no marsh nearby. Maybe St. Elmo's fire. Anyway, some folks say they've heard music deep in the woods, and there's a story about some kids disappearing."

"Kidnapping?"

"No one knows. It happened almost a hundred years ago. Seems some folks went out for a Fourth of July picnic one time, and a couple of kids got lost in the woods."

"Sounds like a movie I once saw."

Jack grinned. "Yes, it was the same sort of thing. These woods can get you pretty turned around, and it was a heck of a lot rougher back then. No highway a mile to the west, just wagon roads. Pittsville was about a tenth the size it is today. No developments, or malls, only a few spread-out farms and a lot of woods. Anyway, they searched a long time and came up with nothing. No bodies, nothing. Some think the Indians killed them."

"Indians?"

"There was a reservation nearby. A small band of Cattaraugus, Alleganies, or some such. They shut it down a long time ago. But anyway, a bunch of farmers marched over there and were ready to start shooting. The Indians said it was spirits got the kids. And the funny thing was the farmers just turned round and went home. There's been a lot of other stuff like that over the years. These woods have a fair reputation for odd goings-on."

"For a southern boy you know a lot about these woods."

"Aggie," he said with an affectionate smile. "She's something of an expert. It's sort of a hobby with her. You'll see what I mean when you meet her. You're going next Sunday, aren't you?"

She smiled at his barely hidden interest. "I guess."

They cleared a thick stand of trees, then suddenly found themselves facing a large bald hillock. It rose to a height of twenty-five feet, dominating the clearing. Not a single plant save grasses grew on it, no tree or bush.

"A fairy mound!" said Gabbie with obvious delight.

"*Erlkönighügel.*"

"What?"

"*Erlkönighügel.* Erl King Hill, literally. Hill of the Elf King, in German; it's what Old Man Kessler's father called it. Erl King Hill is what the farm is officially called in the title deeds, though everyone hereabouts calls it the Old Kessler Place."

"Far out. Is there a story?"

Moving his horse in a lazy circle about the hill, Jack said, "Usually is about such things. But I don't know any. Just that the locals have called this place the Fairy Woods since Pittsville was founded in 1820. I guess that's where Old Man Kessler's father got the notion when he showed up eighty-odd years ago. They've got fairy myths in Germany. Anyway, 'Der Erlkönig' is a poem by Goethe. It's pretty scary stuff."

They left the hill behind and moved down a slight grade toward a path leading back to the farm. As they left, Gabbie cast a rearward glance at the hillock. For some reason she was left with the feeling the place was waiting. Brushing aside the strange notion, she turned her thoughts to how she was going to get Jack to call her again.

9

Agatha Grant's farm was a sea of green bordered by a shoreline of condos. Most of the surrounding land had been sold off over the years, and a new housing development, Colonial Woodlands, loomed up less than a hundred yards behind her barn. Only a large rambling meadow to the north of the house and the woods to the south protected the farm from the encroaching urban sprawl. She literally lived on the edge of Pittsville. The house was another turn-of-the-century marvel, though from the outside it appeared that considerably more thought had gone into its decor, mused Gloria.

Agatha stood waiting for them upon the front stoop, a bright-eyed elderly woman who appeared fit and upright despite the ivory-topped cane she held in her left hand. She greeted Philip warmly and bestowed polite kisses on Gloria's and Gabbie's cheeks. She ushered everyone into the large parlor, where Jack Cole waited, and invited them to take seats. The boys, as one, chose a love seat, fascinated by the strange two-way facing design. Gabbie and Gloria took comfortable stuffed chairs, while Aggie sat beside Phil on a large sofa, his hand held in hers.

Jack opened a breakfront, revealing a fine assortment of liquor, asked people their pleasure, and began pouring drinks. He handed a glass to Phil, who sipped and was pleased to discover a pungent, single-malt scotch. "Glenfiddich?"

"Glenfiddich."

"Thank you, *sir,*" observed Phil with deep appreciation.

Agatha said, "Have you something for the boys?"

Jack presented a pair of tumblers. "Coke. Okay?"

The boys took the offered pair of glasses. Jack passed around the other drinks, then remained at Agatha's side. After a moment Agatha said, "Jack, quit hovering over me. Go sit by that pretty girl over there, that's a good boy." Jack obeyed with a grin, settling upon the arm of Gabbie's chair. Agatha smiled, and Gloria now understood why her husband held her in such deep affection. She was a person of warmth, able to put strangers quickly at ease. She said to Phil, "When Malcolm Bishop ran that little piece in the Pittsville *Herald* saying you'd come home, I could scarcely believe it. What brought you back here?"

Phil laughed, glancing at Gloria. "I decided to return to writing novels."

"No, I mean why William Pitt County?" There was something in her manner of looking at Phil that caused Gloria a moment of discomfort. Somehow this elderly woman still held Phil accountable, as if he were still her student, and from Phil's expression he still felt somewhat accountable to her.

"It's my home. The old family house is small, only two bedrooms, and in a section of town that's pretty run-down now. So I looked around for something bigger and found the Old Kessler Place." He shrugged. "I don't know. I was sick of Los Angeles and the film business. I remember the fields and fishing at Doak's Pond. I remember the stories told about the Fairy Woods being haunted, and how we dared each other to go through them on Halloween and none of us ever did. I can remember the sandlot baseball games and riding my beat-up old bike down dusty roads during the summer. The dumb jokes the kids from Charlestown High used to make about *Pits*-ville High and how we used to get so mad at them and then say the same things ourselves. I remember . . . a home."

She nodded. "Well, you'll find it's changed a lot in twenty-five years." Then she smiled and suddenly the tension vanished. "But there's a lot that hasn't changed." Noticing that the boys had finished their drinks, she said, "Why don't you two run outside and play. We've some new additions in the barn. Our cat's had kittens."

The boys glanced at their mother, who nodded, and quickly made good their escape. Phil laughed. "I used to hate 'grown-up' talk when I was their age."

Agatha indicated agreement. "As did we all. Now, are you writing?"

"Yes, though it's tougher than I remember."

"It always is."

Jack laughed at the remark. "I say the same thing when I'm trying to organize her papers."

"This boy is almost as big an oaf as you were, which means he's a slightly better graduate assistant." Phil seemed unconcerned with the comparison. "Though, of my students, you have done better than most. I am glad you've returned to books. Those films were less than art."

Talk turned to the differences between screenplays and novels, and they settled in for a while, enjoying the rediscovered friendship between Agatha and Phil, and the new friendship between Jack and Gabbie. Gloria remained distant, observing her husband. Phil responded to Aggie's questions, and in a way her prodding produced more revelations about his work in minutes than Gloria had managed to extract in weeks. Not sure of her own reaction, Gloria settled in, considering.

She regretted Phil hadn't volunteered as much to her as to Aggie, but then Aggie was a special person to him. After his parents had died in a car crash, Phil had been raised by his aunt Jane Hastings. But Aggie Grant, Jane's best friend from college, and her husband, Henry, had been frequent visitors. When Phil had graduated from the University of Buffalo he had gone to Cornell to study with Aggie. And Aggie had secured the fellowship that had allowed Phil to attend the university. Gloria conceded that Aggie had been the single biggest influence in Phil's career. She had been a courtesy aunt, but, more than family, she was his mentor, then his graduate adviser, and remained the one person he held in unswerving professional regard. Gloria had read two of Agatha's books on literary criticism, and they had been a revelation. The woman's mind was a wonder, with her ability almost to intuit the author's thought processes at the time of writing from the finished work. She had never gained wide recognition outside of academia and she had her critics, but even the most vociferous conceded that her opinions were worthy of consideration. Somehow Aggie Grant posited theories about dead authors that just *felt* right. Still, in the field of literature, Gloria was simply a reader, not a critic, and some of what had been covered in Aggie's books seemed rites reserved for the initiates of the inner temple. No, if Agatha could get Phil talking about his work, and his problems, Gloria was thankful. Still, she felt a little left out.

Suddenly Agatha was addressing her. "And what do you think of all this?"

Gloria improvised, her actress's training coming to the fore. Somehow she didn't wish it known she had been musing, not following the conversation. "The work? Or the move?"

Agatha regarded her with a penetrating look, then smiled. "I meant the move. It must be something of a change for you, after Hollywood and all."

"Well, the East isn't new to me. I'm a California girl, but I lived in New York City for several years while I worked in theater. Still, this is my first stint as a farmer's wife."

"Hardly a farmer's wife, my dear. Herman Kessler kept only enough livestock to qualify for federal tax exemptions: a dozen sheep and lots of ducks and chickens. That farm has never been worked. Herman's father, Fredrick Kessler, never allowed it, nor did Herman. The meadows have not known the plow or the woodlands the ax for over a century. And this area was never as heavily harvested as others nearby to begin with. The woods behind your home may not be the forest primeval, but they are some of the densest in ten thousand square miles, perhaps the only such parcel of uncleared lowland woods in the entire state of New York."

Phil said, "I was meaning to ask you: when we were at Cornell you were firmly established up in Ithaca. Now you show up in my old hometown. Why?"

She rose and went over to a sliding door. "A moment." She moved the door aside and vanished from view, reappearing almost immediately with a large blue three-ring binder. She returned to the couch and handed the binder to Phil as she sat down.

He opened it and read the first page. " 'On the Migration of Irish Folk Myth and Legend to America in the Eighteenth and Nineteenth Centuries. A critical study by Agatha Grant.' " He closed it. "I thought you'd retired."

"I'm retired, not dead. This has been a hobby piece of mine for more years than I can recall." She seemed to consider. "I began it shortly after my Henry died. I was working on it when I was your adviser; I just never told you about it. Aarne and Thompson did some fine classification that came out in 1961. What I'm doing is using their motif index in following up on the work of Reidar Christiansen. He compared and studied Scandinavian and Irish folklore. I'm trying to do something like that with the older Celtic myths and the Irish folktales which have come to America."

She addressed Gloria and Gabbie as well as Phil. "When I was a girl, growing up at East Hampton, we had a lovely governess, an Irish woman named Colleen O'Mara. Miss O'Mara would tell my brother and me the most wonderful tales of elves and fairies, leprechauns and brownies. All my life I've been fascinated by folk myth. My formal education was in classics and contemporary literature, but I read Yeats's fairy tales as readily as his poetry—perhaps with more enthusiasm. In any event, that is my work now. There were many immigrations from Ireland—besides the famous 'potato famine' one—and thousands of poor, rural Irish came to America. Now, most of those who came settled in the big cities or went west to work the railroads. But Pittsville was one of the few rural communities to capture several waves of these Irish immigrants, many of whom remained farmers. This area is almost a 'little Ireland.' I'm no stranger to the area, having visited my darling Jane many times over the years." She shared a fond look with Phil at the mention of his late aunt. "When I was offered the chair at Fredonia, I didn't pause a moment in deciding where to live. I like Pittsville. We're only a half hour from the campus here. And there were unexpected bonuses."

Phil showed he didn't understand, and Jack offered, "Marcus Blackman lives nearby." He pointed absently toward the west.

"The occult guy?" asked Phil, with obvious interest.

Jack said, "That's him."

"Who's Blackman?" asked Gabbie.

Jack said, "Blackman's a writer, a scholar, a bit of everything. He's something of a character and pretty controversial. He's written a lot of odd books about magic and the occult that have gotten the academic community upset. And he's Aggie's favorite debating opponent."

Agatha said, "Mark Blackman's a bit of a rogue in research and full of indefensible opinions, but he's absolutely charming. You'll meet him shortly. He'll join us for dinner."

"Wonderful," said Phil.

"He's also a fund of information on just the sort of things I'm digging into," said Agatha. "In his library he has some very rare books— a first edition of Thomas Crofton Croker's *Fairy Legends and Traditions of the South of Ireland,* if you can believe—and an amazing number of personal journals and diaries. His help has been invaluable."

"What is Blackman doing in Pittsville?"

"You can ask him. I've gotten nothing like a reasonable answer, though he's very amusing in his avoidance. He has ventured he is working on a new book, though the subject matter is unknown to me. That is all." Agatha paused as she considered. "I find the man fascinating, but also a little irritating with his secrecy."

Phil laughed. "Agatha believes in spreading ideas around." He made the remark to the others over Agatha's protests. "When I began writing fiction on the side, as a grad student, she couldn't understand why I wouldn't show it to her until it was done."

To Gabbie, Agatha said, "Child, your father doesn't write. He brews magic in a cave and woe unto him who breaks the spell before it's done."

Phil joined in the general laughter, and the talk turned to old friends and colleagues from their days together at Cornell.

10

Patrick and Sean hovered over the box in the barn. The cat regarded the boys with indifference as they petted and played with her kittens. Her babies were at that awkward stage just after their eyes had opened, their clumsy antics provoking laughter from the boys.

Patrick picked up a kitten, who mewed slightly. He petted it and said, "Pretty neat, huh?"

Sean nodded as he reached out and stroked another. A scurrying in the hay near the darkest corner of the barn caught his attention. "What's that?"

"What?"

"Over there—something moving in the hay." He pointed. Patrick put down the kitten and rose. He walked purposefully toward the dark corner as Sean said, "Don't!"

Patrick hesitated and turned to face his brother. "Why!" he demanded.

Sean reluctantly came over to stand by his brother. "Maybe it's a rat or something."

"Oh brother!" said Patrick. "You're such a baby." He glanced around and saw an old rusty pitchfork by the door. He fetched it from the wall, barely able to balance the long tool. Slowly he moved toward the corner and began poking at the old straw. For a long moment there was no hint that anything but straw rested beneath the rusty tines

Patrick waved before him. Gingerly he poked the fork deeper into the straw, moving it aside.

Then something appeared from under the straw. It stood less than two feet tall, regarding the boys with large, blinking eyes. It was a little man. From head to foot it was dressed in odd-looking garments: a tall hat, a green coat, tightly cut breeches, and shoes with tiny golden buckles.

The boys stood motionless, as if unable even to breathe. The little man tipped his hat and, with a wild, piercing laugh, leaped from the straw, jumping high between the boys and landing at a scampering run across the barn floor. Patrick echoed Sean's yelp of fright as he dropped the pitchfork and spun around, his eyes never leaving the diminutive creature who leaped high up on the opposite wall, vanishing through a crack between loose boards.

The boys stood silently rooted, their eyes wide with wonder as they attempted to sort out the flashing kaleidoscope of images they had witnessed. Both were shaking, terrified by the vision. Slowly they turned to face one another and each saw mirrored in his twin his own fright. Wide blue eyes, frozen smiles, and rigid posture suddenly gave way to motion as they dashed for the door.

They sped outside, looking back into the barn. Then a shadow loomed before them and they were enfolded in a pair of powerful arms. The boys shrieked in terror as they were tightly held. An odd odor stung their noses and a deep, scratchy voice rumbled, "Here, then! What's it all about, lads?"

The boys were let go and retreated a step; they saw the shadow take shape in the form of an old man. He was broad of shoulder and tall, his grey hair unkempt and his unshaven face seamed and leathery. Redshot eyes regarded them, but he was smiling in a friendly way.

Patrick's heart slowed its thundering beat and he cast a glance at Sean. A thought passed between them, for they recognized the odor that hovered about the man like a musky nimbus. The man smelled of whiskey.

"Easy, then, what is it?"

"Something back there," ventured Patrick, pointing at the barn. "In the hay."

The man passed the boys into the barn, then waited while they indicated the corner. He walked purposefully to where the pitchfork lay and made a display of poking about in the straw. "It's gone now," said Sean. The man knelt and moved some straw about, then stood and used the fork to put the straw back in a semblance of order. He turned a smiling, good-humored face toward the boys. "What was it, then? A barn rat?"

Patrick glanced at Sean and gave him an almost imperceptible head shake, warning him to say nothing. "Maybe," said Patrick. "But it was pretty big." His voice was strident, and he fought to regain control of himself.

The man turned where he stood, looking down on the earnest little faces. "Big, you say? Well, if there were chickens or ducks here, which there aren't, and if it were night, which it isn't, I'd suspect a weasel or fox. Whatever it was, it's vanished like yesterday's promises." The man returned the pitchfork to its place on the wall. He looked hard at the boys. "Now, lads, which one of you wants to be the first to tell me just what you saw?"

Patrick remained silent, but Sean finally said, "It was big and it had teeth." His voice still shook, so he sounded convincing.

Instantly the man's expression changed. In two strides he stood before them, hands upon knees as he lowered his face to the boys' level. "How big?"

Patrick held his hands about two feet apart. "Like this."

The man slowly stood up, rubbing at his whiskery chin. "By the saints. It could have been that big old bandit come looking for a kitten dinner," he said quietly.

"What bandit?" asked Patrick, not understanding why anyone would wish to eat kittens.

The man's attention returned from his musing. "Why, he's a raccoon. An old tyrant of a coon who lives in the woods to the east of here. He's been killing chickens and ducks for a month or so and occasionally chews up cats and dogs." Almost to himself, he added, "Though if it were himself, mama cat here would have been raising a right royal fuss."

Sean nodded, and Patrick said, "Jack said he lived under a bridge."

"He did, did he now? Jack Cole is a fine enough lad, but he's a foreigner, hailing from North Carolina as he does. Still, grown-ups always have to come up with an answer, even if they're wrong." The boys agreed to that. "If the farmers knew where the bandit hid out, they'd have had him out weeks ago.

"Now, lads, I don't think Miss Grant will take kindly to the news a bull coon's poking about her barn and menacing her barn cat's brood. Are we agreed?"

The boys shrugged and said yes. The man rubbed his chin again. "Well, we have your word. So there's an end to it." Changing the subject, he said, "Now, what are you boys doing in Miss Agatha's barn?"

"She said we could play with the kittens."

"Well then," offered the man, "if she did, she did. But they're tiny ones and like all babies need their rest. Why don't we go outside and see the new lambs in the meadow." He gently but firmly ushered them outside. "And who might you boys be?"

The boys offered their names, and the man said, "Patrick and Sean? Sure and those are fine Irish names."

Patrick grinned. "Our mother's Irish. Her name was O'Brien."

"O'Brien!" the man exclaimed. "She wouldn't be an O'Brien from Ballyhack, now would she?"

"She's from Glendale," observed Sean.

"Sure, there's a fair number of O'Briens about and that's a fact." He halted outside the barn. "Well, Sean and Patrick, they call me Barney Doyle, which is as it should be, for that's my name. Pleased to make your acquaintance." He shook hands solemnly with the boys. "Now let's go look at lambs."

As they made their way across the backyard, the screen door opened and Agatha Grant looked out. "Barney Doyle! Where are you going with those boys?"

"To show the lads the new lambs, Miss Agatha."

"And what about my pump? I need water for dinner."

"All fixed and working like new, which, had you turned the faucet, you would have known. I was, this very moment, going to stop off on our way and tell you just that."

Her expression indicated a limited willingness for belief, but she only nodded. "Dinner will be in an hour, so have them back in time to clean up."

"Yes, Miss Agatha."

After she returned inside, Barney said, "A fine lady, even if she isn't Irish. Come now and we can see the lambs."

As they walked down the path toward the meadow south of the house, a car turned up the drive from the road and headed toward the house. The boys ran ahead and Barney reached up to scratch his head. That there was something in the barn two feet long and with big teeth he doubted, for the barn cat would have been hauling her kittens out if a predator had lurked nearby. But that something had frightened the boys there was no doubt. He offered a short prayer to St. Patrick and St. Jude that it was only noises and shadows that had frightened the boys and not what he feared, then hurried after the boys.

11

Two men got out of the car as Agatha watched from her porch. Philip stood beside her, observing the pair. The driver was a tall man, his stride quick and purposeful. His hair was black save for streaks of grey at the temples, combed straight back from a high forehead, but his close-cut beard was black. His age was indeterminate: somewhere between thirty and fifty. He wore a white turtleneck and brown corduroy jacket, despite the warm weather, above brown slacks. As he came up the steps, smiling in greeting at Agatha, Philip noted his eyes were so dark as to be close to black.

"Mark, this is Philip Hastings."

The man shook hands and said, "I've read your books, Mr. Hastings. I'm something of a fan."

"Phil, please."

"And this is Gary Thieus," said Agatha. Philip extended his hand.

"Call me Gary," offered the man with a wide grin that revealed an improbable amount of teeth. His hair was cut very short, nearly a crew cut, and his ears stuck out and were almost pointed.

Mark said, "He's my assistant and is the best cook around—present company excluded."

"Come inside and have a drink. Dinner is cooking and we can all get acquainted." Agatha allowed Philip to hold open the door as she led the others inside.

Philip followed last, behind Gary. Blackman's assistant moved with a loose-gaited walk that suggested a basketball player to Philip, or at least some sort of athletic background.

Jack offered drinks to Mark and Gary, while Agatha removed herself to the kitchen to finish dinner. Jack returned to Gabbie's side; Gloria was smiling at Mark's comment that he had seen her once in a play. When he commented upon a small problem during the second act, she grinned. "You did see the play!" She reached out and squeezed his hand. "In my former calling, you hear a lot of empty flattery."

"No, I did see the play and remember your performance quite well."

Gary said, "Jack, how about a game of tennis tomorrow?"

Jack groaned. "You mean how about you administering another thrashing?" He said to Gabbie, "He knows I've a gimpy leg and delights in embarrassing me."

"Do you play?" Gary inquired of Gabbie.

"A little," the girl answered.

"Good, I'll call Ellen and we can play some doubles."

Gabbie shrugged. Jack said, "At least we'll go down together. Gary's girlfriend is as good a tennis player as he is—which is very good. I hope you can cover a lot of court."

Gabbie smiled slightly, and Gloria grinned behind her glass as she sipped her drink. Mark leaned close and said, "She plays well?"

"Gabbie plays tennis like it's war," whispered Gloria.

"Gary's pretty good; so is Ellen."

"It should be a good match," offered Phil, coming over to sit beside his wife.

"You've purchased the Old Kessler Place," commented Mark. "That's one of the most interesting pieces of land around here. I tried to rent it myself when I first moved here."

Gloria and Phil exchanged glances and Phil said, "It was just a matter of luck I inquired the week it came on the market. It was a steal at the price. But Kessler died only a month before I called the broker. So you must have tried to rent it from the old man himself."

"Not really. When I came to this area, Kessler was in Germany and the house empty for almost a year, but I couldn't find anyone who could tell me how to reach him. Perhaps he was visiting relatives, or friends of his father. That's where he died, you know."

Phil nodded. "That was mentioned. Why'd you want to rent the farm?"

Mark smiled. "There's a lot of history about that place." He paused, then said, "I'm working on a new book myself, and while I'm reluctant to discuss it, let's say that the history of the Kessler family has no small bearing upon the subject matter. Herman's father, Fredrick Kessler, was something of a mystery man. He arrived from somewhere in the south of Germany, or perhaps Austria, in 1905, with a lot of money. It appears that when the First World War broke out there was some minor problem with his citizenship, but other than that he was a model member of the community. He married a girl named Helga Dorfmann and had one son. He built a furniture factory, competing with the larger manufacturers over in Jamestown. His furniture was sturdy and cheap, and he made a lot of money. One of the more interesting stories is that he had a fortune in gold buried somewhere on the property."

Gloria laughed in delight. "Buried treasure! Let's start digging!"

Gary grinned his toothy grin. "You've a lot of property. It could take some time. Besides, it's only a story."

"My interest," commented Blackman, "was in the Kessler library and any other oddities lying about, the ephemerides of the days of Fredrick Kessler's youth, so to speak."

Gloria glanced at Phil, who said, "I've only glanced at the books in the library. The broker had no idea what was in the house. When Kessler died, he owed a lot of back taxes, and the state was in a hurry to sell it. The court appointed Kessler's bank executor. I got the impression things were left a little informal. The loan officer I dealt with was pretty obviously in a rush to unload it; they'd halted the foreclosure and hurried the sale. Anyway, he said there was no family, so he tossed everything into the deal, including old clothes, dishes, the furniture and books. I don't know a tenth of what's there. You're welcome to drop in and borrow anything you'd like."

"I was hoping you'd invite me. Perhaps in a few days. I'll tell you what: if you don't mind Gary and me prowling about for a while, we'll catalog the library as we go, so you'll have a full inventory when we're through. And if anything strikes my fancy, give me first chance to buy."

"You've got it."

Gloria said, "There's a bunch of old trunks in the attic and basement, too."

Gary's eyes almost lit up. "Wonderful. Who knows what odd bits of treasure lurk in the dark!"

Gabbie laughed. "Jack said the woods are haunted; now buried treasure. You sure know how to pick 'em, Dad."

Agatha reappeared and demanded assistance, so Jack drafted Gabbie and the two went off to set the table. Gary mentioned a film of Phil's and the talk turned to stories of Hollywood and the frustrations of filmmaking. Gloria settled back, letting the conversation slip by her. For some reason the talk of buried treasure and haunted woods had made her uncomfortable. And for some unexplained reason she wondered how the boys were.

12

Dinner was superb. True to Jack's promise, Agatha Grant was an exceptional cook. She produced an elegant meal, each dish prepared with an attention to detail guaranteed to make it a treat. Even the twins, who tended to be fussy eaters, finished their food with no complaint.

Gloria had noticed they seemed somewhere else, and occasionally caught them glancing at each other, as if sharing something between themselves. She inquired if they had enjoyed themselves, and they agreed Aggie's farm was pretty neat. "Barney showed us the lambs," ventured Sean.

Phil said, "Who's Barney?"

"He's a man," said Sean. "He was fixing the plumbing."

"Ya, and he smells like Uncle Steve," said Patrick as he impaled a broccoli spear with his fork. "Uncle" Steve Owinski was another screenwriter and a close friend of Phil's, and he was a chronic drinker.

Jack rose and quickly cleared away the dinner plates, carrying them to the kitchen. Agatha said, "Barney Doyle. He's the local handyman." Seeing a small look of concern on Gloria's face, she added, "He's a bit of a tippler, but completely harmless. From what I hear, he was a ripsnorter as a young man, but swore off drinking years ago. Suddenly he's drinking again. I can't imagine why."

Gary said, "Well, you know what they say about alcoholics never being truly recovered." Gloria nodded.

"Anyway," said Agatha, "he's a fine fix-it man, and if you have any problems, give him a call. The service men from the mall stores take forever, want to take everything back to the shop, then keep whatever for months. Barney's reliable and cheap. He has a work shed, little more than a shack, on the other side of my property, right at the end of Williams Avenue. You can cut through the woods from your home." Agatha smiled fondly. "Barney fits my longing for simpler times, when all you had was the local fix-it shop. He's a living American artifact. Besides, I have him around as much for research as the need for repairs. The man was born in Ireland and has an astonishing wealth of Irish oral tradition. In comparing what he knows with what the second-, third-, and fourth-generation Irish here know, I can begin to gauge how much change the myths have undergone in Ireland and America."

Jack stuck his head through the door. "Coffee?" He took stock of who indicated yes, and vanished back into the kitchen.

Gabbie rose. "I think I'll give Jack a hand."

Mark said, "Aggie's picked a tough one. Irish lore, like most in Europe, has been 'frozen' by the printing press. Children now read fairy tales rather than listen at their mother's knee—if they read them at all."

"So you don't think she'll find much variation?" asked Phil.

Mark shook his head in the negative, while Agatha smiled indulgently. "We've had this argument before," she ventured. "Mark is something of a homegrown social anthropologist and claims there is no true oral tradition in Europe or America anymore."

"Well, maybe among the older American Indians and rural folk up in the Appalachians, but nowhere else. Not when you can pick up a book and read the same story in England and America. No, if you're researching myths about cluricaunes, you'll find the same story in William Pitt County as you would in County Cork."

"What are cluricaunes?" asked Phil.

Agatha said, "Leprechauns. They're called lurikeen, lurigandaun, and luricans in different parts of Ireland."

Gloria sat back. There was something passing between the boys, she could sense it. And it worried her. She silently wondered why the talk was making her tense.

Agatha glanced at the boys and asked, "Do you boys know what a leprechaun is?"

"Little men in green coats?" said Patrick, an odd expression on his face.

Sean's eyes widened at Patrick's answer, then suddenly his face became animated as he blurted, "Darby O'Gill!"

Phil laughed. "Just so."

Mark said, "Who's Darby O'Gill?"

"It's a Disney film, *Darby O'Gill and the Little People*. The boys saw it before we left California."

"Yeah," said Sean with a pout. "We had the Disney Channel on cable."

"I rest my case," offered Mark. "The boys are getting their folk myths from television."

Gloria said, "They've been disconsolate there's no cable available out at the farm." She roughed Sean's hair. "Now you'll just have to make do with three channels, like normal people."

Phil said, "I was saving it as a surprise, boys, but I've ordered a satellite dish installed next week."

The two boys' eyes widened. "We'll get hundreds of channels!" shouted Patrick.

Over the laughter in the dining room, Gloria ordered the boys to stifle their enthusiasm. Sean said, "Barry Walter's father has the channel with naked ladies on it."

Gloria said, "We'll talk about this when we get home."

Phil laughed. "It's all right. I got the one with the lock switch. The boys won't be watching any X-rated movies for a few more years."

Jack and Gabbie returned with cake and coffee.

"Speaking of fairy myths, does anyone know what night this is?" Gary asked.

Mark and Agatha looked at each other and laughed, but it was Gloria who answered. "Midsummer's Night."

"Like in Shakespeare?" said Jack.

Phil said, "I thought the solstice was three days ago."

"On the calendar of the Church, it's the twenty-fourth," said Gloria. "The nativity of St. John the Baptist."

Phil said, "I've read *A Midsummer Night's Dream*. I thought it was just . . . a night in the middle of summer."

Agatha said, "There are three days supposedly special to fairies: May first, June twenty-fourth, and November first. This is a night of power and celebration according to legend."

"What are the other two days? I know the first of November is All Saints', but what about the first of May?"

"May Day," ventured Gary. "Fairies are Marxists."

Over the groans of the others, Agatha said, "It's the day after Walpurgis Night, just as All Saints' follows Halloween. Both are Moving Days."

When the others looked uncomprehending, Mark Blackman said,

"In the Irish tradition, the fairies move from place to place on those two days. We're speaking of the Trooping Fairies. Shakespeare had them staying forever in the night:

> " 'And we fairies, that do run
> By the triple Hecate's team,
> From the presence of the sun,
> Following darkness like a dream.'

"But he's alone in that view. According to tradition, the fairies live for six months in a stand of woods, then move to another, perhaps on the other side of the world. And they make the move in one night."

Mark again quoted Shakespeare:

> " 'We the globe can compass soon,
> Swifter than the wandering moon.' "

"It's why fairy stories abound everywhere. Over the ages the fairies have lived in every part of the world," said Aggie. "If you believe in them."

"And tonight's a special night for them?" ventured Gabbie with a laugh.

"According to legend," agreed Agatha. "They'll be throwing a grand party tonight."

Turning to Jack, Gabbie said, "Let's go out to that fairy mound we saw the other day. Maybe we'll see the party."

"I wouldn't," said Mark. All eyes turned to regard him. "Those woods are pretty dangerous in the dark."

Gloria looked alarmed. "How do you mean, dangerous?"

Gabbie made a face. "Ghosts? Indian spirits?"

"Gabbie, let him answer," snapped Gloria. Gabbie flushed and was about to retort when she saw Jack shaking his head and indicating the boys, who sat in rapt attention. Suddenly she understood Gloria's worry, and she felt silly. "Why are the woods dangerous, Mark? Wild animals?"

Mark smiled and tried to look reassuring. "No, nothing like that. No bears or wolves in ages. Nothing much bigger than a weasel or fox since the turn of the century. Just, it's easy to get lost there and there are a lot more woods than you'd think and they're pretty dense in places." Mark turned to Aggie. "Remember Reno McManus? He got lost taking a shortcut in the dark, fell down an embankment, and broke his hip. It was two days before anyone found him. Died of exposure. And he'd lived all his life in the area. It's just a bad idea to be poking about in the woods after dark, that's all I meant."

Agatha said, "Reno McManus was a drunk, and he could have gotten lost in his own bathtub. If Jack and Gabbie take a light and stay to the path, they should have no trouble." Her eyes were merry as she cast a glance at the youngsters, indicating Mark was being obtuse in not seeing they wanted some time alone together.

Mark said, "Well, that's true." He let the conversation fall off.

Agatha rose. "Let's retire to the parlor, like civilized folk, and we can continue this lovely evening." She glanced at Jack. "Fetch the brandy, won't you?"

They left the dining room and were soon all settled comfortably in the parlor, where the talk turned to other topics. Gloria, sitting next to Phil, glanced at the boys, who were being considerably less obstreperous than usual. There was something she had meant to ask them earlier at the table, but she couldn't remember what it was. She let the thought slip away.

13

Gabbie and Jack walked slowly along the path as the circle of light swept along before them, revealing the twigs and other impediments to easy passage. Gabbie had insisted Jack walk in the woods with her, in search of the fairy party. The flashlight flickered, then dimmed for a minute. "Shit!" he said. "Damn batteries are weak."

"I declare," she said with a broad southern accent, "such language! And you a gentleman, sir!" Jack grinned, half-seen in the gloom. "It's okay, Lancelot. I've heard a few Anglo-Saxon expletives in my day. I'm a liberated girl."

Jack laughed quietly. "So I've noticed. And something special, too."

Gabbie turned silent as they walked, then said, "You're not just saying that, are you?"

He stopped, letting the flashlight point down. In the light reflected back from the path they studied each other. He said nothing, but leaned forward and kissed her gently. She froze a moment, then stepped in to him, letting his arms wrap around her. She could feel the strength in his body, and her heart pounded with a rush of excitement. After a time, she gently pushed herself away, softly saying, "Ah . . . that was a pretty good answer."

He smiled. "I guess." Slipping his arm around her waist, he resumed walking slowly, Gabbie matching his pace. "I do think you're special, Gabbie. You've been through a lot, I know, but it's made you thoughtful. Most of the girls your age I've known are a lot younger."

She leaned her head against his arm. "I try to hide it sometimes. You . . . I guess I trust you."

"Thanks."

She let a moment go by where the only sounds were their feet on the path and the breeze through the trees. The evening was warm and damp and the moon hung nearly full in the night, giving the woods a little illumination. Finally she said, "I . . . you seeing anyone special?"

"No one special," he answered without hesitation. He paused, then added, "I had a girlfriend, back at Chapel Hill, Ginger Colfield. We met standing in line at junior registration, Cole, Colfield. We were sort of serious. At least, Ginger was serious. But when I came here it got kind of hard to hold things together, you know? Ginger's down in Atlanta now, working for Coca-Cola, in advertising. I think she's engaged. Since last year, nothing worth talking about. You?"

"Just a high school boyfriend, two years ago in Arizona. Nothing since then. Just dating around."

Jack said, "Never do much of that. I tend to land in a relationship and stay there a long time." He paused. "The last one sort of left me a little beat up, you know?"

Gabbie felt both comforted by the revelation and troubled. She liked Jack a lot, as much as any boy she'd met in a long time, but she was also worried things might get out of hand. "You don't think much of long-distance romance, huh?"

He stopped and said, "You're going back to California in September, right?"

She turned to face him. "Yes." Suddenly she was angry at herself for rushing. "Look, I don't mean to make a big thing out of this, okay?"

He looked away, as if seeking something in the night, then said, "Maybe it is a big thing."

She tensed as if not knowing what to do next. Her feelings were surging up from some deep place, surprising her with their intensity. She was suddenly very scared of Jack Cole and the effect he was having on her. But she also knew that what was said in the next few minutes would have a major impact on her for at least the rest of the summer, and perhaps for a great deal longer than that. With a sigh, a releasing of that sudden energy, she leaned forward, resting her head on his shoulder. "Man . . . what are you doing to me?"

He held her, saying nothing. She felt as if her heart were trying to burst out of her rib cage, as if she couldn't get a breath of air. Softly he spoke into her ear. "You could transfer to Fredonia. I might still be able to get accepted into the program at UC San Diego. We could run off to Paris and live in a garret—except my French stinks." She giggled. "But why don't we just wait and see if you still feel like talking to me tomorrow, okay?"

She smiled up at him, put at ease by his answer. She saw something sweet and caring in his eyes, evident despite the murk of the night. With a sudden surge of warmth through her body, she said, "I could develop a serious case of like for you, Jack Cole."

For an answer, he kissed her. After they separated, she added in husky tones, "Maybe more."

They kissed again. Gabbie was suddenly aware that for the first time since she'd started dating she was with a man who could take her somewhere and make love to her and she would go willingly, without protest or hesitation. Her blood drummed in her ears, and her breath was deep and quick. In an odd detached moment, she wondered, Am I falling in love with this man?

Suddenly Jack stiffened, breaking the mood. She said, "What?"

"Listen," he said softly.

She strained and heard nothing at first, then a faint, unfamiliar sound. It hung just under the masking noise of the branches rustling in the night breeze, a hint of something different, maddeningly close to being recognizable, but just beyond comprehension.

Then there was something else in the air, a terrifyingly sad yet wonderful quality. Something hovered at the limits of understanding, reaching past the conscious mind to touch a more primitive and basic element of their emotions. With a quickening pulse, Gabbie found tears welling in her eyes, and she whispered, "What's happening?"

Holding her close, Jack whispered back, "I don't know, Gabbie. I don't know." He breathed deeply, as if reaching to take control of the alien and powerful emotions that swept through him. Another deep breath, and he said, "Something strange is going on." He looked around. "I think over there."

With those words, the spell was somehow broken. Whatever those astonishing and strange feelings were, they fled as he moved. She also breathed deeply, forcing herself to calm, and followed him.

Cautiously they moved through the woods toward the source of the sensations. As they climbed over a fallen tree trunk, Jack said, "I know where we are."

Gabbie looked about and hadn't the faintest notion where they were. Her attention had been riveted to Jack, and she suddenly felt concern that if anything happened to him she'd not have a hint on how to find help. "Where are we?"

He pointed with the dimming flashlight and softly said, "The Troll Bridge is over there, just beyond that other rise. From there the path goes straight to your back door."

She nodded, relieved to know. Jack moved forward, like a soldier on patrol, slightly hunched over, body tensed, as if expecting an ambush. He worked his way through the trees, climbing a small rise. Near the top, he swore. "What is it?" Gabbie asked.

"Damn flashlight went out." She could hear him hitting it against the palm of one hand, but no light was forthcoming. After a futile attempt at wishing it back into life, Jack put the light in his back pocket. He glanced about, letting his eyes adjust to the gloom. "Come to me," he whispered.

Gabbie climbed up and could see him in the dark. "There's a little moonlight," he offered, "but be careful. You get to where you think you can see and you can still fall and break a leg."

"Should we go back?"

"It's safer if we finish going up, then get the path on the other side of Erl King Hill. Come on." He held her hand and led her the rest of the way to the top of the rise. Abruptly his body tensed. Gabbie squeezed his hand. "What?"

Jack's eyes were wide with astonishment. He could only point. For an instant Gabbie couldn't see what had caused him to halt, then in the gloom she saw it. Across the bald top of Erl King Hill something moved. It was as if a cloud had passed before the moon, making shadows dance. Gabbie glanced up; the sky was clear, without stars because of the bright moon overhead. Slowly her eyes adapted to the light and she began to perceive something moving across the top of the hill. Shapes, suggestive of human form, seemed to be moving in rhythm, a swaying, orderly pavane to an unheard song. On the breeze came a faint tinkling, almost chimes, almost music. And a scent graced the air, a blending of spices and wildflowers, something alien yet familiar.

Jack rubbed at his eyes with his free hand, as if fearing that some affliction was responsible for the vision. Gabbie was about to speak when Jack pulled her back behind a tree. Something was approaching. Jack held Gabbie tight, and for some reason she was terribly afraid.

Something came through the night and it plunged Gabbie into a primitive emotional state, a childlike dread as some unknown terror approached in the dark. She clung to Jack. He stood firm, a rock to shelter under, her protector. In that instant something happened within Gabbie and she understood Jack would defend her. And in that instant her concern shifted from herself to Jack. Suddenly she was afraid of losing him.

The dread rose up within, and Gabbie knew something powerful and wicked loomed close at hand. Whatever it was came within touching distance. Gabbie buried her face against Jack's chest and held her breath, overwhelmed by inexplicable fear. She felt a presence manifest itself nearby, then around them, and whatever it was knew they were hiding behind the tree and was about to reach for them, and if it touched them they would both be lost. Primitive recognition came into focus, and a scream rose in Gabbie's throat.

Then the presence vanished. Gabbie checked the urge to shriek and run, swallowing her own fear. She felt Jack rock-hard with tension, breathing in rapid, shallow rhythm. Whatever had been approaching had turned away, and the sense of dread had turned away with it. Gabbie dug her fingers into Jack's shirt and listened, but the evil presence, the thing of nameless horror, had gone.

In the dark they heard only the sounds of the night, the breeze moving the ancient branches, the rustle of leaves blowing through the woods. A scampering sound here and there would alert them to the passage of a night creature, perhaps a red squirrel fleeing the approach of a owl, or a raccoon foraging nearby.

Gabbie gasped a deep breath, a feeling of relief surging through her. She felt Jack slowly relax. He whispered, "You okay?"

She whispered back, "Yes. What the hell was all that?"

"I don't know." He led her away from the bole of the tree and glanced over the rise. Whatever they had seen before seemed to have vanished without a trace. After a silent moment Jack said, "What did you see there?"

Gabbie hesitated, not certain. "Something. Vague shapes. Maybe that light you talked about when we were riding. You know, St. Elmo's fire. Anyway, it was pretty dim."

Jack remained silent for a long time. At last he said, "Yes, that must have been it."

"Why? What did you see?"

Jack looked at her, his face white in the moonlight. "You're going to think I'm crazy, but I could have sworn for the first moment that I saw a bunch of people dancing across the top of the hill, all dressed up in robes and gowns. Then suddenly it was like looking through a fog."

Without conviction she said, "Too much brandy?"

"Maybe. But one thing is certain, it was weird." He took her by the hand and led her over the rise, down toward the path home. "From now on, when I hear strange stories about these woods I think I'll take them a little more seriously."

Resuming their walk, Gabbie reviewed what had happened. As

they left Erl King Hill, the memory of the figures on the hill became faint, less distinct, until she was certain she had only imagined recognizable shapes, and the terror had been some unreasoning fear in the dark. As they crossed the Troll Bridge and made their way toward home, Gabbie became more and more certain she had been the victim of her own imagination.

"Jack?"

"What?"

"This is going to sound dumb, but . . . what did we see on the hill back there?"

Jack faltered a moment, as if the question surprised him, then fell back into step. "What . . . ? Something . . . I don't know. I think it was a trick of the light. Why? Worried?"

She said not, then fell silent. She couldn't imagine why she had been so worked up over a few strange movements in the distance. She was certain what she and Jack had seen was but shadows and moonlight playing across the bald hill. And her mind was quickly losing its fascination with mysteries in the dark woods. It was turning to the question of her feelings for Jack, and that was enough of a mystery for her.

Behind them, in the gloom, he stepped out from behind a tree, while the sound of the dancers carried past him on the wind. He was black and featureless as he hid from mortal eyes. Then he willed the mask changed and suddenly he was stunning in his beauty, a figure of awesome perfection. His eyes were blue, like the ice of a frozen lake in a winterscape never seen by mortals, and his movements were supple, and he seemed to flow across the landscape without sound. His form was encased in a faint glow, and around him hovered the scent of spices and wildflowers. He was light and beauty and he was evil. He watched until Jack and Gabbie vanished from his sight, then he turned to face in the direction of the other. Her presence so near had halted him as he had thought to trouble the two mortals passing by. Only she could challenge his will. Only she had enough power to possibly balk him. With anger mixed with a hint of fear, he laughed, and the night's blackness was rent by the sound. With a smile that held no humor, he bowed in the direction of the Queen's court and vanished.

Upon the distant hillock the Queen's court paused in their dance, for the music halted. The musicians turned as one, looking past the dancers into the night. All shivered, for they knew he was again upon the night, taking unto himself that which he desired, and save for the Queen's protection, all were at his mercy. They were afraid, for to hear the sound of his laughter was to hear madness.

14

Gloria jumped slightly at the sound of the kitchen door slamming. For just an instant she heard another sound in the distance, the sound of laughter. She put aside her discomfort as she heard Gabbie's and Jack's voices. Gloria thought she'd see how they were doing, then decided the intimate, low tones of conversation indicated any interruption would be unwelcome. Given Gabbie's obvious attraction to the young man from North Carolina, Gloria decided to let things lie.

She glanced over to where Phil sat studying some notes for the next day's work. Then she heard Patrick's voice shouting from the boys' room. "Mom! Dad!" She was out of her chair and moving toward the stairs without thought. The boy's tone had been excited, not alarmed, but Phil followed his wife with an expression of concern on his face, wondering why she was so jumpy.

They entered the boys' room to find both of them seated upon their toy chest, gazing out the window with rapt expressions on their faces. Sean said, "Wow!" drawing out the exclamation. Patrick echoed his brother.

Out by the barn, a dozen tiny lights hung in the night air, pinpoints of blue-green glow, moving through the murk, blinking on and off. "Neat!" said Patrick.

Phil laughed. "Fireflies, boys. You think this is something? One good rain and there'll be thousands of them out there. We'll get a mason jar and catch some." To his wife he said, "You know, I completely forgot about lightning bugs. It's the sort of thing you take for granted when you grow up with them. I didn't think about how the kids would feel seeing them for the first time."

Gloria smiled. Something was making her jumpy and she felt foolish at her alarm. Still, she was the mother. "Okay, back to bed."

"Aw, Mom," both boys said as one.

"Can't we watch a little longer?" asked Sean, his voice pleading.

"Well, for a while. But I'm coming back in ten minutes, and if you're not in bed, I'll . . ."

Both boys grinned. This was not a real threat. "We'll go right to bed," assured Patrick. Everyone knew the boys would be under the covers only as soon as they heard their mother's footfalls upon the stairs.

"Okay, then. Ten minutes."

Phil put his arm around his wife's waist. "Next year you'll hear the peepers."

"What's peepers?" asked Sean.

"Spring peepers," answered their father. "Little frogs, about the size of a pencil eraser; they make the loudest sound. It's fun."

"Neat," said Patrick.

"Good night, boys," said Phil, and the adults left.

Patrick and Sean were as good as their word and went straight to bed a moment before Gloria entered the room. After she had tucked them in and returned downstairs, Patrick fell quickly asleep. But Sean felt a strange restlessness and, after ten minutes of trying hard, gave up and crept back toward the window.

He settled comfortably atop the toy chest and watched as the tiny blue-green lights wove their dance. He was fascinated by the sight. In California's desert climate, fireflies were unknown, and this was as good as anything he'd seen at Disneyland. Then several of the lights moved toward the house and Sean craned his neck to watch them as they vanished below the eaves beneath his gabled window.

He could see a hint of illumination and knew the fireflies were just below where he could see them. Putting his face as close to the screen as he could, he could barely make out their presence.

Then suddenly one came shooting up next to the screen, causing Sean to jump back a little. His eyes opened wide as he saw that before him was nothing that could be called an insect.

Hanging in the night air was a tiny creature of light. A tiny woman, nude and perfectly formed, no bigger than Sean's thumb, hovered like a hummingbird on faintly seen, glowing wings. Eyes that were enormous for her small face regarded Sean with merry amusement for a moment, then the creature sped off.

Sean sat stunned. He glanced to where Patrick lay sleeping, and turned to face the door to the hall, left open a crack so his parents could check up on the twins without making a sound. He was uncertain what to do.

After a long moment of sitting with his heart pounding, Sean returned to bed. Sleep was a long time in coming.

JULY

1

The band struck up "The Stars and Stripes Forever," and while there seemed scant agreement among the brass and woodwinds as to the key, the crowd applauded. The Pittsville High School Cougars Marching Band led the procession down Central Avenue, past the offices of the Pittsville *Herald,* where it would turn onto State Street and make its way toward the municipal park. The annual Pittsville Fourth of July parade was under way.

The boys sat on the curb, below the press of adults, granted a clear view by virtue of their diminutive size. Each held a tiny American flag in his right hand and waved it vigorously. While the televised Rose Parade might hold little interest for them, this celebration of high school band, homemade floats, and local celebrities in cars from the nearby Buick agency fascinated them. There was a raw exuberance, a joyous, genuine feeling of festival, neither had experienced before.

Patrick elbowed his brother. Nearly any excuse was good enough for a sibling brawl and Sean made ready for a scuffle. But he halted when Patrick said, "There's Gabbie!"

Phil and Gloria stood behind their sons and waved as Gabbie and Jack rode into view. A group of local horse breeders and fanciers had organized a mounted company, all decked out in Revolutionary period costumes. Jack sat on John Adams, dressed in a woodsman's outfit, complete with a coonskin hat and a flintlock rifle from someone's attic.

Gabbie wore a fine gown, which probably should have been in a museum, rescued from someone's family trunk for the occasion. It was of rich silk brocade, tight at the waist and low-cut, showing her figure to good advantage and displaying an ample portion of bosom. Her appearance was greeted by several loud whistles from the older boys in the crowd. She blushed and Jack looked irritated. Spying her father and stepmother and the boys, she waved. As she passed, she mouthed the word "sidesaddle" and rolled her eyes heavenward, as if in despair. Gloria laughed and nodded, indicating she understood Gabbie's discomfort.

As the riders passed, Gloria said, "Isn't she lovely."

Phil nodded, his expression revealing his deep love for and pride in his daughter. Gloria smiled to herself as she said, "Jack certainly looked handsome, too."

Phil shrugged as a group of children from the William Pitt Middle School came by, marching with a determination worthy of a military honor guard. "I guess," he said absently. Gloria laughed. "What?" he asked.

"Just your overprotective fatherly instincts coming out again, that's all."

"Me?"

Gloria watched as Jack and Gabbie turned down State Street, out of sight. "I may be wrong, but it looks like things might be getting a bit serious between those two."

Phil looked incredulous. "What? They're just kids."

"Not according to the state of New York, lover. Both can vote and do most of the other things restricted to supposedly responsible adults."

"Well, they're pretty young, any way you look at it." Gloria laughed again, and her husband looked irritated. "I'm being funny, huh?" Gloria only nodded as she sought to stem her amusement. Finally Phil smiled at her. "You think it's getting serious?"

From below, Sean said, "Well, they sure kiss a lot."

Both parents looked down and Gloria said, "Have you been spying on your sister?"

Patrick sounded impatient as he looked up at his mother. "Cripes, they say good night under our window." He puckered up and pantomimed kissing Sean, who laughed and pushed him away. "Kissy, kissy."

"Hey!" commanded Phil, trying to sound stern. "Lay off Gabbie." But he saw his wife's amusement, a reflection of his own.

At last Gloria said, "Cut her some slack, guys. It's not too many years down the road before you'll be doing plenty of the same thing.

And if God's got a sense of humor, your girlfriends will have little brothers."

Both boys made faces, as the suggestion was worthy of a place alongside eating liver and visits to the dentist. "Ugh!" was Sean's comment, while Patrick shook his head.

The parade continued, and when the last of the homemade floats was past, Phil said, "Let's get over to the park." He glanced at his watch. "We've got an hour before all the ceremonies are over, so we can set up the picnic and have the fire going when Gabbie and Jack find us. Then we can take it easy until the fireworks."

A boy appeared as if by magic next to the Hastings family. He looked down at the twins, who returned his appraising look. "You guys play?" he said, pounding his small fist into a beat-up outfielder's mitt. Both boys, as one, raised mitts from where they had lain on the curb. "There's a game at the park. You want to play?"

The boys sprang up, their movement the only agreement necessary. They darted ahead of their parents, only slightly restrained by Gloria's shout to stay close.

2

Gabbie came toward the family picnic site, holding her skirts defiantly above her ankles as she led My Dandelion. Gloria caught sight of her advancing stepdaughter and said, "Oh shit, they've had a fight."

Phil looked up from the charcoal he was poking and nodded. "Yup. She looks just like her mother did when she was going to rip off my head about something. Batten down the hatches."

Gabbie managed somehow to land atop the large blanket with a swirl of silks and linen petticoats about her while still maintaining her angry aspect. "Hello, Gabbie," Gloria said softly.

"Hi, honey," added her father while he arranged coals.

Her answer was something close to a grunt. She looked around and noticed the twins were off playing a ragged game of sandlot baseball with the town kids and everyone else was busy fixing dinners. After several minutes of silence, Gabbie asked, "All right, why don't you say something?"

Gloria took the long barbecue fork from Phil's hand and indicated with a tilt of her head he should go talk to his daughter. Phil hunkered down beside Gabbie and said, "Okay, what's the problem?"

"Oh! A cheerleader. A freckle-faced high school airhead with big tits."

"Jack?" asked Phil, suddenly wishing he'd restricted himself to sons.

"Yes," she snapped. "We were resting the horses before taking them back and this little bitch comes over to talk to him about 'something personal' "—she mimicked a breathy voice—"and he tells me to go on ahead, he'll only be a few minutes. Well, if his taste runs to children, that's fine with me."

Phil glanced at Gloria, his expression begging help. Gloria dropped the pretense of tending the fire and came to her stepdaughter's side. "Maybe you're being a little tough on him, Gabbie."

Gabbie's eyes flashed and she stood up. "I've got to get My Dandelion back to Mr. Laudermilch's stable."

Phil said, "If you're hacking her over to Laudermilch's, how will you get back here?"

Her anger barely contained, she said, "There's a ride for us."

Gloria shook her head as Gabbie hiked her skirts and, in most unladylike fashion, mounted the horse. She kept her skirts pulled up around her waist, revealing her cut-off blue jeans and bare legs, one of which she hooked between the two saddle horns. "God damn, I hate riding sidesaddle!" She reined the mare around and used her riding crop to get her trotting off.

Gloria turned to Phil. "Yes, I'd say things are getting serious."

"At least on one side," he agreed as he rose. "I sort of understood when she got so crazy after her breakup with Danny last year . . . they'd been going together awhile. But she's known Jack a month. I've never seen her like this with a boy before."

Gloria said, "That's because she's fallen in love with a man, boyo. A young one, but a man. The first one's always the toughest."

Phil said nothing, glancing to where his sons played. "Maybe it'll get better," he said.

Gloria laughed and kissed his cheek. "We can only hope."

A short time later, Jack came up leading John Adams. "Hi," he said cheerily. Phil and Gloria exchanged glances as Jack looked around. "Where's Gabbie?"

"She said she had to get the horse back to the stable," answered Gloria.

Jack said, "That's right. But I didn't pass her."

Gloria said, "She rode off that way."

"Oh, damn," said Jack, then he quickly added, "Sorry."

Phil said, "There a problem between you two?"

"Not that I know of. It's just that way you hook along Williams Avenue. She's taking the shortcut through the woods behind your place. She's only ridden those trails a couple of times and could get herself lost. I'd better get after her."

Gloria considered staying silent, but said, "Gabbie seemed pretty upset about something."

Jack mounted. "She was?"

"Something about a cheerleader."

Jack's expression turned incredulous. "She said that?"

"In pretty certain terms," said Phil.

Jack shook his head in wonder. "That's Sheila Riley. She's decided to apply to Cornell and wants Aggie to write a letter of recommendation. She asked me to ask Aggie. She just a little shy about Aggie, is all. Besides, she's dating a guy down at Penn." Jack looked hard at Gloria. "Gabbie really got ticked?"

"Royally pissed," observed Gloria.

"Phil, no disrespect intended, but have you noticed your daughter can get a little headstrong and opinionated from time to time? Not to mention fly off the handle."

"So I have noticed, Jack, so I have noticed."

Jack glanced at the sky. "I better go after her. There's only an hour or so's light left. If she's not through those woods quickly, it could be a pain finding her."

Without further word, he put heels to John Adams, heading toward Williams Avenue. Phil began to laugh, and Gloria said, "What?"

"Just I think I like that guy."

Gloria said, "Me too."

"Hey, look there." Phil pointed.

Glancing over to where the boys were still playing, Gloria said, "What?"

Phil chuckled. "Just that Patrick made a hell of a throw to second to get the runner. Kid's got quite an arm."

Gloria smiled at Phil's proud-father act. "Well, let us commence with the victuals, sir. It's the bottom of the ninth and Mighty Casey's at bat and, win or lose, we're about to have some hungry boys descend upon us."

Phil laughed and put some hot dogs on the fire.

3

Gabbie rode past the shack. Above the door a neatly painted sign proclaimed *Doyle's Appliance Repair.* She urged My Dandelion up over the dirt curb and past the shack. She knew that a few feet into the woods she would be on the corner of Aggie Grant's property. She had never entered this way, but had ridden nearby with Jack a few times. She roughly knew where the path that ran to her own farm was, and from there how to get to the Laudermilch farm. Besides, she didn't want to chance meeting Jack by riding through town, and hacking My Dandelion back to Laudermilch's place was giving her time to think.

Gabbie's anger was fading, being rapidly replaced by a sense of loss. She'd never been this jealous in her life and the strange hollow pain in her stomach was something alien to her. Her only other serious relationship had ended badly, but even then she had felt outrage at being lied to rather than this terrible emptiness. Her cheeks were burning and her eyes seemed to tear without reason. She felt miserable. How could he? she asked herself. Easy, she answered. The little redheaded bitch was a knockout, big breasts without being chunky and legs that took a week to get to the ground. Tears gathered in Gabbie's eyes and she descended into a thoroughly black despair.

Abruptly Gabbie became aware of an odd plopping sound and knew that one of My Dandelion's shoes had worked loose. Before she could rein in, the horse faltered and her walking rhythm shifted. She was limping.

Gabbie was instantly off the horse, inspecting the left front hoof. A bent horseshoe dangled by one nail. Gabbie swore as she pulled it free from the hoof. Holding it up, she saw that the clench on two of the nails had pulled through the hoof, working the shoe loose. My Dandelion had then stepped on the back of the flopping shoe with her left rear hoof, ripping it away. Ignoring the smear of mud My Dandelion's leg had left on the brocade of the dress, Gabbie inspected the hoof. There was one big crack where one of the nails had twisted away, and several small holes where the nails had pulled through. Gabbie swore again and considered the likelihood of a bruise. If the crack didn't go too deep, it could be cross-filed or held together with a metal staple. Otherwise it would continue to split up to the coronet. "Ah, damn!" shouted Gabbie in frustration. "This is one shitty day, world. Thank you very much."

She held the shoe in her right hand and grabbed the reins with her left. She'd have to lead the animal, for to ride her on this rocky path was to risk further damage to the hoof. She looked back and was relieved to see the horse was not favoring her left front leg. At least there was no sign of damage at this point. Still, the path was hard, rocky dirt, and she'd have to be careful where she led the horse. She considered returning to the park, but taking the horse over concrete would be as bad as or worse than over the dirt.

There was a stony rise, which normally she would have ridden over, to reach the path to Aggie's. Now she had to find a way around it. "Which way?" she said to herself.

Picking the left, she began circling. It shouldn't be difficult to find the path, she judged. It just wasn't that far around the rise.

A short time later, Gabbie began to feel the first hints of concern. The rise had been circled, she was certain, but nothing looked familiar. And night was falling unexpectedly fast.

She attempted to judge where the last early evening light was coming from. It was lighter to her right, which she figured had to be the last rays of the sunset and therefore west. She needed to continue south, so she was heading in pretty much the right direction. But there was a gully ahead she'd never seen before.

She led the horse slowly down into the gully and discovered a small rill of water gurgling over the stones. Gabbie halted while she thought. If she followed the gully, she'd be certain to find her way to the Troll Bridge, and from there home was a snap.

She led My Dandelion up the other side of the gully and began to follow it. Soon the shadows of the woods were turning opaque, and

Gabbie felt her worry deepening with them. It was taking too long to find the bridge, she was certain.

Then she heard the sound. It struck at her, startling her. It was a clear, familiar ringing sound, one she couldn't put a name to. It came from ahead.

She halted. The sound repeated several times in succession, and she knew what she was hearing was impossible. It must be something else, she concluded.

She led the horse forward and followed the gully around a leisurely curve, past a sheltering stand of trees, so tightly placed they formed a screen. Beyond the trees a large wagon stood, with an old dapple-grey horse tied to one of the large front wheels. In the back a portable forge burned brightly while a tall man inspected a piece of metalwork he held before him with large tongs. He judged it near ready and plunged it back into the fire. He turned it in the coals and stepped upon something. The forge burst into bright light, and Gabbie saw that he had a foot-powered bellows connected to the bottom of the forge. He pumped the bellows until the coals burned white-hot. After a moment he pulled out his work, placed it upon an anvil resting behind the wagon, and began hitting it with his hammer.

Gabbie couldn't believe her eyes. A farrier stood working in middle of the clearing. She watched in fascination as he quickly turned the metal, a heavy pin of some sort. Gabbie regarded the horseshoe she held and wondered if she was going crazy.

She approached the blacksmith and he glanced at her. She faltered when she saw his eyes. They were so blue they were almost electric. The man was brawny but young-looking and, under the soot and smoke smudge, strikingly handsome. He stood easily six feet two or more, and his arms were heavily muscled. His beard was black, as was the hair that hung below a broad-brimmed hat. He wore an old-style linen shirt, with the long sleeves rolled up over his biceps. Black tufts of hair peeked over the top of his shirt and covered the backs of his arms. His trousers were held up by black suspenders. Suddenly Gabbie understood. There were Amish living over in Cattaraugus County. She'd seen a couple of them at one of the stores in town. They didn't believe in cars or something, but she knew they still practiced arts and crafts like their forebears. And this portable smithy was something out of the nineteenth century.

The man inspected his handiwork and plunged it into a barrel of water. Putting aside the tongs, he came over to Gabbie. He raised his forefinger to his hat and said, "G'day, miss. You havin' some trouble, 'tseems." Gabbie was also surprised by his accent. It was almost Scottish or from the north of England in tone and pronunciation, and she had thought Amish to be German or Dutch.

The man smiled, but Gabbie was struck by something powerful in his eyes. He glanced her over, in a cursory manner, but his gaze was almost a caress.

Gabbie flushed, suddenly wishing the gown's decolletage wasn't so deep. She could feel the blush going all the way down to her breasts. "Ah . . . yes," she answered. "My . . ." Gabbie pulled her gaze from his blue eyes and looked at the horseshoe. "My horse lost a shoe." She held it out. The farrier took it, inspected it, and then took the horse's leg and examined the hoof.

"It's little, though you did well t'lead the beastie. Many a lady would've ridden her regardless, and then complained t'the groom of a lame animal the next morn. We'll have her right in a bit."

"Thank you." Gabbie followed after as he led My Dandelion to the forge and tied her to a rear wheel, slightly confused by the smith's odd remark about a groom. "But what of your own work?"

" 'Tis done, lass. I sheared a linchpin in the wagon tongue and had t'fashion a new one. Soon as we fixed your problem, I'll be on m'way."

Gabbie sat on a fallen trunk watching as the man expertly inspected the hoof again. "We'll need file a bit, t'keep the hoof from cleavin'," he said.

"Staple?"

"Think not, though were it a bit deeper, I'd do so." He looked up from the hoof and smiled at Gabbie, and she felt a hot flush run through her. "You know horses, then, miss. Not many ladies do. Usually they leave such concerns t'their stable men."

He put Gabbie on edge. She found her mind wandering unexpectedly. He was very good-looking in a brutish way, like a handsome wrestler or football lineman. Generally not her type. But damn it, he was sexy. She put her hand to her forehead and it came away damp. Must be from the heat of the forge, and the day was muggy. She took a deep breath. There was something very odd about this blacksmith. "Excuse me for asking, but are you Amish?"

The man laughed and a chill ran down Gabbie's back. The sound was both playful and threatening. "No, lass. I've not the honor t'member m'self with those fine folk. But they're a lot t'understand and respect the old ways, keepin' themselves plain as they do."

The man stuck the shoe into the forge and moved to the horse. He took a large rasp and began to dress the hoof. "The shoe's but a little bent. I'll make it right in a jiffy."

Gabbie shivered again, not knowing why. The woods were darker than she thought they should be by now, and she didn't know where she was. Pushing down her uneasiness, she said, "I didn't know there were itinerant farriers in this area, Mr. . . . ?"

With a quick smile that brought gooseflesh to her arms and breasts, he said, "Smith, Wayland Smith. And there are a few of us about, though I've not always been—how'd you say, miss—itinerant? I'd a forge in White Horse, and for many a year I'd be known for being the fairest smith about, but times change and one must go where there's work. That's truth."

She tried to gauge his age. He could have been in his late twenties or earlier thirties, but his manner made her think he was much older. And there was an aura of power surrounding him, basic, almost primitive, and very sexual.

"I'd have stayed in White Horse, I'm thinkin', t'this day, but my master came for me. . . . I'd fled his service and not followed him. . . ."

His words seemed to fade and Gabbie wasn't making sense of them anyway. Master? Service? He spoke as if he had been some sort of bondsman or servant. Still, whatever curiosity Gabbie felt was fleeting as she watched the smith.

Dropping the horse's leg, he recovered the shoe from the forge. He inspected it, turning it as if reading something in the dull glow. With a grin that made Gabbie shudder, he plunged the glowing shoe into the coals, and began to pump the bellows. He said something to her, but she failed to understand the words. She merely nodded. He pumped up and down in a rhythm, his eyes seeing what only he knew in the burning fire. Then, like a modern Vulcan, he pulled the shoe from the fire and purposefully turned toward the anvil. His right hand seized his hammer and he raised it high, bringing it down on the shoe with a ring that caused Gabbie to jump a little with the sound. Up and down the hammer went, and Gabbie found herself mesmerized by the sight and sound of it. The muscles of Wayland Smith's arms bunched and flexed as he hammered and Gabbie found the sight fascinating. With each exertion he made a slight exhalation, almost a grunt, and Gabbie was reminded of the sounds Jack made when they kissed deeply. The smith grinned, as if amused, and his teeth shone bright and clean against his beard. He hummed a nameless tune and seemed to time the rhythm with his hammer blows, as if beating time to an unknown dance. Gabbie felt the rhythm seep into her soul and she became aware of a moist heat building deep inside her body. Her eyes half closed, as if in dreaming, and she saw that the smith was almost beautiful in his raw power. Images of his body, his skin covered in a sheen of sweat that reflected the firelight as he arched and moved above her, flooded her mind and she gasped. She shook her head, and a distant thought came to her: What's wrong with me? It fled as it had come, quickly, and was barely remembered. She watched the smith.

Sweat gathered below the brim of his hat and ran down his cheeks. His shirt became damp and clung. Gabbie could not think of any man she had seen who had looked this strong. She was sure that he was stronger than any of the football types and weight lifters she'd seen on television. And this man's strength was more basic, more primitive and natural, than that manifested by those who spend hours in the gym. A fleeting image of Nautilus machines and free weights crossed her mind. She made a comparison that made her giggle. Pumping iron was nothing next to forging iron.

The man looked up at the sound of the giggle and smiled at Gabbie. She almost gasped at the force of his gaze. She felt her entire body flush and shudder. A tingling, hot awareness swept through her and coherent thought was elusive. She was becoming aroused as she watched Wayland Smith beat hot iron against the anvil. In a distracted way, she wondered if she was losing her mind. It only took a minute to hammer a shoe; she'd watched farriers since she was a child. But it seemed she'd been watching this man for hours. And with each pump of the bellows, each strike of his hammer, Gabbie felt her mind slip away and a primitive, urgent need rise up within.

Wayland plunged the horseshoe deep into the water barrel, and Gabbie gasped aloud, her eyes watering with tears of sudden sadness, as if her body rather than the hot iron had been plunged into the cold water. A cool breeze filled the glade and she shivered, all at once chilled. God! What is wrong with me? she wondered. Smith took the shoe to the horse, fitted it, and began filing the hoof. The rasp smoothed the cracked hoof, and the smith carefully measured each stroke, so the angle of the shoe would be proper. Pulling nails from his shirt pocket, he began fastening the shoe to the hoof.

Gabbie stood up, in anticipation of leaving, and her knees were weak. She took a step and found her legs rubbery. There was something wrong here, and she was confused and a little afraid. A scent of flowers blew by on the breeze, and Gabbie felt her head swim. There was an odd spicy quality to it that made her blood pound . . . like the rhythm of the anvil, she thought absently.

Then the man rose and said, " 'Tis done, missy."

Gabbie felt perspiration running down her cheek, and the man seemed to be speaking from a long distance away. "Thank you," she said weakly.

She stepped around to take the reins from him. Then she felt his hands upon her waist. Her breath caught in her throat and her body burned as a tremble of excitement rushed through her. She turned, half expecting the man to embrace her. A small, detached part of her mind was frantic, but she was caught up in a hazy cloud of heat and odors. She could smell the salt sweat of him, masked by smoke, mixed with the flowers and spices. Spices? she wondered. Her eyes closed and her lips parted in anticipation. Then the man was lifting her to the saddle, as easily as if she were an infant. She blinked, trying to clear her watery vision. He stood holding up the reins for her. She took them as he said, "Make 'long the gully, Miss Hastin's. You'll find the bridge in no time. From there t'your home is but a few minutes. And go quickly. The light fails and the woods aren't safe after dark."

He swatted My Dandelion on the rump and the horse was moving, taking Gabbie from the circle of light around the wagon. Her head swam and she breathed deeply, trying to catch her breath. She found herself crying, feeling a profound sadness, and not knowing why. Then slowly her vision cleared.

She looked around and found she knew where she was. It was also lighter than she would have thought. She'd easily spent a half hour or more with the smith, and it should have been dark.

What had gone on? She'd almost had an orgasm when he touched her, and that unnerved her in a way she couldn't understand. It was too frightening to contemplate any man having that much sexual power over her. For that was what it had been, a raw, basic sexual power. Embarrassment made her eyes water again and she defiantly wiped them. Damn, I'm no child to be afraid because a guy turns me on. But another voice said that what she had been through was something different from simple arousal. Jack could turn her on. This Wayland Smith could turn her inside out. Suddenly she was afraid. She looked behind and saw no hint of the smith and his wagon. Then she thought, I didn't offer to pay him! On the heels of that thought came the realization that he knew where she lived, and if he wanted payment, knew where to find her. But how did he know who I was! And the thought of his coming to find her both thrilled and terrified her. She looked around as her vision cleared some more. How far had she come in that dream-like state?

The sound of another horse came to her and she wondered if Wayland Smith had decided to follow her. Half fearfully, half excited, she turned and waited and then, with a flood of relief, saw Jack coming down the trail.

Jack reined in beside her, began to speak, and saw something in her face. "Are you okay?"

Gabbie touched her cheeks and found tears running down them. She only nodded. "Gabbie, what is it? It's not Sheila Riley, is it? She's just a kid."

Gabbie looked at him with confusion in her expression. "Sheila Riley?" she asked softly. "No." She leaned across the gap between the horses and kissed Jack, her tongue darting into his mouth. In her hunger, she almost fell from the saddle.

Jack reached out, steadying her as he reluctantly pushed her away, then touched her face. "Christ almighty. You're burning up! Come on, let's get you home."

Gabbie nodded dully. She allowed Jack to take My Dandelion's reins while she held on to the saddle. Images of fires and the smell of spices were fogging her mind and she couldn't understand why she was so confused.

4

Gloria looked up from doing the laundry and saw Jack standing at the back porch door. "Hi. Come on in."

"How's Gabbie?"

"Tired, but otherwise fine. Her temp was normal this morning and the doctor said not to bother bringing her in unless it went back up. He thinks she just caught some bug."

Jack's expression betrayed disagreement. "She was in a pretty ragged frame of mind, Gloria. I'm no expert, but I'm pretty sure she was hallucinating."

Gloria stopped folding towels. "What makes you say that?"

Jack crossed his arms and leaned against the doorjamb. Just then Bad Luck stuck his nose in from the kitchen, saw Jack, snuffed a breath in greeting, and returned to the kitchen. Gloria said, "They're installing the satellite dish and the workmen asked he be kept inside." Jack looked surprised. "He's too friendly. Gets in the way." Jack nodded. "Now, what were you saying?"

"She talked about meeting a blacksmith, a fellow with a horse-drawn wagon, who fixed a thrown shoe. I checked with Mr. Laudermilch's foreman, and he said that he thinks My Dandelion had cracked her hoof a couple of days before and they'd filed 'cross it and reshoed her. He checked and couldn't see anything different. Besides, I was only ten minutes behind her at most, and it couldn't have happened in the time she says. So it must have been a hallucination."

Gloria looked both thoughtful and worried. "Gabbie's not given to flights of fancy. She might have told you about her mother and grandmother—anyway, her childhood was pretty rugged emotionally. She tends to have both feet on the ground. She has a temper, but otherwise she's a pretty down-to-earth girl."

"Well, I got pretty sick when I was a kid, a high fever, and hallucinated giant bunny rabbits hiding in my closet. The human mind is capable of a lot."

"Fever can do that," Gloria agreed, though her agreement seemed tentative. "Maybe she ought to see the doctor anyway."

Just then a voice from the kitchen caused them to turn. Gabbie entered and brightly said, "Gloria, I'm famished—" She halted when she saw Jack and her expression turned dark. "Hello," she said icily.

Gloria put the last towel on top of the new dryer. "I think I'll go see how the workmen are coming." She beat a hasty retreat.

Jack said, "You okay?"

Unexpectedly, Gabbie was taken aback by the question. "Sure? Why wouldn't I be?"

"You were kind of out of it last night, is why."

She looked at him, curiosity softening her eyes for a moment. "What do you mean, 'out of it'? I was just a little—upset." Her expression darkened again. "And now that you mention it, what are you doing here? I thought you'd be out with the balloon queen."

"Sheila?" said Jack, his forehead wrinkled in concern. "I explained all that last night. She wants Aggie to write a recommendation letter to Cornell. She's pinned to a frat rat down at Penn. Gabbie, don't you remember my bringing you home?"

Gabbie's face drained of color. She backed into the kitchen and sat down at the table. "I . . . I remember leaving the park. I rode into the woods and . . . it's a little vague after that. I woke up this morning, so I figured I got home—My Dandelion! I was going to take her over to Mr. Laudermilch's."

Jack pulled out another chair and sat down. "I took care of it last night, after I put you to bed."

Suddenly Gabbie flushed. "You put me to bed?"

Jack smiled, a little self-consciously. "Well, you were feverish and someone had to. I put you in bed, called Mr. Laudermilch's place, and told him what was going on. He sent a couple of boys over to take the horses back, and when your folks got in, I took off."

Gabbie hid her face behind her hands as she uttered a groan. "I'm so embarrassed."

Jack leaned back in his chair. "Yes, I can understand. That tattoo is pretty ugly."

She looked out from behind her hands, half-amused, half-upset, and hit him in the arm. "You bastard! I bet you enjoyed it. Taking advantage."

Jack was caught halfway between a grin and a concerned look. "Actually, I was pretty worried. You were drenched with perspiration, burning up and all. I had to wet you down with a damp cloth." His grin broadened. "Still, I can't say as I didn't take notes as I went."

She hit him again, harder. "Ow!" he protested. "That's enough."

Suddenly she reached out and put her hand behind his neck. Yanking him forward, she kissed him long and hard. He returned the kiss, then, when she pulled away, said softly, "Now, what was that for?"

"For being worried and for not taking advantage."

He shrugged. Gently he said, "Gabbie, when you yank me into bed, I want it because you really want to, not because you're all delirious with fever."

Gabbie's eyes widened. "Yank you into bed?"

Jack grinned even more. "Yes, you . . . ah . . . had some interesting ideas last night."

Gabbie hid her face behind her hands again. "Oh God!" Then after a minute she looked at him. "I thought those were all dreams." Once more her hands covered her face. "I think I'm going to die." She looked at him. "What did I say?"

Jack laughed. "What's it worth to you to know?"

He leaped from his chair as she swung at his shoulder. "You son of a bitch," she said, laughing. "You'd better tell me!"

Jack backed away from her, his hands held out before him in a gesture of supplication. "Now, I don't know . . ."

She jumped forward and he dodged into the service porch. Bad Luck had been lurking under the kitchen table and at the sudden burst of activity began barking, a joyous canine celebration of noise.

"Shut up, you hound." Gabbie laughed. "You," she said, pointing at Jack. "Speak!"

At that, Bad Luck barked. Jack halted his retreat, laughing uncontrollably. "I surrender." Gabbie came into the ring of his arms and he kissed her. "You didn't say much. You said something about a blacksmith fixing My Dandelion's shoe, then were quiet until I started undressing you." She buried her face in his shoulder and made embarrassed noises. "Then you thought to reciprocate."

She laughed. "Whew! I must have been out of it."

"I like that!"

She looked up into his eyes. "Don't fret," she said, kissing him. "As long as you aren't interested in Miss Dock Bumpers, you'll have no problems."

Jack grinned. "You really got jealous?"

Gabbie rested her head on his shoulder. "Ya, I did." Suddenly she was angry. "Damn it," she said defiantly as she pushed herself away and turned toward the kitchen. "It's just not fair!"

He was after her in a stride and took her arm. Her momentum caused her to turn and he drew her back to him. "What's not fair?"

"In less than three months I'll be back in California."

"Hey! It'll be all right."

She looked long at him. "Promise?"

He grinned. "I promise."

She bit her lower lip. "I tried to undress you?" He nodded. "Ow!" she said with a wince as she turned back to the kitchen. "I'm starving. Let's eat."

"Which I take it means you want to change the subject." He admired her as she leaned over to peer into the refrigerator. "Still, you did have me worried."

She looked back over her shoulder. "Really?"

"Yes, really."

She looked radiant. "Thanks." Looking back in the refrigerator, she asked, "Ham or bologna?"

"Ham."

She pulled the fixings from the refrigerator and bumped the door closed. Putting everything down on the table, she paused and looked thoughtful. "Did you say I talked about a blacksmith?"

"Yes, you did. Why?"

"Funny. I just had an . . . image of a man . . . I don't know. It must have been the fever."

Jack only nodded, but he wondered. Too many strange things had occurred in those woods, and he still couldn't shake the feeling he had seen something on Erl King Hill on Midsummer's Night; he just couldn't remember what. And at night he had odd dreams just before falling asleep, ghostly dancers and the faint, inhuman music. He tried to remember the dream in the morning, but it just slipped away; yet he knew there had been something there. He shook himself from his musing and grabbed a pair of plates from the cupboard, handing them over to Gabbie.

Outside he could hear Gloria's voice as she shouted something at the twins.

5

"Okay, monsters, back off."

The boys grudgingly retreated a step as they watched the workmen. The concrete around the pole had been poured a few days before and left to dry, and now the dish itself was being mounted. Patrick and Sean had been hovering around them all morning, asking questions, and generally being underfoot. The two workmen didn't seem to mind, but Gloria was determined to give them a demilitarized zone in which to work. She glanced at the house and wondered if Gabbie and Jack had resolved their differences. She was pleased that Gabbie appeared back to normal this morning, but still felt uneasy about last night. The fever had been sudden and severe. It had been at least a hundred and three, if Gloria could judge from touch. She had nursed two babies through fever and knew Gabbie's had been high. Still, no harm, no foul, as that basketball announcer back in L.A. said all the time.

But there was something about the sudden onset and recovery that disturbed Gloria. It just didn't fit her set of acceptable illnesses. Anything that wasn't clearly a cold, flu, broken bones, or allergy was suspect. Symptoms that didn't make sense were always a sign of terrible things approaching. A deep fear of Gloria's, never shared with anyone, not even Phil, was a terror of illness. Cancer, heart disease, the other lingering, disabling illnesses with long technical names that twisted bones, filled lungs with fluid, robbed the muscles of strength, all were horrors beyond her mind's ability to accept. The strongest, most robust man she had known—her father—had died of cancer. And the symptoms had been misleading at first. His death simply amplified her deep fear of debilitating illness. She gave up smoking in high school when other girls were just beginning. She wasn't a health food fanatic, but she stayed away from refined sugar and high-cholesterol foods and made sure everyone stayed active. She had badgered Phil into running when they had met, and now he was addicted. No, Gloria thought, it was just a bug. But deep inside she wondered if she should press Gabbie to see the doctor.

Ted Mullins, the owner of the local television shop, personally supervised these installations. He had made a fair profit from other farmers nearby and this was the fanciest ground station he had sold yet, so he wanted it perfect. Satisfied all was going as it should, he turned to Gloria and said, "Ma'am, I'll need to hook the cable up inside the house now." She nodded distractedly. "The dog, ma'am?"

Gloria smiled. "Boys, go get Bad Luck and take him for a walk."

"Ah, Mom," Sean began to complain. She gave them both the Look and they fell silent and walked toward the house. "And make it a long walk."

Mullins, a heavy man of middle years, said, "Fine-looking boys. You must be proud."

Watching Sean and Patrick vanish around the rear of the house, she smiled in appreciation. "Yes, I am. They're pretty terrific kids."

"I've got a boy about their age, Casey. Ought to get them together."

Gloria said, "Does your Casey play baseball, Mr. Mullins?"

The man grinned. "All the time."

Gloria returned the grin. "If they haven't met already, they will."

Mullins wiped his hands on his handkerchief and put it away. "We've finally gotten a Little League charter separated from Frewsburg's and we'll be starting teams next year. We used to have our own, but the population fell off fifteen years back when the economy got so sour and factories closed down or moved. Lots of families went to Kentucky or Texas with the factories. We had to take our kids over to Frewsburg. Now we've got that high-tech stuff coming and we've got enough kids for our own league again." He glanced at the dish, obviously pleased at the work. "But until then it's sandlot. Tell them there's a game about every day over at the field. Not the park field, that's for the Muni softball league, but beyond Doak's Pond. Forms up about one in the afternoon."

"That's a little far."

"Not too far. They can cut through the woods and come out over on Williams Avenue. That's only a block from the field."

Gloria didn't relish the idea of the boys' using the woods paths with regularity. But the woods were in their backyard, and it looked as if the Hastings family was settling in for a while, so she judged she should get used to the idea. As she moved toward the house with the workman, she said, "I'll mention it to them."

Mullins turned and shouted some instructions to his companion, who waved in acknowledgment. The boys came tumbling through the door with Bad Luck in tow, and Gloria said, "Mr. Mullins here has a son your age."

Patrick said, "Casey Mullins?"

The man nodded while Sean said, "We played with him yesterday at the park. He's a good shortstop."

Gloria said, "I rest my case."

"Well, he's over there right now. There's a game about every day, over by Doak's Pond. I'm sure they would like to have you aboard." He glanced at Gloria, suddenly sensing he might be speaking out of turn. "If your mother doesn't mind."

Patrick answered for his mother. "She doesn't."

Gloria said, "Well, I like that."

"Can we go, Mom?" asked Sean.

"Just don't be late for dinner, and if anything happens, you call. I'll come get you. I don't want you tramping around the woods late. Got a dime?"

"Phone's twenty-five cents, Mom," said Sean with ill-disguised disdain at such ignorance. "An' we got some money."

"Okay, Diamond Jim. Just be careful."

"Okay!" they chorused as they dashed toward the woods.

Mr. Mullins said, "Seems they already know the shortcut."

Gloria said, "Sure, they're kids. Kids always know the shortcuts."

6

Patrick fumed. "Boy, you sure can be dumb."

"It wasn't my fault!" retorted Sean.

"You don't go running to back up the shortstop on a pick-off, dummy. Anybody knows that!" Patrick's voice was openly scornful. Patrick stopped his brother for a moment. "Look, when I signal a pitchout, you move toward third, see? I almost hit you in the head and Casey didn't even see the ball coming at him. You really blew it."

Sean turned away and plodded along in silence. The misplay had ended up costing their side the game, which alone wasn't a problem. It had reduced their stature in the eyes of the local kids, which was a problem. They would have to endure a long week of being among the last kids picked on each side, along with the nerds and wimps, until they'd established their bona fides again. Patrick was always intolerant of Sean's shortcomings, assuming because they were twins that Sean should be capable of everything Patrick was. Sean was a good pitcher—at least, he had better than average control—while Patrick usually caught, as he could make unerring throws to any base, but the nuances of the game were often lost on Sean in the heat of battle while Patrick always seemed to keep his head about him. The truth was that Sean was just average in many of the areas Patrick was outstanding. Sean's gifts were more in the area of thoughtful consideration, picking his spots as a pitcher. He was a thinker, and possessed an overactive imagination that was part of the reason for his timidity. He was afraid of the dark because of all the things he could imagine lurking in the gloom, while Patrick took the more prosaic attitude that if you can't see it, it isn't there. Sean glanced down at Bad Luck; the dog seemed to have little interest in boyish social concerns.

Finally Sean said, "Maybe we should practice?"

Patrick shrugged. "Okay, if it'll help. But I can't see what the big deal is about getting out of the way when I throw the darn ball."

They turned at the end of Williams Avenue, hiking up the little rise past Barney Doyle's Appliance Repair. The door opened and Barney stepped out. He quickly closed the door behind him and put something on the ground before the stoop. Turning, he spied the twins and said, "Well then, it's the Hastings lads, isn't it?"

Sean shrugged, while Patrick said, "Hi, Barney."

They ambled toward him while he put his keys away. Glancing around, Barney said, " 'Tis certain to be a fair summer night, with a break in the humidity, I'm thinking. We could do with a bit of the dry air, now and again."

Sean noticed Bad Luck sniffing around a saucer of milk before the door and said, "You got a cat?"

Barney leaned forward, patting Bad Luck on the head. The dog seemed to judge him an acceptable human and endured the gesture of friendship with good grace. "Not a cat, lads. 'Tis for the *Daonie Maithe.*" When the boys looked at him blankly, he said, "Which, if your education wasn't lacking, you'd know was Gaelic for the good people."

Sean and Patrick shot each other a glance, each silently accusing the other of betraying a trust. Noticing the exchange and mistaking the reason for it, Barney said, " 'Tis all right, boys. I'm not entirely mad. Many of us from the old country leave milk out for the little people." The boys remained silent, and Barney glanced around as if making sure they weren't overheard. He knelt slowly, age making it difficult, and whispered, "When I was a lad back in County Wexford, I lived on a farm a fair piece from Foulksmills. 'Twas lovely, though we were poor as mice." His eyes, watery and bloodshot, seemed to be seeing something far off. "One fine day in May I was out looking for a bull calf my Uncle Liam had given my father. It was a grand calf, but had a decided tendency to go adventuring. Which was fine for the calf, for he'd see many new sights and make interesting acquaintances, but was a trial for me, for I'd be the one to go and fetch him home—much to the hilarity of my brothers and sisters. Well, that one May day the little bull had wandered halfway to Wellington Bridge—which for your enlightenment is a distant town and not a bridge close at hand—and it was until late after dark I was bringing him home. The night was warm and smelled of flowers and clover, and the wind was fair from the channel, and it was altogether a grand night to be abroad. Being no more than a few years older than you boys now, I was cautious being alone with the calf, but not fearful, for the troublemakers were all in their pubs and banditry had fallen off of late. Then I heard the music and saw the lights."

The boys glanced at each other, and it was Patrick who said, "Leprechauns?"

Barney nodded solemnly. "The whole of the *Daonie Sidhe*," he whispered. "In every shape and size that they come, they were dancing atop a hill, and 'twas a majestic and fearful sight." He slowly rose. "I'd not seen it again since, until this spring."

"The danny she? Are they bad?" asked Sean, his voice betraying concern. Patrick looked at him with a mixture of disdain and relief that the question was voiced.

"It's Daonie Sidhe, though 'danny she' is close enough. Bad?" repeated Barney, rubbing his chin. "Well now, there's a topic. 'Twould be hard to put a good or bad to them, as they are. They can be either, or neither, depending upon whim. It is said they reward the virtuous and punish the wicked, but mostly they leave us alone. Wait here a minute."

Barney stuck a hand deep into one of the pockets of his bib overalls and seemed to feel around for something. Finding what he sought, he withdrew his hand and held something out for the boys' inspection. It was a smooth stone, with a hole in the middle, hanging from a thong of leather. "What is it?" asked Patrick.

" 'Tis a fairy stone."

"Oh!" exclaimed Sean.

Patrick looked unconvinced. "It's just a rock."

"Which is true, to a point. But then, a magic wand is also just a stick, if you look at it that way."

"Is it magic?" asked Sean.

"In its way, lad, in its way. It has the power to keep the good people from harming you, so then it must be magic."

"How can it?" asked Patrick, still unconvinced.

"As to the how, I cannot tell you, save that it does. And not just any stone with a hole will do. You can't grab a pebble and drill through it, you know. It must be a stone washed in a stream, with a natural hole, that is found upon the bank dry. It must be magic, or else why would there be so many rules?"

That made sense to the boys. Patrick showed no great interest, but Sean fingered the smooth stone. Something caused Barney to look about. "I judge the afternoon's ending and you late for dinner. Your mother will be fretting. Now," he said to Sean, "keep the stone, so the Good People cause you no discomfort on your way home, and I'll find another."

"I can keep it?" said Sean in delight.

"Aye, lad, but hurry off now. And don't forget that the Good People will think kindly of you if you leave a bit of milk or bread out for them."

Sean put the thong around his neck, so the stone hung almost to his navel. He'd shorten it when he got home. "Thanks, Mr. Doyle," said Sean.

" 'Bye," said Patrick.

The boys scampered off without further word, Bad Luck loping alongside, and when they entered the woods, began to run. They ran with a delicious sense of danger, as the shadows lengthened and deepened, casting a decidedly menacing aspect to the woods.

They ran and shouted and reveled in the fact of being eight years old with a yet endless summer stretching away before the harsh reality of school intruded. At first they had missed the Valley and friends, but the kids in Pittsville seemed okay and they played ball all the time, which was great. They all missed Little League, but the kids said there'd be a new one next year. It was shaping up to be a wonderful summer.

Then, before they knew where they were, they found themselves crossing the bald hill, the one Jack called Erl King Hill. Both boys grinned nervously and shared a secret thrill at the idea of mystery and things of magic. A sudden, wordless communication passed, and an impromptu game of follow-the-leader commenced. Patrick ran in circles around the top of the hill, while Sean duplicated his movements. Bad Luck tried to play, but couldn't resist running alongside first one brother, then the other. They yelled for the joy of it. Then they were sprinting back into the trees. They dashed through the woods with the endless supply of energy given to children, laughing at the simple pleasure of being alive. Then they reached the bridge.

Both boys halted. Bad Luck stood with hackles rising, a low growl issuing from his throat. Panting, the twins silently understood that the bridge was once again a scary place. Many times since they had first met Jack they had crossed the Troll Bridge, and while it was never a comfortable experience, the bridge had lacked the solid sense of menace they had felt upon first viewing it. But now the feeling of danger had returned, if anything stronger than ever. Patrick rolled the Louisville Slugger off his shoulder and held it before him as if it were a club. Fingering the stone Barney had given him, Sean softly said, "It's back."

Neither knew what *it* was, but both knew there was a malignant presence hiding in the dark place beneath the bridge. Bad Luck snarled and began to move forward. Sean snapped, "Heel!" and the canine reluctantly fell in at Sean's side. He whimpered and growled, but seemed willing to obey. Patrick nodded and they stepped forward, putting foot upon the stones of the Troll Bridge.

Suddenly evil swept up from below, swirling around them like a fetid wind. Both boys moved quickly, eyes wide with fright as they walked purposefully across the bridge. They instinctively knew the rules of crossing. They couldn't look down or back. They couldn't speak. They couldn't run. And they couldn't stop. To do any of those things would allow the thing below the bridge to come rushing up, to grab the boys and drag them back to its lair. The boys didn't make the rules, they just knew them and abided by them.

At the midpoint of the bridge, Sean felt an overwhelming urge to run and shot a glance at Patrick. Patrick returned the glance with one of dark warning. To run was to be lost. With steady steps, he led his more timid brother across the bridge, until they were free of the confines of the ancient dark arch. Bad Luck hesitated, and Sean's hand shot down to grab his collar, forcing the dog to come along at the proper pace. As soon as their feet were off the stones and back on the path, the boys leaped forward as one and were off at a dead run. Bad Luck hesitated an instant, indulging in a defiant bark at the bridge, before he dashed after the boys.

Sean shot a glance rearward, not sure if the rule about looking back held now they were finished with the bridge. As the bridge vanished behind the trees they fled through, he glimpsed the dark presence. It had seen him! Fighting down panic, Sean overtook his brother. Patrick saw Sean pass him, and the race was on.

By the time they reached home, all thoughts of the black presence under the Troll Bridge were forgotten and the only concern was who would be first to reach the screen door. As usual, it was Patrick by a step, with Bad Luck at his side.

Gloria stood in the kitchen, finishing the last preparations for dinner. "Cutting it a little fine, fellows," she said dryly, her eyes upon the clock. They dined at seven during the summer, six during school. "You have just enough time for washing up—and don't simply wipe your hands on the towels!" she shouted after them as they vanished in the direction of the bathroom. Gloria returned to getting dinner ready.

7

"Look at this," said Gary, handing a book to Mark. Mark opened it and read, then grinned.

"What?" asked Phil as he poked around his desk.

"Dirty German poetry," said Gary. "Old Herman had a few vices."

Mark put the book down. "Not very good." To Phil he said, "Look, if we're in the way, let us know."

Phil waved away the comment. "I've finished the first draft and Gloria's reading it upstairs. I'm taking the boys fishing. One of the reasons I left L.A. was so I could spend time with my kids. Being at the studios fifteen hours a day makes for strangers, not families." He put away some papers and moved toward the door. "Gabbie's out with Jack, so you can have the library to yourself."

Mark Blackman regarded the floor-to-ceiling bookshelves and shook his head. "This may take longer than I thought."

Phil turned at the door. "There're more in the basement and attic. Have fun."

"Catch a big one," said Gary with a grin.

Phil stuck his head into the parlor, which was now the family TV room. Sean and Patrick were on the floor before the new big-screen television Phil had ordered the week before. Gloria had said nothing about the purchase—they could afford it—but she couldn't understand why her husband and sons needed to see double plays and touchdowns life size.

"Come on, kids," said Phil.

Sean leaped up and flipped off the ball game. The live feed from Chicago on WGN had begun an hour before, two in the afternoon, local time. The boys loved the idea of being able to point the dish at different satellites and get signals from all over the world, but most especially the superstation baseball broadcasts from Atlanta, New York, and Chicago. Sean grabbed his pole from where it leaned against the wall and happily said, "Padres are ahead by four."

Patrick shook his head in disgust. "Sandberg booted one. Two unearned runs in the first!" He had maintained his allegiance to the Angels, but had decided to be a Cubs fan in the National League. Sean was taking double delight that his favorite team was on the verge of sweeping a three-game series with the Cubbies to the consternation of his brother.

Phil opened the front door and was confronted by Hemingway, who had chosen the middle of the doorway to lie. The cat opened his eyes and regarded three of the people whom he tolerated in his house. Phil looked down and, when it was apparent the old tom wasn't about to move, stepped over him.

As Sean closed the door behind his brother, he said, "Wish us luck, Ernie. Maybe we'll catch you a fish."

The cat's expression showed a less than optimistic attitude toward that outcome.

Gloria heard them leave and smiled to herself. She put the manuscript down on the bed beside her and thought about the chapter she had just finished. Phil's work was good, but the narrative wandered about at this point of the story. She knew that Phil would catch it and tighten it up when he rewrote. But she also knew he'd expect her to point it out to him.

When she heard the car start up, she picked up the phone beside the bed and dialed. It was answered on the second ring. "Aggie?" The voice at the other end answered. "Tell Jack and Gabbie now."

She hung up, a secret, conspiratorial smile on her face. Jumping up from the bed, she padded across the floor on bare feet and headed down the stairs. Reaching the landing, she glanced into the den and stepped back. Gary Thieus was in the fireplace.

Mark Blackman stood with his back to the door, looking over Gary's shoulder while the younger man investigated something in the rear wall. Gloria quietly entered and said, "I don't think you'll find a lot of books in there, guys."

Mark turned, seemingly unsurprised by her entrance. "Look here." He pointed, but she saw only an empty shelf.

"The depth of the bookcase next to the fireplace doesn't match all the others. There's some unaccounted-for space behind the shelves."

From inside the fireplace, Gary said, "Got something."

Gary came out of the fireplace and passed a key over. "A lot of these old houses have little hidey-holes, like behind bricks in fireplaces or under false floorboards, and secret basements. Sometimes two or three different ones in the same house. There's a little hollow on the side of the hearth, covered by a false stone."

She took the key, noticing it was covered in soot, and said, "What is it?"

Mark said, "I don't know. Have you a door that you can't unlock?"

Gloria said, "No, unless there's something in the basement I've missed. I haven't spent a lot of time down there." She absently tapped her cheek with the key, leaving a small smudge. "Mark, just what are you after?"

Blackman said, "I'm not sure. If I were, I'd know better how to go about finding it." He pointed at Gloria's cheek and the key.

"That doesn't make a lot of sense," she said, wiping away the spot of soot.

Mark moved around to lean back against Phil's desk while Gary sat on a stack of books. "Gloria, have you read any of my books?"

"No," she said without embarrassment.

"That's not surprising. Most of them are still in print, but they tend to be in libraries or on the shelves of some pretty strange little stores— you know, next to the books by people who've been to Venus in flying saucers or know where Atlantis is. Most of my work is devoted to finding the underlying truth in myth and legend, especially in the area of the occult and in magic. If there's a real story behind a myth, I want to find out about it. I wrote a long work devoted to the idea that the mystic visions of peyote rites were actually deep racial memories induced by the hallucinogens in peyote. My theory is that the Native American cultures in the Southwest had a different psychological set from European ones, which let those 'primitive' people reach places in their genetic memory, places most 'civilized' people don't know exist within their heads."

Gloria said, "Sounds pretty Jungian to me."

Mark smiled and Gary grinned. "It's very Jungian," said Gary.

"But what's that got to do with your digging around in my fireplace?"

"Look, I don't like to talk about my work before I show it to my editor. Only Gary knows what we're doing, but you do deserve an explanation. But believe me when I say we're up to nothing nefarious. It's just I didn't want to talk about my current work." He paused. "Remember at Aggie's, I told you I was after information about Fredrick Kessler?" She indicated she did. "He's one of a few men I've been able to track who were involved, somehow, in some pretty strange occurrences that I'm interested in."

"Like what?"

Mark said, "Like a lot of things I'm still trying to figure out. But what I know so far is that just after the turn of the century in what is now southern Germany—Bavaria, and parts of Württemberg—there was a sudden return to more primitive attitudes, as if the peasantry were going back to the beliefs of their ancestors of centuries earlier, superficially Christian, but only a Christian patina over a deep, abiding pagan belief system. And doing it in droves. Tales of magic and sorcery ran rampant."

Gloria said, "Great. Now you're telling me Old Man Kessler's father hung out with pagan priests?"

"No," corrected Mark. "I'm telling you Old Man Kessler's father was a mystery man, known beyond what his status as a minor merchant entitled him, at a time when all hell was breaking loose in southern Germany among the peasantry. There were a full half-dozen references to Fredrick Kessler and some other people whom he was known to associate with. But the maddening thing is . . . I'm looking at a black box. Something's in there, I just don't know what." He crossed his arms and obvious frustration showed on his face. "Something odd, and pretty mysterious, happened eighty, eighty-five years ago in southern Germany, and it was very important, but just exactly what it was is not yet clear. And Fredrick Kessler was involved. I wanted to talk to the son, but he was already in Europe when I got here, last year. I tried getting permission from his lawyer to poke around, but he wouldn't allow it. So I snuck out here and checked out the grounds. I didn't break into the house. But the lawyer got wind of it somehow and threatened to call the sheriff if I set foot on the property again. So I spent some time doing whatever research I could in the local newspaper morgue and the area libraries, and even interviewed people who knew the elder Kessler— though there were only a few of them. When Herman died I was down in Washington, checking old banking records. By the time I got back, you and Phil had made an offer on the house.

"What I've pieced together is that Fredrick Kessler and his associates were somehow central to this reversion to pagan beliefs, and it was unprecedented historically. Turn-of-the-century Germany was not exactly the place for such an event. This isn't a case of the peasants in Transylvania suddenly concerned that *Dracul* had risen again from the grave, or aborigines in the outback believing in the spirits of animals. It was as if most every inhabitant of Connecticut in 1905 suddenly believed in spirits, elves, and the older gods again. Then, most surprising of all, the heads of the Protestant and Catholic churches, even the leaders of the Jewish community, which was persecuted by them, all joined with the local authorities to stamp out the sudden reversion to paganism. It was, in a literal sense, a witch-hunt. A lot of people were arrested, some were relocated out of their villages and towns, and not a few simply disappeared—I expect they were executed. It's been hushed up over the years—even a century ago there was concern over P.R.— but it was a regular little inquisition."

"Well, it's a hell of a story," said Gloria. "But why the mystery? Why not tell us up front?"

Mark shrugged. "I don't like talking about my research, like I said. That's part of it. Also there's the question of religion. The established churches don't like to be publicly reminded of some of their past actions. And some people get tense when you bring up the subject of ancient pagan beliefs, even these days."

"*Especially* these days," added Gary. "The fundamentalists can generate a lot of noise if they want to."

Mark nodded. "And there's the stories about the treasure."

"You mentioned it at Aggie's and laughed it off."

"Well, it may not be a joke. Whatever the cause—involvement with this pagan thing or some other reason—the elder Kessler and his cronies left Germany in haste about that time and showed up in Canada, the States, and South Africa. There were about a dozen of them. All of them were traveling light, but all of them were prosperous businessmen within two years of reaching their new homes. Where did the money come from? If you check records, Kessler would have had to have twenty or thirty grand to get started, and it seemed he had more than that."

Gary said, "That's like a quarter million today."

Gloria couldn't shake the feeling that there was more here than Mark was revealing. But before she could comment, the front door opened and Gabbie called out, "We've got it!"

Jack staggered in carrying a large box, put it on the floor by the desk, and hurried outside. Gloria said to Mark, "We'll talk more later."

Jack and Gabbie both brought in several more boxes and quickly opened them.

"What goes on?" inquired Mark.

"It's Dad's birthday," announced Gabbie, removing what looked to be a television from a box. "We've bought him a word processor." With a grin, she said, "It's self-defense. Dad's a lousy typist. At the studios they had people who would type the scripts. Without this, Gloria or I will end up retyping his manuscripts." Inside a half hour, a complete home computer took form on Phil's desk. A printer was hooked up to it, and Jack quickly ran a few tests. "Everything's perfect," he announced.

Mark said, "Well, if you're going to have a party for Phil, I guess we should take off. We'll come back tomorrow."

Gloria said, "No, stick around. Look, Phil's as bad as you are for not talking about what he's working on, but now you've spilled the beans he'll be fascinated. And Gabbie's going into Pittsville for Chinese, so there's no problem with a few extra mouths."

"Okay," answered Mark. "I assume Aggie's going to join us?"

"Of course."

"What do you mean *I'm* going to get dinner?" said Gabbie.

"You've been elected," answered her stepmother. "Besides, I had a call from Mr. Laudermilch and he said it's okay to board My Dandelion here for the rest of the summer now that our barn is fixed. He says you're a pretty good horsewoman."

Gabbie's eyes widened. She turned to Jack. "You creep! You didn't say a thing."

He laughed. "It was supposed to be a surprise. Besides, it was your folks' idea."

Gabbie threw her arms around Gloria's neck. "Thanks, Gloria. She's a terrific horse. I like her almost as much as Bumper. I'll take good care of her."

"You're welcome, Gabbie." Gloria squeezed back. "Phil also got him to let us keep John Adams. But you've got to work them, and teaching the boys to ride is part of the deal."

With mock distaste, Gabbie said, "So now I'll have to put up with *him* every day, I guess," indicating Jack.

"Hey!" protested the object of her bogus scorn.

"Go get the animals, then when Phil and the boys are back, dinner. Okay?"

"Okay!" she said with enthusiasm as she grabbed Jack's hand, and half led, half dragged him from the den.

Gloria watched them exit, then said, "Why don't you go on with what you're doing, and I'll get back to reading Phil's manuscript. We can start over with Kessler's treasure or whatever after dinner. All right?"

"Fine," said Mark.

He and Gary returned to inspecting the books and making a catalog, while Gloria went upstairs. She was not unmindful of the key that
rested in her jeans pocket, and she was certain Mark hadn't forgotten it
either.

In the small storage space under the stairs a black thing listened,
hanging to the underside of the steps. It made a satisfied sighing sound
and judged it time to leave. It moved like some giant black spider, its
long arms and legs seeming to stick to whatever surface it touched. Next
to the baseboard, it halted, regarding the narrow crack between boards.
The creature somehow seemed to shrink in upon itself, compressing
bones and joints, until it could slither through the crack. In an almost
silent whisper it hissed, "The key. The key." Then with a chuckle it
vanished through the crack.

8

At the edge of the clearing, in sight of the Queen's court, he lingered, contemptuous of her power. Within the shadows of the boles he crouched, the mad one of soft light and sweet fragrances, awaiting his servant. The black thing scampered through the woods until he stood at the feet of his master and whispered to him.

His master looked down into the tiny mask of black rage, his own expression a match in anger and madness. Perfect white teeth were set edge upon edge, locked in a hideous grin, while his eyes were wide, orbs of blue insanity glinting with inhuman lights. "Good, good," he whispered back to his servant, stroking its knobby head as a man might stroke a dog. The little apelike creature chittered in pleasure at its master's happiness. It was so rare a condition. "Now return and wait, and when it is time, we shall show them the lock." Without hesitation, the creature scampered back through the woods, with stealth enough that human sight could not apprehend its passage, despite its speed.

The being of light stood, stretched his arms wide, and looked heavenward. With a clap of his hands overhead, thunder rang in the woods.

A sudden breeze blew across the hill, and the Queen rose, her court turning eyes toward the source of the thunder. "You dare . . ." she began, but the shadow was empty. In anger she hissed between teeth as perfect and inhuman as the other's. Again he was gone. She slowly sat, glancing to one who nodded, his eyes reflecting her own hidden fear.

With a wave she commanded, and the musicians resumed their music, but some of the joy had been banished from the circle by the thunder. And all knew that the one who had mocked them could alone dare such an affront. He alone had the power. And the coming night would be colder for that knowledge.

9

Phil led the boys through the door, holding a full creel. "Hey!" he said. "We're home."

Gloria came into the kitchen, and held her nose with exaggeration. "Into the sink!"

Phil and the boys deposited their catch, and Gloria looked at the seven fish. "Don't you clowns know you're only supposed to drown worms, not catch anything." The boys just grinned with pride.

Phil kissed her cheek. "I'll clean them. I've got to teach the boys how to."

Patrick made a face and said, "Ugh, fish guts!" while Sean laughed.

"Wash up first, guts later," Gloria commanded. "I've something to show you."

She bullied them out to the sink in the service porch and watched until they'd removed the fish odor from their hands. "You'll all have to change before dinner, but first come with me."

She led them to Phil's study and slid aside the door. Gabbie shouted, "Surprise!" while Aggie, Jack, Mark, and Gary offered birthday congratulations.

Phil shook his head and said, "I'd hoped everyone had forgotten. At my age I can afford to miss a few." Gloria fixed him with a disapproving look. Then he caught sight of the word processor sitting on his desk, with a big red ribbon stuck atop. "What!" He sat down slowly at his desk.

"Happy birthday, Daddy!" said Gabbie, hugging him from behind.

Phil sat staring at the blank monitor, silent for a long minute. Finally he said, "How do you work it?"

"Jack can show you."

Phil vacated the chair, while Aggie commented, "It's a lot like the one I use, just more snazzy."

Phil laughed. "I thought you used an old Remington Noiseless."

"My boy, we live in a technological age, if it has escaped your notice," she chided. "Don't let this thing scare you. Once you get used to it, you'll throw rocks at your old typewriter. Now, something a little more traditional." She handed a box to Phil. "Happy birthday, Philip."

Phil opened the box and revealed a beautifully ornate silver letter opener. "Aggie! This was Henry's. I can't take it."

"Of course you can, you silly man. I'm going to die one of these years and I'd rather you had it than the state of New York." She looked at the beautifully fashioned sheath of silver. "I got it for him when we were honeymooning in Mexico. It was made up in the silver country somewhere. You have to clean it regularly. It's pure silver handle, blade, sheath, and everything, and tarnishes dreadfully." She smiled. "No, you keep it, Philip."

Phil seemed genuinely moved by the gift, a personal belonging of Aggie's husband's. "Thanks," he said, rising to kiss her on the cheek.

The boys clustered behind Gabbie, inspecting the computer, and Sean said, "What kind of games can you play on it?"

"Can you do *Spy Hunter*?" inquired Patrick.

Jack laughed. "Well, you can play games, but—"

"No games!" said Gloria. "This is for your father and it's no toy. One computer game and he'll never get to use it."

"Aw, Mom," protested Patrick.

"Don't 'Aw, Mom,' me," she said in mock indignation. "You two go clean up. Dinner's in a half hour." The boys gave in and trooped up the stairs to completely wash up and change into clean T-shirts.

Phil hovered over Jack's shoulder while the young man showed him the basic operation of the system. He indicated the manuals and said, "If you run into a problem, give me a call—"

"He'll be out in the barn," interrupted Gabbie.

Jack grinned. "Probably."

Gloria said, "Well now, who wants a drink?"

"That's my cue," said Gabbie.

"What?" asked Phil.

"Dinner. I've got to go fetch it. Loo Fong's best Hunan and Szechwan to go. Back in fifteen minutes."

As Gabbie hurried out the door, Gloria said, "You play with your new toy, Phil. I'll go do something with those fish."

He nodded absently as he poked experimentally at the keyboard.

Gabbie's Porsche 911 Turbo was back in California, awaiting her return for the school year, so she took her father's Pontiac, driving as she usually did, fast but not recklessly. She hated to dawdle. The food was all bagged and waiting in two cardboard boxes, so all she had to do was negotiate the boxes into the backseat of the car. Gabbie pulled an illegal U-turn on McDermott Street—after making sure no one was coming either way—and headed for what the locals called a highway. To Gabbie it was a glorified two-lane country road, and a little one compared to what she'd grown used to back in Southern California. Hitting the highway, she drove at five miles over the speed limit, sure the local police considered that within the legal amount of fudging. She was approaching the turnoff to home when a shaft of light momentarily dazzled her as the sun appeared between some trees on a distant hilltop. She turned her head slightly and flipped down the sun visor. Then her eyes widened and she looked back toward the sunset. Atop a hill on the road leading away from the highway something was outlined against the sky.

A blast from a car horn pulled her attention back to her driving, and she hit the brakes and swerved. She had been drifting off to her left, and the angry driver of the car in the oncoming lane threw her a black look and flipped her off as he sped past. Gabbie's heart pounded as she negotiated the turn off the highway. She was doubly shaken as she pulled the car over to the shoulder and came to a complete stop. She took several deep breaths, then checked the backseat to see nothing had spilled before resuming her trip home.

Gabbie muttered to herself that she must have been imagining things. For an instant, outlined against the evening sky, she had seen something that had looked like an old wagon pulled by a single horse. A vague memory came to her, one which she almost recaptured, but which then fled. All she was left with was the name Wayland. And she couldn't understand why she felt tears running down her cheeks.

10

After dinner, the adults sat around the living room while the boys retired to the parlor for a little television before bed. Jack and Gabbie were out in the barn, checking on the two horses rented from Laudermilch, even though there was little reason. Gabbie already had plans for new fences from the barn around the south pasture, so the horses could be allowed to wander. Gloria had observed to Phil that she was making some long-term plans for a kid heading back to California soon, a remark that Phil shrugged off.

Everyone had overheard Gabbie's remark, and Gary said, "She's in for a shock when she sees what that much fencing's going to cost."

Phil and Gloria burst out laughing. Mark and Gary exchanged glances, and Aggie said, "Money's not a problem."

Mark said, "You must have done very well with those *Star Pirates* movies, Phil."

"It's not my money we're talking about." When Mark looked uncomprehending, Phil said, "Gabbie doesn't like us to talk about it, but it's public record. She's an heiress."

Aggie said, "The Larker family of Phoenix."

Mark blinked, then said, "Of course. Her mother's Corinne Larker."

Aggie nodded. "Who was disowned by Helen Larker, making Gabbie sole inheritor of the estate."

"But she's . . ."

"What?" said Phil.

Mark shrugged. "I don't know. Normal? Un-rich-kid-like—how's that?"

Gloria said, "Gabbie's got a good head on her. She doesn't go in for ostentation. She got only a small allowance while in school, until she was eighteen. She learned to get along on a modest income. Now she can get whatever she needs from the trustee of her grandmother's estate with a phone call, which suits her just fine. She's only had two indulgences: her horse, which set her back more money than I care to think of, and her Porsche, which she drives too damn fast. Other than that, she gets along on very little. The trustee'll turn the whole thing over to her when she marries or turns twenty-five."

"If it's not too tacky," said Gary, "can I ask how much?"

"I don't know," said Phil, "but many, many millions."

"Well then," observed Gary, "if she wants a fence, she'll get a fence." A mock-evil grin was followed by, "I wonder how expensive it would be to put a hit on Jack?"

They laughed and Mark said, "Ask Ellen. You go after Gabbie and she'll put a hit on you."

"True."

"When do we meet this girlfriend, Gary?" said Phil.

"Well, Mark and I were going to have you over to the house soon, and she'll be there. We're sort of unexpected guests tonight."

Phil raised an eyebrow and Mark explained about the key. He repeated his surmises about Kessler and the possibility of there really being a treasure, and when he was finished, everyone was silent for a minute.

"Well, it's a wild story," said Phil. "What about the treasure part? Do you really think it's hidden somewhere around here?"

"It's possible, I guess. Kessler came from Germany, started a major enterprise without local capital, and ran in the red for two years before breaking even. It's pretty clear he must have carried a tidy fortune out of Germany. In Germany there's almost no information about him, so where he got the money is anyone's guess. But there's a small item I uncovered in some banking records in New York. An agent for one of the equipment firms reported that the bank draft Kessler used to pay for his first shipment of heavy equipment was marked 'funds secured by gold,' an unusual notation. And he paid the note from his factory's profits, so the gold was never touched as well as I can make out."

"So," said Phil, "you think Kessler might have plundered some secret gold hoard in Germany to start his factory?"

"Sounds pretty silly when you put it that way," agreed Mark. "But before I start manufacturing theories, I need more facts. I don't even have enough for a good historical novel, let alone a history."

"What about the key?" asked Gloria.

Mark stood up. "If you can find the door that key opens, you might find something that will tell me what I want to know about Fredrick Kessler: what he and his sudden wealth had to do with all the strange goings-on in Germany at that time, and all the rest."

"And," added Gary, "you might find his treasure—if there is one."

"We should be off," said Mark. "If you've no objection, we'll continue with the books tomorrow."

"Of course you can," said Phil, showing them to the door.

When they were gone, Gloria said, "I still have the feeling that there's more here than he's telling."

Aggie said, "Mark tends to the mysterious, but he's harmless, dear. Besides, he always turns up these marvelous and wildly improbable bits of nonsense."

As Phil returned, Gloria asked, "You think this is all nonsense?"

"No," said Aggie. "I just refuse to indulge in Mark's tendency to jump from fact to fact and assume causality. Mark's work is fun to read, but I don't take most of it seriously. He's obsessed by ancient secrets and lore, and he can't stand not knowing. He's not as bad as that Dutch fellow with his gods being astronauts rubbish, but Mark isn't a rigorous researcher either. He has many critics, and not without justification.

"But, in his defense, a lot of Mark's work has an element of brilliance in it. There are some things he claimed that were later borne out by more scholarly research. No, Mark's not a quack. He's just a lot more like Indiana Jones than Margaret Mead." She paused. "But ask yourself who you'd rather have chasing after buried treasure, Indiana Jones or Margaret Mead?" Rising, she said, "Well, it's late and I should be off. Let me know if you turn up any more wonders."

They saw her to the door, and Phil walked her to the barn to fetch Jack. Gloria stuck her head into the parlor and informed the twins it was bedtime. Ushering them upstairs, she couldn't shake the feeling that Mark had revealed only a small portion of what he was after. And she reminded herself to have a look for a lock to match the key in her pocket.

AUGUST

1

August days are dog days, when Sirius, the Dog Star, rises. In baseball, with the long season two-thirds completed, the heat and humidity begin to take their toll. Averages dip and pitchers' arms begin to wear out; chronic injuries become acute and teams start to look to the minors or to trades with other teams for that player to fill the gap; front-runners begin their slides and teams talking World Series at the end of July by September first are saying, "Wait till next year." A team holding the division lead throughout August is a good team.

Gabbie dreaded August, for behind August came September, and with September would come the decision: return to California or stay in Pittsville. Already August was a week gone, and time felt as if it flew by. She and Jack had talked, but there was something preventing either of them from making the commitment that would keep her in New York. Gabbie felt suddenly frightened as she turned straw with a pitchfork. She halted her work in the barn and leaned upon the handle of the fork, thinking. Jack had gone to New York City with Aggie, to meet with the members of some committee or another. He'd been gone for a week and it had given Gabbie a chance to reflect. She was in love with Jack, or at least she felt more for him than she ever had for any other boy she had known. And that caused her concern. Was she in love? Sometimes she felt like a little kid and everything scared her. She had made her way through life with an ability to hide her fears from others, to look calm and collected, even tough. Through private school she had been the object of scorn by most of the other girls, both for her good looks and for her money, but her protective façade never broke. Gabbie could be bleeding inside, but she'd never let on. But just because she didn't show it didn't mean she wasn't hurting.

In high school she'd had only one serious boyfriend, Danny. Gabbie had thought herself in love with him. He had seemed different from most other boys. She had thought the relationship would endure beyond his leaving for college. After he'd enrolled at Stanford, she had three letters from him. The third one had told her he had met another girl.

Gabbie's face flushed in memory. She had flown into a rage, jumped into her car, and driven north, stopping only once for gas. She had her Porsche clocked at over 120 miles an hour at several points along Interstate 5, and had made the trip to Palo Alto in under five hours. She had stormed around Stanford until almost one in the morning, when Danny came back to his dorm from seeing his new girl. The confrontation had been humiliating. Danny's new relationship was nothing but sex. Gabbie and Danny had never had intercourse. Their love play had always ended with Gabbie having to hold him at bay. In their last few weeks together they had passed the heavy-petting stage, each bringing the other to climax, but Gabbie still refused to permit the final act. Somehow she couldn't let Danny inside of her, as if to do so would be an admission that it was love. And this girl had slept with him on the first date. He was totally infatuated with her, sexually obsessed, and regarded Gabbie as an unwelcome intrusion from his past, best disposed of quickly and without tenderness. He had called her a prude and a cock-teaser, then described in graphic detail the sexual antics of his new girl, as if her willingness to engage in them somehow proved her love for him. Gabbie had fled in shame and pain.

She'd expected to catch hell from her dad and Gloria, but they had been wonderful, offering support and no criticism over her flying off the handle. She had never communicated with Danny again. Now she understood that her reaction had been wounded pride and possessiveness. The jealousy that had attacked unexpectedly at the Fourth of July picnic had been something completely different, a terror at the thought of losing Jack.

Gabbie resumed turning the hay and smiled at the thought of Jack. There was such a difference between Jack and Danny. Danny had been a nice boy, most of the time, but he'd been a boy. Jack was a gentle and loving man. He never spoke about Ginger, the girl down in Atlanta, except to answer a direct question from Gabbie's. He had told Gabbie he was a little beat up from that relationship, and she attributed his reluctance to speak of the future to that. Whenever Gabbie would become concerned about tomorrow, all Jack would say was "It will work out."

Gabbie thought, Damn right it will work out, Jack Cole. Feeling a sudden surge of strong feelings for him, she found her eyes brimming with moisture. Damn it, she did love him. And she knew that soon she was going to drag him off someplace and make love. He'd never pressed and never accused, seemingly satisfied to take his lead from her. Twice now she'd regretted his not being a little more commanding. Ever since that first walk in the woods, since that night at Aggie's, she would have let Jack make love to her. But the fact of his restraint only served to make her more sure of his being just the right man to be her first—and maybe only—lover. Gabbie took a deep breath, suddenly aware she was nervous. Jack was due back in an hour or two and Gabbie considered that this might be the night.

Gabbie finished freshening the straw in the stalls and put the fork away. The horses were out in the pasture and this time of year stayed out at night, but the hay still got moldy. The boys had taken another riding lesson before their regular afternoon ball game. Gabbie was surprised to discover how much she enjoyed teaching them. When she had arrived from Arizona, the twins had been six, cute but underfoot a lot. Now they were turning into regular little guys, complete with personalities. They even managed to complete the small chores given them around the barn with a minimum of grumbling. Despite their teasing her about Jack, they seemed to hold their older half sister and her boyfriend in genuine affection and showed gratitude after each lesson. And she loved them, despite a maddening tendency on their part to barge into the bathroom without knocking. Several leisurely baths had been terminated with Gabbie throwing bath sponges at one brother or the other.

Gabbie wiped perspiration from her brow. She didn't know if she'd ever get used to the humidity after years in the dry heat of Arizona and Los Angeles. The unexpected summer showers were alien to her, and the one that morning had been a beauty. Even in the early evening, with the sun dipping behind the hills to the west, it was like a steam bath in the barn. She pulled at her shirt, letting the air in. She rarely wore a bra, and the air felt cool on her breasts. She unbuttoned her shirt and flapped it, allowing the evaporating moisture to cool her. She regarded herself as the cooling caused chill bumps to form on her breasts. Not as big as Sheila Riley's, maybe, but not so bad, she thought, absently touching herself. As her fingers passed over her nipples they came erect, and she thought of Jack. "Christ," she muttered aloud, "I've got sex on the brain."

A noise caused Gabbie to freeze. It had been a laugh. She spun around, rapidly covering herself. She sought the source of the sound and glanced up at the hayloft, hidden in the almost evening gloom. "Is someone up there?" From within the shadows a laugh erupted, boyish in timbre. "Sean? Patrick?" Again the laugh. "Are you monsters spying on me?" Her tone was angry and she felt herself blush.

The laugh continued, and suddenly Gabbie was afraid. It wasn't Sean or Patrick. There was something unnerving, almost mad, in the sound. Gabbie was turning toward the barn door when a whispering, musical voice said, "Hold, and abide awhile, Gabrielle."

Gabbie whirled and beheld a boy, no more than fourteen or fifteen from his appearance, hunkering down at the edge of the hayloft. He was partly hidden by shadows. "How . . . ? Who are you?"

The boy jumped, and Gabbie felt her heart skip. She regarded the drop, over twelve feet, but he landed like a gymnast coming off the high bar, both feet planted firmly on the ground. He wore an odd-looking pair of trousers, of coarse linen, it appeared, tied with a thong. They reminded her of the hospital pants worn by some of the kids at school. He was barefooted and bare-chested, and he stood slightly taller than she. His body was muscled, but smoothly, less like a man's than an athletic boy's, and his hair was a tangle of brown curls, of a color different from anything she had seen, looking like nothing as much as the color of tree bark. His face was young, but odd—high cheekbones, a high brow, almost cruel lips, and wide, deep eyes. The blue of those eyes struck her, and she was certain she had seen them before. Softly, feeling confused, she said, "Who . . . are you?"

"A wanderer, a seeker, fair one." He stared at her, his eyes passing over her body as if caressing her. His expression was appraising, openly desirous. "Do not leave yet, for your society is most pleasing." He spoke in a funny way, with an accent impossible to place but somehow familiar. He reached out, and Gabbie's heart skipped again, and she felt terror building within her. She was on the verge of crying out, or running, but was somehow unable to accomplish either. The youth touched her hair, then her cheek. As his fingertips brushed her face, Gabbie's body tensed, for a thrill ran down her neck, between her breasts, to her groin. Her nipples hardened again and her body flushed with heat as she trembled. The odor of flowers and spices assailed her nostrils and her head swam.

Teetering she stood while the youth walked around her. Gabbie was unable to follow him, as if her head refused to turn and her eyes were fixed forward. From behind her the youth leaned toward her until his face was next to her cheek, his chin resting upon her shoulder. Softly he said, "I would not have troubled you, Gabrielle, save that your longing sings to me. Your heat is felt and, being felt, warms my desires." He giggled, a sound that caused a shiver to run up Gabbie's spine. "Pleasing, your form is a delight to my senses. To you shall I return such delight, for your needs are as apparent to me as a storm in the sky is to the raven." She felt his hand press against the small of her back, then slide down over her right buttock. She shook, unable to move, trapped like a deer in the headlights of an oncoming car at night. Her mind shrieked and yet she could make no sound; and from deep within, a desire was building. The youth moved in front of her and she saw him clearly again. He wore nothing beneath the trousers, and she could see he was in a state of arousal. His eyes were electric, a blue like flashing lightning. His boyish features were masked by a shadow of ages, both childlike and ancient. He was beautiful and terrifying to gaze upon. He moved close to her, and all she could see were his eyes. Blue, like the shimmering surface of lapis lazuli, like perfect ice, his eyes drank her will. His voice caressed her, soft and sensual. "Shall such a flower wither for want of tending? Nay," he whispered in her ear. His hot breath blew over her cheek and ear and she shuddered. "If the bloom is to be lost, then it shall not wither, it shall be plucked. Come, follow, child." He gave her a small push and she found herself moving toward the barn door. The youth half skipped, half danced, reaching the door a moment before her. He paused to glance out and, satisfied that nothing was amiss, pushed wide the barn door. Gabbie found herself moving despite any wish of her own.

Her mind felt detached from her body, robbed of any volition. She moved in rhythms odd and jerky, as if whatever commanded her was unused to her body. Her body? her mind wondered. She fought to halt, and felt her body held at the door of the barn.

The youth spun to face her, a smile of searing heat burning her eyes like the crack of lightning. In a voice like music he said, "You know your desires. Do not pause. Come, come with me." He made an airy gesture with his hand, a lazy half circle, and said, "Listen, listen, Gabrielle."

From the distance came the sound of music, a sobbing melody so lovely it brought tears to Gabbie's eyes. Grand themes overwhelmed her, though the sound was little more than a quintet, a harp and three flutes, with another, unrecognized woodwind. Still, it swept over her like a wave, freeing emotions that came flowing up from some place deep within. Gabbie cried, for the song was too lovely to be mortal, both wonderful and sad. It was the loveliest song she had ever heard and the most melancholy.

Then the theme of the music turned sprightly, a jaunty tune of merry syncopations. Gabbie felt her body respond, felt her pulse quicken, as she moved in time to the music, half walking, half dancing behind the strange young man. He turned and capered around her, and from somewhere he produced pipes, four reed flutes fastened together. He played in counterpoint to the music, and Gabbie felt like laughing, yet it was an urge to a laughter caught between joy and insanity. A tiny part of her stood aloof, attempting to sort out the madness that had enveloped her, but that lonely part was the only logical being in an insane universe, for everything around Gabbie had become fey.

The barn looked blurry, as if seen through a smeared glass, and the light in the sky was electric, a searing blue vibrant with energies never seen, only felt. The trees rustled in the breeze and they spoke in an ancient language. Even the mud beneath her feet seemed lovely, a moist and warm carpet to dance across.

The boy moved through the pasture, Gabbie at his side. She was a puppet, a marionette whose strings he deftly manipulated. She found herself spinning, making running circles as when she had been a child, moving for the sheer and simple joy of movement. A gleeful sound echoed her own laugh and she saw the boy grinning at her.

Seemingly without effort, he vaulted the fence with but one hand upon the top of a post. Gabbie climbed, but even that normally awkward movement was in time with the song, all rhythm and harmony. He led her into the woods, into the cool green of the forest. And in the gentle evening the trees sang and Gabbie listened.

Never had the woods looked like this, alive, throbbing with life and energies she could see. The gloom became soft sheltering darkness, transparent to her eyes, as a new dimension was revealed to her. She could see every branch and leaf, and every tree, each unique. She saw that there was another world, a hidden world, contained within, surrounded by, the world of her birth. She knew that this other world had always been there, but that she had never before been able to perceive it. Now, in the midst of this mad and joyous dance, she could see that other world. And in the darkness the boy glowed with his own faint blue light.

Then the boy was dancing around her in a circle, all the while playing on his pipes, spinning like Pan at a bacchanal. Gabbie watched the boy's shoulders and back while he spun, young muscles cleanly outlined under the skin. The scent of wildflowers, honey, and spices assailed her nostrils as the boy moved closer and closer to her. God, he was beautiful, she thought, as she felt his nearness. When he spun, she could see that despite the mad dance, his erection was still there, a homage to her loveliness. Gabbie was overwhelmed with desire for this boy. Her own body became a thing unto itself, alive with awareness; each fiber of muscle sought to bend and twist, to flex and release, and the dance was joined. Her skin was electric, her hair flying around her like a dark halo. Her nipples were hardened to a painful state and her stomach and groin were awash in damp heat. A distant voice deep within screamed in terror, pleading with her to flee. She dismissed that voice.

Without knowing how he had come to stand before her, Gabbie was vaguely aware of his hands unbuttoning her shirt and felt the cool air against her breasts, as his tongue lightly darted against her cheek. Her body tensed, suddenly coiling like a spring, and then he lightly touched her left breast. She exploded in a flash of wet heat, her body releasing in a wild uncontrolled spasm.

Gabbie's knees went weak and she began to collapse, but a surprisingly powerful arm encircled her, holding her upright as if she were a child. Her skin was drenched, as perspiration coursed down her, and she gasped for air. In a distant corner of her mind the conscious being named Gabbie suddenly cringed in terror, as her body went out of control, becoming a thing apart. She felt her fall turned into a gentle descent to the ground. She shuddered as waves of pleasure coursed through her, numbing her last shred of volition. Softly he said, "Come, young beauty, come, and let me gift thee with delights." He bent over and kissed her. And then he drank her soul.

He deftly unbuttoned the fly of her jeans. His hand traced circles of fire across her stomach and her breath caught in her throat. He lowered his head and kissed her breasts and she felt the spring inside her groin winding tightly again. Her mind was overcome by hot wet longings and she couldn't think. He slipped his hand below the elastic of her panties and between her legs. Gabbie shook and thrashed and bucked like a wild animal, sounds of primitive pleasure erupting from her lips.

Trapped within herself, isolated from her own body, Gabbie's mind was smothering. And through that palpable heat she could see images, a kaleidoscope of memories, brilliant colors scattered behind her eyes, dancing like translucent colored beads swirling in blinding light. She could see every man who had ever attracted her, each remembered in detail. They stood before her, all aroused and ready, each an object of her desire, each content to wait upon her whim. From her days at school she remembered a stallion ready to mount a mare, and the laughter of the girls as they watched one of the stable men holding the stallion's huge member and trying to guide it into the brood mare while not getting stepped on by the inflamed animal. The giggles were transformed into sighs and moans of passion as the girls suddenly shared the act with the mare. Then the girls were surrounding Gabbie, and the hated shower in the gym was transformed into a sensual arena, as firm young bodies writhed in the hot steam and glistened under the blue lights. Desires undreamed of rose inside and she lusted to caress those slender bodies, to explore their moist mystery, and to taste their lips. Red lights burned—no, fire, she could now see—and a giant of a man stood revealed before her. His arms flexed as he pounded upon an anvil, his perfect body drenched in sweat. Wayland, she thought. Then she knew the boy was beside her, his tongue probing the soft contours of her stomach.

Through a crimson haze of her own pounding blood, she could see the youth moving to position himself over her. His face blurred and shifted and for an instant another gazed down upon her, one whose aspect was madness made solid by a demented artist. A face of cruel beauty regarded her, then that face lowered to meet hers. His hot breath was as sweet as mulled cider, his thrusting tongue hinting at peppercorn sharpness. His kiss seared her lips; his touch shocked her skin, and pleasure mounted to levels of intensity beyond her capacity to endure. The burning wet heat between her legs became electric, and as she climbed new heights of desire, the gratification of that desire remained just beyond her reach. Seeking unobtainable release, Gabbie crossed the boundary between passion and torment. Desire fled as, in that instant, pleasure turned to pain.

Gabbie knew agony. And terror engulfed her. Fear profound and uncontrolled, the knowledge that she stood poised at a point of being lost beyond redemption, swept over her, carrying her beyond concerns of flesh and passion; she verged on becoming lost in spirit. Within her own mind she screamed out in terror, but her lips only moaned in pleasure, as her body remained a thing apart from her. Trapped within herself, she knew this was nothing of love. Love was a giving thing and this was a taking, a ripping away of something precious. Gabbie screamed again in her mind, but her body only made hoarse sounds of sexual satisfaction.

The youth attacked her with animal fury, his teeth and nails leaving fire upon her white skin, each nip and scratch eliciting a yelp of pleasure. Deep within herself, Gabbie shrank away in fear, a spectator to her own body, so mindless in its grotesque lust that even this pain became a delight. Silently, inwardly, she wept in mortal terror. Gabbie felt the boy's hands work perverted magic upon her flesh and knew he was about to take her. And she knew that once he had her, she would never return to the world she had known. For, deep within herself, she knew that beyond this pleasure and pain lay only death.

Even as the passion and terror mounted toward climax, a sound intruded, and that distant, trapped part of Gabbie's mind turned toward the sound. Someone called her name. It was a distant voice, but coming closer. Then she heard a familiar voice call, "Gabbie?" Searing agony passed through her groin, feeling like an electric shock applied to flesh too sensitive to endure the most gentle caress. She arched and twisted as if current passed into her body, silently gasping, unable even to scream so intense was the jolt of energy. Yet even at that instant she knew this was but a promise of the full measure of agony yet to come. She could only silently whimper as waves of heat and pain raced to consume her, and she understood that she would endure them for an eternity before death arrived.

Then the red heat vanished and the pain remained. Gabbie felt something akin to a cascade of frigid water pour over her feverish body. Her heart seized up and her breath froze within her as she went rigid. Then her heart resumed beating, and a single gasping breath drove slivers of ice into her lungs. She lay cold and sick, her ravaged body shuddering in reaction to the wrenching transition from sweltering heat to icy darkness. Something was removed from her, leaving her adrift upon a frigid jet sea, the pounding in her ears the sound of distant breakers smashing upon ebon rocks. In that lightless arctic ocean she floated. The first sensation to intrude into this blackness was a smell. Damp earth. No longer did her head reel from sweet fragrances; now she smelled the richness of loam, and the blend of wood and leaf fragrances, the odor of grasses and the musk of a distant vixen, all carried on the cool night air. In an uncoordinated, tentative way, her mind was rejoined with her body. She became aware of a trembling, a sensation somehow coming closer, until she realized it was her body shaking, her teeth chattering audibly. She moved her head, and the pain shot behind her eyes, making her cry out. Then it was light, almost blinding. "What!" said the distant voice. "Gabbie! Oh my God!"

Gabbie felt the inky haze lifting. She blinked and shook her head. The terror had vanished, as if someone chased it away, but much of the pain and the terrible cold remained and she couldn't stop shivering. Then Jack was standing over her.

He put down the lantern, and she turned her head away from the blinding light. "Oh God, what's going on?" he said in a hoarse whisper. Her eyes refused to focus and she could only vaguely sense Jack's words; their meaning slipped away before she could apprehend them. The fragments of thought began to coalesce, and she looked down. Her body was near-nude, her shirt unbuttoned and pulled back, her jeans and panties yanked down around one ankle. She was lying in the mud alongside the path toward the Troll Bridge in the woods. Her breasts were covered with teeth marks and scratches, as was her stomach. Her nipples were throbbing from the cold, and pain shot up into her groin each time she moved. Gabbie became aware of her damp hair matted on her head and face, obscuring her vision, and she feebly attempted to brush dark strands of it from her eyes. She blinked in confusion and began to cry. She weakly reached toward Jack. He said, "Oh God, Gabbie, what happened?" as he cradled her in his arms.

Finally she spoke. "Jack?" Her voice was a dry half-whisper.

Gabbie felt him quickly pick her up. As he bore her back to the house, she felt her control slip away. The last hint of the soul-shaking terror and the memory of the insane, blinding lust vanished, replaced by a revulsion so deep it caused her mind to knot in torment. She cried, deep sobs racking her body with uncontrollable trembling. Her stomach knotted a moment later and she turned her head and vomited. Between sobs she whispered, "Jack, I'm so scared." She was still crying when he carried her into the kitchen, just before she slipped into unconsciousness.

2

Gabbie blinked. Her head pounded and her mouth was dry. "Water," she said, and her voice was a dry croak. Gloria poured her a glass from a pitcher and helped her lift up to drink. Gabbie's head reeled with the effort, as she was overcome with dizziness. The water was cool and fresh, and Gabbie drank deeply. Quickly the dizziness passed and she took in her surroundings. She was in her own bedroom.

Gloria stood beside the bed, Phil just behind her. "You okay, honey?" asked Gloria.

"Sure, I guess." Gabbie smiled weakly. "What happened?"

Gloria glanced at Phil, who said, "We were hoping you could tell us. Don't you remember?"

"Remember what?" Gabbie asked.

Gloria sat on a chair next to the bed. "You went into the barn about seven-thirty yesterday. Jack showed up at eight and I thought you'd come up here to your room. When I discovered you weren't here, Jack grabbed a lantern and went to the barn. You were nowhere to be found, but he saw footprints in the muddy ground, heading across the meadow toward the woods. He followed them and found you on the path."

Gabbie's brow furrowed as she thought. "I . . . I remember going to turn the hay for the horses, and I was thinking . . ." Her voice trailed off. "I can't remember anything else." Suddenly she was visited by dread; but she couldn't identify the source of that feeling. It was only a nameless and numbing terror. The color drained from her cheeks and she whispered, "What happened?"

Phil said, "Honey, someone tried to rape you."

Gabbie fell silent. Somehow that didn't seem possible. She thought that if someone tried to rape you, you'd remember. Softly she said, "Rape?" She looked at her father and saw that his face was a mask of controlled anger. For the first time since she had come to live with him, she saw her father truly enraged. "Someone tried to rape me?"

"You were pretty beat up, honey," said Gloria. "And you were burning up with a fever. You'd been left . . ."

Gabbie looked down at herself, as if trying to see through the covers and the T-shirt she wore, as if trying to see inside her own body. "Did . . . was . . ."

Gloria took Gabbie's hand. "The doctor will be here soon. Look, we can talk about it more later. You need your rest."

Gabbie lay back against the pillows. "I'm not tired. Just confused."

Phil said, "You don't remember anything?"

Gabbie felt her fears diminish. The possibility of rape seemed somehow distant. She felt bruised and battered, but somehow not . . . She didn't know what she felt. Then she said, "Jack?"

"He's downstairs, waiting," said Phil. "He's been here all night, slept on the couch, if he slept at all."

"The boys?" Suddenly Gabbie was concerned for her brothers. If some maniac was on the loose, they might be in danger.

"They're okay."

"Can I see Jack?"

"Sure," said Gloria, rising from the chair beside the bed. Phil kissed Gabbie and followed his wife from the room. Almost instantly Jack was beside Gabbie. He looked haggard, unshaven, and rumpled. He smiled down at her. "Hi."

"Hi yourself," she said, returning his smile. "Don't I get a kiss?"

He leaned over and kissed her. "Are you all right?"

She said, "I . . . don't know. Ah, I don't remember much." She studied his face and saw he was working hard to maintain a light manner. Behind the soft words and quick smile, he was seething and deeply troubled. "Are you okay?"

The mask broke and tears gathered in his eyes. His voice became thick with emotion. "No, I . . . I'm not doing real good with this." He took a deep breath. "I'm not a violent person, Gabbie, but I swear if I get my hands on that animal, I'll kill him."

The strength of his emotions startled Gabbie. "Hey! Take it easy."

Jack's control was lost and tears ran down his cheeks. He took her hand in his and looked at her. "I . . . I love you, you know?"

She smiled. "I know. I love you, too."

He sat on the bedside and leaned over, kissing her again. "If anything happened . . . I'd go nuts, you know?" he whispered.

"Ya, I know," she whispered back, holding his head so his cheek rested against hers, ignoring the rasp of his beard stubble. At that moment she felt the bond between them and knew that whatever doubts she had felt were gone. There was a long silence, then she said, "It's funny, but I don't feel raped." Jack stiffened, and she said, "Hey, calm down, Jack. I'm serious. I feel . . . tired, and bruised, but . . . somehow I don't think . . ." She looked at him. "I think I'd know." Her eyes closed as she kissed Jack. She loosed her arms from around his neck and he sat back. "Something happened," she said softly. Her voice lowered to a near whisper as fragments of images flashed past. "But . . . it wasn't what they think."

Before Jack could answer, one of the boys shouted from below, "Doctor's here!" The downstairs door could be heard opening, then slamming, as Sean or Patrick provided a loud welcome. A moment later Dr. John Latham entered and chased Jack from the room while he checked on his patient. Jack went downstairs and found Phil and Gloria talking to a man in the living room.

The man looked up as Jack entered and Phil said, "Jack, this is Detective Mathews." The police detective had arrived on the heels of the doctor and returned to what he had been saying when Jack had entered. "I'm sorry, Mr. Hastings, but if she can't remember details, there's little we can do."

Phil looked incensed. "My daughter was raped and you can't do anything?"

The detective held up his hands. "Mr. Hastings, I know you're upset, but we won't know if she was raped until the doctor says she was. From what you say of her condition, we can pretty well rule out that the girl beat and bit herself black and blue, so there is ample evidence of an assault. But unless we have a physical description of a suspect, we're stuck at a dead end. We'll have a car make additional patrols out here for a few days, and we'll keep an eye out for any strange characters who might come through town, but we don't have a lead. Hell, if it's a transient, he could be halfway to anywhere by now." He paused, and added, "I'm no lawyer, but even if we found someone, we still might not have a case for assault. Without a positive identification, we couldn't tie him to this crime."

Phil said, "Look, I don't care what you charge the bastard with. I just want him caught."

"We'll do what we can. Now, as soon as your daughter's able, I'd like a few words with her." He turned to Jack. "You're the one who found her?" Jack nodded and the detective took him aside to ask some questions.

A while later Dr. Latham came down the stairs. He said, "She's fine. Just keep an eye on her for a day or two, and let me know if that fever comes back." He looked disapprovingly at Phil and Gloria. "I wish you'd brought her in to the emergency room last night."

Gloria looked self-conscious. "I . . . it didn't look especially bad, I mean the swelling of those bites and scratches didn't start until this morning, or during the night." Her voice trailed off as she added, "I have this thing about hospitals. . . ."

"Well, I've given her a tetanus booster, and a shot of tetracycline, so those scratches won't do much, but . . . look, I'm not going to lecture you. Just don't be so quick to make a diagnosis in the future, all right?"

Phil said, "We won't," and cast a sidelong glance at his wife. Last night Phil had been beside himself, and Gloria had appeared an island of calm, reassuring her husband that Gabbie was only a little bruised. He had been forced to agree, as he had helped put the feverish girl to bed, that the scratches on her breasts and stomach had looked minor. Gloria had judged Gabbie's temperature to be little more than a hundred degrees, so he had grudgingly agreed not to rush her off to the hospital. This morning, when Gloria had looked in on her, the fever was still there and she had tossed off her covers in the night. Gloria had seen the welts that had come up during sleep and had rushed to the phone, getting Dr. Latham's name from Aggie. It had taken all Gloria's persuasiveness and dropping Aggie's name to get him to agree to the house call.

Phil said, "Doctor, what's the story? Was Gabbie raped?"

Dr. Latham said, "My best guess is not. There're no physical signs of penetration."

"Are you sure?" asked Phil.

The doctor understood Phil's concern. "One hundred percent? No, anything is possible, but I'd bet thirty years of practice she wasn't entered. No, your daughter was roughed up a good deal—those teeth marks are a symptom of a pretty sick mind at work." He looked thoughtful a moment. "The marks are odd, more like burns than abrasions. And I swear there are tiny blisters on the skin below her pubic hair." He regarded the puzzled expressions of Gloria and Phil, and said, "No, I don't think she was raped." After a short silence he said, "But, to all intent and purposes, it's pretty much the same thing. She was violated and she needs to have some help dealing with that. I can recommend someone if you'd like."

"A psychiatrist?" said Phil.

"Or a psychologist. Or someone from the rape assistance center up in Buffalo, maybe. Sign of emotional difficulty may not surface for a while, so keep an eye out. If she's troubled, or has difficulty sleeping, or shows any unusual behavior, like becoming suddenly agitated or manic, or going quiet for long periods, just let me know. I'll give you a referral."

Phil thanked the doctor, and the detective went up to question Gabbie briefly. When they had both left, Gloria went upstairs to sit with Gabbie. Phil and Jack stood in the living room and exchanged a look that revealed they both felt the same things: outrage and helplessness.

3

_____

"Hey!" Gabbie shouted. As usual, her protests were ignored and the twins continued their battle. Pulling aside the covers of her bed, she got up and stormed down the hall to their room. Sean and Patrick were rolling on the floor, their tussle approaching the point where play verged on battle. "Hey!" Gabbie shouted again.

The boys halted their struggle. Looking up, Sean said, "What?"

"Take it outside," ordered Gabbie.

"Take what outside?" said Patrick with that evil expression only little brothers are capable of.

"Your noise, your brother, and yourself," she said, her patience at an end. "Or when Gloria and Dad get back, your little fannies'll be in a sling." She turned on her heel, not staying to hear their rebuttal. Then a shout caused her to look back. "What!"

Patrick stood there, trying to pick up Sean. "You said to take him outside." Both boys collapsed to the floor with uncontained mirth.

"Oh!" said Gabbie as she retreated to her bedroom. She had gotten exactly twenty-four hours' consideration from the boys since Jack had carried her home. All day yesterday the boys had practically tiptoed around and spoke in whispers, so as not to disturb Gabbie's rest. Now it was business as usual. She gave up on the convalescing and took off the big T-shirt she used as night clothing. She paused a moment to regard her nude body in the full-length mirror hung on the door and shuddered. The welts had gone down, but now angry marks, like tiny sunburn blisters, had formed, puffy reminders of some terrible encounter she could not remember. Sighing, she pulled a pair of panties out of the dresser and stepped into them. Dressing in a shirt and jeans, she pulled on her boots, determined to put all this strangeness behind her. Besides, she needed to work the horses.

Back in the hall, she found that the boys had left, and assumed they were heading out for the afternoon baseball game at the park. Phil and Gloria were up in Buffalo for the day. Phil had been asked to speak at a library luncheon, and Gabbie had almost had to throw a temper tantrum to get him to go. He'd wanted to stay close despite her assurances she was all right. Phil consented to go when Mark agreed to baby-sit the place, so he and Gloria had decided to make a day of it, staying for some shopping, then dinner at the Cloister, which was reputed to be one of the best restaurants in the state.

Passing the library, she spied Mark sitting behind her dad's computer and stuck her head through the door. "Hi. How's it going?"

Mark looked up and smiled at her, and Gabbie was suddenly struck by the thought that he was a very nice man. She'd spent only a little time with Mark and Gary, more with Gary, for Jack and she would play tennis with Gary and his girlfriend, Ellen. But when she was around Mark, she found him pleasant company.

He said, "Pretty good. Just about done here, and getting ready to brave the basement tomorrow. How's it with you?"

She shrugged. "I'm still bruised. But I'll live."

"That's good."

"What's with Dad's computer?"

"I'm using it to catalog the library. I'll dump a hard copy for myself, and your dad'll have these discs to keep. He can update them when he buys or sells something."

She shook her head. "I doubt he'll remember. He likes the word processor, but all the other stuff is from another planet as far as he's concerned."

Mark laughed. "I know. I wrote the program for the catalog."

Gabbie lingered at the door, seemingly unable to speak for a while. After a bit, Mark said, "Want to talk about it?"

"It's pretty weird."

"Weird is my business." He looked hard at her. "Gabbie, if you don't want to talk, my feelings won't be hurt. But if you need an ear, I'll be more than happy to listen." He smiled. "And I am a psychologist."

"I didn't know that." She seemed surprised.

"Most people don't. I don't practice, but I have my Ph.D. in abnor-

mal psychology and a license from the state of New York which says I'm
a shrink. That's how I got into the occult in the first place, investigating
weird psychological phenomena. The first book I wrote was on paranormal psychology, and that led to other things in the occult field. I'm sort
of distant from when I did my clinical internship, but I still know how to
listen."

She paused, as if considering what he said. Then at last she said,
"Confidentially?"

"Absolutely." He punched some keys, saving whatever he was
working on, while she went over to a chair. He sat back, the desk
separating them, and said nothing.

After a while she began, "What has me worried is that I don't
remember much. I mean, I've heard of people having blocks and the
like from trauma, but I don't feel especially . . . traumatized, you
know?" He nodded. "But it's like a . . . dream. Like when you wake
up and almost remember what you dreamed, maybe an image or something, but you can't remember most of it."

"What do you remember?"

"I remember . . . hearing something. And I remember . . .
smelling something."

"What?"

"Wildflowers, I think. At least, it smelled like flowers. And it had to
be pretty strong for me to smell it in the barn." She laughed, looking a
little embarrassed. "This is pretty stupid, huh?"

"No, not at all. Smells are pretty basic, stronger than you'd imagine.
You can look at a picture of your grandmother, for example, and not
remember her, then smell her favorite cologne and trigger vivid memories. It's common."

"Well, I don't think I've smelled anything like this before. It was
spicy. I'd have remembered . . ." Her voice trailed off and her eyes
widened.

"What?" Mark asked softly.

Color drained from Gabbie's face. "I *did* smell that flower smell
before. I . . . I'm surprised I didn't remember right away, 'cause that
was pretty weird, too."

"When?" said Mark, obviously interested.

"When My Dandelion threw her shoe, on the Fourth of July." She
told him about her encounter with the blacksmith. Mark moved forward, so that his elbows rested upon the desk as she spoke. "That's so
strange. I didn't remember anything about that until just now. Must
have been the flu."

"What flu?"

"I got a bug on the Fourth. Jack found me. He thinks this black-smith was a hallucination. I don't. I think he was one of those Amish guys from Cattaraugus. He looked like one, wide hat, suspenders, heavy boots. And he had an accent. He had this old wagon, with a portable forge in back. But it looked . . . you know, really old, not like the modern ones in the back of trucks. I don't know how to describe it, really."

Mark didn't say anything; at last Gabbie said, "You know, I was pretty upset with Jack, and I thought that smith was pretty nice. I sort of thought I might like to meet him again, but I guess an Amish guy wouldn't . . . I don't know, date outside his faith? Whatever."

Mark smiled and spoke softly. "No, I don't think so. Look, Gabbie. There may have been a blacksmith. I don't know much about the Amish, but I could check it out for you. Did he tell you his name?"

She wrinkled her brow, then her eyes widened. "Smith. That was it. His name was Wayland Smith."

The only change of expression on Mark's face was a slight tighten-ing around the eyes. "Wayland Smith," he repeated in flat tones.

"Yes." She seemed to be struggling to remember something. "He said he was from someplace called White Horse. I guess it's his home-town. That's about all, except . . ." She lowered her eyes.

After a long silence, Mark softly said, "What?"

"Well, he sort of . . . got me turned on, you know."

Mark was silent, absently tapping a pencil against his cheek. Then he said, "Did this disturb you?"

Gabbie's eyes met his, and she looked embarrassed. "Yes, sort of. It's like there's two different people, see"—she tapped her chest with a finger—"inside." Gabbie paused, fighting for words. "Me, the real me is, you know, normal." Her voice lowered, showing discomfort. "I've got urges, you know. I get . . . excited, by Jack, you know."

Mark smiled. It was reassuring and warm, not mocking. "Yes, I know."

Gabbie grinned self-consciously. "I do that when I get nervous. You know, you know, you know." She shook her head. "Grandmother used to really get on my case about ending every sentence with 'you know.'" The mood seemed to lighten, and Gabbie began to relax. "Look, when I'm with Jack, I get pretty turned on, but it's sort of a normal thing. . . ." She began to say something, then halted and changed it to "see?"

The both laughed. Mark said, "I do."

"But with this blacksmith . . . well, he was nice and all, but while he was working, all I thought of was his body." She sighed loudly. "I mean, he was something else, but . . ." She thought for a long time and finally said, ". . . but I don't normally think a lot about a guy's body. I mean, Jack's got a terrific body, and I'd have trouble with somebody who repulsed me, but what a guy says and thinks, how he feels, those are the things, I guess, that make me take notice." She seemed again to be fighting for words.

"And this Wayland was different?"

Gabbie said, "God, yes!" She fell silent once more while she remembered. "I watched him work, and I was sweating all over, and all I could think of was getting my hands on his body." She laughed self-consciously as she made a grasping gesture, and shook her head in amazement. "He lifted me to the saddle, after he'd finished the shoeing, and when he put his hands on me, I just about came in my jeans." Gabbie's tone shifted from embarrassment to distress. "Mark, it scares me. I'd have balled his brains out right there on the ground. I mean, I wasn't thinking about love or loyalty to Jack or my virginity or anything. I just wanted to pull his pants off and screw." Her voice lowered. "It was like he had this power over me. Am I crazy, or what?"

Mark smiled. "My guess is you're a little more 'or what' than crazy." Gabbie smiled back. "Sex is a pretty heavy experience in any case." He studied her for a moment. "Especially if you're kind of new at it. You may get a little better at dealing with sexual attraction as you get more experienced, but it's still something that can badly shake you. Every once in a while we'll meet someone who just makes us go batty without our knowing the first thing about him or her. Most times, we need some sharing, trust building, and time together to build a relationship, you know?" They both smiled at that. "But this other thing, chemistry, love at first sight, lightning striking, whatever you call it, is pretty scary stuff. Even old guys like me have it from time to time. Just a year ago, I met someone at a writer's convention . . . well, without details, when we shook hands to say good-bye, it was like an electric shock. Damn near knocked my socks off."

Gabbie became animated. "That's it! I nearly jumped out of my clothes when he touched me." She lowered her eyes. "It was almost an orgasm."

"It's a powerful and basic thing. And it doesn't make a whole lot of sense. It's the reason people get so deeply involved with partners who are no damn good for them."

Gabbie nodded. "Like my mom and dad?"

"I never met your mom, but from what little your dad has said, it might have been like that. I've seen pictures of your mom, and she's a killer." He winked at her. "And so's her kid." Gabbie smiled at the compliment without embarrassment. "And your dad was pretty young when they met. By all accounts, it was a whirlwind courtship. Even now *they* might not be able to tell you what they saw in each other back then." He paused. "So what I'm telling you is that when we run up against this chemistry thing, it's overwhelming and it doesn't make sense. And you get scared. Also, it gives you the feeling someone else has power over you, and that's usually not pleasant. We often come to resent those we love, just for that power they hold over us." Gabbie still appeared worried. "Look, you said you had the flu, right?" She indicated yes. "Well, when we're feverish, we can act in some strange ways. I'm not an M.D., but I do read the journals, and I know fevers do weird things to hormones and other things in your biochemistry. Maybe this fellow's effect on you was due in part to the fever. Or at least you responded more strongly than normal because your body chemistry was a little messed up and your normal inhibitions were dampened. Or something like that."

Gabbie sighed. "I hope so. I . . . hope it isn't something . . . you know, like something I really wanted . . . secretly or something." She looked down at her hands, folded in her lap. "Like maybe this guy in the woods . . . saw something in me. . . ."

Softly Mark said, "Gabbie, getting excited by a good-looking, strong young man isn't the mark of a slut. It doesn't put a neon sign on your forehead inviting every passing man to jump on you. And even if you were into sports sex, even if you'd had a dozen lovers by now, rape's a different thing. Very different."

Mark studied Gabbie for a moment without speaking. His expression was serious, but his tone remained reassuring as he said, "It's not uncommon for victims to get confused and lose sight of what's reasonable and what isn't. You can get pretty messed up, feel somehow responsible for being victimized. Understand?" Her expression showed she still had some doubts. "Look, you can find yourself saying, 'I should have prevented this somehow,' or 'I must have secretly wanted to be raped,' or 'God must have had it in for me,' or some other such thing, and the guilt comes pouring out."

She raised her eyes a little. "I sort of thought things like that. I thought maybe he . . . you know, that I invited him . . . that it was my fault."

"It's not. But you can get scared and confused and think it was." He looked hard at her. "And sometimes those around us also get confused and reinforce those feelings. Like boyfriends or fathers. Any problems like that?"

"No, Dad and Jack have both been perfect." Her eyes seemed to light up at that, and she smiled. "Ya, they've been great."

Mark smiled again. "Remember, it wasn't your fault. Okay?" She nodded. "Now, any improvement in remembering what happened in the barn?"

She shrugged. "I don't know. I can remember that smith better than what happened in the barn. The guy in the barn? Just he was young, like maybe younger than me. And he was . . . cute, but sort of spooky, too, even crazy. Charismatic maybe. He talked to me, but it's like I can see his lips move but can't hear the words, like watching a movie with the sound off. Then suddenly he was all over me. I don't remember much, really. I don't even remember how we got into the woods." She leaned back. "So I'm not nuts?"

He laughed. "No . . . well, maybe just a little." She smiled. "There is no 'right' way to feel about this sort of thing, Gabbie. Anger, regret, hostility, depression, even euphoria, all of them are possible at different times. Just make sure you're straight with yourself about how you do feel at the moment, and if things get rough, don't be shy about giving me a holler, okay?"

Gabbie nodded. "I've been pretty good about staying in touch with my feelings. I had to deal with a lot growing up."

"So I've been led to understand." He paused. "If I were you, I'd just get on with living. Not try to forget, but just let whatever comes out of your memory come out, and not worry about the blank spaces for a while. It will come to you when it does."

She stood and said, "Well, that makes sense." She bit her lower lip as she thought. "I think that smell was . . . somehow part of the whole sex thing." She sighed. "Well, if I remember anything else, can I talk to you?"

"Sure, anytime."

She moved toward the door. "I've got to check out the horses. Jack might have messed things up, you know," she said lightly.

"You okay with the barn?"

She smiled. "I don't think he's still lurking there, do you?"

"If you want, I'll go out there with you."

"No, that's okay. I'm a big girl." She started to leave, then stopped and said, "Thanks, Mark."

"You're welcome, Gabbie." He watched her leave. She was a lovely youngster. He smiled as he remembered Gary's remark about putting a hit on Jack. If she'd been ten years older he might have thought the same thing. Hearing her slam the back door, he sighed and added to himself, Or if I were fifteen years younger. Chuckling, he amended that to twenty years. He passed off the thought with amusement and picked up the phone. It was answered after the second ring. "Gary? Do me a favor. Go to the file and look up the name Wayland Smith. See what we've got on him. Don't call back. Keep it until I get home." He listened. "No, I'll be here until about eleven, I guess. Phil and Gloria should be back by then. You and Ellen enjoy yourselves at the movies." He hung up. Sitting back, he thought for a long time on what Gabbie had told him. Finally, resigning himself to waiting upon this newest mystery, he turned back to the computer, which waited patiently for his next input.

4

Gary was waiting up for Mark when he got home, in the room they used as an office. Blackman put down the printout he'd dumped from Phil's computer and said, "You're back earlier than I expected."

"Ellen's got to work, remember. Unlike some of us, she can't beg an extra hour of sleep in the morning. Want a brandy?" Gary indicated his own glass. Mark shook his head no.

Gary said, "I looked up Wayland Smith in the files."

"What'd you find?"

"He's a character of folklore, who appeared in the Old English poem 'Deor's Complaint' and later in Scott's *Kenilworth*. He's seen as a cognate of Volund; in that form there's a long story about him in the Elder Edda. He's supposed to be some sort of supersmith, like what Paul Bunyan was to lumberjacks. All of which I expect you already knew. Now, want to tell me why?"

Mark said, "Did you notice where he was supposed to live?"

Gary grumbled as he stood up and went to the heavily littered desk. He pulled out a stack of cards and flipped through them. Finding one, he put the rest down. "All it says is White Horse."

"Look up White Horse in my place file."

Gary did as he was bid and soon was reading from another card. "White Horse. Uffington, near Wantage, southwest of Abingdon on the Berkshire Downs. The White Horse is a monument of unknown origin,

possibly predruidic, formed by cutting away the top layer of turf, expos-
ing the chalk substratum of the hillside. Others are found in Wiltshire,
Yorkshire, and elsewhere, but Uffington is the most famous." Gary put
down the cards. "All right. So now are you going to tell me what's going
on?"

"Gabbie said she met Wayland Smith on the Fourth of July."

Gary sat down. Quietly he said, "Shit."

"Well put, as usual."

"No, I mean, maybe the name is coincidence."

"An itinerant smith, with an ancient portable forge in the back of a
wagon, whom she took to be Amish because of his old style of clothing
and speech? Who says he lived at White Horse?" He went on, explaining in detail what Gabbie had told him. "And remember, this is a
consult, almost-a-doctor, for I've promised confidentiality."

"Since when do candidates in historical linguistics do psychological
consulting?" Gary waved away the question. "Joking. I won't tell Gabbie you've been gossiping about her sex life." He sat back, tapping his
fingers on the chair arm. "It just doesn't make any sense, Mark. It's like
paddling down the river and meeting Huck Finn on a raft. Someone's
got to be putting her on."

Mark was silent for a long time. "It's just possible that there's a
series of coincidences here. Perhaps Gabbie's right and it is an Amish
smith from over in Cattaraugus, who's named Wayland and who comes
from a town called White Horse. Though I don't think there's a snow-
ball's chance in hell we're going to find any Amish carrying an English
name."

Gary was up again, pulling an atlas from a shelf and thumbing
through the index. "Here. There are two towns called White Horse.
One is one word, Whitehorse, Yukon, Canada—"

"I think we can rule that one out."

Gary frowned at the interruption. "The other is"—he smiled as if
vindicated—"in William Pitt County, New York." He flipped to the
indicated map page. "It's about spitting distance from the Cattaraugus
county line, halfway between here and Pearlingtown, so it may have
Amish living nearby."

"Do me a favor."

"I know, go there and check out if there's a blacksmith named
Wayland Smith working in the area."

"Yes. He won't be in the phone book if he is Amish." Mark sighed. "I
don't think you'll find him, but we should be thorough.

"This one's got me bugged. Either the gods of coincidence are having a field day or Gabbie's had the most outrageous paranormal experience we've ever encountered."

"Or someone's running a pretty wild scam," offered Gary.

"What are you thinking?"

Gary looked at Mark over the rim of his brandy glass. "Maybe somebody's got the kid marked for a major league con job."

"Why?"

Gary leaned back against the desk. "Millions of reasons."

Mark said, "Her inheritance?"

Gary nodded. "I did some checking at the library in town, in some back issues of *Fortune* and *The Wall Street Journal*. Phil wasn't kidding about millions and millions. I doubt even Gabbie has a notion of how far-reaching her grandmother's holdings were. Eldon Larker, Gabbie's great-grandfather, was a regular robber baron, a minor leaguer compared to the Vanderbilts and Mellons of the world, but still pretty good at finding ways to make money. And her grandfather built upon that with major success. We're talking Middle Eastern oil, South African gold and diamonds, high-tech companies in California, a shirt factory in Taiwan, a perfume concern in Paris, a percentage of a small but profitable nationwide car rental company, a dog food plant, a chain of Christian bookstores in the Bible Belt . . . dozens of other things. And unless Gabbie's mom finds a way to break the will—which appears unlikely; Helen Larker's lawyers are too damn good—the kid's rich with a capital letter *R.*"

"How big an *R?*"

"Quick cash? Three, four million maybe. But if she divested herself of holdings, who knows? Her net worth would be, I figure, over eighty million."

"Why your interest?"

Gary shrugged. "Curiosity." Then he grinned. "And maybe I'll drop Ellen and give Jack a run for his money—make that her money."

"That'll be the day." Mark lapsed into silence.

After a while Gary said, "This is really bugging you."

"It makes no kind of sense." He sat back. "I'll take that brandy, please."

Gary fetched him one. Mark said, "If someone was after Gabbie's money, there'd be a thousand more likely ploys. I'd be a lot more suspicious of a smarmy young tennis pro with Hollywood good looks, a Latin accent, and a marathon runner's endurance in bed than a rural blacksmith. I don't know. But I think a scam to get her money is the long shot."

"If that's the long shot, what'd you call meeting a walking, talking folk myth?"

Mark closed his eyes, suddenly tired. "I don't know. But I'll bet you a dinner in town that you'll find no Wayland Smith in White Horse, New York."

Gary said, "No bet. I've learned not to argue with your hunches." He sipped his drink. "Okay, so I go there and turn up empty. Then what?"

"I don't know. I really don't know." After another long silence he said, "When's Aggie getting back?"

"I think in another two days. Jack went back to New York to help her lug all her stuff home. Why?"

"Give her a day, then stop by and see her. Be as circumspect as you can, but I'd like you to feel her out about something that's starting to come together in my head."

Gary put down his drink and got pencil and paper. When things began crystallizing in Mark's head, it usually led to a new project or a breakthrough on a current one. "Aggie will know more than most about the folk myths of the British Isles and their relationship to historical events. See what she knows about the druidic priesthood. . . ." Mark instructed Gary to inquire after a long series of seemingly unrelated topics. He finished by saying, "See if she knows the Smith legends."

Gary ended his note-taking. "That's going to be something to dress up in cocktail talk."

Mark smiled. "You'll find a way."

"Yes, sahib." Gary rose. "Now I'm for bed. Between an athletic girlfriend who beat me straight sets, then laughed about it all through the movie, and a strange boss, I'm grumpy and bushed. And it looks like a long day tomorrow."

Mark waved good night and sat for a long time staring into his brandy. His mind turned things over and he kept coming back to the feeling that the answer that was the least probable, even apparently impossible, was somehow going to prove to be the right one. And that certainty filled him with a strange and exhilarating dread. For if he was correct, then whatever mysterious thing had rocked Germany at the turn of the century was occurring again, in William Pitt County, New York.

5

Patrick looked about and Sean signaled all clear. They opened the back door and hurried down the three steps. Patrick placed the saucer of milk on the ground and the boys scurried back inside. For a few moments they watched the milk, then Sean said, "Maybe they won't come if you're watching. Like Santa."

Patrick shrugged. "Maybe. Come on. If Mom catches us, we'll really get it."

They left, avoiding the wrath of their mother, who was watching some dumb movie with their dad in the parlor. Tiptoeing up the stairs, they reached the haven of their bedroom. In a trice each was in his appointed place, deep under the covers.

Their visits with Barney Doyle had become more frequent, as he held them spellbound with his wild stories of great Irish heroes and their magic. It was his placing the milk out by the door that had caused them to begin doing likewise. They could hardly sleep for the anticipation of going down in the morning and discovering if the good people, as Barney called them, had taken the milk.

Below, the milk sat unattended, until a glowing pair of eyes spied it from under the house. Moving silently, a form came out into the moonlight and regarded the saucer. Ernie's nose sniffed delicately and, finding the unexpected treat fresh, he began to lap.

A slight sound caused the tom to turn. Behind him, approaching cautiously, was something odd and confusing. A little man, no higher than the cat, was approaching, waving a tiny walking stick at Ernie. In words high and faint he cried out, "Shoo! Be off!"

The cat backed away, at first tempted to paw at the man, but something registered in the old tom's head and he backed off. There were others coming behind, and some innate sense told the cat they were not to be played with. These were not food, or enemies, just strange. Ernie retreated a short way off and sat down to watch the creatures. There were a half dozen of them, all little people, some with tiny wings on their backs, some dressed in odd fashion, but looking wrong and smelling alien to the cat. They circled the milk, then one dipped a finger in and pulled it out, tasting it. He nodded and they all bent over the dish and began to drink.

Then something else emerged from the dark: something dangerous. The cat's back went up and he hissed. A thing black and fearsome came out of the dark, something so evil that the cat rose up and danced backward, hissing and yowling. The little people turned and saw the black creature approaching, and all backed away from the milk, waving their tiny fists in frustration and anger. But they, too, left the milk uncontested before the approaching evil, fleeing under the house. Ernie hesitated only an instant longer before quitting the field. He turned and ran toward the barn, leaping high into one of the small, scruffy apple trees. Reaching the highest branch that could hold his weight, the tomcat hunkered down and watched as the black thing came before the milk. It moved with strange articulation of its joints, as if monkey had been mated to spider. All these concerns were beyond the tom's understanding, save one thing: this creature was dangerous. It gave off a dark aura and an evil stench as it hunkered down before the milk, making soft noises of delight while it drank.

6

Gabbie stuck her head through the door. "Mind some company?"

Mark looked up the stairs from where he sat on the floor of the basement, amid a pile of old books and trunks, and said, "Nope."

Gabbie came down the steps and sat on the bottom riser, so Mark was forced to look up at her. "Troubles?"

"Just some nightmares." She was silent for a while, as if reluctant to speak. She looked about the confusion in the basement. "What have you found?"

"A ton of oddities. Both Kesslers were into some pretty diverse stuff." He held out a book. "Thomas Mann; it's either a first edition worth hundreds or it's worthless. I'll have to write to a bookseller friend to find out." He picked up another. "And this is Herman Hesse's *Magister Ludi,* definitely a first. And just when you think Kessler *pater et filius* were literary gourmets you find stuff like this." He waved to another stack. "Badly written junk on the occult, snake-oil medical theories like mucus-free diets and the benefits of ice baths, pornography, potboiler best sellers from a hundred years ago to today, crackbrain philosophy, all sorts of crap. I don't know where they found it all." Mark stood up. "There's little sense to it."

Gabbie reached over and took a book from the top of a pile next to the stairs and read the spine. It was Thomas Keightley's *The World*

Guide to Gnomes, Faeries, Elves, and Other Little People. "This worth anything?"

Mark said, "I've got the original, published in 1850 as *The Fairy Mythology.* That is a recent reprint of no worth." He glanced about. "There's probably no reason for me to be curious, but it strikes me the Kesslers had some reason for this eclectic gathering of oddities." He sighed. "What do I know? They might have been the sort of people who like to buy books by the yard, in the proper color bindings to fill bookshelves so the decor is right."

Gabbie laughed. "Old Man Kessler was not concerned with matters of decor, if Gloria's frustration is any indication." She noticed a small piece of paper in the book and opened it to page 317. There was a reprint of an old drawing. Gabbie squinted and said, "The light down here is going to make you blind." She stood up and walked up to the top of the stairs, to better see the book in the light from the door. Mark turned back to his sorting and picked up another book from an open trunk. He chose which pile to put it in and decided it was a big enough stack to warrant carrying it upstairs and begin putting data into the computer. Then something in the air caused him to look up.

Gabbie was studying the picture with intense concentration, seemingly unable to take her eyes from it. After a while she softly said, "This is wrong."

Mark put down the book he was examining and came to the foot of the stairs. "What do you mean it's wrong?"

"He's too young." She looked down at Mark, and in her eyes he saw unfiltered fear. Her words came thick and choking, as if she had to cough them up. "This is him as a baby, a little boy. He's older now."

Mark hurried up the stairs and gently took the book from Gabbie's trembling hands. "What do you mean?" he said quietly.

Tears welled up in Gabbie's eyes. "Look at the face. It's hard to see, but it's him."

"Who?"

Gabbie had to swallow hard. "It's the boy from the barn. The one who tried . . ." Mark gently reached out and let Gabbie come into his arms. She shook like a frightened animal. "Oh God!" she said, a desperate, terrified whisper. "I'm going crazy."

Mark let Gabbie cry as he held her. The part of him that was the psychologist knew the release of pent-up terror and other dark emotions would be healthy in the long run, and questions of sanity were but momentary concerns. The real work with Gabbie would now begin, and with luck would not take long, for she was basically a resilient, well-adjusted, and healthy kid. But the investigator into dark mysteries was astonished that he felt no surprise at her revelation. He held the book behind Gabbie's back, where he could see the illustration she had looked at. The word scribbled in the margin by the younger Kessler, in an old-style, formal Germanic script, was *Butze.* He knew it was a variant of *Putzel* or *Putz.* He glanced at the picture and shook his head. Could he have become so desensitized to wonders that the impossible failed to move him any longer? For if Gabbie wasn't insane or terribly confused, or the gods of coincidence weren't on another rampage, the same girl who had met Wayland Smith in the woods had been assaulted by Puck.

7

Phil looked at Mark with open disapproval on his features. When Gabbie and Mark had come up from the basement, the girl had been close to hysteria, unable to stop crying. Gloria was upstairs with her, and Mark had suggested that if she didn't settle down soon, Dr. Latham should be consulted. Phil had barraged Mark with questions and had been unsatisfied with the answers.

"Phil, I know she's your daughter and that you're upset, but I can't discuss what she's told me without her permission."

Phil seethed. He stood in the hall, hands upon hips, unable to articulate his anger. Finally something inside seemed to break, and he visibly wilted before Mark's eyes. In an instant his anger was changing to concern. He took a deep breath and said, "Sorry. I was out of line."

Mark shrugged. "Not really. You make good father noises."

"Come on. I could use a drink and I don't like to drink alone."

Mark looked at his watch. It was a little after noon. He usually didn't drink this early in the day, even at publishers' business lunches, but Phil looked in need of an ear.

They had just poured a couple of scotches when Gloria appeared. Her anger was barely contained. Taking Phil's drink from his hand, she took a healthy swallow, then said, "Thanks. Pour one for yourself." Phil did as she bade while she sat opposite Mark. "Now, just what the fuck is going on?" Phil looked at his wife, who usually avoided strong language.

He could see she was as upset over Gabbie's condition as she would have been where the boys were concerned. In a strange way it made him feel better to see his wife so protective of her stepdaughter.

Mark said, "I just told Phil that I can't talk about what Gabbie's going through without her permission."

"What are you, her doctor?" said Gloria, obviously upset. "I left a kid up there crying herself unconscious. She looks like hell. She's obviously scared shitless. Goddamnitall, Mark, what's going on?"

Mark leaned forward. "First, yes, I am her doctor." Gloria blinked. Mark told them of his credentials, and went on, "I'm listening for free, but I'm bound by the same considerations as if she were paying me seventy-five bucks an hour to sit in a Park Avenue office."

"Damnit," said Gloria with sudden anger, "she's our kid! And she's a basket case. Now, what's going on!"

Mark was visited with a sudden insight as Phil sat next to his wife, regarding her with a mixture of pride and concern. Gloria was as scared as Gabbie, and Mark understood why. The idea of mental illness— maybe illness in any form—terrified Gloria. Mark balanced his concern for Gabbie with a newfound wish to make things as easy as possible for Gloria. Slowly, so as not to upset her any further, he said, "Look, I can tell you a few things. After Gabbie wakes up, I'll tell you whatever she says I may. But if she says not, I can't. You understand." He hurried on before Gloria could issue any ultimatums. "Gabbie had a pretty frightening encounter, shocking her so badly she didn't know she was shocked until this morning." He paused, letting that sink in a moment, then he continued, "I don't want to do a clinic on victim counseling, but she's just left the denial stage of the normal reaction, and now she's dealing with the terror. But she's not emotionally ill." At this, Gloria seemed to lose some of her steam. "She's reacting the way most any normal person would to having the shit scared out of her by a madman.

"Rape is not a sex thing, it's assault. It's a power trip; a rapist wants total domination over women. He loathes women. He's trying to humiliate his victim, not . . . love her. And sex is the weapon, not the goal. That's not theory; it is accepted canon." He paused. "It's a brutal act of physical and psychological violence. The victim's loss of control is as scary as any other aspect of the experience. It's the helpless, dehumanized feeling: being at the mercy of someone who can violate you at will. And there's always the threat of additional violence or death throughout." Mark shook his head. "That's about as scary as anything gets. That's why Gabbie still reacts like it was a rape even without the sex act. She's angry, and guilty, and ashamed, and a lot of other things.

"Now she's dealing with the pain. The best thing we can all do is be supportive. Right now what she needs most is not to be hassled." Mark rose and tried to be as reassuring to Gloria and Phil as possible. "She'll be fine. I know it's not much, but I'm afraid that's all I can tell you without Gabbie's say-so. Okay?"

Gloria looked hard at Mark, as if trying to see something behind his professional mask. At last she said, "Okay." The last objection seemed to slip away. "Ya. Okay. Damnit."

"Look, I'm not trying to be mysterious about this. If you want to talk more, I'll be more than happy to listen. Your own reactions are just now coming out. For now, I think I'll head down to the basement and work." He took a sip of the half-finished drink, then put it aside. He glanced toward the stairs. "I'll hang out until she's awake. She may want to talk again." He rose as Gloria and Phil nodded. "If you need me, I'll be downstairs."

Gloria sagged as Mark left, resting her head on Phil's shoulder. After a moment he said, "You okay?"

Quietly she answered, "No."

8

Mark was sitting reading when Gary entered. Gary went over to the bar, poured two stiff scotches, and handed one to Mark. Mark raised an eyebrow. "You'll need it," said Gary, peeling off a light windbreaker emblazoned with the logo of the Seattle SuperSonics.

"All right, you've got me on the edge of my chair. What did you find?"

"White Horse is about as Amish as Salt Lake City."

"So you didn't find Wayland Smith."

"No, you owe me a dinner. I found him."

"Oh?" said Mark, now interested. He'd be relieved to find any concrete evidence to bear out Gabbie's experiences. "Did you speak to him?"

"A little tough. He's been dead awhile."

"Okay, talk."

"I got to town and asked around if there were any blacksmiths in the area. The local tack shop owner was very helpful. There's three smiths that work the area, and all live in other towns close by. Then he asked why I didn't use the phone book, so I had to explain that the smith I wanted might be Amish and wouldn't have a phone. He said he'd never seen any Amish smiths, and even if there were one, he assured me, it was unlikely they'd find a lot of work in White Horse. The population is decidedly mainstream and, I think, slightly bigoted. In any event, later on I met this old codger, name of Ry Winston, who remembers his father talking about Wayland. He steered me to the graveyard, and there was a small stone marker with Smith's name. Seems he died in 1905."

Mark shook his head and groaned. He took a drink and said, "Just what we need. Ghosts." He frowned. "Why is that date familiar?"

"I'll get to that."

Mark sighed. Gary had a flair for the dramatic and hated to be rushed in telling a story. "So we've got a spirit encounter?"

"We can pretty well rule out a bizarre scam. If it is, it's a world record for off-the-wall ideas. I can't see any point in impersonating this guy. I did a lot of checking. Smith was a regular 'local character,' so there were lots of stories among the old folks, Ry's father's generation, and Ry had heard most of them. And the library had some pretty interesting stuff. An obit from the local paper was pretty frank on his reputation. It took me half the day to find the issues I wanted in their morgue." He drank and said, "Seems old Wayland was sort of a local Wee Geordie, the strongest kid on the block. He won all those weird contests they used to have, you know, like tossing horses, biting anvils in half, lifting buildings, or whatever."

Mark laughed. Gary had a tendency to colorful images when he got going. Gary continued, "One of the strangest things about this is that the guy lived locally for only half a year or so."

"He must have been something for old Ry's father to remember so much about him."

"Notorious, to say the least, a world-class hell-raiser, almost a legend in his own time. He worked out of the local saloon, the Rooster Tavern, where he tied up his wagon. Rented a loft over the taproom there. He allegedly died in 1905, but they never found the body. He vanished one night after a party. Supposedly, he got too drunk to function and fell into the river near the tavern. The marker was put up as a memorial by his local pub buddies. Seems he was the leader of the equivalent of that day's biker crowd. 'Ruffians of all stripe, teamsters, field hands, and unemployed layabouts,' in the words of the paper. He also, according to old Ry, jumped every pretty girl in town regularly, including a fair number of the young wives. Seems there was some mystery about it, 'cause it wasn't hushed up, and that's something Ry can't understand. They're a pretty straitlaced lot now, so they must have been downright puritanical back then. But consider this: I said to Ry it's strange no husband tried to blow him away. Even if he was the local strong man, a rifle from behind a tree is a hell of an equalizer. Ry's answer was to shrug and say, 'That was Wayland. Pa said no man'd raise a hand against him. He had the power.' "

Mark considered. "What power?" He was silent for a while, then said, "What else?"

"With all that sex, I asked Ry if Wayland might have some descendants around, and Ry said, 'Old Wayland never did leave kids, on one side of the blanket or the other.' The best Ry could figure was that the old boy was sterile, and that's why the ladies liked him so much, no problem with getting preggers."

Mark said, "So he was a Casanova."

"Yes, but here's why the date tickles your sensitive curiosity. He showed up the same day as Kessler."

Mark's expression showed keen interest. "What?"

"I found mention of Kessler's arrival, a 'German gentleman seeking investment opportunities,' in the same paper that announced Smith's setting up for business. Both men arrived on May 4, 1905."

"But Kessler didn't come to Pittsville until June 2."

"Right. Kessler rented a room for a few weeks in White Horse, at the Rooster Tavern—part of the time we assumed he was still in New York City—then pulled up and came to Pittsville."

"Okay, mark that down as coincidence for a moment. What else?"

"Here's the best story of all. A few years earlier someone imported a bunch of poor Germans—sort of an unofficial indentured servitude, working off passage with several years' labor. It was probably illegal, and just as probably the town officials were in on it. Anyway, there's one real juicy story about Wayland, a local matron, and a German maid. Seems one night the matron walked into the kitchen and found Wayland humping the maid's brains out on the kitchen floor while she was supposed to be serving hors d'oeuvre to guests. Anyway, there was a row, and it turned out he was boffing the old gal as well, and that made for just the sort of scandal these little towns love so much. But the kicker is the matron was the mayor's wife and the girl was Helga Dorfmann. The mayor married her off to Kessler just after that to get her out of the house and, it seems, out of town."

"Kessler's wife?"

"None other. They married less than a week later."

"So there was a good chance Kessler and Smith knew each other, or at least knew of each other." Mark sat silently for a while, then laughed a beleaguered laugh. "Why couldn't you have found me an Amish smith, Gary!" he said with mock anger. "Okay, so we have a regular folk hero in New York who sounds like a match for the one in Uffington. But what do we have to link him to the Wayland Smith that Gabbie met?"

"How about his wagon being pretty much as Gabbie described it to you?"

"You saw it?"

"In the paper. The picture was old and grainy, but it was there. They shot a picture of him after he ate a tree or something in a Fourth of July contest. And his horse was an old dapple-grey."

"I don't suppose you got a copy?"

With a grin and a flourish, Gary produced a photocopy. The reproduction was bad, but there was the smith standing before his wagon. The caption read: "Wayland Smith, recent arrival to White Horse, victor in the Independence Day horseshoeing contest."

"What do you think?" Mark looked disturbed. "Parapsychological phenomena? Is Gabbie seeing ghosts? Is she picking up on some sort of psychic field in the area? Maybe we got evidence of our first true time fugue, and for a while she passed back to 1905? Or he came forward in time for a few minutes? An other-life experience?" He sighed in resignation. "I don't know what to think."

"I don't know either, but rule out subconscious suggestion, hysterical self-delusion, and the other hypnotic schtick. Gabbie's new here and has not heard those stories. I doubt ten people here in Pittsville have."

Mark drummed on the arm of the chair. "Maybe she'd let us test her for paranormal abilities."

Gary looked hard at Blackman. "I've known you too long, Mark. You've already thought of something. You just don't want to tell me."

Mark covered his eyes as if tired. After a moment of silence, he said, "You're right. Let me think for a while."

"Okay, you think. I've got to call Ellen. I'm late and I owe her one."

Gary hurried upstairs to use the phone in his room. Mark sat alone, nursing his scotch while he pondered an answer forming in his mind. It was so fantastic he wanted to exhaust every answer more probable. And there were still too many blanks. He sat back and suddenly wished he had stayed in experimental psych as an undergrad. Rats and pigeons never gave one this much trouble. Or this much potential for terror.

9

The rain pounded. It beat on the boys and Bad Luck like a thousand tiny hammers, insistent, unrelenting, stinging eyes and somehow getting up noses, making them sneeze. Patrick and Sean marched purposefully through the woods, drenched to the skin already. The rain was cool but not yet chilling. Their moods matched, caught between irritation at the rain-out and delight in getting sopping wet and muddy with a good excuse. They had never seen a sudden summer thundershower in California to match this one. The peals were deafening and the lightning flashes impressive. The dim, late afternoon light, almost forgotten behind the thunderclouds, made distances odd; the woods looked flat and impossibly dense. Bowers became caverns of menacing gloom, with familiar boles now sinister shapes of black against dark grey. The boys took delight in the delicious scare the shadowy woods provided, as if they were embarking upon an adventure of gigantic proportions. Bad Luck seemed not to mind the rain, or at least he was more caught up in the boys' fun than in concern over wet fur.

They cut across Erl King Hill, as usual in coming back from the park, and when they topped the hill, a staggering blast of lightning and thunder caused them to halt. As one they jumped, for this display was considerably more terrifying than those before. Patrick let out a yell, something between a shriek and battle cry, and ran down the hill, Sean a step behind. Halfway down the hillock, Patrick clutched his chest and fell, shouting, "I'm hit!" He rolled, and Sean rolled after him. Both boys reached the bottom covered in wet grass, mud, and stickers. They were now a complete mess. Bad Luck barked in joy and nuzzled first one brother, then the other, licking faces already wet. Patrick leaped up and ran to the trail that led home.

The rain drove them on, an insistent pressure. Where drops fell unobstructed by branches, they struck muddy ground, exploding upward in rebound, splattering the boys with droplets of mud. The cuffs of their jeans turned black. Where the drops struck branches, they gathered, combining, then shot downward larger, somehow wetter, and struck the boys with an audible plop. Never had the twins known quite so magic a rain. Even while menacing, it was the most wonderful, most excellent, best ever rain.

Patrick veered off the trail and down the bank, toward a shortcut they used across the creek. Sean yelled after his brother, who ignored him. Sean didn't know if Patrick chose not to hear or couldn't because of the sound of the rain and the wind in the trees, but he was upset at the slight.

At the base of the cut in the woods he grabbed Patrick, swinging him around. "Hey!"

"What!"

"Don't go down there."

"Why not?"

"We got to go back and use the bridge. Jack said there could be floods."

Patrick gifted his brother with a look that said his concern was unfounded and resulted from lack of nerve rather than thoughtful concern over risk. "It's too soon. The rain just started a half hour ago. Boy, you sure can be chicken sometimes."

Sean stood speechless. There was something he fought to recall about Jack's warning, but he couldn't remember—something about rain in the hills. Patrick turned and walked down the short distance to the edge of the stream, halting there. The stream was now swollen to ankle depth or more, and the swift-moving water presented a different picture from the meandering rills they were used to seeing. Bad Luck waited, halfway between Patrick and Sean, uncertain which brother to follow. Patrick hesitated, seemingly on the verge of turning back, but he caught sight of his brother and his decision was made. He plunged into the water.

"Patrick!" Sean yelled. "Mom's going to get you!"

Patrick waded out, finding the water already up to his knees.

"Why? You going to tell?" He turned to face his more timid brother, a defiant look on his face. "Huh?"

The rain had begun in the hills two days before, at first a gentle sprinkling, but growing in strength each hour. Pools formed in the rocks, gathering until they found escape downward. Trickles became rivulets, which gathered into streams. Near Wurtsburg the level of the water in the flood control basin had risen until the operator decided to bleed it off and opened the valve. That small flood rushed down the usually dry stream bed toward Munson Springs. At Dowling Mills the water swirled down a broken culvert, diverted to a small creek that turned it toward Pittsville. At the north end of the Fairy Woods, the water gathered behind a clog of branches, leaves, mud, and debris. It leaked through, causing the stream which ran below the Troll Bridge to rise as thousands of gallons of water raced over normally dry rocks. Then the surge from Wurtsburg, turned aside at Dowling Mills, struck the clog of wood and brush. The inadvertent dam held, then suddenly disintegrated and was swept away. A crest of water two and a half feet higher than before rolled down the stream bed.

A deep thunderpeal and the masking noise of rain was counter-pointed by a more ominous sound, a rolling, surging rumble. Patrick hesitated, and that moment trapped him, for he turned to look up-stream, rather than move toward either bank.

Sean looked where his brother's eyes fastened, and down the gully the wall of water moved. "Patrick!" he shrieked as the water engulfed his brother. He scrambled down the bank, seeking to reach Patrick.

The water was little more than waist-high, but it knocked Patrick down, then picked up the boy and bore him along. Sean watched his brother's head vanish below the roiling brown foam. With a cry of terror he jumped forward, grabbing Bad Luck, who had been about to leap into the water after Patrick. Sean's mind reeled, but he knew that no matter what Patrick's fate, the lab would also be swept away. He pulled hard on the dog's collar and scrambled back up the bank, his feet churning the mud as he sought to race to the Troll Bridge.

The rain turned everything to a chiaroscuro, a grey haze devoid of color, and suddenly Sean was lost. Crying in terror, he shouted his brother's name while he spun, seeking the path he had stood upon a moment before. Bad Luck hesitated and with a bark bounded off be-tween two trees. Sean ran after the dog, hoping he knew where the path lay.

Patrick choked as he fought vainly against the force of the water; then he came up, spitting and coughing. The stream wasn't that deep, but it moved with staggering force against the little boy's body. And the rocks seemed uniformly slippery, so that no handhold was possible. He tried to shout for help, but each time he opened his mouth, he sucked in water. Trying to keep his head, he struggled against the stream, but in vain. Something he had been taught while playing at Santa Monica beach, about rip currents in the ocean, intruded on his panic-stricken thoughts, and he attempted to move at a right angle to the flow. All he succeeded in doing was turning himself in circles and bouncing off rocks. The boy was terrified, and his natural bent for keeping calm was escaping him. Then suddenly he was in darkness.

Instantly he knew: he was under the bridge. And so was the Bad Thing.

Claws seized him, and he felt his T-shirt rip, while pain erupted on his arm. He struck out with small fists, which hit something soft and fleshy. He felt himself being lifted up, and his nose was filled with the stink of rotting meat.

The Bad Thing hung by three limbs beneath the bridge, upside down like a giant spider. It clutched the boy's arm in one clawed hand, and above the pounding sound of the water Patrick could hear its inhuman sounds. The boy vomited, his stomach constricting in terror. He kicked and hit, and screamed for his mother and father.

The water pulled him under again and sharp claws tore at the child's flesh. As the Bad Thing sought to grab the boy, claws raked along Patrick's face and chest. He was seized and lifted, and for a moment lightning illuminated the area. A strange and distant snapping sound briefly intruded on the boy's awareness before horror filled his world. A black mask with yellow eyes hovered scant inches before his face. An evil sharp-toothed monkey grin split that face as the clawed hand painfully pulled Patrick closer. The Bad Thing was smaller than the boy but impossibly strong.

Another wave, courtesy of the flood control basin at Wurtsburg, raced down the stream. The wave slammed against the sides of the bridge and hesitated as the barrier repulsed its first onslaught. Then it forced through the opening, rising in level and picking up speed. Patrick felt the water hit him, tugging him free of the Bad Thing's grasp. Choking on water and fear, he felt himself being pulled along. The claws gripped at him again. An inhuman shriek sounded in his ears in counterpoint to his own cries of terror, cries choked off by water rushing into mouth and nose. Patrick spit and vomited. His lungs burned for air; he tried to inhale, but there was nothing there, and his lungs spasmed, ejecting the water. He inhaled, managing only a single breath while his head bobbed above the water. Again he heard the snap-snap sound; then darkness washed over him and water filled his nose. Blood welled into his mouth as he bit his own tongue. Pain revisited him as claws once more seized his arms, cutting him cruelly.

Then the water moved him and the claws were forced to yield their prey. Patrick struck the stone sides of the bridge with stunning force and felt consciousness slipping away as fatigue, pain, and terror took their toll. He was being lifted up, and he felt water exploding from his lungs as he coughed, spit, and vomited water a last time.

In a distant fog he heard his name called and vaguely understood it was Sean's voice. The snap-snap sound resolved itself into Bad Luck's barking. He forced open his eyes and realized that a familiar face was looking down on him. Through near-blinding rain, Jack hovered above him. "It's okay, Patrick. You're okay."

Patrick felt Jack cradle him in his arms as the young man began to run—a slightly awkward, limping gait—through the woods toward home, Gabbie and Sean beside him, Bad Luck at his heels. Patrick wondered, in a strangely detached way, how Jack and Gabbie had come to be at the bridge, and why the Bad Thing had let him go. Then he passed into unconsciousness.

10

Gloria's face was set in an emotionless mask. She kept her eyes on Patrick while the doctor ministered to his wounds. When the boys had been late coming home from the game, and given the sudden rain, she had become worried. Jack and Gabbie volunteered to backtrack through the woods. They were only fifty yards from the bridge when they heard Bad Luck's barking. Gloria opened the kitchen door at Jack's shouting, to discover her son a mass of bleeding wounds. Not waiting for an ambulance, they had quickly done what they could on the fly, bundling Patrick up and driving through the rain to Pittsville Memorial Hospital. Gloria called over to Aggie's, where Phil was discussing his newest manuscript.

Now they were all waiting to hear how Patrick was doing. Phil had rushed to the hospital and together with his wife pieced together what had happened.

For the fourth time she said, "If I ever catch either one of you near that stream again . . ." She let the threat fall away.

Patrick squirmed. Sean was a few feet away, outside with his father, Gabbie, and Jack, and it was unusual for only one of the brothers to be taking the brunt of their mother's ire.

Through the door to the waiting area, Sean sat with eyes fixed upon his brother. Gloria glanced in his direction and he seemed to shrink within his chair. Somehow he had gotten the message he was equally responsible for Patrick's recklessness. He had been scared for his brother, but he was also angry that he was being blamed for Patrick's stupidity. Letting his voice rise, he said, "It's not my fault, Mom. I didn't go down there. Patrick did." His father looked down at him, shook his head, and smiled. It was okay, he seemed to say. It's only Mom being angry. It will pass.

Gloria looked back to where the doctor tended Patrick and tears threatened to form in her eyes, but she said nothing.

The doctor left it to the nurse to finish the last bandage and smiled reassuringly. He led Gloria back to where Phil and the others sat, then said, "He's fine."

Gloria felt relief break inside and the tears came. "Thank God," she said in earnest.

The doctor was a young resident, barely older than Jack. He smiled as he said, "He's pretty banged up and a few of those cuts look nasty, but most are superficial." He glanced around. "Just how did he get so many cuts?"

Jack said, "He got caught in the stream over in the Fairy Woods and swept along under the Troll Bridge. There was a block of tree branches under it and he was pulled through."

The doctor winced at the description. "It looks like it. Anyway, the cold water cut down on blood loss and we've sutured the one big gash on his scalp. We've bandaged the little ones and given him a tetanus shot. I don't think there's anything else wrong with him. You can take him home. Just keep an eye out for fever or other signs of infection. I'll want him brought in in a few days to change the dressings. In a week the stitches can come out."

Gloria said, "What about . . . scars?"

The doctor shrugged. "Nothing to worry about. He'll have a couple on his upper arms and chest he can brag about to his friends. They'll all fade by adulthood. And his face has only a few minor scratches. He's not disfigured, if that's what's worrying you." The last was said softly, but with a firmness showing it was not worth considering that possibility.

"Well, he looked so bad," said Gloria softly, obviously relieved.

The young doctor nodded. "A lot of things look worse than they are until you clean them up. Scalp wounds are messy and Patrick had a beaut. That's where most of the blood came from. He really wasn't as bad as he looked."

Gloria nodded. "It's just there was so much blood."

The young doctor spoke in calm, firm tones. "As I said, it's not as bad as it looked."

Phil comforted his wife and said, "Thank you, Doctor."

"You're welcome. Before you leave, check in over at administration and they'll do the insurance stuff. I'll leave his chart at the nurses' station for your own doctor to review in the morning, before it gets buried in the administrative archives."

"We haven't gotten around to getting a local doctor yet, though I guess you could say Dr. Latham. He took care of our daughter."

"Well, John Latham's a good choice. He's one of the last true general practitioners left. He's good with kids, too. He'll be checking on his patients tomorrow. I'll give him Patrick's chart." He shook hands with Phil and left.

Phil said, "Jack, if you'd take everyone home, I'll stick around and do the paperwork."

"Sure," said Jack.

Gloria walked next to Patrick while he was wheeled from the hospital. He seemed to be half-asleep. Sean walked silently behind. They left the waiting room while Phil headed for the admitting desk. Outside in the parking lot, water reflected back a low-hanging moon that peeked through the clouds. Softly, almost to himself, Sean said, "It wasn't branches. It was the Bad Thing."

No one seemed to hear, though Gabbie tightened her grip on his hand. Patrick was held on his mother's lap and he didn't protest being treated like a baby, as he usually would have. Sean retreated inside himself, sure he should not repeat what he'd said about the Bad Thing. There were some things destined to be kept to oneself, and he suspected that the final confrontation with the Bad Thing was allotted to him and Patrick alone, and no grown-up could help them. As the little boy climbed into the backseat of his mother's station wagon, he considered this. Despite the terror he felt in contemplating the Bad Thing under the bridge, he felt a strange sense of fate. Patrick had survived. Somehow he had won past the first test. Sean felt what could only be called cold comfort at that fact. And while resting against his sister's side, he drifted off to sleep, a strangely disquieting doze where the dreams were of slipping down muddy banks and of yellow eyes in black faces.

11

Patrick shouted, "Dad! It's doing it again!"

Phil came in from his study and regarded the large television screen. The picture was breaking up, and both boys sat with disappointment on their faces. The Phillies were playing the Mets in a crucial series, while the Cubs were due to start a game with the Pirates in another hour. The boys were looking forward to the doubleheader. But for a week the television had been acting up. Twice Mr. Mullins had been out to check it out and both times had found nothing wrong. He had expressed sympathy to Phil, saying nothing was as irritating as an intermittent failure. Phil picked up the phone and called and after exchanging greeting said, "Look, I know you haven't found anything, but isn't there something you can do?"

Patrick shouted, "Tell him to put in a Low-Noise Downblock."

Phil blinked, then said, "Young Tom Edison said we need a Low-Noise Downblock." He listened and laughed. "Yes, they do know everything." After a little more conversation, Phil hung up. "Mr. Mullins is going to come out with a new amplifier and simply swap it. He'll send ours back to the manufacturer and have them test it. In the meantime he'll check the lines and make sure everything else is okay. And you should be able to watch the games. And it's a Low-Noise Block Down Converter, smarty."

Sean smiled, while Patrick only nodded. Patrick had been more subdued of late than was normal, and refused to talk about his experience with anyone. Phil had begun to think the child was more deeply disturbed by the accident than he had first shown. The bandages had come off a week ago, and the scars were beginning to disappear under summer tan. But where a usually loud and playful boy had been, now a thoughtful, introspective child resided. Sean had also become more subdued, but as he usually took his lead from Patrick, Phil thought nothing of it. Slowly the boys stood and Sean flipped off the television set.

"You going to the park?" asked their father.

Patrick shrugged. "Maybe," answered Sean.

"Well then, you'll need these." He pulled open the closet door in the hall, took out a brand-new bat, and handed it to Patrick. Patrick had lost his bat and glove in the accident under the bridge. Both boys said thanks.

Then Phil gave Patrick a new catcher's mitt, saying, "You'll have to break that in."

Patrick looked appreciative; Sean tried not to look envious and failed. Phil paused a moment, then produced a brand-new fielder's glove for Sean. "I figure you both needed new ones, anyway. Why don't you donate your old one to the boys' club, Sean?"

Sean grinned and pounded his fist into the stiff new leather. "Sure."

Phil said, "Let this be a lesson to you. You can mess up and still come out ahead, sometimes. Just don't make a habit of it, okay?" Both boys agreed.

Phil thought about his sons as they left. The thing that caused him the greatest concern was that the boys hadn't played at the park since the accident, two weeks before. School was due to start up soon, and Phil had hoped the boys would have some vestige of a normal summer before having to adapt to a new school environment. He watched as they walked out the front door, none of the usual scampering in evidence. Even the new equipment didn't seem to get them back to their old selves. Just as he wondered if he should consider having them talk to a psychologist, Patrick's voice cut through the still air. "Mail's here!"

Phil smiled. Some things hadn't changed. Patrick would never walk back to the door and tell his father something when he could yell it across the yard.

Phil hurried out the door and met his wife coming around from the back, where she and Gabbie had been overseeing the installation of new fencing by the barn. Gloria smiled at him. "I almost got run over."

"The boys?"

"Yes. They're off to somewhere in a hurry."

Phil felt relief, without knowing why. Just the fact they were back to moving from place to place at full speed seemed to him a reassuring sign. He and his wife reached the mailbox and laughed when their hands brushed together reaching to open the box. "After you, my dear Alphonse," said Gloria.

"Thanks, Gaston." Phil opened the box and took out the mail. He quickly sorted through it and handed several envelopes—mostly advertising and giveaways—to his wife. He opened one and read while she opened another.

"Listen," she said, "Tommy will be passing this way next week and is going to drop in."

Phil said, "That's nice. How's Superagent doing?"

"He doesn't say. And what brings him out this way, I wonder?"

"Well, knowing Tommy, it's not just social. He didn't drop by once that time he was just over the hill at the Beverly Hills Hotel for two weeks. We had to go there. Maybe he has a job offer for you."

Gloria snorted derisively. "That'll be the day." They began walking back toward the house. "I haven't worked in New York in almost ten years. The attention span of the average producer on Broadway regarding young actresses is about ten minutes—unless you've won a Tony—and then only if you're sleeping with him or owe him money. And as you may have noticed, I didn't exactly stand the town on its ear."

"Stranger things have been known to happen. Here." He handed her the letter he had opened.

She quickly read it, then hit him in the arm, hard. "You shit. You let me prattle on and didn't say a word." She grabbed him and hugged him hard. "Congratulations."

"Well, I haven't agreed. They want some things—"

She silenced him with a kiss. "Oh, shut up. That's what agents are for. You'll work out the details. I'm so proud of you, darling. The first publisher out of the bag and you get an offer." She stepped away and said, "The money's not great, but it's not chump change either."

"Well, you've got to remember, I didn't exactly tear up the New York *Times* bestseller list with my books. My credits in film count spit in publishing."

"Look, it's a deal, as my father always says. Get the deal, then worry about the details."

"Come on. We're going out for dinner tonight."

"Good idea." She smiled and walked with her arm around his waist. Since the night of Gabbie's assault, this was the first time Gloria felt relaxed.

12

"Help!"

Gabbie turned from hammering at the plank Jack held in place and they exchanged startled glances. Then Jack dropped the plank and they ran toward the front of the house.

They rounded the corner and discovered one of the workmen hanging from the lintel under the corner of the roof, while Phil frantically tried to right a stepladder the struggling man had kicked over. Ted Mullins was hurrying toward the accident. Phil held the ladder while Jack scrambled up and grabbed the man. Through gritted teeth the workman said, "My hand's caught." He managed to get his feet back on the ladder, but he was unable to free his hand.

Jack looked up and saw that one of the strange gargoyle-like carvings had twisted, capturing the workman's hand like a vise. Jack said, "Give me a pry bar or a big screwdriver."

Ted removed a very large screwdriver from the toolbox and handed it up. "Get ready to catch him," said Jack as he levered the screwdriver between the carving and the next one. Then, with all his strength, Jack lifted up, using the large screwdriver as a lever, pushing the carving upward so the man could slip his hand out from between the clamping jaws.

The man fell away, caught by Phil and Ted. Jack inspected the carving. "It broke loose," he observed. The carving had pulled away at the top, causing it to tilt forward. The lower part of the carving had struck a support beam under the lintel and the ugly head had cracked behind the alligatorlike jaw, but not broken free. If it had broken, the man would have simply fallen. As it was, the carving had caught the man's hand, his own weight acting as the force to keep the hand pinned between the jaws.

"It's like the damn thing bit me," exclaimed the workman, wrapping his hand in a handkerchief. The skin had broken and the white handkerchief was stained red.

"You'd better have that looked at," said Phil.

"I'll take him to the hospital," said Ted.

He took the man in tow and Phil looked at Jack and Gabbie. "That's pretty odd."

"It's freaky, all right," agreed Gabbie. "What was he doing there anyway?"

"The cables from the dish run into the house there."

Jack looked. "I don't see them."

Phil showed him where the coaxial cable and the control lines ran up the support closest to the dish and disappeared into a hole at the base of the lintel. "They must run inside."

Jack climbed back up the ladder. "These carvings are all set into a big piece of wood. There's some new screws here." He looked down. "See that pile of them down there." Phil saw the dozen or so screws near the base of the ladder. "He was taking the last one out when the board shifted—strange, it looks like it's been pushed from inside." Jack unscrewed the last fastener and put it in his pocket. He grabbed the line of gargoyles.

"Careful," admonished Gabbie as Jack moved the cumbersome piece of wood outward.

After several inches, Jack could see the cable. "They move along here," he said, sighting along the board, "and run toward the parlor."

"They come out there. Mullin's put them back there for appearance," said Phil.

"Tidy. But it does make checking for damage a pain in the ass." Jack looked down the board; something caught his eye back under the roof. "Thought I saw something moving. Ernie? You crawling around in there?" He squinted, as if trying to pierce the gloom by force of will. He looked down at Phil. "Got a flashlight?"

"Yes, I'll get it," said Gabbie.

Jack was left holding the long wooden facing with the odd carvings while she hurried inside. She returned and handed the light up to Jack.

Jack shined it into the darkness. "Hello, what have we here? There's something back in there."

"What?" asked Phil.

"I can't tell. Even with the flashlight it's awful dark. And it's a fair ways back."

"How did you see it?" asked Gabbie.

Jack tossed back the flashlight. "I thought I saw something move for an instant. A trick of my eyes, I guess."

He put the board back in place and quickly returned the one screw holding it up. Hurrying down the ladder, he said, "Mullins will want to check the cables, so I'll leave it like I found it."

"What about that thing you saw? Can you fish it out?" asked Gabbie.

"It's pretty well back. Even with a broom handle I couldn't reach it."

"Well, how did it get there?" wondered Phil.

Jack regarded the roof line. "That's the boys' room up there?"

"Right."

"Can we take a look around there?"

"Sure." They hurried inside and up the stairs. In the boys' room Jack went to the window and looked out to judge his location relative to the porch roof. "I think about here," he said, pointing at where the wall met the floor.

He moved a toy chest and inspected the wall below the window. After a few minutes, Phil and Gabbie joined him. Nothing appeared out of the ordinary, until Phil noticed an odd depression near the base of the wall. "Give me that screwdriver," he said.

Jack and Gabbie watched as Phil put the screwdriver in the indentation and pried upward. A section of the floor moved just enough to slip his fingers under the side, three boards cut to fit so closely they looked one with the rest of the floorboards. The lid was an odd one, for the boards were of unequal length, the trap lid cut along the natural lines of the boards so no unusual seams could be seen. "Well, I'll be go to hell," said Phil.

Jack grinned. "There's a lot of this in these old houses. They were built before the government insured banks. Most folks down home can show you where great-grandfather hid what little they had from the Yankees. You wax them a few times to fill the cracks and you can run your hand over them all day and never find them."

Phil shined the light down and the beam fell upon a pouch or packet of some kind. Jack reached in and gingerly removed what appeared to be a wrapped bundle of papers. "Treasure maps, do you suppose?" said Phil.

Jack observed the package. It was a white-flaked bundle of some sort of cloth. "Let's get it down to the study."

They took it downstairs and put it on the desk. Jack regarded the white substance on his hand and said, "I think this is wax."

Phil was gingerly poking at the cloth. "Feels pretty brittle. Must be old."

"Maybe not." Jack rubbed the flakes between his fingers and smelled the residue. "Paraffin," observed Jack. "It's used for water-proofing. Only problem is it burns really well. We used to dip match-sticks in it in the Boy Scouts."

"I didn't know you were a boy scout," said Gabbie in a teasing manner.

"Lots of things you don't know, darlin'," Jack teased in return.

"Can we open the package?" said Phil.

"I think," answered Jack. "It's the wax that's brittle, not the paper or whatever." Jack's guess turned out to be correct, as the wrapping turned out to be light oilcloth. Inside they found several documents.

Jack and Phil scanned them and Gabbie said, "What is it?"

Jack shrugged. "They're all in German. All I managed was a C minus in high school, and that was a while ago. Can you read kraut?"

"Only Spanish and then pretty badly," admitted Gabbie.

They could hear the sound of a car in the drive. Gabbie looked out the window and said, "We're saved. It's Mark." She ran from the room.

Phil glanced at his watch. "He's a little early."

Jack smiled. "I like a man who knows how to time his entrance."

Mark and Gary entered the room, Gabbie at Mark's side. Jack glanced at them, then did a double take, noting with some discomfort the manner in which Gabbie clung to Mark's arm. Since they had begun regular therapy sessions, Gabbie had started to speak a lot about Mark. Jack struggled to put aside an unreasonable stab of jealousy.

Gary said, "Gabbie says you found something interesting."

Phil indicated the pile and Mark picked up a paper. He quickly scanned it and handed it to Gary. One after the other, they looked and then laughed aloud. "This is wonderful!"

"What is it?" asked Gabbie, excitedly jumping up and down.

"Fredrick Kessler's records. The old scoundrel was a con man."

Gary pointed at a paper. "He was, to put it bluntly, a swindler."

"What?"

Gary said, "I'll have to read these carefully, but it seems he had odd transactions going on with several banks at the same time. And if I'm

not mistaken . . . humm . . ." he compared three different papers.
". . . he was using the same collateral for all three loans." With a toothy
grin he said, "And I do believe that sort of thing is frowned upon."

"At least by the banks," said Mark. Then his smile vanished. "Look
at this."

Gary did so and whistled. "I'll be damned. That's unbelievable."

"What?" asked Gabbie, delighted with the find.

"It's a notation from a bank president, ah, a Mr. Schmidt at German
Manufacturers Trust of New York, that certifies he's seen the gold that's
used for collateral." He quickly searched through the other documents.
"See, there are several others. This is from the First German American
Bank of Brooklyn."

Gary said, "All these bankers had German names and all the documents are in German."

"That was common enough," said Mark. "Immigrants like to deal
with their own people. Bank of America was founded as the Bank of
Italy in San Francisco years ago."

"Could they have had connections back in Germany?" wondered
Gary.

"I don't know, but it's a possibility. Maybe mutual business acquaintances from the old country. German-American banks with offices in
both countries, perhaps. Anyway, one thing is certain: that old swindler
used the same gold several times as collateral for loans."

"How could he do that?" asked Jack. "Didn't the banks check to see
if there were papers out on that gold? Or take possession of the gold?"

"Things were a lot looser before the big bank collapses during the
Great Depression," observed Mark. "Back then they sort of shot from
the hip. Without much government control, banks could be anything
from stuffy old countinghouses to fast-and-loose investment cartels,
playing the stocks or commodity markets with the investors' savings.
There was a lot more potential for abuse. Banks used to go bust regularly." Mark continued looking through all the documents and at last
said, "But there's still nothing that tells us what he did with the gold."

"Maybe he sold it off?" said Jack.

"If he had, I'd expect him to have left a record." He indicated the
bundle.

Gary nodded. "He seems to have been fastidious in everything else.
These records could have hung his butt if the banks had found out
before he paid off his notes."

Gabbie seemed disappointed. "I hoped for a treasure map."

"And I hoped for something to tie Kessler in with all the odd goings-on in Germany at the turn of the century," said Mark. "Still, this is another piece of the puzzle."

"Maybe there's another secret hideaway around here somewhere."

Gary grinned. "Want to play treasure hunt?"

"You four can if you want. Gloria and I are having dinner in town," said Phil. "As you are all here, I'll tell you now. I got an offer for my book."

The announcement was met with general congratulations all around, and Gloria, who had been in the shower, shouted down from the second-story landing, "What's going on down there?"

Phil shouted back to her, "Come on down. We're having a party!"

"Not until I put on more than a bath towel. Wait until I get dressed!"

A few minutes later, Gloria entered wearing a robe, her hair still damp from the shower. "What's it all about?"

"Treasure maps and lost gold," said her husband with a happy little dance around the desk. "Tales of corruption in high circles. Bankers in league with mysterious Germans." Mark and Gary began to laugh loudly. "Scams to make a patent medicine salesman blush. And secrets of the ages, wonders and terrors, all wrapped up for a grand adventure." Kissing her lightly on the cheek, he added in bright spirits, "And celebrating a true miracle, an editor who recognizes genius when he reads it."

Gloria smiled. "So it finally hit you." He grinned back and kissed her again. Then she hugged him tightly. Over her shoulder she said, "Well, I guess we have a party. Gabbie, call the pizza man. Jack, break out the beer." She shrieked in mixed pleasure and annoyance as Phil bit her neck and patted her on the rump. "You animal!" As Gabbie left the room, she shouted after her, "And find the boys!"

Above, in the narrow space between the ceiling and floor, the Bad Thing moved. The package had been discovered and the master would be pleased. Things were always better when the master had been pleased. The simple creature, evil in most ways, truly desired to please the master. And the master had been wroth when he had discovered the Bad Thing had attacked the boy under the bridge. And the Bad Thing didn't like it when the master was angry. He had not wished to ignore the master's will, but the boy had entered his lair, and he had smelled so fresh and young, so warm and tender. For a moment the Bad Thing shuddered in pleasure, remembering the warm, wet scent of Patrick's blood. Then it remembered the master's displeasure and the pain and its shudder became one of fear. With a soft sound, like a baby's sigh, it moved like a spider through the secret crawl space between the floor above and ceiling below, hanging upside down most of the way. At the lintel, at the corner below the boys' room, it pushed aside a narrow board and squeezed out, scampering down the drainpipe. It didn't like being about in the light, for the daylight made it remember vague images of a time long forgotten, when the Bad Thing had been young. Such memories hurt. And the light gave it few places in which to hide. But the afternoon was waning and the shadows were growing longer, so it could reach the woods safely. Besides, it considered, nothing in the house posed a threat. Nothing there could harm it. Nothing.

13

Patrick displayed his scars with a mixture of pride and anxiety. Proud of his badge of courage, he was anxious over what Barney would say about the Bad Thing under the bridge. They stood before the handyman while he perched on the stool next to his workbench. A disassembled electric mixer was spread before him.

"Well, he cut you good and then some, didn't he, Patrick Hastings?" He regarded the boy with the bleary gaze they had come to expect.

Patrick nodded. "He tried to bite me. But I got away, Barney."

Barney sighed and took a drink from the bottle he kept nearby. Moving from the stool, he led them out the door and sat on the porch. He glanced about as if expecting to see something. "A little more than two months. We've only got to get through the next two months and a bit." He took another drink.

"What's two months?" asked Sean.

"Moving Day, Sean. The Good People will pack up and be on their way by midnight, gone before sunrise on All Saints' Day." He took another drink and then a deep breath. "And if we're lucky, we'll not see their like again in this life. Twice in my life is two times too many." He winked conspiratorially at the boys. " 'Tis the reason I'm a drunk once more. The Good People have a soft spot for fools and drunkards, 'tis said, and they trouble me not so long as I've the smell of barley on my breath." He winked again, tapping the side of his nose with his index finger.

"The troll'll be gone?" asked Patrick.

"Aye, and all his ilk, though I don't think he's properly a troll, now. A troll's a large and fearsome thing and springs out upon any that trespasses. I think you ran afoul of a beastie of the dark folk, those wee ones who've lost hope of God's salvation. Perhaps even . . . well, then there's no use dwelling on what it might be." He made the sign of the cross. "But if it were a troll, you'd have had no chance to cross the bridge. This Bad Thing keeps to itself underneath. But the river swept you through its lair, and once inside you're fair game. Stay out from under that bridge and you'll be fine. Such as he won't venture into the light, as a rule." He thought. "Though from time to time the rules get broken."

With sudden fervor, Patrick said, "I want to get it."

"You what?" said Barney, his grey eyebrows coming up in amazement.

Near tears of anger, the little boy said, "I want to get even. It hurt me and I want to hurt it back. I'll make it go away."

"Easy, lad," said Barney putting his hand upon the boy's shoulder. "Now, in the first, you don't have the magic. In the second, it's certain it's but a little fellow of its kind, and to cause it harm might bring you to the attention of some of its larger, even less caring kin. If it's what I think, it's in the service of just such a one as to cause you no end of misery. And in the third, it'll be off by November. My advice is to let things lay."

"No, I want to get it back."

Seeing the determination, Barney shook his head. "Well, that's a large order." He sat back with a sigh, looking thoughtful, and after a moment asked, "Can you wheel a sword?"

Patrick said, "I can swing a bat."

"Sure then, that's a fair style, if you're running amok with a great two-handed bastard sword, thrashing about in wondrous abandon. But this beastie sounds a quick and agile fellow, difficult to hit." Barney looked hard at Patrick. "How are you with the bow? Have you a silver arrow to shoot it with?"

"That's werewolves," said Sean, in disbelief.

"That's as may be, but it's for the Good Folk as well. They have little enough love for metals, disliking iron—though I think they have no true trouble of it, as some tales tell you. Otherwise they'd have vanished long since when man first came to the forge. And they love their gold, hoarding it in great troves, beneath the earth—valuing it as men do. But silver, blades and arrows, or shot from sling or gun, no, they do not like silver. It's the metal of the moon, as they are creatures of the night, and it is at one with their powers, so they fear it." He stood slowly. "I must get Mrs. Macklin's mixer finished." Looking down on Patrick, he said, "So get yourself home, and when you've a bow with silver arrows, or a silver sword, come on back and I'll tell you what to do next."

"Aw, Barney, that's not fair!" complained Patrick.

Barney leaned over, hands on knees, and said, "And as my sainted mother—God rest her soul—was heard to say upon more than one occasion, 'What has fair to do with it? That's the way it is.' Now get along home, before it gets dark and that thing under the bridge gets restless."

That was all the urging the boys needed, and as one they were off and running toward the woods and back home. As they vanished from sight, Barney shook his head and muttered, "And if blessed St. Patrick is looking after his namesake, Patrick Hastings, you won't be getting your hands on any silver swords soon."

14

The party was the more enjoyable for being impromptu. Aggie came over after a phone call, and when Ted Mullins returned from taking his worker to the emergency room, he was co-opted into the festivities. The boys arrived just as the pizza was delivered and dug in with abandon. Gloria noticed they were still subdued, but showing signs things were returning to normal.

Suddenly Gabbie said, "Oh, damn. I left the tools sitting around. I better get them." Without comment, Jack rose and went outside with her.

As they reached the fence, Gabbie said, "You've been quiet. Something on your mind?"

Jack shrugged. "I didn't think you noticed. You seemed pretty involved in your conversation with Mark."

Gabbie looked hard at Jack a moment, then bent to pick up the tools. Keeping her eyes on the ground as she put long nails into a sack, she said, "Well, he's pretty terrific company."

Her bantering tone was lost on Jack. "Must be," he said flatly, gathering up the hammers and putting them in the open toolbox.

Gabbie smiled to herself. Jack was silent as he picked up the toolbox and level; then he said, "I'll put these away. You want to put the lumber in the barn?"

"No. Let's just toss a tarp over it."

Gabbie lingered by the door as Jack went inside and put the tools on the shelf to the left of the door. Sounding casual, she said, "I figure, if we do it right, it'll be four or five weeks before the fencing is done all around."

There was silence inside the barn, then Jack emerged from the dark. "You staying?"

Gabbie decided to keep him in his place. "I haven't decided. But I figure I can hire someone to finish it for me, if I go." Jack's expression darkened. "I'll still be coming back over Christmas and next summer."

Without a word, Jack walked past her, grabbed a stack of fencing boards, and carried them inside, ignoring Gabbie's suggestion of using a tarp. Gabbie began a slow burn. Jack could be a doll one moment and a dumbass the next. She'd already decided to stay, but she was damned if she tell him until he said something. She was ready to do anything for Jack, but, damnit, a girl wanted to be asked. And, liberation notwithstanding, she wasn't about to ask him. Whatever had happened to him with Ginger had left him reticent about any final promise or commitment, and Gabbie wasn't about to let him take anything for granted.

She sighed as she heard him rattling around in the barn, stacking wood. She didn't like seeing him so upset. Maybe hers was a childish attitude after all, she thought. She was on the verge of speaking when something caught her eye. In the gloom, with the western sky turning from pale blue to rose above a line of indigo woods, at the edge of the trees stood a glowing figure. And the scent of flowers and spices assaulted Gabbie's nostrils.

Gabbie screamed.

Jack was out of the barn in an instant, while inquiring shouts came from within the house.

"What?" demanded Jack.

With tears in her eyes, Gabbie pointed toward the woods. "Him!" she managed to say.

As the kitchen door opened, Jack said, "Stay here." He vaulted over the fence of the corral and sprinted toward the woods and the vanishing figure. The boys dashed toward their sister, followed closely by their mother's orders to stay in the house.

Phil, Gary, and Mark reached Gabbie, and Phil ordered the boys back to the kitchen. Mark said, "What is it?"

"I saw him." Gabbie pointed toward the woods. "I saw the boy who . . . was in the woods."

"Are you certain?" said Phil. He glanced about, and without words it was clear he didn't understand how she could see anything in the faint evening light.

Gabbie only nodded. "Where's Jack?" asked Mark.

"He went after him," she said, pointing.

Without a word, Gary leaped the fence and went running toward the path in the woods.

A short time later, Jack and Gary both appeared in the kitchen, where the others waited. Jack, who was limping, said, "I think I saw him, but this damn gimp leg let me down."

Mark asked Gary, "See anything?" Gary shook his head no.

"I called the police," said Phil. "They'll have someone here soon."

Aggie and Ted Mullins both rose at the same time. "I'd best be off," said Aggie.

Mullins agreed, saying the hour was getting late and he'd return the next day to finish checking out the satellite dish. He said he'd escort Aggie to her car and follow her to her home, then drive on. The boys were hurried off toward their room, even though it was an hour before bed. Over their complaints, Gloria ordered them to find something to do for a while.

Mark said, "Jack, what did you see?"

"It was the damnedest thing," he said, absently rubbing his shoulder. "I think I saw a boy of about maybe fifteen. And I swear he was glowing. It must have been the evening light. But I could see him through the trees well enough to follow him across the bridge and toward Erl King Hill."

Mark and Gary exchanged glances and Mark said, "I think I'll take a look around."

"Don't you think you should wait for the police?" said Phil.

"I'll go, too," said Gary. "If it's a kid . . . well, he might jump a girl, but I doubt he'll come after two grown men. Got a lantern?"

Gloria took a Coleman lantern out of a cupboard by the pantry entrance and handed it and some matches to Gary. He took the proffered lantern and quickly had its mantles glowing brightly. With a grin and a wave, Gary said, "We'll just make sure he's not hanging around, and we'll be back soon."

Jack sat rubbing his shoulder. "Maybe I should go, too."

Gabbie said, "No, your leg is hurting. And what's wrong with your shoulder?"

Jack looked surprised at the question, then realized he had been massaging his shoulder. "I don't know. I must have wrenched it or something when I jumped the fence."

"That settles it," said Gabbie. "You sit."

Mark said softly, "We'll be all right." And without further word they left.

Gloria said, "Will someone tell me just what the hell is going on around this crazy place?"

Phil said, "I wish I knew."

15

Gary pointed. "Over there," he whispered.

Mark nodded. "I'll go that way." He made a circling motion and Gary headed off, the lantern clearly marking his progress while Mark crept through the gloom.

They had been tantalized by dimly perceived movement for ten minutes, as if someone lingered at the edge of their light, just close enough to mark his presence but without fully revealing himself. Mark moved with stealth, making as little noise as he could manage, but to his ears it still sounded as if he were crashing through the brush. He wondered if it was really true that Indians once moved through these woods without sound.

A high-pitched laugh from above almost made him jump. He craned his neck, trying to see what was in the trees. "Who's there?"

Again the laugh, followed by a scurrying sound, as if something was moving among the branches. Then Mark heard the sound of someone or something large landing in another tree. Whoever was up there was moving through the woods, jumping from tree to tree like Tarzan. Mark hurried after the sound.

Mark moved as quickly as possible, but the dark and the close-packed trees caused him to lose ground on whoever was up there. He hit a tree with his shoulder and cursed aloud, and was startled to hear a childish laugh ahead. He followed the sound and discovered after a few moments that he was lost.

Halting, he called out, "Gary!"

Instantly his call was echoed by a distant voice, mimicking him. "Gary!" it shouted. Mark tried to gauge the direction of the sound and again called Gary's name. The echo sounded, a mocking mimicry, but this time from another direction.

Mark looked about with no idea of where he was. He attempted to judge the position of the rising moon, but couldn't see through the thick branches overhead. Then he heard his name called in the distance.

As he took his first step toward the voice, it repeated from another quarter. Mark halted. Whoever had mocked him was now imitating Gary's cry. Mark was suddenly afraid. Someone was playing with them.

Slowly and carefully Mark looked for anything like a clearing or path. He glanced behind him as he tried to ascertain where Gary was. He stepped around a bole and started forward. And froze.

Mark's chest constricted and he couldn't catch his breath. He blinked, as if to clear his vision, and his legs began to tremble. He forced himself to take a halting backward step and then another. Slowly he retreated from the sight that greeted him. No more than twenty feet ahead of him were three women of astonishing beauty.

Dressed in thin white gowns that swept the ground, they smiled, a seductive twist to their full lips as they held their arms out toward him, moving with a swaying, inhuman grace. He gasped, forcing himself to breathe, and ran his left hand through his hair. "My God," he whispered, unable to move another step. He swayed and reached out to grip a nearby tree bole with his right hand. He was certain that could he see their feet, he would see each woman had bird claws or goat's hooves, for the legend said such was the case. And he was looking at a legend come to life: the White Ladies. Mark was overwhelmed with the scent of flowers and spices, and a rush of heat struck him in the pit of his stomach. He felt his head swim as lust rose up in his groin, making him ache to go to them. His body shook with desire so intense he felt his chest constrict; breathing seemed impossible. He felt as if the air were sweltering and humid, a hot August night in New Orleans with not a hint of breeze. He forced himself to suck in air. Perspiration broke out on his forehead and he pressed his right hand against the tree so hard the bark dug deep into his palm. The pain of it was all he could find to keep him sane. That pain in his hand was real.

His mind swam. He tried to move but was paralyzed with wonder and fear. He knew the tale of the White Ladies, and he knew their embrace meant death. Summoning all his strength, he pulled back his hand and jammed it hard against the rough bark, scraping it sideways. The pain of broken skin shot through the hot wash of desire, giving him a moment of clarity. He struggled to take a step backward. He remembered a snatch of lore, and with it a prayer reputed to give protection from the White Ladies. Barely able to speak, he whispered the Old German words.

A look of regret passed over the White Ladies' stunning features. The central one of the three seemed sad, while the others simply turned away, vanishing from sight, as if stepping through doors into another world. But the sad one followed, her diaphanous white gown clinging to her body, revealing it in tantalizing detail. Erect nipples, outlined by the thin gauze, and moist, desire-swollen lips hinted at promises of sexual rapture beyond human imagining, and Mark almost cried from the conflict between terror and passion. Except for the feet, which were hidden from sight, the woman was perfect, and in that perfection terrifying, for no human woman could possess such beauty. To know her embrace would be to know ecstasy beyond endurance. She would kill with love. In a distant corner of his mind, Mark thought she would literally screw him to death. A soft, moist smell touched his senses, a faint odor of spices and flowers, mixed with a more pungent odor, that gave a clear message to some deep center of his brain. Dimly he thought of some sort of pheromones. Mark fought down the nearly overwhelming drive to go to her and slammed his palm against the rough bark again, tearing the meat of his hand, using the pain as a shield. He forced himself back another step and again repeated the centuries-old German prayer. Terror redoubled struck Mark like a physical blow, for this time the prayer seemed to have no effect upon the vision. She moved to within touching distance of him, and he felt himself swaying as she reached toward him. His mind seemed entombed within himself, witnessing his body going out of control. Ignoring the pain in his hand, he took a small step toward his destruction. Within the prison of his own mind, Mark cried out in despair.

Then the White Lady spun as a distant horn was sounded, followed by a laugh of mad delight. The hunting horn trumpeted in the night, and the pounding of hooves echoed through the trees. As she hesitated, Mark felt her power over him lessen. She looked at him and he felt the passions explode within his body once again. She stepped forward, hand outstretched. Suddenly a figure dropped from the trees above, a boy or small man. Stepping in front of Mark, he held up a hand, palm out toward the White Lady. She shrank away and suddenly was gone, as if slipping through an invisible door, seen from the side.

Mark didn't hesitate but turned and fled, stumbling through the gloom, away from the madness. His foot snagged a root, and he fell. He attempted to rise, but could only manage to sit up. He felt feverish, his strength gone. It sounded as if riders were speeding through the woods toward his location. He struggled to his feet, gripping a tree, and breathed deeply to clear his head. Forcing himself to calmness, he glanced about. He had no idea where he was. From behind, the sound of riders became louder.

Mark turned toward the sound, then shrank back against the bole; tiny figures could be seen bursting from between the trees. Dozens of glowing bodies no bigger than sparrows, some the size of insects, sped through the night. The beat of their tiny wings was a hum of almost hypnotic music, a counterpoint to the pounding blood in Mark's throbbing temples. One creature darted past Mark's tree, visible for a moment—a tiny woman, smaller than a canary, nude, with golden hair, the faint blur of hummingbird-like wings on her back, and bathed in a blue-green nimbus of light. Little figures smaller than humans but larger than the fliers bounded by, leaping like grasshoppers through the woods. Mark felt his mind slipping away as he regarded little men in cutaway coats of green and red, little women in dresses of gossamer and light. He felt tears run down his face and knew fear. He wondered if he was going mad, for these creatures were both impossible and all too real. But they were colored strangely, as if fashioned by a nature that required all flesh to glow from within, for the gloom of the night did nothing to hide them. Each stood forth in sharp detail as it sped past, each clearly seen, as if a soft light was forever fixed upon the creature.

The crashing sound of horses' hooves knocking aside brush heralded the arrival of the next assault upon Mark's senses. Riders of incredible appearance raced toward him, and he felt a scream building up in his throat. Then a hand covered his mouth as the young man abruptly reappeared before him. He grabbed Mark in a surprisingly strong grip and dragged him around the tree, pinning him so that he sheltered Mark from the riders' sight. Mark was held in a viselike grip, hard against the tree, the youth's body pressed against his. The same odor of wildflowers and spices Mark had smelled upon first sighting the White Ladies assaulted his nostrils, but the effect wasn't erotic or intoxicating. It was rather the opposite, almost sobering. The woods echoed with the sound of the riders as they sped past, apparently unable to see Mark and his protector. Mark could only wonder how they could fail to notice the pair pressed against the tree as horses galloped within touching distance. Mark glimpsed figures of inhuman beauty speeding past upon horses unlike any he had seen before, strangely graceful beasts with eyes aglow, who almost seemed to float as they ran, so smooth were their movements. The animals were an impossible white, a glowing snow color dancing with ice-blue highlights, and in the gloom their long flowing manes and plumy tails seemed shot through with silver and gold light. The riders wore armor of odd hue and cut, magnificent in design, though somehow wrong. Ornate helms were bedecked with protrusions that would catch a sword blade, not turn it, one surmounted with eagle's wings of ebony, another with a bull's horns of ivory, a third with stag's antlers of gold. The helmets and long spears and slender lances they carried seemed inured to the snagging branches of the trees as the riders raced along. Breastplates were fluted and covered with scrollwork, and greaves, chain, and gambeson all looked decorative, not functional. Still, they were figures of awesome appearance, and Mark was staggered at the sight.

They vanished in the woods and Mark was still held tight against the tree. From above a sound came, as if something scampered through the branches at a furious rate, in a vain attempt to keep up with the riders. It scurried through the foliage like a monkey, swinging overhead, and for an instant Mark felt the presence of something evil and dangerous, and his fear deepened. Then the pressure on Mark's chest was relieved as the other stepped back.

Mark slowly collapsed to the ground, his knees too wobbly to hold him. He leaned against the tree and wiped his brow. His hand came away dripping, whether with perspiration or blood he didn't know.

Forcing himself to breathe slowly, he regarded his protector. He was a boy, a teenager matching the description of the one who had assaulted Gabbie. Mark looked up into the boy's face and studied it. Then he knew. There was nothing young about the face that regarded him in the gloom. Ages looked out through those eyes. Softly the boy said, "The Fool and his coursers ride the night. To be seen by them is to be lost."

In a voice barely more than a croak, Mark whispered, "You . . ."

"I am not the one you think," the boy interrupted, his face a stern mask. Softly he spoke. "All is not revealed to you, Mark Blackman. Know that what was done was done by another's hand." The stern aspect softened. "And what was attempted was only because the girl's desires call his attention." The youth's eyes narrowed, and even in the gloom, Mark could see a fey blue light in them. "I serve another, one who would prevent such harm to the girl and others like her and so becomes your benefactor." Almost absently he said, "Later, all may be made known to you." The boy's face split with a mischievous grin. "Or perhaps not. Now you are in my debt, lore keeper. Forget." With a wink he sprang upward toward a branch and vanished. Mark crouched low, hugging himself against a chill in his soul; tears rolled down his cheeks and he openly cried. He reached into his coat pocket and pulled out the tiny microrecorder he carried for dictation. He thumbed the record button and began to speak into the condenser microphone on the side, attempting to put some order to the mad scene he had just witnessed. He vaguely noticed the blood from his torn hand smeared on the recorder as he forced himself to speak. It was a difficult task, even for a man of his stern professional discipline and experience, for his voice broke and he was forced to pause while sobs broke uncontrolled from his throat and his chest constricted in icy pain. And he found that the images, so incisively etched in his mind, were becoming less distinct, more diffused, each passing moment. Mark hurried to recall every detail, but one thing did not lessen. For the first time in his life, Mark was truly terrified.

16

Gabbie looked up as Gary and Mark entered. One look at Mark told her something was wrong. A smear of something brown crossed his forehead, looking like dried blood. But more than that was the way he looked: his face was set in a mask, with no expression, but it was drawn and without color. The others noticed at once and Gloria said, "You all right?" She pulled out a chair and Blackman sat.

Mark nodded. "Yes. I just did something stupid. I got separated from Gary. You don't really know how scary those woods can be until you get turned around in the dark out there." He forced a smile. "I guess I'm just a little shook up." He held up his hand. "I fell and tore this up trying to catch myself on a tree."

Gabbie made a face and said, "Ugh, that's gross."

"Just some torn skin," said Mark. Gloria hurried out and returned momentarily with a first-aid kit and began to dress his hand.

"You should get this looked at," she said when she had finished.

"I had a tetanus booster less than two months ago. I'll be fine."

"You want a drink?" asked Phil.

Mark shook his head no. "I think we'll be getting on home, now that the police are here."

Two police officers had found Mark, sitting on the ground. Gary had been attracted to their lights. He had brought Mark back. The officers were still out looking for the suspect, but held little optimism about finding him. They had also made plain what they thought of Mark and Gary chasing after possibly violent criminals in the dark.

Gary bade the others good night, while Mark said nothing. It appeared he was concentrating on something, but from his shaken appearance, all sensed he was disturbed and no one took exception to his departing without a word. Reaching the car, Mark pulled out his recorder and gave it to Gary. "Tomorrow, before I wake up and get out of bed, I want you to play this back to me." He thought, then said, "Have another tape recorder running, will you?"

Gary said, "You've got an idea something's going on that only your subconscious may be understanding, that it?"

"Something, but I want a night to let this computer"—he tapped his head—"churn it around a bit."

Gary started the car, then said, "Are you all right?"

Softly he replied, "Yes. I'll be all right."

"What happened out there? Something hit you hard." He received no reply. After a moment Gary said, "I thought for a moment I heard . . . I don't know. It sounded like horses. And some sort of odd music. What happened?"

Mark started to speak, then closed his mouth. "I don't know if I can describe it. I don't know much of anything right now. I'll tell you tomorrow after you play that tape for me."

Gary knew Mark too well to argue. He would be told in good time. With a sigh of resignation, he put the car in gear and drove away from the Hastingses' house.

17

Gary looked down at his employer and friend. Mark's breathing was slow and steady, but his eyes were moving under his eyelids. He was in REM—rapid eye movement—state. He was dreaming and would be susceptible to suggestion and able to recall things buried in his memory. They had used this technique three times before and always had interesting results.

Gary had listened to the tape before going to sleep, and wished he hadn't, for it had both piqued his curiosity and disturbed him to a point where he had been awake since dawn, drinking coffee in the kitchen. He had decided to let Mark sleep in until just before his usual wake-up time of eight. It was not quite seven forty-five. Gary crept to Mark's bedside and knelt. He thumbed the switch on one of their portable tape recorders, making sure it was on record and that the condenser microphone was pointed at Mark. Softly, so as not to awaken him, Gary played back the other tape. He regarded the brown smear of blood on the small machine as Mark's voice came through, strained with a note of fear Gary had never heard before. In the years they had been together, in more weird situations than most people could ever imagine, Gary had never known Mark to show the first sign of fear. "Dark woods in the night. A mocking voice shouting my name. Three women in white, the goddamned White Ladies. God, oh God." There was an audible sob and then some sniffing. "Lights and tiny figures . . . oh God. It's fairies!

Little goddamn fairies. Naked little people with wings. Oh, Christ. Leprechauns and brownies, skipping by. . . ." More sobbing. "Then riders. Oh God, it's the Wild Hunt. Then a boy who smells of spices. Horsemen in armor are all around us. The boy keeps them from seeing me. Oh my God. Oh my God." Mark's voice trailed off as the recorder was put into his pocket. There was no sound for a long time, Gary knew, then, just before the tape ran out, the distant muffled sound of a policeman's voice, and Mark's answer. He had regained most of his composure by then. The exchange ended as the tape ran out. Gary turned off the machine, for he knew Mark had no interest in that section of the tape.

Gary looked at Mark's face as he rewound and replayed the tape. The second time through, he noticed that Mark's REM had become more pronounced, and a sheen of perspiration was forming on his face. His breathing became more shallow and the rate increased. Then he began to make sounds and abruptly he shouted an inarticulate cry and sat up, eyes wide and awake.

He blinked, grabbed the tape recorder Gary had left beside him, and spoke into it. "It was . . . night. We were in the woods looking for Gabbie's assailant. I shouted your name, Gary, and someone mocked me. Then I thought I heard you call, but the voice came from all directions, as if someone imitated you. Then I turned and saw three *Weissen Frauen,* who beckoned me to join them. As I tried to break away from their spell, the sound of horses came and from the trees . . ." His eyes held a haunted look. "Hundreds of tiny creatures, glowing, came past me, flying and leaping and running. They were followed by riders. It was the Wild Hunt. Then a boy, a teenager, I think the same one who tried to rape Gabbie, jumped from the tree and shielded me from the riders. After the riders had passed, he said, 'The Fool and his coursers ride the night. To be seen by them is to be lost.' Then he said he wasn't . . . something to do with why he . . . tried to make Gabbie . . . he was serving someone, and now he wasn't . . . something like that . . . and . . . then he smiled and said, 'Now you are in my debt, lore keeper. Forget.' He then vanished." Mark ran a hand over his face. "That's all I remember."

Gary hesitated, then asked, "Did you see the horsemen?"

Mark got out of bed and put on a bathrobe, Gary pointing the mike of the recorder at him. "Yes. They weren't human and I've never seen horses like the ones they were riding." He briefly described the alien armor and animals.

"Did the leader have a stag's head?" Mark blinked. "The leader of the Wild Hunt has a stag's head in some of the legends."

Mark shook his head. "I saw one, he might have been the leader, whose helm was crested by antlers. Maybe that was it." Mark looked drawn again. "I need to wash up. We'll talk when I'm done showering."

Mark walked slowly to the bathroom, while Gary ran downstairs and made a pot of fresh coffee. When the coffee was finished he took two mugs up to Mark's room. Mark was out of the shower and half-dressed when Gary entered. He took the proffered mug and drank. After a moment he said, "What a dream. I must be reading too much of that stuff we dug up on Kessler. Maybe I need a vacation."

Gary blinked. "What?"

"I said I must be working too hard. You wouldn't believe the dreams I had last night."

Gary walked over to the tape recorder, the one used by Mark in the woods, rewound the cassette, and played it back to Mark. As Mark heard his own voice, he paused in dressing, his arm put through his pullover shirt sleeve. When the tape finished, he slowly resumed dressing. As he sat down to pull on his heavy hiking shoes, he said, "They make you forget."

Gary said, "Who?"

"The fairies. The elves, whoever—whatever—they are. That's why Gabbie had only some of the normal reaction a rape victim would have. She forgets the incident unless someone else brings it up." He looked down at his shoes, elbows on knees. "By the time I had gotten out of the shower, I thought that whole thing a dream. I thought I hurt my hand running after the boy in the woods, and we'd never found him." He ran his uninjured hand over his face. "It makes sense."

"Good," said Gary, sitting on a chair by the dresser. "Then you can explain it to me."

"Whoever these people are, they can make humans forget contact. Don't you see, that's why they're considered myths, because no one can remember seeing them. All we've ever heard are partial reports, fragments, bits and pieces. And given the superstition of earlier centuries, people were likely not to ask a lot of questions anyway. Suppose for a minute you're a peasant farmer in the Middle Ages and someone comes running into your hut, babbling about little glowing critters or something, then the next day can't remember anything. It's how the legends get hatched."

Gary thumbed the tape machine and asked, "What do you remember of last night?"

Mark thought. "We went looking for Gabbie's assailant. We . . . got separated." His brow furrowed. "I thought . . . I thought I saw someone, maybe more than one person. I tried to follow. I . . . think I

. . . There was someone else there. He . . . said something. There was noise. Maybe the wind. Then I was alone and the cops and you showed up."

Gary rewound the tape and played it again. Mark listened and again his face drained of color. "We need to make copies of that. I don't want to risk losing the only thing that can make me recall what I saw. Then you're going to hypnotize me and condition me not to forget. And I'm going to do the same for you. It may not do any good, but it can't hurt." He looked at Gary. "You and I are going to spend all our time seeing what we can find out about Kessler and the time between his getting to America and showing up at White Horse. And we're going to do some digging on Wayland Smith. And digging around in the Hastingses' attic and basement for . . . I don't know." He rubbed his face as if he hadn't slept. "There's got to be some sense to all this."

"Mark, just what the hell is going on?"

"If you apply that ample imagination of yours to this, you'll have no problem in seeing the obvious. Whatever it was that happened in Germany at the turn of the century is happening again right here in William Pitt County, New York."

Gary grinned. "If you're right, it could be the coup of the century for you."

"I don't even want to think of all the possibilities right now. I just want to get a handle on what we've experienced so far, and I think Fredrick Kessler's the answer. Whether we're dealing with ghosts, aliens from Planet Ten, or fairies, Kessler's the key—"

Gary's eyes widened. "The key! I'd forgotten about it."

"We've got to dig around some more and find the lock that matches that key."

Gary stood up. "You know, I'm sort of excited by all this. It's amazing stuff."

Mark finished tying his shoelaces. "Just remember what happened in Germany."

"You mean all the old folk rites and stuff?"

"I mean a lot of people died."

Gary's expression turned somber. "Yes, I see what you mean." With no further comment, he went down the stairs.

SEPTEMBER

1

"Mark!"

Mark pushed himself away from Phil's desk, not even bothering to save off his program, so urgent was the note in Gabbie's voice.

He entered the kitchen to find Gabbie helping Jack to a seat at the table. Perspiration ran in streams down Jack's face, and his shirt clung to him, almost completely soaked through. Given the day's heat and humidity, it was likely he'd sweat, but this was far beyond normal. Despite working alongside him on the fence, Gabbie's face showed only a light sheen of moisture.

Mark said, "What is it?"

"Jack's sick, but he won't go home." Her tone was both scolding and concerned as she looked down at the young man.

Jack tried to downplay his condition. "I'm okay. It's just a bug. Give me a few minutes to catch my wind, and we can get back to work on that fence."

Mark reached down, saying, "Jack, if you're sick, take it easy—"

His words were cut off as his hand touched Jack's shoulder. The younger man cried out in pain. Gabbie's hands flew up to her mouth and she jumped slightly at the unexpected cry. "Jack, what is it?" she asked, her eyes wide with concern.

Mark knelt. "Let me look at that shoulder."

Jack nodded weakly, allowing Mark to unbutton his shirt. Mark fumbled awkwardly a moment, his bandaged right hand encumbering him. He got the buttons unfastened and gently pulled the shirt back.

"Oh Christ!" said Gabbie, looking down at Jack's shoulder. It was aflame with infection, a dome of red flesh rising up above the joint. The center of the swelling was almost purple, while the flesh at the edges of the swelling was hot red.

Mark said, "This is no bug, Jack. You've got a killer infection. We've got to get you to the hospital, now. I'll drive. This looks like an invitation to blood poisoning if I've ever seen one."

Jack looked down at his shoulder, attempting to focus his eyes. "It was all right this morning," he said, his voice sounding weak.

"Well, it isn't all right now," answered Mark, digging his car keys out of his pocket. Handing them to Gabbie, he said, "Let me turn off your dad's computer and you go get the car started. Drive it around to the back and I'll help Jack outside."

Gabbie hurried out toward the front door, and Mark gently replaced Jack's shirt over the inflamed shoulder. Within a minute the computer was off, the doors locked, and Mark's car turning down the road toward Pittsville Memorial Hospital.

2

The young doctor in the emergency room examined the shoulder, touching it lightly, but even that gentle touch caused Jack to wince and grunt. Gabbie stood by his side, while Mark stood a short distance off, watching through the E.R. door.

The doctor said to Gabbie, "I think you should wait over there. This isn't going to look very pretty." Gabbie said nothing, only shaking her head once.

The doctor ordered novocaine and injected Jack just above the swelling, in still-healthy tissue. The pain from the needle caused Jack to grip the edge of the examination table where he sat, but he said nothing. "That shoulder's really hot. This will take the sting out in a moment." He waited, then touched near where he'd injected. When Jack didn't complain, the doctor injected closer to the center of the inflammation. As he waited for the entire shoulder to go numb, he said, "You really shouldn't have let it go this far, Mr. Cole. It may have been only a boil a week ago, but now it's a world-class infection and you're a hairbreadth away from septicemia."

"I didn't have a boil a week ago," said Jack, his color returning a little now that the pain was dulled. "Doctor, I didn't have a boil this morning."

The doctor looked skeptical. "I'm not going to argue, Mr. Cole, but that couldn't have popped up in a few hours. Didn't you have any discomfort in this shoulder recently?"

Jack shook his head, but Gabbie said, "You were rubbing it the night before last, after running into the woods, remember? And you were sort of moving it around all day yesterday, like it was stiff. I saw you."

Jack said, "I thought I'd just wrenched it going over the fence." Then he thought and said, "Yeah, it was sore yesterday."

The doctor only nodded, as if this was an admission of neglect on Jack's part. He took a scalpel and said, "If blood makes you queasy, I suggest you look at that pretty girlfriend of yours." He cut into the center of the swelling, and the nurse at his side began to sponge off the blood. "Whew, what a mess." The doctor probed deeply. "If I'd known it was this deep a pussy mass, I'd have sent you into O.R. and called in a surgeon." He ordered another tray to catch the discharge and nodded to the nurse. Another nurse came and moved Gabbie away, and without saying anything, they turned Jack and made him lie down. The doctor ordered a shot of antibiotics and continued to drain the infection from Jack's shoulder.

He probed into Jack's shoulder, seeking to lance the core of the infection, and said, "What's this?" He kept the lancet in place and asked for a long retractor, pulling open the incision. Then he went after something deep inside and came away with a tiny white object. "I think we've found the problem." He deposited the object on a clean green cloth and said, "I think you had a bone chip work loose and get infected, Mr. Cole."

Jack's voice sounded weak. "I've never had any trouble with my shoulder, Doctor. I shattered my leg a few years back." He closed his eyes a moment, then said, "If I had a bone chip there, I wouldn't be surprised." He described his sailing accident while the doctor cleaned up the shoulder.

When he was done, he ordered Jack to stop at the pharmacy and pick up a week's supply of penicillin and told him to take it easy for a couple of days. He said Jack should have the shoulder looked at the next day and again in a week, and Jack said he'd check in with Dr. Latham.

Gabbie and Mark took Jack outside and the doctor looked at the cleanup in progress in the E.R. He went to the instrument tray to inspect the bone fragment and saw that the cloth it lay on was missing. Looking around, he was about to comment on its absence when a warning siren intruded. An ambulance was approaching the E.R. door, and the doctor quickly forgot Jack's quirky bone fragment as he pulled off dirty gloves, moving toward the sink to scrub once again.

3

Mark sat quietly behind his own desk. Gary was out having dinner with Ellen and Mark expected he wouldn't see his assistant until the morning; it was likely Gary would sleep over at Ellen's tonight, as they preferred the relative privacy of her apartment. Mark had been silently staring at the hospital-green cloth he had deftly pocketed in the E.R. It was stained by a now brown spot of Jack's blood, and upon the bloody spot a tiny white object lay.

Mark had been staring at the object for nearly an hour. He sighed and opened a desk drawer. Mark was an infrequent pipe smoker, and the ignition of tobacco in his study was a sign of deep concern or worry. Had Gary entered, he would have known in an instant that something was wrong. The tobacco was dry and half-stale, but Mark packed the pipe anyway. It would burn hot and cook his mouth a little, but the ritual and smell of the pipe had a calming effect upon Mark, and at this moment he felt the need of a calming influence.

When the pipe was burning, Mark rose and poured himself a brandy from the nearly empty decanter on the bar. He'd have to remember to purchase some more in town, or remind Gary to, he thought. They'd had a bit more than usual, a sure sign of stress, as they both tended to drink only after a long day's work.

Mark returned to his desk and put the drink down and the pipe in his seldom used ashtray. He picked up the small Bausch & Lomb reading glass that had come with his compact edition of the Oxford English Dictionary and looked closely at the white fragment on the towel.

What the doctor had taken for a bone chip was a triangular piece of white flint, little more than an eighth of an inch long. It tipped a tiny piece of wood, the presence of which had been hidden from the doctor by the mass of puss built up around the flint. Mark opened the bottom drawer of his desk and pulled out a box of X-acto tools. To the usual collection of blades and handles he had added a long pair of tweezerlike tongs, used by stamp collectors, and two pairs of small needle-nose pliers.

Mark used the tongs to pick the tiny arrow up off the cloth, carefully, as his bandaged palm made handling things awkward, and hold it underneath the glass, turning it to inspect it from every angle. His mind struggled to accept what he held, and he silently sought to determine how this tiny missile could have come to be.

He sat back, placing the glass down. Without thought, he transferred the little arrow to his uninjured hand, noticing it felt almost without weight. His mind cast back two days as he attempted to organize the fragmented and shadowy images of that strange encounter in the woods. A dozen times he had listened to the tapes, and Gary and he had hypnotized each other against forgetting, but even just after hearing the tapes he found that the memories were distant, colorless things, lacking substance, as if a dimly seen movie were being recalled, not one of the most terrifying moments of his life. What power could cloud a man's mind? he mused. The Shadow? he answered, knowing the glib quip was born of frustration at not understanding what force moved out in the woods.

Suddenly his reverie was broken by a small prick in the palm of his left hand, as if an insect stung him. He jerked it involuntarily and then looked down. The tiny arrowhead was now stuck in the fleshy part of his palm, under his thumb. He wondered how he had managed to stick himself. He didn't feel alarm; the pain had been barely noticeable. He reached for the tongs to pull it out, then felt his heart skip a beat as he saw the tiny missile vanish into his hand, as if sucked in by his own flesh.

Mark sat stunned and flexed his fingers. He experienced an odd discomfort in the palm of his hand, as if he had strained a muscle, but otherwise no pain. Then he knew. He grabbed up one of the X-acto knives in the box on the desk and, gritting his teeth, dug an incision where he had seen the arrow vanish. The pain struck him like a hot wave and his eyes watered, but he pressed the knife deep. Blood flowed copiously, and he held his hand above the hospital cloth. Mark quickly dropped the knife and picked up the tongs. He pressed the bleeding wound against the cloth, and for a moment the pressure and absorbed blood cleared the wound. In the incision he could see the tiny arrow, and he plunged the tongs in, gripping it. Ignoring the jolt of electric pain, he blinked furiously to clear his eyes of tears. They flowed down his cheeks as he pulled the arrow from his hand, depositing it on the now blood-soaked cloth.

Mark rose and found his knees weak. He made his way to the bathroom, managing not to drip blood on the floor along the way, and tended the wound. Luckily, he had acted quickly and the missile hadn't moved deeply. He used a gauze pad to stanch the flow of blood, elevating the hand above his heart to hasten clotting. Then he inspected the damage. What had felt like an amputation and had bled like a mortal wound was only a cut a little longer than an inch and perhaps a quarter of an inch deep. He applied copious amounts of Neosporin ointment to the cut and bandaged it. The cut would heal without needing stitches. Now both of Mark's hands hurt, but the discomfort was among the least of his concerns.

He returned to the desk and picked up the little arrow, being careful to employ the tongs. With real regret he reached over to his butane lighter and flicked it on. Without hesitation he placed the little arrow in the flame, watching as the slender wooden shaft burned in an instant and the flint turned black. When he had finished, he rubbed the blackened arrowhead between his thumb and forefinger. As he expected, it crumbled like so much soot.

Mark sat back, then took a long pull from the neglected brandy. He had seen and been injured by a genuine elf-shot. He had destroyed the evidence, but he felt no further need for evidence. He was convinced, and he knew that convincing others was not a prime concern at this point. Now he knew what lurked among the trees of the woods behind the Hastings house.

Jack had been wounded by one of the tiny creatures Mark had seen bounding by in advance of the Wild Hunt. Now Mark understood why medieval legends told of such wounds causing death. The tiny weapon was beyond the ability of the healers of the day to detect and the infection came fast. Without antibiotics, Jack would already be close to death.

Mark considered and then rose. He began to pace the living room. For hours his mind wrestled with the problem of what to do next.

As dawn approached, he began pulling books off the shelves around his desk.

Three hours later, Gary entered through the front door and saw his employer hard at work behind the desk. One quick glance told Gary that Mark had been up all night, and the pungent odor of stale pipe smoke still hung in the air. Gary skipped his usual wry quips and said, "What is it?"

Mark absently waved to the books. "We've got to dig out some things from a lot of garbage." He looked up at Gary. "The other night, when we were all out running around, Jack was elf-shot."

Gary sat down, his eyes wide. "Right."

"I'm serious." Mark held up his left hand. "I made the mistake of putting the damn elf-shot on my own flesh and it dug itself in."

Gary began to say something, but halted himself. He looked at Mark, started to speak again, then stopped. Finally he could only shake his head and say, "Coffee?"

"Good idea."

As Gary rose and turned toward the kitchen, he said, "What are we doing?"

"Digging out every description we can find of how fairies behave and what to do about them." He looked up at Gary. "Not all the cute, fanciful stuff, but any reference to how to deal with them—rituals, prayers, customs, protocols, anything. When we're done, I want a handbook on what you do to deal with fairies."

Gary stood dumbfounded. He was silent a long time, then again started to speak. One more time he halted, unable to articulate his astonishment. At last he said, "Coffee," and turned toward the kitchen.

4

Gabbie heaved and the trunk rocked slightly. Jack said, "Here, wait a minute. That's pretty heavy."

He came around a stack of magazines and stood next to the girl. Together they pushed, and the large trunk slid slowly along the floor, revealing the bottom half of the bookcase it had blocked.

Mark and Gary hadn't been around for almost two weeks, since Mark had taken Jack to the hospital. Mark had called to say they'd stumbled onto something, but they'd be back at work on the cataloging soon. Then last night Gary had called to say he'd be taking Ellen for a long weekend to New York City, while Mark was up at Buffalo, lecturing at SUNY that afternoon for one of their Friday colloquium series, a favor he had promised months before. Neither would return until late Sunday night.

Gloria had decided that someone should at least continue digging stuff out of the basement for Mark to catalog, so she had volunteered Jack and Gabbie. A dozen old trunks had been plundered and their contents sorted somewhat, waiting for Mark to make final disposition. Jack knelt and began scanning titles. "Some of these I can read, others not. My German's pretty fractured." He pulled one out. "Some sort of physics text, I think."

The door at the top of the stairs opened. Gloria shouted down, "Gabbie, Tommy's here."

"Great!" said Gabbie, jumping up. "Come on. You'll like Tommy. He's a real character."

Jack wiped dusty hands on his jeans and followed Gabbie up the stairs. In the hall, Phil stood shaking hands with a large man, at least three hundred pounds on a six-foot-two-inch frame. His red-brown hair was combed straight back in a rakish style and his beard was so red it was almost orange.

Gabbie hugged the large man and endured a playful pat on the rump as she said, "Tommy, it's good to see you."

The man called Tommy squeezed her. "Gabrielle, you are so lovely, I think I'll leave my wife and run away with you."

Gloria laughed. "Tommy, you're not married."

With mock surprise, Tommy said, "What! Did Caroline divorce me already?"

Taking Tommy's elbow, she answered, "Yes, about five years ago."

With mock regret, he said, "Ah me. Wives are so difficult to keep track of. That makes four, I believe. Gabbie, would you care to be Mrs. Raymond number five? You have the best figure and would be the prettiest of the lot. I could drape you in jewels and slinky clothes and show you off everywhere."

Gabbie laughed and said no, while Gloria steered Tommy into the living room. "How long are you staying?"

"Just until after dinner, I'm afraid," he said as he sat heavily in the overstuffed chair. "I've made plans to continue on to Erie, Pennsylvania, if you can imagine. I've a stepsister who is marrying off her daughter tomorrow, so I decided to combine all my travels in one pass, as it were. A daring sojourn beyond imagining, I know, but necessary. If the fates are kind, I will soon be back in my own little nest in Manhattan, none the worse for the journey."

Gabbie laughed. "Little nest." She said to Jack, "It's a penthouse that's easily two million bucks' worth."

Gloria said, "Tommy, this is Jack Cole. Jack, this character is Tommy Raymond, formerly my agent."

Jack's hand was engulfed in Tommy's giant fist, as the large man half stood. "Jack Cole! Good, I was going to have Phil call you over if you weren't already here." He sat back in the chair.

Jack looked surprised. He couldn't imagine why Gloria's ex-agent would have even known he existed, let alone wish to see him. He snuck a peek at Gabbie and saw her shaking her head no while an alarmed expression crossed her face.

Blind to her warning, Tommy Raymond continued speaking. "I'd owed these lovely people a visit for some time, and after reading your work, I decided to combine a little business with pleasure while passing through."

Jack was obviously stunned, blinking like a startled owl. "Reading . . . my work?" He turned to stand outlined against the window, his face a mixture of surprise and displeasure.

"Yes," said Tommy. "The manuscript portion that Phil sent me."

All eyes in the room turned upon Phil, who looked uncomprehendingly at Tommy. "I didn't send you any of Jack's work, Tommy."

Then slowly all eyes moved from Phil to Gabbie, who stood looking guiltily at Jack. "Ah . . . I used to forge late passes my senior year in high school, Dad. I've got your signature down pretty good."

Jack looked irate. "You sent copies of my stuff to him!"

Instantly Gabbie took the counteroffensive. "Yes, I did!"

"That stinks!" Jack almost shouted.

"Hey, cool off, you two," said Phil to no avail.

"The deal was we read each other's work, not show it around," said Jack.

"It had some good stuff in it."

"I don't care! I didn't want anyone reading it."

"Hold it!" said Gloria.

Both Gabbie and Jack fell silent. Gloria said, "All right. Now, what's going on?"

Gabbie said, "Jack and I agreed to show each other some things we'd written over the last few years, you know, sort of a mutual consolation society. But some of his was really good."

"So you sent it to Tommy?" asked Phil. "Why didn't you show me?"

Gabbie shrugged. "You're my dad. And I thought maybe if Jack heard from a pro who wasn't a friend that his stuff is good, he'd go back to writing."

Jack was doing a slow burn. "You didn't have the right," he said, softly and angrily.

Tommy's laughter interrupted any rebuttal Gabbie was preparing. "Right or not, young Jack, she did and I read it. Now, do you care to hear what I think?"

Jack's curiosity won out over his anger. "Yes, I guess."

"Well then, you are a very bad writer of prose fiction." Jack's expression darkened again, but Tommy pressed on. "But you write excellent dialogue. In fact, you may be one of the best natural writers of dialogue I've read. Your characters are like little lumps of lead until they open their mouths. Then they dance and caper about the page, all light and wonder. Your proposed book *Durham County* would, at best, make a bad parody of Edna Ferber as prose. I think, however, in a different medium, it could be excellent."

"A play?" said Gloria.

"Perhaps, but I'm more inclined toward a screenplay. I think it could make a wonderful motion picture."

Jack was caught completely off guard. "A movie?"

"Yes. Perhaps even a television miniseries. I primarily represent actors, but my agency handles all manner of theatrical and film folk, writers and directors as well as actors. So we have agents on both coasts who are familiar with working with writers. And you have one of the more successful screenwriters in recent years sitting a few feet away, and if I read this situation correctly, he would be willing to help you get the project into shape as well. When you feel it's ready to present, I'll be more than happy to see you're properly represented to the studios."

"Will another agent want to work with me just because you ask?" Jack still appeared confused.

Tommy laughed. "Son, you misread the situation. Of course an agent in my office will agree to work with you. I own the agency. I am, in short, the boss."

Gloria inclined her head toward Tommy. "Jack, if I was half the actress Tommy is an agent, I'd have been a star. Do it."

Tommy laughed. "You, my darling, were a thespian of marked gifts. Your only shortfall was a decided lack of ambition. That is why you made the right choice to get married and leave the theater." He said to Jack with a smile. "Well then, Jack Cole, what do you say?"

Jack sat back on the windowsill. "Ah, thanks. I . . . this is all sort of a shock. I'll need to think about it."

"Well, there's no problem." He looked at Phil. "Might I have a brandy?"

Phil laughed. "Of course, Tommy. One brandy coming up."

Jack looked like dark thunder for a moment. Then softly he said to Gabbie, "You. Outside." He didn't wait for an answer but moved purposefully toward the door. The entire way down the hall and out the door, he didn't look back to see if she followed. When he reached the rail around the front porch, he turned and said, "You really didn't have the right."

Almost defiantly she said, "Okay, so maybe I didn't. But Tommy said you're good."

Jack looked off into the distance. "I'm sort of messed up about this. I don't know if I should feel betrayed or if you're proving something to me."

She came close and looked up at him. "You're a dumb shit at times,

Cole." She stood on tiptoe and kissed him. "Why do I put up with you, anyway?"

All anger fled as he put his arms around her. After a moment he said, "So what am I to do?"

"What do you want to do?"

He was silent for a while. "How about we get married?"

She clutched at his shirt as she rested her head on his shoulder. Then her arms slipped around his waist and she hugged him tightly. Tears came to her eyes. "It works for me." She kissed him long and hard and said, "I love you so very much."

He held her close. "I love you too, Gabbie." He was silent for a while again, then said, "You know, I was getting pretty frantic about your heading back to the coast. I didn't know what I was going to do."

"Like I said, you're a dumb shit at times. It's the tenth of September. Classes at UCLA begin in two weeks. I'd have to be out of here next week if I was going back. Have you seen any sign I'm getting ready to leave? I've already written to UCLA telling them I'm staying here. And it's all because of you, idiot." She paused. "But maybe I should write again and tell them I'm coming for Winter Quarter."

"Why?"

"Look, if you're going to write a screenplay, we'll have to go to the Coast and find a place for you to work."

"Wait a minute." He looked troubled. "I've got to finish my dissertation and get my Ph.D. I can get us on the list at Graduate Housing, or we can both stay at Aggie's, but I can't afford to support a wife in L.A. while I'm trying to get a career started in screenwriting." He paused. "Besides, I'm not sure if I really want that. But if I try, I'd be an idiot not to let your dad help me if he's willing, which means staying here. Look, this is all coming on so damn fast."

She started to say something, then stopped; Jack was on the verge of saying something important, she was certain. At last he said, "When I graduated at UNC, Ginger and I were full of plans." He paused, remembering. "Well, mostly she was full of plans. But . . . well, I got timid. Maybe I wasn't really in love with her." He looked down into Gabbie's eyes. "Maybe I wasn't. Or maybe I just wasn't willing to open up and take what she had to offer. But the thought of marrying her just scared me silly. Anyway, I came here and she went to Atlanta and after a while we just sort of weren't going together anymore. I guess it was mostly my fault. I didn't want the responsibility, I guess, of taking care of someone else."

Gabbie smiled. "You *are* a dumb shit, Jack." She said it with a mixture of affection and irritation. "I mean it. You don't have to take care of me. I'm a tough kid and I've got resources. What you're going to have to learn is to let me take care of you . . . if your southern male ego can handle it."

"Why? You going to work while I write?"

She shook her head. "Let's see how liberated you are, boy. How about you write and I go to school while we live off my money."

"Look, I can't let your dad support us—"

"I didn't say a damn thing about Dad's money, Jack! I said my money." She looked away, uncertain about how he'd react to what was coming next, but at last plunged in. "If you haven't figured it out by now, you're probably not going to without my telling you." She paused and took a deep breath. "I'm rich. Buckets of money rich." When he looked uncomprehending, she said, "Remember when we first went riding, I told you the Larkers were serious money? We're talking *major* serious money. And when Grandma Larker died, I got it all. She cut my mother out of the will. Except some money she left to charity and Arizona State University, every penny comes to me. It's tied up in a funny trust; the trustee has to approve any amount over an allowance I ask for—he gives me whatever I want, anyway—but when I marry or turn twenty-five, the trustee goes away, and I get everything without strings. I don't think we could spend it all if we tried."

Jack looked astonished. "You're kidding."

"Nope. We're going to get many, many millions on our wedding day, sport."

He whistled. Then he grinned. "I always wanted to marry a rich girl."

She returned the grin. "Well, you will. Can you handle having me pay the bills for a while?"

He nodded. "I think. But even if this writing thing does work out, I'm still going to get my doctorate and teach part-time, okay?"

"Okay. But let's not worry about that now." She hugged him and kissed him. "Let's go tell the folks, then get out of here and go somewhere so we can be alone."

"Aggie's in New York for the weekend. There's no one at her place." He looked deep into her eyes. "You sure?"

"Damn sure," she said, her eyes shining.

They returned to the house and shortly had Gloria in tears and Phil breaking out a bottle of chilled champagne. Phone calls to distant friends and relatives were made and Tommy Raymond insisted on taking everyone out for dinner before he dashed off to the wilds of Erie. But eventually Gabbie and Jack stole away, taking her dad's car to drive over to Aggie's.

5

A loud noise woke Gloria. She listened for a moment in sleepy disorientation before she sorted out what the racket was. Somewhere below, Bad Luck was barking loudly, while inquiring voices from the kids were beginning to fill the night. She glanced at the clock while Phil was already rolling out of bed. The luminous dial said 3:10 A.M.

"What the hell is this?" Phil said.

"Be careful," she urged as he slipped his bathrobe on. For an odd moment she considered the quirky nature of the human mind. Phil might be going down to confront a prowler, but he refused to do it naked. His pajama bottoms were tossed somewhere in the corner, the result of some enthusiastic lovemaking earlier that night.

Phil hesitated. "What are we supposed to do? Call the police?"

"I don't remember. Make noise or something. Scare them away, I guess."

"I don't want to scare the kids. Sean and Patrick would want to capture the guy and hold him until the sheriff's posse got here."

A dull thump came from downstairs and Bad Luck continued to bark. Gloria started at the sound. "Well, do something."

"I'll go look. You call the cops."

Gloria began dialing while Phil moved cautiously down the hall. Passing Gabbie's room, he noticed her standing at the door, an anxious look on her face. "Stay here, honey," he cautioned as he passed her. Her worried look spoke volumes about her concern for her father. The boys were outside their own door, Patrick armed with their baseball bat. Phil relieved them of the would-be cudgel, saying, "I'll take that. You two guard the stairs." Patrick seemed on the verge of protest when his father said, "Take care of the women." Sean and Patrick both positioned themselves resolutely at the top of the stairs, arms folded, daring any invader to attempt to pass them.

Phil slowly crept down the stairs, listening. Nothing alerted him to a prowler's being close, as the only sound was Bad Luck's barking. He absently hefted the bat, holding it as one would a quarterstaff, ready to swing or thrust. He felt a little silly, but somehow more confident for having some sort of weapon.

A snarl and yowling sound, followed by a loud thud, caused Phil to jump. Instantly Bad Luck resumed barking at an even more furious pace. The Labrador was standing before the door to the basement, barking and whining to get in. The sounds of movement and banging came from below, as if someone was knocking things around. Then came a yowling cat cry. Phil laughed self-consciously as he moved toward the door to the basement. It sounded as if Hemingway had encountered a trespasser in the basement and was discussing issues of feline territoriality and rights of passage. Another thump was followed by a painful screech, rising to a pitch of agony. Phil flung open the door to the basement, while questions came from above.

Bad Luck charged down the stairs, barking loudly, while Phil flipped on the light and hefted the bat. If something besides a stray cat had wandered into the basement, Hemingway might need rescuing. Phil had vague recollections of Jack or Gabbie or someone telling of a raccoon that was a terror in the area. Phil hurried down the steps.

Something black and agile, and damn big compared to the cat, leaped from a stack of books to a high basement window and vanished outside before Phil could get a good look at it. Bad Luck leaped after it, scrambling up a fallen pile of books to the worktable below the window. He stood on hind legs, barking in outrage at whatever had escaped. Phil shouted, "Bad Luck! Shut up, hero! Get down!" After a last bark, the dog ceased his racket and jumped down from the workbench with a defiant snort. Phil glanced around and said, "Hemingway?"

A weak, pitiful meow answered him as he located the cat beneath a tilting bookcase. Dozens of books lay strewn across the floor as the case leaned forward over three trunks. The cat lay amid the confusion. "Hemingway?" said Phil softly, reaching in. He touched something wet and warm, and a screech of pain erupted and claws struck the back of Phil's hand. Snatching away his hand, he swore. Hemingway had never scratched anyone in the family. Phil pushed up the tilting bookcase and Hemingway lay revealed in the glow of the bare light bulb above.

"Oh God," whispered Phil. The cat lay atop a pile of bloody magazines and books, his stomach ripped open from forelegs to hind legs. What seemed an impossible length of intestine was spilled below Hemingway's stomach. Gloria came to the top of the stairs. "Phil?" she asked.

"Don't come down!" said Phil. The cat looked up at him. Hemingway's expression seemed to be asking Phil to make things better. His tiny tongue darted out, licking his nose, and he seemed disoriented. As much as anything, he looked distressed to be found in such an undignified state. Hemingway tried to mew, and it was a strangled, pitifully weak imitation of his usual tomcat yowl. The cat's head tilted to the side slowly, lowered until it touched a green-covered book, then lolled to one side at an odd angle. Glassy eyes stared blindly up at Phil. Hemingway was dead.

Gloria ignored Phil's instruction and came down the stairs. At the bottom, she glanced at the mess and for a moment seemed unsure of what she was seeing. Then she said, "Oh shit," softly.

"Something got in and Hemingway tried to chase him out. Whatever it was . . . gutted him."

Gloria turned as the twins appeared at the door. "You two, *stay out of here!*" Her tone said in no uncertain terms how much the twins could get away with: nothing. They backed out of the door, and Gabbie came to the landing.

"What happened?" she asked.

"Something big got in and . . . killed Ernie," answered Gloria.

Gabbie's eyes welled with tears. "Ah no," she said softly. "Poor Ernie. What was it? Another cat?"

"No," said Phil. "It was too big. Maybe a weasel or fox or something. I couldn't get a look at it. It was too fast. Looked sort of like a big black tomcat. Maybe it was that raccoon Jack told the boys about. Anyway, it was huge."

The boys heard from the hall and silently exchanged glances. They knew. They nodded as wordlessly they said, *The Bad Thing.*

Gabbie came down the stairs as Phil used an old newspaper to cover Hemingway. "Christ, what a lot of blood," she said. She glanced at the mess. "How'd they knock over that bookcase?"

Phil looked and shrugged, "Hemingway was next to it."

"I don't think a cat could knock that over." She glanced around. "Jack and I spent a day stacking all this." She left unvoiced the complaint that they would have to do it again. Hemingway had been her dad's cat, and she knew he was deeply feeling the loss, despite his outward calm.

"We'll bury Ernie," announced Sean.

"By the apple trees," agreed Patrick.

Gloria said, "All right, in the morning. Early. School day tomorrow. Now, back to bed." Her eyes widened. "Oh, Jesus! I better call the police back and tell them it was a cat fight. They're sending a car out this way."

As Gloria herded the twins ahead of her up the stairs, Gabbie said, "Look at this."

Phil came over to his daughter, who was peering at something behind the bookcase. "It's a door."

Gabbie said, "What's it doing hidden behind the case?" She climbed atop a trunk and leaned forward, putting her right hand on the wall. She reached over with her left and tried the knob. "It's locked."

Phil said, "Maybe that key Mark found will open it. Let's try tomorrow."

Excited, Gabbie said, "At least go get it and let's try now."

"You're going to have to move all that crap before you can get the door open." Glancing around, as if unable to decide what to do first, he added, "And it's pretty nasty right here. I don't think we should be shoving things around until we clean up."

Gabbie turned to face her father. "Okay, but if we try the key in the lock, we can see if it's worth while moving all that crap."

Conceding the point, Phil went upstairs and fetched the key from where Gloria had put it in the dresser drawer. As he came downstairs, Gloria was just hanging up the phone; she said, "What?"

He explained as they returned to the basement. Phil passed the key along to Gabbie, who hadn't left her perch. Gabbie leaned over and put the key in the lock. "It fits!" she announced. She gave it a turn. "It works!" The door opened a few inches and she said, "I can't see anything."

Gloria said, "Come on, then. You can putter down here tomorrow. You and Jack can dig around all day if you want. But now let's clean up this mess, then back to bed."

Gabbie nimbly jumped down from the trunk. "All right. But I'm dying to know what's in there."

"Probably more junk," muttered Phil as he gently gathered together the papers around Hemingway. Gloria and Gabbie retreated up the stairs, leaving Phil alone with his cat. Phil ignored the wet, sticky softness beneath his fingers and carried the cat over to an empty cardboard box. Lowering the bloody mass into the box, he said, "Just like

Papa himself. You thought you could do anything, take on anybody, didn't you? Well, you dumb shit, you finally overmatched yourself." He sighed, not fighting back the tears that gathered in his eyes. "Well, you were pretty good company for a lot of years, Hemingway." He sighed and left the box by the door on the top landing, so the boys could bury him in the morning. Without another word, Phil wiped away the tears in his eyes and flipped off the light.

Outside the basement window the black thing watched the light go out. With a sick sound, a twisted laugh, it retreated from the house. Its master would be pleased. Its only regret was that the man had come before it had finished tormenting the cat. Chasing the cat around the basement so the humans would find the lock had whetted the creature's appetite for sport. It had enjoyed gutting the cat, then pulling out the steaming intestines, but the cat had still been alive when the black thing had been forced to flee. It hadn't been allowed to prolong the torment a few moments longer. It felt cheated. Perhaps another time. Perhaps the master would let it play with one of the boys. Considering that happy possibility, it scampered off into the dark.

6

Jack seized a shelf, lifted the side of the case, and swung it around in an arc, letting the other corner act as a pivot. He sat it down with an audible grunt, then flexed his sore shoulder. In the two weeks since it had been drained, it had reinfected, and Dr. Latham had had to reopen it and clean out the wound, giving Jack a second course of antibiotics. Everything seemed under control at last, but the shoulder was still tender. Before the case had touched the concrete floor, Gabbie had the door open.

She pointed the flashlight she'd brought down and flicked it on. She took one step into the large room and halted. "Jack," she said softly.

"What?" he said, stepping around the mess on the floor and halting behind her.

"Get Dad."

Jack took one look through the door and nodded. He ran up the stairs, and in a few moments Phil came to stand behind Gabbie. He watched as she played the light over the interior of the small room.

It had been excavated out of the earth next to the house so that no hint of the room's existence could be gleaned from the floor plan. The ceiling was reinforced so no depression of earth outside would betray its location. Hooks were placed along the right wall, from which hung musty robes. They were white save one, which was red, and from the way the light scintillated across them, they could have been silk.

Seeing the robes, Phil said, "What? Kessler was a Klansman?"

"I don't think so," said Jack as Gabbie played the flashlight around the room. On the other wall were shelves on which both books and rolled-up scrolls had been carefully placed. At the rear, a wooden table stood topped by a funny-looking lectern, with a large book resting upon it, flanked on either side by candles. The wall behind the table was hung with a tapestry depicting some sort of hunting scene, done in Renaissance fashion, showing a group of riders, all bedecked in strange armor, exiting a forest. To the right of the riders, lovely women in white danced in a circle before a throne, upon which sat a beautiful queen. At the right edge of the tapestry, the subject matter turned decidedly erotic, as members of the Queen's court had doffed their clothing and were embracing one another. Those depicted at the farthest right edge of the tapestry were engaged in blatant sexual acts, in couples and groups. At the far left, game from the hunt was hung as trophies. Gabbie felt her gorge rise as she saw that some of the game hanging from the trees was human. Beneath the table, in odd contrast to the rest of the room, was a fairly modern banker's box, metal, with two drawers.

"What is this place?" said Gabbie.

"I don't know," said Phil softly. "We'd better call Mark."

7

Mark and Gary arrived fifteen minutes later. Phil, Jack, and Gabbie were taken aback by both men's appearance. Mark looked as if he hadn't slept for a week and Gary's color was bad, as if he was fighting a cold or flu. It was clear both men had been working hard, and something in their manner suggested they were under a great deal of stress. As soon as Mark saw the contents of the room, he became animated. "Did you touch anything?"

"No, we just sort of stood around in awe," answered Phil.

"Good." Glancing down at the bloody mass of scattered books and magazines next to the case, he said, "What's all this?"

Phil said, "Something killed Hemingway last night." When both Mark and Gary looked blank, he added, "My cat."

Mark said, "Killed it?"

"Eviscerated him. The boys buried him before Gloria took them to school."

Mark and Gary exchanged glances; Mark said, "Did the room smell strange?"

Phil said, "Not that I noticed. Why?"

Mark knelt a moment to inspect the mess, then stood, shaking his head as if the question was trivial. "Just that foxes or other wildlife can give off a pretty strong odor. Well, I'm sorry, Phil."

Phil seemed to have accepted the cat's death. "It's okay. He was a tough old coot and was going to go out fighting one day anyway."

Mark nodded. "Who's seen this?"

Phil said, "Just us. Gloria stayed in town to grocery-shop after dropping the kids off at school. She should be back in the next hour."

Mark said, "And I'd just as soon no one outside of here knows about this just yet."

Phil said, "Why?"

Mark sighed slightly. "I'm not sure yet just what's going on, Phil." He paused, thinking a moment. "All this," he said, waving at the room, "has to do with the mystery surrounding Kessler. And maybe some other strange things, as well. Anyway, until I get a few facts nailed down, I think it's a good idea not to let anybody know about this until absolutely necessary. We'll tell Gloria, of course, but if the boys can be kept away, or at least cautioned not to talk about this at school . . ."

Phil said, "We'll tell them you just found something secret. I know my boys. They'll be pains if we try to keep them away. If we let them in on it, they'll stay quiet about it—for a while, anyway."

Mark reluctantly agreed. It was Phil's house and his property, so he decided not to make an issue of the boys' seeing the secret room. He turned to Gary, handing him some keys. "Get the big tape recorder and some blank cassettes, both cameras, and a stack of legal pads, then we can start." As Gary headed up the stairs, Mark called after, "And get the sack in the trunk, too, if you would." To Phil he said, "Can you get a lamp and an extension cord in here?"

Phil hurried upstairs and returned with a lamp from the living room and a long extension cord from his study. Mark removed the shade and plugged in the lamp to the extension cord while Phil plugged the other end of the cord into a socket in the basement wall. The room was illuminated by a harsh white light.

Mark pulled out the little recorder he carried in his pocket and flipped it on. "This is Mark Blackman. The date is September twelfth. I am standing in the basement of the Philip Hastings residence at 76 Frazer Road, Rural Route 6, William Pitt County, New York, this residence also being known locally as the Old Kessler Place or Erl King Hill. I am recording the findings of a hidden room discovered at—"

He flipped off the recorder. "When did you find this place?"

"About three-fifteen this morning," answered Gabbie.

Gary returned down the stairs with the equipment Mark had requested and began setting up to take pictures.

Switching on the recorder, Mark continued. ". . . approximately 3:15 A.M., this date. The room is approximately thirty feet deep by fifteen feet wide by ten feet in height. Exact measurements will be made." Even as he spoke, Gary was unlimbering a builder's tape measure that he had pulled from the sack. "It was excavated to the east of the house proper, the location giving no sign of the room's existence to casual observation. The ceiling is braced with double joists and cross-member supports, preventing collapse from above. The wall construction is not visible to casual inspection. Upon the right wall, as viewed from the door, are eight hooks, spaced approximately a foot apart. From each hangs a robe, white in color, except the farthest from the door, which is red. They appear to be silk or satin. Upon the left wall are floor-to-ceiling bookshelves. . . ." He continued his description of the room, noting in detail everything he saw. When he reached the altar, he said, "The candles appear to be common wax, but may be more exotic in composition. Analysis will be made. The holders appear to be gold. The—"

"Gold!" blurted Gabbie, and Jack shushed her. Everyone was fascinated by Mark's work.

"—table seems fashioned from ash or another wood of similar appearance, perhaps olive." He inspected it from below without touching anything. "The workmanship is typical of nineteenth-century manufacture of the area. As speculation: it may have been manufactured at Kessler's factory, or even handmade by Fredrick Kessler himself. The book is open. It is approximately fifteen inches high by nine inches wide, page dimensions. It is written . . . in German, in Gothic script, but in a dialect I do not know, perhaps Old High German or Middle High German." He described some of the properties of the writing and finally said, "It is most probably a copy of a more ancient text, for it appears to be no older than a hundred years." He turned his attention to the tapestry, turning off the recorder for a moment.

Looking at Phil and Jack, he asked, "Can you get more light in here?"

Phil said, "I've another lamp we can bring in, and a two-way plug adapter."

Gabbie said, "There's a work lamp in the barn, the kind you can hang from a hood when you work on a car."

"Get them, please," said Mark.

Jack said, "I'll fetch the one in the barn," and accompanied Phil up the stairs again.

"Gabbie, if it wouldn't be too much trouble, maybe you could rustle up some sandwiches. Or if you'd prefer, I can contribute to a hamburger run. We're going to be here awhile."

"Ah, I can cut up some of that turkey we had last night. And I'll make a pitcher of lemonade." She glanced at her watch. "Lunch in about two hours?"

"That's fine." Mark removed his corduroy coat and tossed it carelessly across a dusty trunk. He resumed his narration, describing in detail the illustrations on the tapestry, then opening the top drawer of the banker's box. "The banker's box is metal, appearing to be no more than twenty years old. Inside the top drawer are what appears to be correspondence and other documents." He closed the top drawer, opened the bottom, and found more of the same. "It appears there are possibly two or three hundred documents in the box." He snapped off the recorder. Gary reached into the sack and removed a roll of masking tape, and a black marker, which he gave to Mark. To Gabbie he said, "Now we start cataloging everything."

"This is fascinating," said Gabbie, wide-eyed.

Mark smiled. "Tell me that in about six hours when we're still at it." Gary tore off a piece of tape and handed it to Mark, who numbered it with a big "1." He put it on the uppermost shelf in the bookcase, at the left, beneath a rolled-up parchment. He continued until Jack and Phil returned and set up the lights. Then he took out the Polaroid and shot a few pictures to determine exposure. Judging the required numbers, he took the Nikon and began shooting pictures of everything. Gabbie, Jack, and Phil settled in to watch.

8

Three hours later, Mark was still at it. Phil had returned to working on the final draft of his manuscript, making last-minute revisions before the publisher put it into production. Gloria had come home and been shown the discovery. She had watched Mark and Gary a bit, then vanished upstairs when the twins came home from school. Keeping the boys out of the basement had proved little trouble. A few minutes of watching Mark talk into his tape recorder while he pulled down parchments and opened them, and Gary took pictures of them, was all it took to drive away their interest. *Indiana Jones and the Temple of Doom* this wasn't. They promised to keep mum about the room, certain none of their friends would be impressed anyway.

Gabbie and Jack watched with interest. As a rule, Gabbie wasn't given to long periods of inaction, but she found Mark's work riveting. Jack was also curious; as a student of literature, his knowledge of any sort of fieldwork was nil, and watching the way Mark ensured that each item was clearly identified before it was moved was instructive. Nothing would be misplaced or lost if possible, and the exact order in which things were done was recorded as Mark spoke continuously into the recorder and Gary shot picture after picture. Mark had gone through two ninety-minute tapes and was into the third. He switched off the recorder and stood up, groaning audibly. "These knees are getting too old to camp out on cold concrete this long." He left the lights on as he exited the room. "Time for a break."

They went upstairs, where a stack of sandwiches waited. They had been prepared at noon, and it was now past three. Removing the wax paper covering, Gabbie put sandwiches on plates and handed them around while Jack retrieved a pitcher of lemonade from the refrigerator. Hearing them in the kitchen, Gloria and Phil wandered in.

"Find out what that stuff is?" asked Phil.

"Not half of it, and it's incredible stuff," said Mark.

Gary nodded agreement. "Those scrolls are written in Greek, Old High German, Old Russian, Amharic, and a few in Latin, Hebrew. . . . Some I don't know. I'll have to dig out some books, but I think a few are in Pahlavi."

"What's Pahlavi?" asked Gabbie.

Gary looked at her and said, "Medieval Persian. It's a dead language."

Jack and Gabbie exchanged glances. "Persian?" wondered Jack. "What's Kessler doing with parchments covered in Persian and those other languages?"

Mark shrugged and looked at Gary. "Can you translate them?"

Gary spoke around a mouthful of sandwich. "Some. My practical linguistics is a little rusty. I'd do better with Old Church Slavonic or Old Prussian, but I can handle the Russian and German, and the Latin, too. The Pahlavi . . . ? Indo-Iranian languages were never my thing. I only touched on Pahlavi once or twice. I can get some reference books and take a crack at it, but it's a little too far east for me." He shook his head. "But I know someone at Washington who could read it like it was the funny papers. We can photocopy the scrolls and with express mail have an answer in a few days."

Mark shook his head. "See what you can do first. We can call your friend if we need to."

"What about the robes and all?" asked Gloria.

"I've a few vague ideas, but I'm going to hold off talking about them until we get some of those books and scrolls translated. The German I can read, freeing Gary for the others. I can even read the Old Middle and Old High German, slowly, with a dictionary in hand. And if any of them are in French or Flemish, I can translate them, too. It will take a while, but I think we've found the stuff I've been after for the last two years. Whatever was going on in Germany in the early 1900s was connected to Kessler and his cronies, and . . ." He paused while he thought. He seemed disturbed, despite his outwardly calm appearance. At last he said, "Somehow, something went wrong, terribly wrong, and

Kessler and his friends had to flee. There are things involved here that are so . . . outrageous, I don't want to even hint at them."

Gloria asked, "Nothing dangerous, is there?" She was obviously thinking of the boys.

Mark thought a minute, then said, "Possibly. But I don't think so. At any rate, as long as we don't spread news of this find around, we should be okay."

"Mark," said Gloria, "I don't like this. What's going on?"

Mark glanced at Gary, and the younger man shrugged. Mark chewed silently a moment, then said, "I don't really know. I've told you a little about what I know about Kessler and his lot back in Germany, and all the strange things that were going on at that time. It may be . . . there may be some interest in all this. That's why I want to keep quiet. I'll have a better idea of what's going on after we finish here."

"How long will that take?" asked Phil.

"We've about finished the rough catalog. There're less than a dozen documents to record. Then we get to open the banker's box and count letters. Then I can start translating the German and French"—he grinned—"while Gary gets headaches with the Pahlavi and the others."

Gary said, "I'll start with something less exotic, then work my way up to the Pahlavi. I'll have to run back to the house and find my linguistic references. I hope I can remember where I put them."

"Most of your college texts are on the lowest shelf behind my desk."

Gary nodded, finished his sandwich, and said, "I'll go now."

"Good," answered Mark. "Gabbie and Jack could help me. If you don't mind," he directed toward them.

"No," said Gabbie.

"Sure," said Jack. Both seemed pleased to be included.

Finishing his sandwich, Mark killed off the last of his lemonade and said, "Well, let's go." Seeing Gloria's concerned expression, he reached out and touched her arm. Looking her in the eyes, he said, "There's nothing dangerous about this, Gloria."

She returned his look and slowly nodded. She turned away to clean the table as Phil returned to the study and Gabbie and Jack headed toward the basement.

As he left the kitchen, Mark wondered if Gloria could tell he was lying.

9

_____

The last document from the shelves was a rolled-up light vellum. Mark had Jack and Gabbie hold the large sheet flat while he photographed it. Speaking into the recorder, he said, "Document 136: a single sheet of what appears to be vellum, measuring"—Gabbie had the tape out and she and Jack quickly measured, giving Mark the dimensions—"twenty-four by thirty inches." He knelt to study the vellum. "No writing apparent. Seven lines, in staggered order, placed along the edges to the right as photographed. A single line from the bottom at approximately a 60-degree angle to the bottom running . . . seven inches, then turning to approximately 250 degrees to the original angle, running for eleven and seven-eighths inches. The line ends in a circle of less than a half inch in diameter. Three marks are clustered in the upper left corner. A line runs in a tightening coil from the circle to a larger circle"—he counted—"encompassing nine full turns counterclockwise before terminating. The nature of this document is not apparent."

He had them roll it back up and said, "Well, that does it. Now we can begin translating." He smiled, obviously pleased with the finding. "Let's take a short break until Gary gets back."

Over coffee in the kitchen, Mark said, "I think we'll have the answers we've been looking for. I can almost feel it within reach." He seemed both pleased and disturbed.

"What exactly got you started on this thing?" asked Gabbie.

Mark thought back. "About ten years ago, I was doing work on a book about secret societies; it never got written in the end. I couldn't get a publisher, because two similar books had bombed. Anyway, I was digging around for some stuff in Germany, in Münster—where a secret society called the Holy Vehm had operated in the late fifteenth century —when I chanced across some letters from a Catholic priest in Ulm, which is near Stuttgart, dated October 1903. The priest he wrote to in Münster was a friend from his seminary days. The letters were misfiled in the archives of the local diocese and probably should have been buried deep in a Vatican vault. They told of some 'trials' and hinted at execution. The priest in Ulm was deeply disturbed by both the events taking place in his parish and the Church's reaction. That was the first hint I had that something very unusual had taken place in the south of Germany at the turn of the century.

"What I've been able to piece together is pretty much what I told Phil and Gloria before: all sorts of pagan practices were revived." He fell silent for a minute. "People were returning to a set of beliefs rooted in Gotho-Germanic culture and myth, some involving primitive rites centered on the worship of the White Goddess: much like the druidic practices of ancient Britain. From what I could discover, it got pretty bizarre for a while. There were hints of terrible things . . . even, possibly, human sacrifice." Again there was a moment's reflection, as if he was uncertain what he should say next. Then he relaxed and said, "It fired my imagination. I've since worked on other projects over the years, but always had it in the back of mind that one day I'd find out what the hell went on back in Germany eighty-five years ago." He smiled in recollection. "When I finished my book on voodoo two years ago I decided to take a vacation. I guess my subconscious was at work, for I picked Germany. I did the Oktoberfest in Munich, then wandered over to Ulm to poke around. Again I got lucky. I couldn't get a thing out of the local Catholic or Lutheran church records, but I found a little bit in the archives of the local paper about a group of local businessmen who had suddenly departed for the States, Canada, and Africa. That's what put me on to Kessler and his cronies." He shook his head. "Whatever they were involved in, they took great pains to cover their tracks, and some records were lost in both world wars. I couldn't even get agreement from story to story on how many men were in . . . whatever they were in. Sometimes it was as many as twenty, sometimes as few as ten. And they changed names—even nationalities along the way, if they could.

"I chased three others of that group to dead ends, losing track of one in Alberta, Canada, another in New South Wales, Australia, and the third in what was then German East Africa. Then I followed Kessler. If I'd picked old Fredrick first, who knows? I might have uncovered some of this stuff earlier. But it doesn't matter now." There seemed to be some hidden meaning in those words, and Gabbie was about to comment on his mood when Mark pressed on. "When I came back from Germany, I spent a few weeks in New York, called Gary back from Seattle, and moved to Pittsville. We started poking around after news of old Fredrick Kessler, trying to uncover the truth. And at last it looks like it just may happen."

Gary returned, carrying three large books under one arm and several more in a book bag in the other hand. "Well, I may not be able to decipher those scrolls, but I'm as equipped as I'll ever be."

Mark put down his cup of coffee. "Good; let's get started."

10

Gloria stuck her head through the basement door and said, "Mark! Are you two going to work all night?"

Mark looked up from where he sat with open notebook, translating one of Kessler's books, and glanced at his watch. "It's after eight?"

"Yes. You've worked straight through dinner." Mark recalled her announcing it and his saying he'd be up, then proceeding to forget to eat. "Aggie's here, and getting ready to go home. Why don't you two call it a day and come up for a bite and a nightcap?"

Gary stood slowly, limbering joints stiff from sitting on a concrete floor, and said, "I'll second that."

In a few minutes they had put the basement in order, even to the point of closing and locking the door to the secret room.

Upstairs, Phil offered both a brandy and Gloria gave them plates of reheated dinner. Gary asked, "Where are Gabbie and Jack?"

Phil shrugged, but Aggie said, "Over at my house, I expect."

Phil sipped his drink, then said, "Well, we're dying to know what you've uncovered."

Mark and Gary exchanged glances and Mark said, between mouthfuls, "I'd prefer to dig deeper before I make any guesses about what we've found."

Gloria took him by the arm and steered him to a chair. Sitting him down, she said, "But you're with friends, so you don't need to worry about having to retract later what you say now, and if you don't share, I'll bop you one over the head with the biggest book down there." Her bantering manner did little to disguise her concern.

Mark smiled as he held up a hand in a defensive posture. "All right, I give." His smile slowly faded as he paused; at last he said, "I've got a pretty wild idea." He glanced at Gary, who seemed content to follow his lead. "But keep in mind we may have to modify our theories as we go. It may turn out Kessler was someone like us who was investigating, something like an amateur historian."

"Who hides his work in a secret room?" scoffed Aggie.

Gary said, "A paranoid amateur historian?"

They laughed, then Gloria said, "So what's your wild story, boys?"

Mark said, "I've only managed to translate a part of one book—we're skimming to get the sense of these things, not being particularly exhaustive. But it seems all those books and scrolls are related to some sort of . . . tradition."

"Tradition?" said Phil. "I don't understand."

"Maybe a religion of some sort, a cult. Remember I was investigating secret societies when I stumbled across the letter that first began all this. Anyway, if Kessler and his cronies were responsible for, or at least involved with, all the weird business in Germany at the turn of the century, then that was only part of something much larger."

"Can you be more specific?" said Aggie, obviously fascinated.

"Not until we've spent several weeks translating. Some of those documents, if authentic, date back a long time."

"How long?" asked Phil.

Gary said, "Those Pahlavi scrolls to the eighth, maybe seventh century. A couple of the Greek are . . . maybe centuries older. Maybe as far back as first century B.C."

"Is there a problem with condition?" asked Gloria. "I've read those old scrolls can crumble."

"No," said Mark. "These are in surprisingly good condition. Someone's ensured they were stored well. If you check that room in the basement, I think you'll find it's been insulated against cold and dampness. Also . . . they may be copies, not originals. We'd need the equipment to test the materials—parchment fibers, ink or whatever they used to write with—to be sure. But since they're that old, we're running into the usual problems with ancient documents: scribes who misspell, who have their own little shorthand, or who use provincial dialect. The chance of screwing up is pretty high." He sighed, started to speak, halted, then started again. "Phil, I don't like saying this, but . . . I would think it best to keep this secret for a while longer."

"You said something earlier," said Gloria. "Would you mind elaborating?"

Mark said, "I . . . I'm not sure, but it's possible someone"—his hand swept about in a general gesture—"might be interested in all this."

"If those documents are as old as you seem to think," interjected Aggie, "I'm sure any number of historians would be interested."

Mark shook his head. "No, I mean someone might be interested in keeping things hushed up." He put aside his now empty dinner plate and sipped a brandy.

Gloria looked upset. "Do you—"

Mark interrupted. "Probably not. I'm saying 'just in case,' and I can't emphasize that enough. Don't get worried over this until we know for certain."

Aggie shrugged. "Mysterious Mark Blackman."

Mark seemed on the edge of a sharp retort, then said, "Sorry. I'm tired. Really, I don't think there's anything to worry about. Let's just say I'm being overly cautious, okay?"

Phil said, "Okay by me. I'd rather take it slowly anyway. I've a book to finish, and a house full of historians would be a little disruptive."

Gary drank his coffee and said, "It's going to be a while before we know exactly what we've got here, anyway. I'm cracking this Russian thing, a church letter, from down around the Black Sea somewhere, and it keeps referring to things the reader's supposed to know about. I get phrases like 'I agree with your conclusion,' and I don't have a hint what that's about. I hope the letter that the writer's answering will be there, so I know what he's agreeing to." His bantering, pained tone made them all laugh.

"Do you find a lot of stuff like that in this sort of work?" asked Phil.

"We don't usually do this sort of work. There're centuries of collecting in your basement," said Gary. "There's stuff from all over the world. We've got letters, scrolls, books written in Hebrew, classical Latin, Church Latin, ancient Greek, Old High German, Middle High German, Middle English, others I don't even know what they are, Chinese, Japanese, Korean, or some mix of Asian languages. At some point we're going to have to farm some of this out to experts, people who can get the translations right." He looked knowingly at Mark. "Soon."

Mark shook his head no. "Not until we have an overall sense of how this stuff is likely to fit into a larger pattern, how it all hooks together. There's some central core of . . . something here.

"If we were archaeologists from the future, and we blundered into part of a library, we might struggle for years before we figured out that the only things the section we found had in common was that the authors were listed alphabetically. Or we might hit nonfiction and find the section on contemporary politics. Those books, scrolls, and letters are about something. Once we discover what that something is, a cult, religion, secret government organization, whatever, then we'll get into the detail stuff."

Aggie rose. "Well then, I'm for home."

Mark and Gary agreed it was past quitting time, and bade Phil and Gloria good night as well. They walked Aggie to her car, then followed her out the driveway.

As Mark's car pulled away, Phil said, "Secret societies, huh?"

Gloria was quiet, then said, "And weird documents. It's all kind of scary, somehow."

Phil looked at his wife. "Scary? I would have said exciting. And there's still the question of the gold. Maybe that wasn't such a story after all."

Almost sarcastically, Gloria said, "Want to get a shovel and go look for buried treasure?"

Grabbing his wife playfully, he swung her about and said, "Got all the treasure I want right here." He kissed her, slipping his hand down to squeeze her rump. Gloria remained tense, not returning Phil's playful affection. "Hey, what's wrong?"

Gloria put her head on Phil's shoulder. "Mark's lying to us, Phil. He's been covering something up since he set eyes on the room."

Phil looked down at his wife. "Aren't you making a bit much of this? Aggie told us Mark likes to keep quiet on his work. He's even said he doesn't like talking about it. He's just being cautious."

Gloria sighed. "Maybe you're right." But she knew he wasn't.

11

Gloria hung up the phone. "That was Mark."

Phil, sitting behind his desk, looked to where his wife stood in the hallway and said, "What's up?"

"He's flying out to New York tonight. He says they've hit a wall, so they're going to consult with some people. Gary's taking copies of some of the more exotic stuff to his friends at the University of Washington and Mark's going to talk to some people he knows at NYU."

Phil was alerted to an odd note in his wife's voice. "Something worrying you, hon?"

Gloria stood hugging herself and shook her head as if clearing it. "No, I don't think so. It's just . . ."

"What?"

"I don't know, but I had the strangest feeling when Mark hung up that . . . that I'd never hear from him again."

Phil began a quip, then stopped himself as he realized that his wife was really disturbed. He rose and went over to her. "Hey, Irish, what is this?" he said softly, taking her into his arms and holding her gently.

"You haven't called me that in years," she said. She rested her head on his chest. "It's just a cold feeling."

Phil hesitated a moment, then reached around his wife and picked up the phone. He dialed as Gloria said, "What?"

"Wait." The phone at the other end rang, then was picked up. Phil said, "Mark, Phil. When are you leaving?" An answer came, and Phil said, "Well, look. Why don't you and Gary both come by, then we'll all drive up to Buffalo together for dinner? Then we'll hang out with Gary in the airport bar until his plane leaves. That way he won't have to sit around the terminal by himself for two hours. And you won't get stuck for long-term parking fees. No, no trouble. We'd enjoy it." He hung up.

Gloria said, "What was that?"

"Mark's plane leaves at ten tonight and Gary's catching the red-eye at midnight. And this way you can shake that feeling you'll never see Mark again." He glanced at his watch. "You can see him in about two hours. He'll be here at five."

Gloria smiled. "Thanks."

"For what?"

"For not making fun."

He shrugged off the remark as the door in the kitchen banged closed behind the twins. "Ma!" echoed through the house as Patrick announced his brother's and his arrival. The swinging door opened and the twins marched into view, Sean holding a bunch of envelopes. "Mail's here," he informed them.

Phil took the mail as Gloria said, "Guess who baked some tollhouse cookies today?"

With a shout of approval, the twins moved with their mother toward the kitchen while Phil employed the silver letter opener that Aggie had given him to discover how much this month's American Express bill would prove to be. The opener reminded him of Aggie and he shouted to his wife, "Better call over to Aggie's and tell Gabbie we'll need her to watch the boys tonight." He shook his head. Without fanfare, Gabbie had begun spending nights over there and for the last few days had hardly been seen by the Hastings household, except in the barn. No matter how much in love with Jack she might be, she'd never neglect the horses. Then Phil glanced at the last letter in the stack; he looked at it again, staring at the return address as if for a moment he couldn't believe his senses. Then he shouted, "And tell her she's got a letter here. From her mother."

12

Gabbie's face was an unreadable mask as she finished the letter. Folding it slowly, she looked at her father and began to laugh. "Mom got married."

Phil blinked and said, "She's married?"

Gloria watched the reaction with interest. The only subject in Phil's past that had been off limits had been Corinne. Phil had given Gloria the barest facts and refused to discuss his first marriage further. When they had begun dating, Gloria had worried that Phil carried a torch for his first wife. She quickly learned that was as far from the truth as anything could be. Gloria knew there was a lot of hostility and anger still dormant within Phil, but there were also other feelings, feelings not shared. It was the only thing Gloria felt left out of where Phil was concerned.

Gabbie continued her laughing, a deeply amused sound tinged with a note of bitterness. "She married Jacques Jeneau."

Gloria's eyes widened. "The French millionaire?"

Phil's mouth turned up at the corners, and his eyes brimmed. For a moment Gloria feared he was on the verge of crying, but suddenly he threw back his head and laughed. He was nearly convulsing, laughing so hard he fell back over the arm of the small couch opposite his desk, landing with a thud. He lay back, laughing. "Jeneau!" he croaked.

Gabbie's laughter echoed her father's and she had to wipe a tear away as she became caught up in her father's hilarity. Their laughter bounced back and forth, feeding off itself, until Gabbie had to sit down and hold her breath to stop.

Jack, who had been quietly standing by the hall door, said to Gloria, "What's so funny?" She shrugged, indicating ignorance.

Phil lay back, arm over his eyes, for a moment, his laughter diminishing to a continuous chuckle. At last he took a deep breath and then sighed. Gabbie covered her face with her hand, wiping away the wetness on her cheeks. Jack politely asked, "Who's Jacques Jeneau?"

Phil sat up, also wiping tears from his face, as he said, "Ah, therein lies a tale."

He got up and went to kneel beside his daughter. He put his arms around her shoulders, hugging her tight, a rare display of physical affection between them. "You all right, kiddo?"

Gabbie's laughter had halted and she looked at her father, her eyes red from tearing. She sniffed and nodded. "Yup." She kissed him on the cheek, then said, "Some joke, huh?"

Gloria said, "If it's not a bother, what's so damn funny?"

Phil continued to kneel beside Gabbie. "Jacques Jeneau is a French playboy who spends his time with slow boats and fast women. His hobbies are losing yacht races and divorce suits." He sat on the floor, his arm resting across Gabbie's knees. "We met him at a reception in New York, in '66, I think. It was some charity thing. Anyway, Corinne got a fair share of invitations to those affairs because of her family, even though we were poor and just getting by. And we went to a number of them—the ones we didn't have to contribute to get into, anyway. There were always plenty of free drinks and pretty good buffets. At this one Jeneau made a pass at Corinne." He smiled in remembrance. "This was before she got radical, but even then she called him a parasite. We saw him a half-dozen times after that, and every time he came on to her. We treated it like a joke. He's been chasing her on and off for twenty years. Look's like he finally caught her. Some joke."

Gabbie said, "The joke is this letter." She sighed and looked at Jack. "So much for the grande dame of the Left. Will you look at that engraved stationery! It must have come from some designer shop in Paris, for Christ's sake."

Gloria couldn't stand it any longer and took the letter from Gabbie's hand. She read it, then said, "So she's sorry for the lost years and wants you to come visit?"

Gabbie stood. "It's a little late." She went to stand next to Jack, who put his arms around her.

"Don't be too hard, Gabbie," said Phil as he stood up. "Maybe she's mellowed in her old age."

"If she married Jeneau, she didn't mellow; she moldered." She made a face. "I met him at a rich people's reception at Grandmother's. He made a pass at me! And I was all of fifteen!"

Jack grinned. "So? You were probably pretty hot stuff for a fifteen-year-old, or is he just a dirty-old-man type?"

"Old?" Gabbie sighed in resignation. "No, in fact he's gorgeous. Like a Robert Redford with big brown eyes and ginger hair, with perfect grey at the temples. And a body like a gymnast's. All dripping with Gallic suavity. It's just he's so damn obvious. He's used to having women throw themselves at him. I think he was halfway shocked and amused when I walked away from him."

"Like mother, like daughter," said Phil. "He's been intrigued with Corinne for years. I guess he just couldn't stand being turned down."

Gloria tapped her chin with the folded letter. "As the Chinese say, 'May you live in interesting times.' Well, it's been yucks, kids, but if you're going to have any dinner, I still better check on the roast. Mark and Gary should be here soon." Passing Gabbie, she handed back the letter.

Phil headed toward the doorway, saying, "It might not be too bad a honeymoon, kids. The South of France isn't hard to take."

Gabbie looked at Jack. "What do you think?"

"I think we'll do what you want. We could always work it so we pass through Nice for a day. Cocktails on the yacht; that sort of thing. Then we could split if it gets too uncomfortable."

Gabbie sighed. "I'll think about it. Maybe we should see Mom, at least once."

Phil said softly, "Ah, now you know where she is, maybe you should invite her to the wedding?"

"I'll think about that, too." With a small hint of anger, she said, "She didn't invite me to hers."

Phil put his hand on his daughter's shoulder. "I understand. Whatever you want, okay?" The sound of a car approaching the house intruded. "That'll be Mark and Gary. We'll be back after midnight."

Gabbie nodded. "Have a good time."

Gloria appeared and took her coat from the closet as Mark knocked on the door. Quickly Gloria gave last-minute instructions about dinner and stuck her head into the parlor to say good night to the boys. Soon Mark's car was heading out of the driveway and Gabbie and Jack were alone in the study.

Jack studied Gabbie's face in the soft glow of the porch light coming in the window and wondered what was going on in that complex head of hers. He knew she was enduring mixed emotions where her mother was concerned, but he also knew she'd decide to do what was right for her, with no bullshit or apology. It was one of the qualities that made him crazy about her. She sighed and put her head on his shoulder, without words, and they fell into that warm glow simply being together gave them, while from the parlor the sound of gunfire informed them the twins had discovered something diverting among the hundred-plus channels Phil's dish could pull in. For a quiet time nothing was spoken, then Gabbie kissed Jack lightly on the cheek and said, "Come on, lover. Let's feed the monsters." With a mock groan at being forced to quit the comfort of the couch, Jack rose and followed Gabbie to the kitchen.

OCTOBER

1

Gabbie rushed down the hall as the phone rang for the fifth time. She was dripping wet and furious as she attempted to keep the towel wrapped around her. As she sped past the twins' room, she said, "Thanks, brats!"

Sean and Patrick looked up from where they were reading comic books and exchanged questioning glances. They had no idea what she was talking about. They had both been off in a four-color world populated by costumed superheroes and space adventures, and something as mundane as a phone ringing was not going to break their concentration. Patrick looked out the window, heavily streaked by rain, and silently wondered, *Is it ever going to stop?*

"Sure," said Sean. "Just in time for school on Monday." Neither thought it odd they shared that silent communication from time to time. They had been doing it since birth.

Patrick returned to his comic, grumbling inaudibly. School was more than a month old and the rain had seemed constant since the second day. Either it was pouring, or the ground at the park was too muddy to play ball. Now another Saturday was almost shot. They hadn't played an inning in three weeks and both were feeling deprived. The kids at school didn't want to play baseball much anymore, anyway. It was football season, and while both twins liked touch football, it wasn't the same as a good baseball game. It was a sure sign the summer was long gone, the next an impossibly distant time away. Besides, next year was Little League, and while excited at the prospect of organized play, the boys also sensed that some element of freedom was slipping from their young lives.

Sean studied his brother. His own sense of gloom was reflected back by Patrick's, but with that reflection came a darker shadow. Sean knew Patrick still seethed inside to get back at the Bad Thing, but hoped that with school occupying his energies Patrick would become content to wait through the last two weeks of October, until November 1, when all the Good People left. But deep within he knew it was unlikely. Patrick was an open book for Sean. Sometime soon Patrick would act.

Gabbie stormed back in the other direction, halting long enough to say, "Damn salesman! If the phone rings again while I'm in the bath, one of you monsters better pick it up or I'll . . ." She let the sentence go unfinished as her little brothers showed nothing resembling concern over the vague threat; she hadn't the faintest notion of what she'd do if they didn't. And the towel was small enough that it didn't quite cover most of what Gabbie wanted covered. The comic struggle with the towel undermined her attempt at looking menacing. She gave up and left.

Patrick observed, "She takes a lot of showers and baths."

Sean nodded. "Girls do that. They don't like dirt." With that sage insight they returned to their comics.

After a while the phone rang again. Sean looked up and saw that Patrick was lost in the latest adventures of Wonder Woman. He listened and heard Gabbie's voice echo down the hall: "Get the phone, damnit!"

Sean rose and hurried to the phone, picked up the receiver, and said, "Hello."

"Patrick? Sean?" said the voice on the phone, made scratchy by long distance.

"Sean."

"This is Mark. Is your father home?"

"No. Mom and Dad are shopping. They'll be back for dinner."

"Is Jack or Gabbie there?"

"Jack's coming over. Gabbie's in the bath. You've been gone a long time. When you coming back?"

"Soon. I'm in Germany. Now listen carefully, Sean. I want you to give your dad a message. It's important. I don't know when I'll be back. . . ." A squeal of static erupted, then Mark said, ". . . but regardless of when, tell your dad to leave the stuff in the basement alone until I get back, no matter *what* he finds. And if he finds anything else, anywhere on your property, tell him . . ." Again static obscured his words. "It's very important that he doesn't touch *anything*. You got that?"

"Sure. You're in Germany and Dad's not to mess with the stuff in the basement."

"Okay. Now, tell your father I've got some of the translation of the parchment and some other new information—" A sudden loud burst of static sounded as lightning flashed outside; the phone went dead at the other end. Sean listened for a moment as series of clicks sounded, followed, after a long silence, by the dial tone. Something in the tone of Mark's voice and the sudden silence on the phone disturbed Sean. He held the phone until it began a recording telling him to hang up. He did so and headed back toward his room.

Gabbie opened the bathroom door, allowing a cloud of steam to escape, and said, "Who was that?"

"Mark. He's in Germany."

Gabbie emerged from the bathroom wearing a white terry-cloth bathrobe, a puzzled expression on her face. "He called from Germany?"

Sean nodded. "Yeah, he's in Germany. He said to tell Dad that he shouldn't do anything in the basement until he got back."

Gabbie toweled her hair. "I wonder what that's supposed to mean. Germany? I thought he was in New York all this time. Was there anything else?"

"Yes . . ." Sean thought a long moment. "But I forget."

"Great. Well, you better remember before Dad gets back. When's Mark coming here?"

"He said he didn't know." Without further comment he entered his room and returned to the latest adventures of the Batman. For a long time Sean scanned the brightly colored pages, but he couldn't shake the odd quality in Mark's voice. Sean couldn't judge such things, but he thought Mark had sounded scared.

2

Phil wasn't pleased by the lack of agreement about what had happened. He said, "So he said not to do anything?"

Sean nodded.

"Anything what, honey?" asked Gloria.

Sean struggled to remember. "He had something for you, I think. Anyway, he said he'd tell you when he got here."

Gloria regarded the pouring rain outside. "But he didn't say when that would be?"

Sean shrugged. "He just said soon."

Gabbie ate silently. She had avoided responsibility for the lack of a complete message by insisting on her right to an uninterrupted bath. The boys were old enough to write down messages. Her father had agreed in principle, but he still looked irritated with his daughter. He had left her in charge.

A knock on the back door was followed by Jack's entrance. He was dripping but smiling. "You ready?"

"Wait a minute," Gabbie said, jumping up from the table. "We're running late tonight."

"We've got time. The movie doesn't begin for another hour."

"No, you leave now," said Gloria. "With this rain I don't want you rushing, and I know how Gabbie drives." Gabbie ran from the room and up the stairs. Gloria regarded the dripping Jack. "Why in heaven didn't you let her pick you up? Even with that slicker, you're drenched."

Jack winked. "Because if I'd stayed at Aggie's, Gabbie'd have waited until the last minute to collect me, and I know how she drives, too."

"I heard that!" came down the stairs.

"Gabbie says you're taking off for a few days," said Gloria.

Jack unbuttoned his slicker. "First thing tomorrow. I've got an old friend at Fredonia who's going to help me organize my material, then prep me for my second orals, week after next."

"This is it, then?" said Phil.

Jack nodded, betraying a slight nervousness. "If I get past these orals, I advance to candidacy. My doctorate won't be automatic, but it'll be just a matter of doing the work right. But this is where they wash out the students they don't think can cut it, the final culling of the herd."

"You'll do fine," commented Phil.

Gloria changed the subject. "Mark Blackman called. He's in Germany."

"Germany?"

"If Sean heard right, he's been in Germany for the last two weeks."

Jack looked confused a moment. "This all has to do with the stuff in the basement, I guess. Germany? Fancy that."

Phil said, "I guess." He put down his fork. "That still doesn't clear up the mystery of what happened to Gary. I expected him back a few days ago."

Patrick looked up from his plate, a guilty expression on his face. "He's still in Seattle."

Phil said, "How do you know that?"

"He called."

"When?"

"Last week. I forgot to tell you. He said Mark had gone to Germany from New York and he was going to stay in Washington for a while."

"I think tomorrow I buy an answering machine." Phil was caught between anger and resigned amusement. "With five people living in this house, why isn't it humanly possible to get messages . . ."

3

Gabbie jumped up at the sound of a car coming up the drive. She let the book she'd been reading fall to the floor as she peered through the window. Jack was barely out of Aggie's car when she was flying down the porch steps to leap upon him. He staggered back against the fender of the car, dropping the book bag he had been carrying. He held her up as she kissed him. When at last she broke away, he said, "Hey. I've barely been gone a week."

She kissed him again, lingering and hungry. "It seemed like a month." She said with a grin, "I'm so damn horny, I can't believe it."

Jack returned the grin. "We'll have to do something about that." She stuck her tongue in his ear, something she had discovered made him absolutely crazy, and he jumped and shivered. Quickly he disentangled himself from her. "But not until tonight, you shameless hussy." Over her mock pout he said, "Aggie's got some local matrons over for tea. She's picking brains for her book again. Unless everyone here's gone off somewhere?" he hopefully asked.

"No such luck. The twins will be home from school in an hour and Gloria's doing kitchen stuff. Dad's in playing a game on the computer, though we're all supposed to think he's hard at work." She pinched Jack on the rear. "We could grab a blanket and sneak off to the barn."

Jack jumped and laughed. "You are insatiable, woman." He kissed her. "And those brothers of yours have radar. They'd come rolling into the barn at the worst possible moment. Besides, it's starting to get wet and the barn roof leaks, and it's *cold*. Now, be good!"

Hugging him again, Gabbie grinned. "Good? I'm great. You've said so yourself."

Jack laughed in resignation. A scattering of drops announced the arrival of a rainstorm that had been glowering in the sky all day. "Let's get inside," Jack said.

She put her arm around his waist and they walked toward the house.

In the den, Phil was hunched over before the computer, concentrating hard on what he read on the screen. After a moment he opened the bottom drawer of his desk, pulling out a pencil and a legal pad. He consulted his notes and typed in the instruction to return him to where he left off last. Somehow, some way, he was determined to finish this and, without help from anyone, get a perfect score of 400 playing Zork. He looked up and smiled at Jack. "How are things?"

"Pretty good. I think I'm ready for my orals next Tuesday. My friend Mike came up with questions I don't think even Aggie could have thought of. Speaking of Aggie, I thought I'd hang out here for a few hours before going home. Her coffee klatch should be finished by then."

"Good," said Gabbie. "We can put the time to good use."

"What good use?"

"We've still got a bunch of trunks in the attic we haven't opened. Let's go poke around and see if we can't scratch up something interesting."

Jack said, "Toward what ends?"

"Who knows? Maybe we can find something that will help out Mark and Gary when they get back." It was already three weeks into October, and Mark and Gary were still on their respective sojourns seeking insights into the odd findings in the Hastingses' basement. "Gary called a couple of days ago. He's bogged down with his linguist friends in Seattle. And he's lost track of Mark and wanted to know if we've heard from him."

"Lost track?" mused Jack. "That's strange."

"Gary didn't seem particularly distressed. He said Mark often gets sidetracked while traveling. He must've uncovered something diverting after he said he was about to return. So I volunteered us to go snooping in the attic. Anyway, it'll give us something useful to do this afternoon."

Jack shook his head. "All right. You've talked me into it, you silver-tongued devil."

Phil's attention had already returned to his computer screen. "Have fun, you two," he said absently.

Gabbie said to Jack, "Come on, let's go into the attic and poke."

Presenting an evil grin as they climbed the stairs, he whispered, "You know that sounds dirty."

A short elbow to the ribs was her only answer as they headed for the stairs to the attic.

4

It seemed impossible. If you tried to get through the gas-filled room with a lit torch, you blew up, but if you put out the torch and moved in the dark, the hideous grue got you. Phil was diverted from the computer screen by the sound of rain on the window. He glanced over and discovered the sprinkle had become a steady downpour. Then the sound of water striking glass was cut by Gabbie's and Jack's voices. He glanced at his watch and saw he'd been playing for almost an hour and a half. Quickly he saved his location in the game and turned off the computer.

Jack entered with a roll of paper. "Phil, take a look at this," he said.

Phil studied the paper for a moment. "It's a map of the property." He noted the yellowish color and condition of the map and added, "And it's an old one from the look of it."

Jack pointed to a title block in the lower right corner and said, "Nineteen hundred and six, according to this. That's about when Fredrick Kessler bought the property."

Gabbie said, "The barn's in a different place. And it's smaller."

"Must have had a new one built later," observed Phil. He read the small notations and said, "It's certainly the original plot plan for the property. There's no gazebo and no tool shed beside the barn, and the drive heads off at a slightly different angle." Something about the map bothered him, but he couldn't put his finger on what it was.

He looked up to see Jack studying him. Jack said, "You too?"

"Something's funny about this map, Dad." Gabbie shook her head.

"Yes, but what?"

"It's like something we saw already, but different," observed Jack.

"I don't recall seeing any maps of the property, except at the bank when we bought this place, and those were the little ones provided by the land title company."

Gabbie looked hard at it, as if by force of will she'd make it yield its secret. Then her expression turned to one of understanding. "I've got it!" she shouted.

"What?" asked Jack.

"Stay here and I'll show you." She ran from the room and Jack and Phil could hear the basement door under the stairs open. They heard her footfalls on the wooden stairs to the basement, then the distant sound of the door to the secret room being opened. In a moment she was back with a parchment. "It's this odd thing we found when we helped Mark." She unrolled it and they again regarded the strange unmarked vellum with its odd lines and circles. "Look at the seven lines at the right and look at the underlined words on the map!" Her tone was excited.

Jack said, "Gabbie, you're a genius! It's an overlay. Watch." Jack laid the translucent vellum atop the map. "By pressing, you can see the map underneath."

Phil looked and said, "Barely."

"Maybe they didn't have onionskin paper back then," said Gabbie.

"Or they wanted something that would last a little longer," said Jack. He pointed. "Look at these seven lines on the right."

Each line on the vellum underlined a word of description on the map, part of a notation made by the records clerk when the map had been filed at the turn of the century.

"That coil of lines wraps right around the base of Erl King Hill," said Jack. He moved the overlay and read the paragraph below. It began, "From the median line of county road 15, at a distance of exactly two miles south of the junction of state road 7, to the point described as a meeting of lines extending from . . ." It went on describing the property limits of the farm using geographical locations of the day. The word "to" had been underlined. The entire paragraph was strictly *pro forma* legal description, but the last line read, ". . . the property commonly known as Erl King Hill," with the words "Erl King" underlined, completing the message.

Gabbie read the seven words aloud. " 'To the home of the Erl King.' What's that mean?"

"I think it's a code within a code," ventured Jack. Gabbie and Phil looked at him questioningly. " 'The home of the Erl King' meant something to Kessler and maybe some others, but . . . you know, in case someone like us found the map and the overlay, we'd still not know what it showed the location of."

Phil's eyes followed the long lines and saw that the larger circle was located a half mile behind the house. Pointing to the coil with circles design, he tapped it with his finger. "What's that?"

Jack's voice sounded excited. "I don't know. But the large circle is at the base of Erl King Hill." He looked at Phil and Gabbie. "Know what I think?"

Phil said, "You think that's where Kessler buried his gold?"

Jokingly Gabbie said, "What happened to 'X marks the spot'?"

"That's a long shot," commented Phil.

"What else could it be?" asked Jack. "Why this much trouble to mark one place on the side of a bald hill? And this overlay and code business. There's something hidden there."

Phil looked at the other lines. "What about this other circle here?" He pointed to a smaller circle on the map, located about a hundred feet or so to the east of the larger one.

Gabbie moved the vellum aside and read a note on the map. "That's where that big oak stump sits. See, here it's noted as 'a lightning-struck oak, needing to be cut.' "

Phil grinned as Jack's smile faded. Phil shrugged. "If I was burying gold, I'd put it somewhere I could find without the map, like the base of an easy-to-find tree stump."

"Then what's this other circle?" wondered Jack.

Phil returned to his seat. "Maybe a covered well? Or some other mundane thing a property owner might like to know about."

Jack shook his head. "Not with all this other secret bullshit going on, Phil. Look at all these weird lines and things. One of these two circles is where Kessler buried his gold. I'll bet on it."

Phil laughed. "Well, if you want to go digging, you have my permission. Just fill in the holes when you're done, okay?"

Jack smiled, half self-consciously. "Well, okay." To Gabbie he said, "Come on, let's go take a look."

"In the rain!" she said in disbelief.

"We'll just poke around, nothing serious. All right?"

With a groan of resignation, Gabbie threw up her hands and said *sotto voce* to her dad, "Watch him stop in the barn for a shovel."

Gabbie followed Jack from the room and Phil sat back, half-amused and half-curious. Maybe in a little while he'd don his raincoat and go out and give Jack a hand. He flipped on the computer and returned his attention to getting through the gas-filled room without blowing up.

5

"Dad!"

Phil was out from behind his desk and moving toward the kitchen the instant he heard the excited tone in Gabbie's voice. He pushed open the door and halted when he saw his daughter. Gabbie stood dripping wet, covered in mud, while Gloria and the boys looked on in astonishment. "You've got to come. We found something!"

"What?" said Phil, not believing what he had just heard.

"Beneath the stump, like you thought. We poked around there and found a hollow among the roots. Water's been eroding the ground for years. Jack only had to stick the shovel in and it collapsed. He moved the mud around, and after digging less than a foot, he hit the top."

"Top of what?"

"I don't know," said Gabbie. "There's something down there. We shined the light down there and Jack's digging for it now. I couldn't tell what it was, Dad, but it's big."

Phil said, "I'll get my coat."

Gloria said, "I'll get mine."

The boys were dashing toward the hall—where the raincoats were hung—in an instant, and Phil halted them. "Hey, where do you think you're going?"

"Aw, Dad," began Patrick. "We want to come and see, too."

"Wrong. You guys stay here and watch TV or something, and listen for the phone. And write down messages!" he shouted after the disgruntled boys as they left the kitchen.

Within minutes the three adults were hurrying across the Troll Bridge. They discovered Jack digging at the stump a short distance from the bridge. Phil studied the hole Jack had dug. It had filled with water, and Jack hastily dug at the side until a small channel was fashioned to lead the water away. Then he knelt and shined the heavy rubber-encased flashlight into a depression under the stump. Phil hunkered down and peered into the hole. A glimpse of an odd shape greeted him as the water washed the dirt from atop something in the hole. For a long minute Phil was silent, then he stood up while Gloria and Gabbie regarded the hole.

"What do we do, Dad?" asked Gabbie.

"Let's see if we can wrestle this thing out." He motioned for Jack, who put down the shovel and knelt beside Phil. Together they reached in and each took a grip on what felt to be a large wooden chest. They pulled, but the thing wouldn't move. "Christ!" swore Phil. "This thing weighs a ton."

Jack began digging around the box, while Phil played the light over the chest. Soon Jack stood knee-deep in mud as he moved shovelfuls up and over the edge of the hole. Phil motioned for Jack to push away some dirt from the front and said, "That thing's got a handle on it. Gabbie, there's a rope in the trunk of the car. Would you get it? Jack, use the shovel to make a ramp in the mud." She took the keys and ran off, while Phil shined the light on the chest and Jack continued to dig furiously.

By the time she returned, Jack had dug out a smooth ramp of dirt down to the chest, angling under the old stump. "If it weren't for this rain," Jack observed, "this would have taken hours." Still he was panting, and under the hood of his slicker perspiration ran off his forehead with the rainwater. "Let's see if we can pull it out."

They tied the rope to the metal handle closest to the ramp. Phil and Jack pulled, and when no movement was apparent at first, Gabbie and then Gloria grabbed hold. They pulled, but the chest didn't budge. Jack yelled for a halt and sat on the ground in the hole. He stuck the shovel in between the chest and the ground. He then jumped up and leaned on the handle.

"What are you doing?" shouted Phil over the now pounding rain.

"Suction. I'm trying to break the vacuum between the chest and the mud."

Phil nodded and stepped down on the handle, his foot next to Jack's, adding his weight to the shovel. After a long minute of the two of them putting their full weight on the shovel, it moved. Phil barely

avoided falling on top of Jack and jumped back. Jack pulled out the
shovel and scampered out of the hole. He signaled the others to grab the
rope and they all hauled on it. The footing was slippery, but after a long
pull the chest moved slightly. Then it halted. Jack said, "It's like the
roots of the stump are holding the box in place." He jumped back into
the hole and used the edge of the shovel to slash at the roots, to little
effect.

After a few minutes of futile hacking, Gabbie said, "I'll get the ax
from the barn." She dashed off and returned shortly with both the ax
and a hatchet. Jack spent the better part of a half hour cutting at the
roots atop the box. Several loud clangs informed them there was metal
on the box.

Jack tossed the ax out of the hole and went at it with the hatchet.
After he thought a way out of the root tangle had been secured, he said,
"Let's try it again." All four grabbed the rope. They moved in concert
and slowly it came out from under the stump. As it continued to slide,
momentum aided their efforts, and once it cleared the lip of the ramp
Jack had dug, it slid cleanly into view. It was a wooden chest two feet on
each side, fastened round by two iron bands, with iron reinforcing at the
corners. The metal was brown with rust but still looked substantially
intact; silver glints peeked through scars formed by Jack's ax blows.
There was no apparent latch or lock, simply an iron hasp over an iron
ring. Without waiting, Gabbie said, "What's inside?"

She knelt and opened the lid, while Phil shined the light down on
her. She lifted the lid, revealing the interior. Shimmering reflections
danced from the golden coins that nearly filled the chest to overflowing.
Softly Jack said, "No wonder it was so heavy."

Gloria said, "Shit! An honest-to-God treasure chest!"

Gabbie said, "Kessler's gold. It's real."

Then Phil began to laugh, and in a moment all were whooping and
hollering. After this short burst of enthusiasm, Gabbie said, "What do
we do now?"

"I think we go back to the house and have dinner," said Phil.

Gloria looked up at her husband. "You think we should tell someone?"

"I'll call Darren in the morning and have him start looking up laws
on property rights or mineral rights or salvage rights or whatever the
hell else it is that applies here."

"Darren?" asked Jack.

"The family lawyer," said Gabbie.

"For all we know," added Phil, "we might have a German national
treasure here, or something someone else has a legal claim on. So let's

get it safe into the house and find out. Until then we keep our mouths shut, and I mean especially the twins. Now, come on. Let's get dry and fed."

Jack pushed the mud back into the hole, causing it to fill quickly. He then grabbed one of the two handles of the chest, and he and Phil lifted. It was heavy but, free of the mud's pull, manageable. They returned across the bridge, heading back to the dry and warm kitchen at home.

Among the trees two pairs of eyes followed their travel. The tall figure held the small black one, cradling it like a baby. Long fingers stroked the leathery hide of the thing's stomach, then paused. With a sudden jab that brought forth a squeal of pain from the small one, the tall being with the mad eyes said, "Ahh! It is near!" The sound was one of frustration. Gripping the black thing by the neck, he spun it around to face him and said, "Soon, my pet. Soon."

With a half toss, half slap, he deposited the little black creature on the ground. The Bad Thing struck the mud with an audible splash, but turned and rolled, scampering to its feet, already moving to do its master's bidding. "Go and watch, small one," he whispered, his voice an echo of ancient breezes. "Go and keep it safe until the deed is done." Then he threw back his head and howled in pleasure, his shrieks hidden by the rolling thunder in the skies. Then, with a twinkle of light in the gloom, he was gone.

6

The rain had halted the next day. As Phil hung up the phone, he laughed, a short amused bark. "Darren wasn't amused. He thinks I'm crazy. But he's going to look up whatever information he can about lost treasure, as he calls it, and he'll get back to us. He did say not to move it until he gets back to us. Which should take a few days because, as he puts it, he's got to waltz around with the IRS and the police without letting them know what's going on. Otherwise one or the other's likely just to seize everything and let us go to court to get back any share we're entitled to."

"Do you think it's safe?" asked Gloria.

"Sure. Jack filled the hole with mud, and after the rain there'll be little sign of digging. Besides, how many people have come tramping over that way since we moved in? Just some of the boys' chums from school, and Jack. No one knows the chest is in the basement. It'll be all right down there for another few days."

Gloria sat on the couch opposite Phil's desk. Gabbie and Jack hadn't come in from a ride, their first in over two weeks, and the boys were off at school—after a long lecture on not sharing the news of the gold with anyone. Gloria said, "Do you think we should call Gary?"

"Sure, if I knew how to get a hold of him. Maybe I could track him down through the University of Washington's Linguistics Department." Phil studied his wife. "What's on your mind?"

Gloria sat quietly. "Phil, I'm scared. I mean down to my booties scared. Stuff's going on around here that's . . . impossible to explain. I don't know. But with what happened to Gabbie, and all those things Mark and Gary said about Kessler, and the way Ernie was killed . . ."

Phil came from behind the desk and sat next to his wife, putting his arms around her shoulders. "Look, honey, there's a simple explanation for all this, I'm certain. I don't know exactly what it is, but I doubt there's anything terribly menacing about it. Sure, the thing with Gabbie was frightening, but Mark said she was coming out of it with no apparent problems, and now she's got Jack. That rapist is probably a thousand miles away by now. And this mystery of Kessler and his buddies in Germany? Well, I think it will all turn out to have—"

"I know, a perfectly rational explanation." She crossed her arms. "Look, maybe somebody's going to come looking for that gold."

Phil shrugged. "Why now? The house was empty for a long time between when Herman Kessler left for Germany and we moved in. Anyone who knew about the gold could have waltzed in and dug it up without anyone ever suspecting. Besides, who else could know about it? I'm sure this is the gold Mark told us about, that Fredrick Kessler used to make those shady loans."

Gloria seemed unconvinced, but she halted her protestations. Something gnawed at her, a deep sense of foreboding. Her thoughts were diverted by the arrival of the twins, home from school. They wandered in and Phil said, "Hi, guys. How were things today?"

They both shrugged in that shared gesture which indicated it was nothing to talk about. Sean said, "Robbie Galloway got sent home for tearing Maria Delany's sweater."

Gloria tried to look interested, but her thoughts were on her disquiet. Patrick said, "Ya, he was trying to tickle her. He likes to tickle girls. The teacher says he's got to have a talk with Robbie's father."

Phil smiled knowingly as Gloria threw her eyes heavenward. Under her breath she said, "Let's not have any early puberties in this household, please, Lord."

Phil said, "Well, finding Mark's out of the question, so I'll try to track down Gary, somehow, and let him know what's going on." To the boys he said, "Does anyone know where Gary's staying in Seattle?"

Patrick said, "Lupinski's."

"Who?" said Gloria.

"He knows this guy from college," explained Sean. "He told us. The guy works for the SuperSonics. Gary used to go to a lot of games with him. He said that's where he got his neat jacket and that's the guy he stays with." Almost guiltily he added, "I asked if he could get us jackets like his."

Phil glanced at his watch. "It's noonish on the Coast. I'll call Seattle information and get the SuperSonics office. . . ." He called and got the number, then dialed it and waited until the ring at the other end was answered. "Hello, may I speak to Mr. Lupinski, please." He nodded as he was put on hold. After a moment he said, "Mr. Lupinski? My name is Philip Hastings . . . how do you do. I'm trying to track down Gary Thieus. . . ." Phil's eyebrows raised. "He is? Please." After a long second he said, "Hey, Gary, how're you doing? I didn't think I'd find you this easily."

He listened silently for a moment, then said, "No, everything is fine here. But are you ready for a shock? No, nothing terrible, thank heaven. It's just that Jack and Gabbie have uncovered Kessler's gold." He grinned at the response on the other end, and even Gloria could hear Gary's exclamation as Phil held the receiver away from his ear. "No, I'm not kidding, old son. That odd-looking piece of vellum you and Mark found was an overlay to a map Kessler had stashed in a trunk in the attic. Jack and Gabbie simply went to where some marks on the map indicated, dug a bit, and *voilà*, gold."

He hung up with a chuckle. "He said, 'I'm on my way,' and hung up. He'll call from Sea-Tac airport and let us know when he'll be landing in Buffalo."

Gloria stood up. "I think I'll make a pot of tea. Want some?" He indicated yes as she crossed to the door. "Come on, guys, let your dad get back to work." The boys moved past their mother into the hall. Standing by the door, she said, "And, honey, thanks."

"For what?"

"For telling me everything's all right."

As she and the boys vanished from sight, Phil leaned back in his chair and sighed. The twins exchanged glances which asked what that was all about, but despairing of understanding grown-ups, they decided to find something entertaining to do and quietly left. Phil hoped fervently that he hadn't been blowing smoke at Gloria just to soothe her nerves. Since Gabbie's assault, he had also been feeling something alien, something disturbing . . . something impending.

He pushed aside those feelings, judging them nothing more serious than being sensitive to Gloria's worries. He turned his computer on, booting up the word-processing package. Zork was put aside for a while, both because of his frustration in not getting through the gas-filled room, and because he had a notion for another book and wanted to put some things down on paper. He chuckled to himself at that last thought, considering the electronic "paper" he was using. He put a fresh disc in the second drive and began to write. Soon he was lost in thought and caught up in the excitement of a new project begun.

7

Gary whistled in disbelief at the sight of the open chest on the kitchen table, his tired eyes almost lighting up. "I'll be damned." He had taken the red-eye in from Seattle to Buffalo.

Jack, who had picked him up at the airport, said, "Something else, ain't it?"

Gloria handed Gary a cup of coffee, saying, "I've got to admit when you and Mark first told us all those stories about Kessler and the rest, I half didn't believe it. But with the junk in the basement and now this, well . . . you've got to believe."

"Any idea what it's worth?" asked Phil.

Gary took out a coin and examined it. Years of rain had deposited a slight silt crust on it, as the chest was not waterproof. No one had touched the coins since they had been carried two nights before. Gary washed the coin off in the sink and dried it with a paper towel. His eyes widened. He yanked the roll of towels off the holder and began furiously cleaning the dirt off coins at random, laying them out on the table. "I don't believe this."

Phil said, "What is it?"

"I don't know what half these coins are, but I recognize a few." He pointed to a tiny coin resting upon the paper towel. "This is worth maybe a thousand dollars to a collector."

"Really?" commented Phil, beyond surprise at anything at this point.

"It's a five-dollar gold piece, and the only reason I know it's a collector's item is because of a term paper I wrote in high school. I've seen some of these others in textbooks." He held up a large coin. "Unless I'm mistaken, this is an imperial Austrian mark, from the late nineteenth century. This one,"—he indicated a rough coin sitting next to the five-dollar gold coin—"is a Spanish real, about seventeenth-century. And this little guy here is an eight-escudo piece from"—he squinted at the faint lettering—"Peru. Spanish colonial period." He shook his head. "These few are worth easily ten thousand dollars or more, Phil." As if suddenly weary, he pulled out a chair from the table and sat down. He pointed to a coin that was almost worn smooth. "I think that one's Roman."

"So all these have collector's value?" asked Gloria.

"I doubt if more than one coin in fifty in that box isn't worth a lot more than the price of the gold used to make it. Some, like this Roman baby, are maybe worth hundreds of times their weight."

Suddenly the implication of what Gary was saying sunk in. Phil's mouth opened. "My God. That means this box is worth . . ."

"Maybe a million," Gary finished.

"What do we do?" asked Gloria.

"I think," said Gary as he stood up, "you call your lawyer back. Me, I think I'll go home to get some sleep. I've got to call back to Seattle and give some more instructions to the guys and girls working on translating those photocopies I gave them. I left in something of a rush." He half smiled, fatigue evident on his face. Softly he added, "And maybe Mark'll call again one of these days. I'm not worried, but . . . well, I just wish I knew what he's digging up in Europe."

"Yes," said Gabbie, from where she sat on the drainboard. "What have you guys come up with on those documents?"

Gary shrugged. He appeared to be weighing something, as if unsure what to say. At last he said, "Nothing that makes a lot of sense yet. But pieces are starting to fall into place. The best I can judge, Mark was right about there being some sort of secret organization." He seemed about to add something, but stopped.

Gloria noticed and said, "What?"

"Nothing, really," replied Gary. "I'm just tired."

Gloria regarded Gary a moment. "No, you were going to say something. What?"

Gary sighed deeply. "Okay, just for a moment, suppose there was some organization Kessler was involved with. They might know about the gold. And they . . . well, they might not like the idea of someone else's digging it up."

Color drained from Gloria's face, and she threw a look at Phil as if Gary's statement refuted his reassurances of only a few days before. "Maybe we shouldn't tell anyone?"

Phil said, "That cinches it. I'm going to call the police. I'll put this all in the police property room. Then I'll tell the paper about the gold, making sure Malcolm Bishop prints that all the gold is moved. If someone's after this gold, they can try to knock over the police station."

Gary said, "Don't be rash, Phil." Phil's expression showed his surprise at Gary's remark. "I mean, it sounds good to me." He seemed to be forcing a lighter tone to his voice. "You know, I gave up an exhibition game between the Sonics and the Lakers to see all this. But it's worth it." He grinned weakly. "I was coming home soon anyway. I've got to take a trip up to Canada shortly—maybe I'll leave tomorrow—to check up on some things Mark asked me to look into on my way back from Seattle. So, no rest for the wicked." He paused, the smile fading. "Look, what I meant was that maybe your lawyer will consider it rash to tell anyone about all this, even the police. Maybe you should call him back?" Phil considered and Gary added, "Well, can someone drive me home?"

Phil rose. "Sure, I'll get my coat."

Once outside the house, Phil said, "Something really eating you. What is it?"

Gary opened the car door and got in as Phil slid behind the wheel. He was silent a long time while he considered what to say. He was still struggling with what he and Mark had uncovered in the last month. So much of what they had learned was so utterly fantastic, so outside the normal bounds of experience, that even Gary could scarcely believe it. And he was fearful about Mark's absence. He decided to wait a bit before sharing more than was necessary. Perhaps if Mark wasn't back when he returned from Canada, then he might tell Phil what he knew.

Gary looked over to discover Phil regarding him intently. He said, "I didn't want to say anything in front of Gloria. She seems a little . . . on edge these days."

"Well, this stuff in the basement, and the gold . . . it all adds up to some pretty spooky possibilities."

Gary thought about the tape Mark had made, that night in the woods, and for a moment wondered if he wouldn't feel better sharing what he knew with someone. He decided to stay with his decision to wait until after he returned from Canada, and said, "I can't argue with that." He let silence pass between them until Phil started the car and put the transmission in gear.

As they rumbled down the drive toward the road, Gary stared off into the distance. Finally he said, "I didn't mean to upset Gloria back there, Phil."

Phil made a noncommittal noise.

Gary thought about whoever had almost ridden Mark down and the mysterious youth who had saved him, and Mark's claim that Jack's infected shoulder was the result of his being elf-shot. There were possibilities here that deeply disturbed Gary. He was silent until Phil pulled up before the house he and Mark rented. As he reached for the door, he said, "Well then, I'm off to the Great White North tomorrow. If I discover anything that has a bearing on the gold I'll call; otherwise I'll talk to you when I get back."

Phil said good-bye and, the entire way home, couldn't shake the feeling that the discovery of Kessler's gold was destined to be more curse than blessing.

8

Gabbie sat at the kitchen table, attempting a rough organization of the coins. She constantly consulted a pair of primers on coin collecting she had fetched from the local library, which both lay open on the table beside her. The largest pile was German coins, but many others were mixed in. British, French, and Spanish coins from the seventeenth, eighteenth, and nineteenth centuries abounded, but some were much older. Gabbie held out one. "This is Greek, I think."

Jack took it and said, "Look at the color. It's full of impurities, almost red in places."

"Copper," said Gloria from the sink. "That's how they make red gold."

"It's really old," said Gabbie. "And these look like Roman over here."

Jack sat down next to Gabbie. "Someone's been gathering this gold for a hell of a long time."

Phil entered the kitchen; he had returned from taking Gary home and had walked into the house just in time to answer the phone. "Darren called. He's flying out."

"Really?" said Gloria. "He must think this is important stuff to get him out of L.A."

"Important enough he said not to tell anyone about it. He'll be in Buffalo tonight. He's having a notary public meet him at the hotel, first thing tomorrow. They'll be here about ten. He says he wants statements under oath from all of us. He says the best thing to do is to dump this on the IRS, hold our breath, and wait. If no one else has a claim, and there're ways of checking that out, he says, then we'll get it all. We'll have to pay taxes, but under the new tax laws we'll keep more than half. He said otherwise the feds might simply take it and let us bring suit to get it back, which could keep us in court for years."

Jack said, "Half? That's still a lot of bucks."

"Do we call the IRS, or does he?"

Phil said, "He said, 'Do nothing, big en, little oh tee aitch eye en gee.' "

Gabbie said, "Daddy, some of these coins are very rare. There's a couple here that this book say are worth twenty, twenty-five thousand dollars just for one." She grinned. "This is something else. Now I know how those guys who found Tut's tomb must have felt."

Gloria said, "Cursed." The others looked up with startled expressions, and she said, "Just joking, folks." She looked out the window at the deepening rain and wondered why she felt so empty. Somehow she couldn't share in the others' wonder at discovered treasure. Something stirred in the woods, a brief flickering of movement, and was gone. For an instant she felt cold pass through her: what her mother would have called "someone walking on my grave." Then the feeling was gone, leaving behind a residue, a strange mixture of foreboding and resignation. Something was about to happen and she was powerless to stop it. No one could stop it.

Among the trees, under the mantle of rain and wind, they moved. The tall one with the mad eyes, who led, stood closest to the edge of the woods. He looked down upon the human home, with its metals and electricity, and considered. To his companions he said softly, "Soon they will move the hoard off this land, thinking to keep it safe." With a grin, like the rictus of a death's-head, he turned to face his followers. "Then shall we roam unfettered once more." The sky spit lightning and boomed its annoyance, and the glade was empty, as those who had assembled only an instant before were suddenly gone. They vanished into the woods, fading from view like the drops of rain flowing into puddles in the mud.

9

For three days the Hastings house became a camp. Darren Cross, the Hastingses' attorney, had taken one look at the gold and called in a private security agency. Two somber, large, and intimidating men were brought in to ensure that no unpleasant surprises occurred. One was constantly walking perimeter around the house and barn while the other stood quietly in the corner of the kitchen, overseeing the work. At three in the afternoon, they would be replaced by two equally somber, large, and intimidating men who were relieved in turn at eleven by another pair who stayed until seven the next day, when the first two returned. All six men were polite but taciturn, refusing to engage in conversation. Sean was convinced they were CIA.

Darren Cross took depositions from the entire family, including the boys, then packed the notary off with healthy bonuses to ensure silence. He called in an appraiser to develop as clear a picture of worth as possible, as well as an inventory. The coin dealer had almost fainted at the sight of the chest's contents. After only an hour's examination, he had urged that a colleague be called in, maintaining some of the coins were antiquities and outside his expertise. Darren had acquiesced, but only after making sure that security was not compromised, which slowed things down considerably.

The two coin dealers had been housed in the boys' room, at Darren's insistence, to minimize the chance of the story's leaking prematurely. The boys were bunking in their sister's room, while she was staying with Jack at Aggie's. Now the two men had finished the tally and, after several minor arguments, had agreed on the final figures.

Cross, a fat, balding man who thought fashion began and ended with the three-piece grey-pinstriped black suit, sat in the living room, Phil at his side. Gloria sat on the arm of the couch. Nelson Toomes, the first coin dealer consulted, and Murray Parenson, the antiquarian, were sitting in chairs on the other side of the coffee table.

Darren looked at the papers that summarized the find. At last he said, "To all appearances, this is something of a major find, I take it."

Parenson, thin and afflicted with a chronic nervous smile, said, "That is certainly the case. Some of the coins in Mr. Hastings's possession may be one of a kind. There are sixteen that are unique. For that reason their values are hard to determine—we'd only know their true value after seeing what they'd fetch at auction. But despite those small oddities, the bulk of the coins in question have some clear historical value. That value varies from trivial to profound, but there are fewer than a dozen coins worth only slightly more than their gold weight. Those are a few of the more common American and British coins minted in the early part of this century."

Toomes, the coin dealer, interrupted. "Those may not have historical value, but they have collectors' value."

"What's the bottom line?" asked Phil.

"The bottom line is that you're a very rich man," said Cross. "Before, you were simply well off. Now you can retire if you choose."

"How much rich?" asked Gloria.

"We shall have to bump heads with the IRS. They will treat this as found money, much like gambling winnings. They will also closely audit the sales figures. And the market will fluctuate slightly." He glanced at Toomes.

"Very slightly. There are not enough of a single coin, same year and minting, to affect its market value in any significant way."

"So, for the moment, we'll accept these figures." He passed the paper to Phil and pointed at the bottom numbers.

Phil read, blinked, and reread it. Softly he said, "Two million dollars?"

"And some change," said Cross. He pushed his glasses up from the tip of his nose. "About three hundred thousand dollars' worth of change. After taxes, closer to one point four million. Though we can shelter a bit of it, and set up a corporation for you and stick some more in a tax-deferred pension. But you'll give almost a quarter to Uncle."

Phil said, "How do we do this?"

It was Toomes who answered. "There are several major firms across the country who can buy up to a million on the spot. By setting up a syndication of four or five of them, we could take the entire find off your hands for a lump price. The other option is to sell on your behalf, brokering for a fee. You might realize a small price advantage, but it could take a great deal longer, perhaps up to a year to dispose of all the coins."

Gloria said, "Darren?"

"Sell it in a lump, Gloria. You'll lose less than 10 percent by a quick sale, and regain that by investing advantageously over the time it would take to sell it by the piece. Also you'll have it off your hands and off your mind."

"Can you do that?" Phil asked Toomes.

Toomes said, "I'll need permission to forward copies of the inventory we've created, but we'll have no trouble establishing a syndicate. We should be able to agree on a price within a week and make an offer."

"There's no offer," said Cross. "You have the inventory. We'll discount 20 percent for cash. For the sake of simplicity, call the change three hundred thousand. We'll ensure some provision for changes in the market over the next ninety days—the period of time the police will insist the gold be impounded pending any claim. Assuming no such claim is forthcoming, on day ninety-one deliver a check to my client in the amount of one million eight hundred forty thousand dollars and you can send the Brink's truck to pick up your gold. Otherwise, we'll pay your appraising fee and contact your competitors and see who else is willing to establish a syndicate. I assure you, gentlemen, the more work I do, the higher the final price. Should we go to auction, you know the end price will be at least 30 percent higher than the price we will take today. But you must agree now."

Toomes didn't look pleased, but he said, "That should be acceptable, I expect."

Cross smiled a small, tight-lipped smile. "Anything else, gentlemen?"

Parenson said, "There's the matter of those unique coins I mentioned. May I urge you to consider withholding them from sale. By donating them to museums, you could realize some tax advantage, and they'll be held in trust for the public rather than buried in some private collector's vault."

Toomes seemed on the verge of protesting, but Cross cut him off by saying, "I see here that no value was established for those coins, because of their uniqueness. It seems, then, we were speaking of the value of the collection less those . . . ah, sixteen coins." Toomes was clearly becoming irritated. "We shall let you know, gentlemen," Cross said. "If we choose to sell the coins, Mr. Toomes, we shall ask a price adjustment. Otherwise, we shall consider your suggestion, Mr. Parenson. Now, I thank you for your good works, gentlemen, and I'll have a car round to return you to the airport." He glanced at his watch. "You should be leaving within ten minutes if you're to catch your planes."

They left, and Cross said, "I depart tonight, Phil. I've let far too much work go idle on the Coast while we've played treasure hunter. I think all is well in hand here."

Phil said, "I don't know how to thank you, Darren."

"You don't have to thank me. You're about to pay for my grandson's college education. And he will go to Harvard, I expect." Phil laughed. "Now I will go pack, while you call the police. They will want to send a car, and you will insist we bring the gold in ourselves. They shall send a car and escort us as a compromise. We shall provide an inventory and they will want their own property-room people to match the coins to the inventory, which should prove amusing. Then we shall have a final dinner, and I will go back to California. These chilly nights are bothering my arthritis." Without further remark, he trundled up the stairs to pack.

Gloria said, "I'm glad it's over."

"You've been quiet all week, kiddo. Troubles?"

Gloria said, "It's been *Alice in Wonderland* time around here for two weeks. And I'm worried about Mark. He's been gone a lot longer than Gary expected—Gary won't say so, but he's getting worried, too. I'm afraid something may have happened. And I'm still worried about what Gary said."

Phil hugged his wife. "It'll all work out. Now we've this gold business over, we can get back to normal. Loud kids, leaky roofs, a wedding next spring—you know: regular stuff."

She sighed and hugged him back. "Hope you're right. Oh, there's a school Halloween party the boys want to go to. They need some permission slip signed."

"No problem." He stopped and thought. "Halloween's only five days off, isn't it? We'd better stock up on candy."

"Nope. No trick-or-treaters. Some trouble a few years ago with bad candy, so now they have the school parties—one at the primary school for the little guys and another at the high school for the big kids. All we have to do is deliver them and pick them up."

Phil said, "That's simple."

Gloria felt another chill of anticipation, the same that had been troubling her since the gold had been found. Shrugging it off, she said, "Well, we still have to eat. Lunch?"

He smiled. "Thought you'd never ask." Phil slipped his arm around his wife's waist and walked with her toward the kitchen.

10

The police car's motor rumbled, being slightly out of tune. The two officers were relaxed but alert as they observed Phil and Jack lift the wooden strongbox into the trunk of Phil's car. Moments later, Phil and Darren were inside the car and it was crawling down the drive toward the road. Gloria watched it pull away and turned back into the house, closing the door behind her.

From the woods another pair of eyes watched the cars as they moved along the narrow drive to the edge of the property. Phil's car hesitated at the road as cars passed. When the way was clear, it swung out into traffic and picked up speed, the police cruiser following closely.

With a note of satisfaction, echoing menace, the watcher in the trees whispered, "The Compact is broken!" With a spin and a glimmer, he vanished. His companion, hanging from a bare branch above, watched with glowing yellow eyes as the cars disappeared over the hill. The Bad Thing didn't understand all its master's concerns, for it was a simple creature, its intelligence blunted over the years by pain and perversion. But it knew its master was happy, and that was good. That was very good. Perhaps now the master would let him have the dog, or the girl, or better yet, one of the two boys. With a slight sigh, and nursing odd visions of murder in its twisted heart, the Bad Thing crawled up the side of the tree, vanishing in the russet-colored foliage above.

THE FOOL

11

The twins tried to settle in and fall asleep, but couldn't. The wind outside was making odd sounds. The weather had turned cold and blustery in a way alien to them. It was a mean and stinging wind, sucking warmth from the body when it struck, despite the new quilted down jackets purchased from Sears over at the mall. The wind seemed to have started blowing within moments of their father taking away the gold that afternoon. And there was an electric quality to it, a sizzling hum as it tormented the leaves and branches of the tree outside the window. It made Sean feel as if he was holding his breath, waiting for something to happen, as if something was coming closer every minute and now almost upon him. In the upper bunk, he absently rubbed the fairy stone Barney had given him, comforted by its presence. Putting aside his disquiet, he softly called his brother's name.

"What?" came Patrick's sleepy reply.

"What you going to wear?"

Patrick knew Sean was speaking of the Halloween party the following Saturday. In the chaos surrounding the discovery of the gold, no one had talked to the boys about costumes. Then, suddenly, Mom had remembered. They were to have made up their minds by breakfast, and no changing once decided, no getting upset because the other's idea sounded better. There was a momentary pause, then Patrick said, "Dunno. What?"

Sean understood his brother. "Pirate. Captain Billy Kidd."

Patrick laughed. "You dumbass. It's Captain Kidd. Billy the Kid was the outlaw."

Sean lay back staring at the ceiling, feeling slightly embarrassed. "You know what I mean. What are you going to wear?"

"I don't know," answered his brother, his voice betraying an odd irritation. "I was sort of having this dream when you woke me up."

"You weren't asleep," replied his brother, refusing to allow Patrick the opportunity to cast blame.

"Was too," insisted Patrick, but instead of pressing the argument, he said, "In the dream I . . . saw this guy in a neat knight's suit. You know, armor and swords and a horse. Maybe I'll go as a knight."

Sean said, "Dream?"

"Yeah, a creepy one. But the knight suit was neat. It had these horn things, you know, like deers've got, on the head. And the guy rode a neat horse. And he was shining."

Sean didn't answer. He had lain awake while his brother had the dozing dream. But in Sean's imagination he had seen the alien knight, despite his attempts to turn his thoughts away from the figure. He had watched in silent darkness as the figure had become more concrete in appearance, more distinct every passing minute in his mind. But Patrick was wrong about the dream, or vision, as Sean thought of it. It hadn't been creepy. It had been terrifying. Sean almost audibly sighed. Patrick was often amused by what frightened Sean. The more timid brother hid those things from Patrick, for it was the one area where Sean felt inadequate. He might be more sensitive than his twin, but like all children everywhere, he felt the need to avoid being labeled different by anyone in his peer group. There's nothing worse than being called "wimp," "spaz," or "nerd" by your classmates.

The twins lapsed into silence. Soon Sean was in a half-dreamy state, lulled in part by his brother's rhythmic breathing as Patrick quickly fell asleep. But each time sleep approached Sean, a change in the wind, an odd noise—the house creaking, perhaps—something would yank him awake again. For a long time this condition persisted. Sean forced himself to close his eyes. For a while he lay silent, attempting to sleep, but he only managed a restless half-doze. The fluting wind outside heralded something approaching, getting closer by the minute. Sean tossed fitfully, unable to rest, for each passing minute the feeling grew stronger. Something *was* coming.

Sean's eyes snapped open and his little heart pounded as he sensed the inpending arrival of something terrible. Then a gasp of fear jerked him rigid, as he was struck by a suddenly overwhelming sense of danger. It wasn't coming! *It was here!*

It was the same terror as the night the Bad Thing had come into their room, but it was now ten times worse. Sean lay frozen, afraid to look, barely able to breathe. There was an odd sound in the corner, a movement, a slight scrape of weight shifting against the wall, but it also echoed with an overtone like music, alien and terrifying. Then the smell of flowers and spices reached Sean. With a sharp intake of breath he pulled his covers up to his face, peeking over to look across the room.

Someone stood in the corner.

Hidden in the darkness of the farthest corner, he was motionless, but his outline could be faintly seen. Then he moved slightly. A hint of silver-blue shimmers, like luminosity on a warm ocean tide at night, flickered across his body, as if the act of moving released energies. Instantly after being seen, the luminosity faded and the shape faded into shadows, motionless, silent, and unseen, but there.

Sean *felt* him there. Cold terror clutched at the boy's chest. He fought to will breath into his lungs, so he could shout, but sound lay beyond his ability. He could not move. Time ceased to pass and in the boundless space between moments he lay trapped, motionless, petrified by the knowledge that something waited across the room, unmoving, soundless, invisible, but its presence made known by an aura so chilling it froze the boy's heart. And it stood only three strides away. Sean's teeth began to chatter and his hands shook as he clutched the blanket under his chin. Then, with a sound little more than a strangled sigh, the thing in the corner moved.

Sean could make out no detail of appearance; he could see only the faint blue shimmer briefly across the thing's body, as if dim phosphors were painted on a featureless black mannequin. The silhouette was of a tall, thin man, his body moving with the controlled flow of a dancer, his muscles as smooth as unrippled water. Details of appearance, color of hair and eyes, tone of skin, shape of face, were obscured by either inky blackness or bluish glow. All this was insignificant to Sean. He only knew the man was there for the boys.

And he knew one other thing: this blue-glowing, dark man was an evil far beyond the Bad Thing.

The dark man moved to stand in the middle of the room, his face almost but, maddeningly, not quite seen. The shape of his head was long, the chin somehow too narrow, but no detail of eye or lips, hair or brow showed. He laughed, a distant, wind-hollow echo, a sound from ages past. Sean lay motionless, the covers pulled up to his face, as his stomach knotted at the sound. He followed the movement of the dark man as he slowly walked toward the door near the head of the bunk beds. The boy following with his eyes until the dark man was at the limit of his field of vision. From the corner of his eye, Sean suddenly caught a glimpse of a face. He turned to look again and detail vanished, as if to look straight at the man lost one the ability to see him. Sean sat up, terrified that his movement had somehow betrayed him, but unable to remain motionless. Still he could see only the hint of a figure in the room. In silent fear, Sean turned his head away. As he did so, the man's face reappeared for an instant. Sean tried to avert his eyes, as if not looking would make the faintly glowing, spectral figure go away, but he couldn't. His gaze was trapped and held by a terrible fascination. He sat motionless save for his trembling, his breath coming in shallow gasps, his teeth chattering. For an instant he could make out features in the dim mask, as the man smiled. His teeth were perfect, meeting in a grin like a skull's, seeming to glow in the black face. And in that death's-head grin Sean saw terror and madness come to steal Patrick and himself away, before the features vanished again.

With a silent gasp, a gulping of breath, Sean flattened his back against the wall, halfway between the foot and head of the bed. He tried to close his eyes and will away the vision, but couldn't. All he wanted to do was curl up in a ball and hide in a warm safe place. But he could not move. He was held motionless by something alien to his child's nature. He was frozen by hopelessness.

The dark man stepped forward, closing the distance to the bedside, as if to get a better look at the boys. Other shapes moved at his feet, as if smaller creatures accompanied him. Sean forced muscles locked with rigor to move and slowly turned away, his cheek and side pressed against the wall, watching the terrifying man from the corner of his eye. "Patrick," he barely got out in a hoarse croak. Then the man stood beside the bunk beds.

Softly, with a voice like a thousand whispers, the man spoke. "Two." It was a hot summer night's breeze giving voice to a word and that word was despair.

To Sean it felt as if a hand had reached into the pit of his being and seized him in a searing grip that would never let go. Then came the small, mad chuckle and Sean's eyes watered with tears of fright. His stomach knotted again, as if he was going to vomit, and he swallowed hard, forcing back the sour taste rising into his mouth. He wished nothing more than to scream for Mommy and Daddy, but no sounds came forth. The scream was trapped within, fighting to escape. He couldn't take his eyes from the figure by the bedside. Seen this close, the man was glowing, surrounded by a faint nimbus of silver-white light, cut with blue energies, his features still unseen. But now Sean could see the suggestion of eyes in the black face.

The dark man bent down, a moment out of Sean's view, and the boy felt an odd, cold stab in his chest, as if the hand that had reached inside a moment earlier had torn something precious from deep within. He knew the man had Patrick! Sean felt the scream within battering against whatever held it in check, frantic to get out. Sean swallowed hard, his throat constricted in fear, and managed to gulp down a breath of air.

Then the dark man rose up before Sean, Patrick lying asleep in his outstretched arms. Suddenly the man shifted Patrick, holding him cradled like a rag doll in his left arm, as his right hand snaked forward toward Sean.

In a hoarse whisper, little more than a dry croak, Sean said, "Mommy."

A whispering echo played in the room, mocking him as it sang, "Mommy, Mommy, Mommy," getting fainter and fainter.

The faint, glowing hand hesitated and the dark man withdrew it. In a harsh whisper he uttered a single word. "Ward."

Sean gripped the fairy stone tightly, shaking his head as he repeated his almost inaudible cry: "Mommy." Again came the mocking echo, repeating the word over and over, softly, quietly, offering no hope of being heard outside the room.

The dark man, his ghost voice sounding like a thousand fluting reeds in the wind, spoke. "Remove it."

Sean suddenly moved, his skin prickling with an alien fever, as if this dark terror radiated heat. He scuttled to the head of the bed, trying to get as far from the glowing black figure as he could. He pushed himself as deep into the corner as possible, his small feet scraping against the sheets and covers. Tears ran down his face as his eyes were locked, staring at the invader. Patrick nestled in the man's arm like a kitten and his eyes were vacant, his expression slack-jawed. He seemed without color, faded to grey half-tones. "The ward, boy!" The voice was as soft and quiet as before, but more commanding. When Sean remained motionless, the dark man signaled toward him.

Suddenly the Bad Thing sprang from the floor to the foot of the bed. It scampered forward, to squat before Sean. Large brown eyes, surrounding whites a luminous yellow, were set in a face like a demented monkey's, with the fangs of a baboon seeming to glow as it grinned at Sean. Its body looked like a tiny man's, but with too many joints in the too long arms and legs, and its skin was a sooty charcoal color, like an ancient mummy's or a bat's. It stank of things dead for ages, and its hot and repulsive breath blew in Sean's face as it made slobbering, sucking sounds. A taloned hand reached for the boy, but hesitated.

Suddenly another figure leaped up from below, and Sean's heart jumped. Patrick stood crouching upon the foot of the bed. Then Sean saw that it wasn't Patrick, but some evil caricature of himself! The boy was physically identical to Sean, but was nude, and his head moved in an odd fashion, much like a monkey's in the way it turned one way and another as he regarded Sean. The doppelgänger absently played with himself as he watched Sean, again like a monkey in the zoo. An evil leering grin was fixed in place as he reached out to touch Sean. Like the Bad Thing, when he came close to the ward he yanked his hand away.

Sean's eyes were wide, whites showing completely around the irises, and tears streamed down his cheeks. His nose ran and his mouth worked silently. The creatures seemed to struggle against something as they reached toward the fairy stone around the boy's neck. Once, twice, three times in turn, each tried to grasp the ward, only to halt scant inches away. At last the Bad Thing turned to face the dark man and spoke. Its words were twisted, a mockery of human speech, slurred and thick, as if the tongue were the wrong size and the mouth filled with cotton. "Master. Hurts." The false Sean's mouth opened wide and he hooted, a mad monkey sound.

Sean's tremble turned to more violent shaking, a near-uncontrollable palsy throughout his body. His skin burned with a poison fever. A miasma of evil washed over him, filling his nostrils, forcing breath from his lungs, choking him, threatening to drown him in mindless panic. Sean's jaw worked as he struggled to cry for help, but all that came forth was short, pitiful yelps, almost inaudible against the wind howling outside.

Sean saw the Bad Thing turn to regard him once more, and again the clawed black hand came forward, as if to touch him.

For a terror-torn instant, Sean's mind sought to flee his body, and he felt himself almost lift from the bed by force of will. Like an overwound watch spring, the tension became too much to endure. Like a captive animal crashing the bars of his cage, he sought escape and, finding none, redoubled his fury. Again the Bad Thing reached toward the boy, and withdrew his hand. Sean whispered, "Mommy."

The strangled note of a tormented violin mocked him as the Bad Thing grinned and repeated the word. "Mommy, Mommy, Mommy," it sang, its breath filling Sean's nostrils with the stench of decay, its face set in a happy mask, as if something in that word amused or pleased it. The mock Sean mouthed the word as the Bad Thing sang it, but the sound produced was an animal grunt.

Then the dark man leaned close, until his face was scant inches from Sean's. Suddenly he was alight, in an intense glow that hurt Sean's eyes. And for the brief instant of that shining brilliance, Sean saw the face of the man. Eyes, set in deep sockets, locked with Sean's and Sean felt his mind twist, as a long, low, pain-filled sound at last escaped the boy's lips. For in those eyes Sean saw lightning dance, as electric-blue orbs sought to burn his soul. A beauty so pure it was terrifying greeted Sean in that instant, something alien, beyond the ability of the human mind to accept. And in that instant Sean wanted nothing more than to give up all will and go with the man, and in that rush of unexpected longing came a desire so concrete Sean's body rocked. For that desire was something he was not ready for, something reserved for changes not yet come, when love and tenderness turned to passion. But now it struck Sean with a wanton heat, a hunger so intensely sexual that his body could not interpret his desires. Sean found his child's penis stiffening unexpectedly, while his body shuddered and his skin prickled with chill bumps. Perspiration poured off his body, soaking his pajamas. He looked over at his false twin and found a leering creature squatting a few feet away, his tongue lolling out of his mouth as he fondled himself, rocking from side to side, a reflection in a befouled glass made solid. The evil twin's eyes were wide like Sean's, but, rather than terror, his expression was one of perverted, inhuman desire.

Sean's heart pounded in his chest and he could endure no more. His bowels contracted, and his tiny erection vanished as his bladder emptied. His stomach spasmed as if a knot were pulled tight. And in that instant of blinding light, of adult longings shocking his child's body, of beautiful passions twisted to black lust, Sean knew a thing. It was a thing that he had thought he had known before, when the Bad Thing had first come to their room, or when Patrick had been swept away in the storm. But those encounters had been but grey shadows compared to this ultimate black. The thing Sean knew was horror. It had passed through him and surrounded him, and now it was made solid. And it stood before him in the guise of the being he would ever after know as the Shining Man. That recognition triggered the release of all that was trapped inside.

Sean screamed.

Beyond anything he would have dreamed possible, he screamed, a sound to pierce the soul. He screamed so loud that it seemed his mother's voice was answering before the sound had finished echoing down the hall to the stairway.

Time froze for Sean, and a dozen images came crashing in upon him. The light about the Shining Man vanished, returning him to darkness surrounded by a faint blue glow. He moved, and Sean glimpsed his face from the corner of his eye. For an instant Sean saw an inhuman expression of hate so evil and demented that nothing in the world could frighten the boy after seeing that. Sean continued screaming. The Bad Thing tumbled back, away from the sudden sound, unsure of what to do, while the false Sean rolled backward with a monkey's shriek, to fall out of sight, landing at the foot of the bed.

Sean could see the Shining Man holding Patrick in his arm like a baby doll. His brother seemed pale, without color. Sean's screaming continued. From the hallway he could hear his parents calling his name and his brother's, Gabbie's voice asking what was wrong. Bad Luck was scrambling up the stairs, his bark challenging anything that would harm his family. Sean continued to scream.

The Shining Man again stepped toward Sean, reaching for him. He snatched his hand away, as if conceding Sean was beyond his ability to capture. A hollow sigh of resignation was followed by the distant voice saying, "We will meet again." Then came a laugh so chilling it punched through the scream.

Sean knew despair.

The Shining Man retreated into the corner. The Bad Thing and the false Sean scurried to stand at their master's feet, while the Shining Man held Patrick in the crook of his arm as if he weighed nothing. The remaining glow around him faded, and gloom drank all sight of the four figures in the corner.

Then the room light blazed into being and Gloria stood in the door. She froze for an instant as she saw the dark creatures crouched in the corner beneath the man figure that held one of her sons in his arms. All were still shadows, as if the room light couldn't quite vanquish the murk. Then the dark figures were gone. Gloria paused in mid-step, blinking in confusion, not believing her senses. The instant passed. Gloria shook her head slightly, as if clearing her vision. She glanced down to see Patrick still in his bunk, asleep, as she moved to the bedside. Reaching for Sean, she said, "Honey! What is it?"

Sean shivered and quaked, unable to control himself. He had wet the bed and filled his pajama bottoms. His eyes refused to focus. His mouth was wide, the jaw flexing as his throat-tearing shriek continued, saliva running down his chin, and his body was drenched in sweat. His breath was sour with fear. He could only make one sound: *the scream.*

The scream became reality for Sean. It was something tangible in a world twisted to insubstantial insanity. He could hide within the scream, cover himself in it, wrap it around his family and shelter all within its folds, shaped and molded into a safe place to hide. His throat was raw, and his body ached with tension and pain where fear tried to seep through the skin like a thick burning poison, but the scream continued, reassuring and real. It filled the room, surrounding him and his family with a concrete barrier, as real as wood, or stone, or steel. The scream went on and on, for Sean knew that the moment he stopped, the Shining Man and his companions would come back and get Sean's mother and father and Gabbie.

Phil entered the room and came to the bedside; Gabbie stood in the doorway, her expression one of alarm as Phil knelt by the lower bunk. Gloria reached out to touch Sean, but the boy pulled away, as if trying to crawl deeper into the corner. "Sean! What is it, baby?" Her voice rose, as if her disorientation at what she had glimpsed as she entered the room was being compounded by his terror. "Baby, what is it? Please stop screaming. It's all right." Her eyes were brimming and her face reflected the pain and the fear she felt within him.

Sean wanted to tell her it wasn't all right, and he knew his mother understood it wasn't all right, she was only saying that; he could see that in her face, but he knew he couldn't stop the scream to tell her. If he stopped, they'd all be trapped by the Shining Man. All he could do was point at the corner, point and scream. He pointed and tried to make them understand. His right hand pointed and his left pounded the wall, to make them understand. He rocked back and forth and shook from side to side, hitting the wall to make them understand. Gloria stood with her hand poised halfway to her son, made helpless by something beyond her ability to comprehend. In her son she saw torment visited upon the innocent and she stood powerless to help him. Sean screamed.

"Oh my God!" cried Phil, and Gabbie gripped the doorjamb, her knuckles whitening.

"What!" demanded Gloria, almost jumping with fright at his tone.

"Patrick's unconscious. He's burning up with fever. Oh God. Gabbie, call the hospital and tell them we're coming." Phil bundled Patrick in a blanket and carried him down the hall.

Gloria forced herself to reach out and touch Sean, and said, "He's burning up, too." Spurred by the need to care for her son, she ignored the wet blanket and the soiled condition of his pajamas and swept the still-shrieking boy into her arms, gathering the blanket around him. Letting the urgency of the moment banish from her memory the confusing, frightening sight that had greeted her at the door of the boys' room, she raced down the hall after her husband.

Gabbie hurried back into her room and grabbed the receiver off the phone by her bed, dialing the operator, asking to be connected to the hospital emergency room. From outside she heard her father's car starting up, then the tires spraying gravel as he sped down the drive. And into the night, seemingly long after she stopped hearing the car, Gabbie could hear Sean screaming.

12

The emergency room staff was ready even before Phil's car had halted before the hospital entrance. Phil held Patrick's limp form while Gloria carried Sean. He had not stopped screaming the entire way to the hospital, but his throat was worn to the point where he could manage only a faintly scratchy, hoarse sound. The E.R. staff's professional detachment was unexpectedly reassuring to Gloria, as if whatever was wrong with her boys was only an interesting problem to be solved, nothing to get excited about. The boys were placed on examining tables. Each boy had two nurses beside him. The young doctor in charge, a thin man with a slight New York City accent, listened to the nurse reading vital signs while he examined the boys. He ordered a mild sedative to calm Sean, then became alarmed when the nurse read him Patrick's temperature. "One hundred six."

In calm tones he said, "Okay, it's spiking. Let's get him monitored and bring that sucker down."

A nurse wheeled over a digital thermometer and inserted a rectal probe into Patrick while another began rubbing him down with alcohol. The LED readout on the thermometer's display showed 106.2. After a few minutes it rose to 106.4. "Doctor," said the nurse in a calm, professional manner. "It's going up."

The young doctor glanced at the machine, nodded curtly once and said, "Right; let's pack him in ice."

They picked Patrick up and put a rubber sheet under him. A male nurse brought out two large buckets of ice and began putting handfuls around Patrick, while another nurse held the rubber sheet to keep the ice from spilling from the table. When the ice was covering Patrick, she folded the sheet across his body. The doctor turned away from Patrick to examine Sean. Gloria said, "What are you doing to Patrick?"

To Phil the doctor said, "Why don't you take a seat in the waiting room and I'll be with you in a minute." When Gloria seemed ready to argue, he said calmly, "Lady, we've got a couple of very sick kids here. Let us take care of them, all right?"

Phil guided his wife from the room and they sat on a vinyl-covered couch. The only sound beside the soft voices of the emergency room staff was the whir of a loud electric clock on the wall. Phil glanced at it and saw it read twelve-twenty in the morning. Phil's fog of concern was pierced by the realization that Gloria was trembling.

Gloria kept her eyes upon the emergency room, where strangers worked quickly to save her children, but her mind's eye kept seeing a remembered image, a strange momentary flicker of darkness in the corner of the boys' room when she had first entered, and the certainty, for just an instant, that Patrick had been in the corner, surrounded by that darkness. She couldn't put that image, or the feeling that somehow it was something dimly remembered from her own childhood, from her mind. She sighed and steeled herself against the doctor's confirming her worst fears, that somehow her boys were lost to her forever.

Phil reached out and gathered his wife to him, letting her rest her head on his shoulder. He attempted to reassure her with a squeeze, but both knew there was no reassurance for either of them this night. They settled in to wait.

13

Jack passed coffee around. He and Gabbie had arrived twenty minutes after Phil and Gloria. Gabbie had called over to Aggie's and he had come at once. He had scouted out a coffee machine and brought a cup for everyone. Gloria's sat cooling before her as she leaned forward in her seat, motionless, eyes fixed upon the door to the E.R.

A half hour after Jack and Gabbie arrived, the young doctor came from the emergency room, a file under his arm and a mug of coffee in his hand. Gloria almost jumped to her feet. "How are our boys, Dr. . . . ?"

"Murphy, Jim Murphy, Mrs. Hastings." The doctor sat opposite them in the waiting area. He sipped the coffee, and Gloria suddenly became aware she was the only one standing. She sat as Dr. Murphy opened the file and said, "The boy who was conscious—"

"Sean," supplied Phil.

"Sean," continued the doctor, "was pretty agitated. But besides a high fever—with no obvious cause—we've found nothing wrong with him. We've sedated him and are moving him to the pediatric ward. If nothing turns up in a day, he can come home. The other boy"—he glanced at the file—"Patrick, is another matter. He had a spiking fever, over a hundred six and . . . well, we've got it down, but we need to watch him closely." Even as he spoke, two orderlies were wheeling Patrick out of the E.R.

Gloria watched the gurney roll out of sight and said, "Where are you taking him?"

There was a note of panic in her voice that made the doctor look at her a long moment before answering. Softly he said, "We need to watch him very closely. We're moving him to intensive care."

Immediately panic was apparent in Gloria's eyes. "Intensive care! My God, what's wrong!"

The doctor attempted to be reassuring. "Mrs. Hastings, Patrick had a very high fever. We've lowered it to around a hundred and one degrees, but we're keeping it there for a while. With a very high fever, the body often loses its ability to regulate its own temperature. We just want to watch Patrick closely for the rest of the night as a safety measure." He glanced back at the forms Phil had helped the admitting nurse fill out. "The truth is we don't have a clue to what is wrong with your boys. We can rule out a lot of things just due to their not having any complaints before bedtime. It might be some odd sort of food poisoning, but the rest of you weren't affected."

"Dr. Murphy, the boys were fine at bedtime," said Phil.

"I know, Mr. Hastings. My guess is we've got a pretty rugged virus that hits hard and fast. But until we get some lab work done in the morning, we are only guessing. All we can do now is make the boys comfortable, stay alert, treat them symptomatically, and begin work first thing tomorrow. And the rest of you should take it easy. If it is a virus, something they picked up at school, it may hit you as well in the next few days. If any of you start feeling poorly, at the first sign of a symptom I suggest you check back here at once. If it's a virus, it's a nasty customer."

Gloria seemed unable to move or speak, her eyes wide with an almost panic-stricken look. She seemed to shiver. The doctor said, "Ma'am, we're doing everything possible." She didn't speak, managing only a tiny nod. The doctor said, "I'm going to write out a prescription for a tranquilizer, Mr. Hastings. I think it might be a good idea for you and your wife to each take one tonight. We won't even begin to have a picture of what's going on until tomorrow afternoon."

Gloria leaned heavily against Phil, who said, "Thank you, Doctor."

The doctor rose and crossed to the nurses' station, where he scribbled on a prescription tablet. He handed it to Jack. "You can fill this at the pharmacy in the front lobby. They're open all night." Jack hurried off. The doctor said, "You folks really should go home. I'm afraid this may take a long time. You should count on Patrick's being here for a few days at least."

Gloria leaned against Phil, her head on his shoulder. She closed her eyes a moment and again saw the image of the darkness in the corner of the boys' room. A faint memory of a sound, like wind chimes in the distance, and a vague spicy smell of flowers were recalled, and for an instant she felt a stab of panic.

Gloria stood disoriented, as if trying to focus her vision. Phil saw the panic in her eyes. He held tight to her hand and said, "It'll be all right, honey. They're doing everything possible."

Gloria seemed not to hear her husband. She looked wildly around the room. Suddenly she let out an anguished cry. "Patrick!" She moved forward, as if to run toward the ICU. Gabbie and Phil restrained her, and her voice held a hysterical note as it rose in pitch.

The doctor yelled to the nurses' station for a sedative, which a nurse quickly produced. He injected the frantic Gloria, and within a minute she lapsed into a half-dazed state. Jack returned with the prescription and took in at once what had occurred. The doctor said, "I think you should all get home and salvage whatever's left of a night's sleep. And before you come back, you might do well to take one of those pills I prescribed, but have someone else drive you."

"Thank you," said Phil. He said to Jack, "See Gloria and Gabbie get home, will you."

Gabbie put her hand upon her father's arm. "Dad?"

"I'm staying."

The doctor was about to protest, but something in Phil's eyes caused him to relent. "All right, I'll pass word to the nurses on the Peds floor that you're allowed to spend the night in Sean's room. But the ICU's off limits." Phil looked as if he was going to object, but the doctor said, "That's not negotiable. No visitors in the ICU longer than ten minutes and then only during visiting hours. No exceptions, Mr. Hastings."

Phil agreed and sent Gabbie and Jack off with his wife. He thanked the doctor and took the elevator up to Pediatrics, noticing from the directory on the elevator wall that the ICU was two floors below. He checked at the nurses' station and was told that Sean was in room 512. He went there and found Sean asleep in a semiprivate room. The other bed stood empty.

Phil leaned against the railing of the bed. He looked down at his little boy's face, and in Sean's face he saw Patrick's. He hid his eyes and began to weep. Throughout his life Philip Hastings considered himself a rational man, one who had had to deal with the craziness of a first wife with a capricious nature and a career in a field where abrupt and unpredictable changes were the norm. He had thought himself a man able to cope with the unexpected. But this was bringing him to his knees.

Never comfortable with displays of strong emotion, Phil struggled to pull himself together. He considered the empty bed for a moment, then decided against it. Something about using a hospital bed repulsed him. He crossed to the large chair next to Sean's bed and settled in. Within a few minutes the late hour and emotional fatigue took its toll and he drifted off to an uneasy doze.

Phil felt himself adrift in a grey landscape, a place of half-light dotted by lightning-shattered black trees, a murky and lifeless forest where shadowy figures moved just outside the range of his vision. Odd-sounding whispers, almost understandable, tantalized with their near familiarity, but comprehension eluded him. Then a distant voice called to him. It was Patrick! He could hear him calling, "Daddy!"

Phil sat bolt upright, heart racing, as the calm voice on the hospital's public address system repeated its message. He blinked, found himself bathed in a cold sweat, and shook his head to clear his foggy brain. The voice again repeated its message. "Code Blue, ICU. Dr. Murphy to ICU, stat."

Phil was moving past the nurses' station before the duty nurse could speak to him. He passed the elevator and took the stairway down, two steps at a time. Two floors below Sean's room he pushed on the crash bar of the large door and entered a lobby. Double doors proclaimed he stood before the ICU and that admittance was restricted. He pushed through and found himself next to a nurses' station composed of six sets of monitors, opposite a glass wall through which he could see six beds. Over one a group of doctors worked furiously, while a nurse charged out to intercept Phil.

Without apology, she roughly grabbed him. "Sir, you cannot stay here."

Phil, half-numb, allowed himself to be pushed back through the doors by the small woman. Outside he said, "What . . . ?"

"The doctor will speak to you as soon as he's able." She hurried back through the doors and left Phil alone in the waiting area.

An hour later Dr. Murphy came out and sat down before Phil. "Mr. Hastings . . ." He paused. "Look, I've never been good with bedside manners, so I'll just come out and say it. Patrick's had what we call a cardiac episode."

"A heart attack?" said Phil in disbelief.

The doctor looked fatigued. "Not quite. A mild fibrillation. It's under control, and we're watching him closely. The boy's body has undergone a lot of punishment in the last six hours . . . and sometimes things like this happen. A lot of the body's regulatory functions get fouled up."

"But he's okay?"

"As far as the cardiac part is concerned, I think so. There are some tests down the road we can do to determine if there's been any permanent damage to the heart muscles. But . . ."

"What?" said Phil, feeling a dread certainty something terrible had taken place.

The doctor rose. "Come with me, Mr. Hastings."

Phil followed the young doctor back into the ICU and saw another doctor and several nurses standing in the hall between the nurses' station and the beds, watching the displays above Patrick's head with rapt expressions on their faces.

With a note of fatigue in his voice, Dr. Murphy said, "Mr. Hastings, Patrick's fever was terribly high and lasted . . . who knows how long? I'm afraid we may find some pretty serious neurological damage."

"Neurological?" Phil whispered, as if the word was alien, the meaning unknown.

"Brain damage, Mr. Hastings," said the doctor, obviously finding the words distasteful.

Phil's eyes closed as he winced at the words. "How badly damaged?" he asked quietly.

The doctor shook his head. "Normally, I wouldn't think he'd make it."

"What do you mean, 'normally'?"

Dr. Murphy pointed to the array of machines attached to Patrick. The screens were alive with dancing lines, flipping around at a frantic rate. "See those monitors, Mr. Hastings?" Phil nodded. "They tell us what's going on with Patrick, moment to moment."

He crossed to one screen next to the bed. "This is an electroencephalograph, an EEG." His finger pointed to three jagged lines on the screen, moving furiously. "If Patrick were brain-dead, these would be flat."

"Then he's all right?" said Phil.

Murphy said, "Mr. Hastings, I'm only a second-year resident. Right now I don't know my own name. I've never seen anything remotely like it—and I doubt our resident neurosurgeon has either. This is as far removed from a normal brain wave pattern as anything I've seen in any text on the subject. Right now I can't even begin to tell you what's happening with your son."

"Is Patrick all right?"

Murphy crossed back to Phil's side, took him by the arm, and steered him back toward the door to the waiting area. "Mr. Hastings, I don't have the faintest idea." He took Phil outside.

Phil sat down and looked at the doctor. "What do we do?"

"First thing tomorrow, I'm going to call in Dr. Wingate, he's head of service in neurosurgery. He may be able to figure out what's going on, but beyond that I don't have a clue."

Phil sat back. After a minute he closed his eyes. The doctor sat there a long minute at his side. Then a call sounded over the public address, announcing another emergency in E.R. Dr. Murphy stood up. There was nothing more he could do here.

While Phil sat numbly outside, one of the ICU nurses glanced through the glass at Patrick's bed. For a brief instant she could have sworn she had seen a flicker around the boy, as if some sort of energy had glowed forth, then faded. She chalked it up to the frantic Code Blue and fatigue, and all the weird displays. She glanced over at Patrick's monitor screens, duplicates of the ones in his room, and shook her head. If anything went wrong, how would she know? The screens were unreadable. She looked at her watch and saw she would be off in two more hours; then it would be someone else's headache. She returned to filling out her half-hourly reports.

In the bed behind the glass, beneath the white sheet, Patrick's feet moved, an imperceptible flexing of muscles as if, in a dream, he was dancing in glee, and a tiny smile creased the corners of his mouth for an instant. Then the movement stopped.

14

Gabbie stood in the doorway, looking down at her father as he sat staring at Sean. Jack had dropped her off at the entrance while he went to hunt up a parking place. She had arrived a moment before. She looked over her father's shoulder at the sleeping boy, who moved restlessly. Finally she said, "Dad?"

Phil looked up and Gabbie felt as if her heart were about to break, seeing the pain in his eyes. She hurried to his side and knelt. Gripping his hand, she said, "Dad?"

With a voice made hoarse by emotion he said, "Hi, honey."

Gabbie's eyes brimmed with tears, for without his saying anything else, she knew something terrible was happening with Patrick. Gabbie fought grief for a long, silent time, until Jack quietly entered the room.

As if by signal a nurse arrived to inform them there were too many people in the room. Something in her manner triggered Gabbie. Like fury embodied, the girl stood to confront the nurse and snapped, "Where's the doctor?" She kept her voice low, but her tone was sharp.

The nurse, a veteran of many a tragic scene, was nevertheless caught off balance by the girl's sudden, angry tone. She backed off a step. "I'll have Dr. Murphy paged . . . miss."

Jack came up behind Gabbie and said, "Patrick?"

Gabbie only nodded her head slightly, and she felt Jack tense as a sad and resigned sigh escaped from his lips. Shortly after, Dr. Murphy appeared. Gabbie spoke softly, but there was no hesitation as she asked, "Doctor, is my brother dead?"

Dr. Murphy glanced past her at Phil, who nodded. The doctor motioned for Gabbie and Jack to join him in the hall. Outside of the room, he said, "No, Miss Hastings, your brother isn't dead. He suffered a terribly high fever last night, which seems to have done something odd to his higher brain functions. Right now we've got him hooked to a battery of monitoring devices, but to be honest, we don't have a clue to what's going on with your brother."

"Is he going to be all right?" Gabbie demanded.

The doctor seemed uncertain for a moment. "Miss, we just don't know yet."

Gabbie stood as if struck. Then at last she softly said, "When will you know?"

"We're having Dr. Wingate, our very best neurosurgeon, look at him right now. He's very sharp. He'll . . . level with you and your dad. I noticed that Patrick had been admitted for some cuts a while back and you indicated John Latham was your doctor. He'll be here shortly and I'll speak to him first thing. They'll come talk to your dad."

Gabbie nodded as she glanced through the door at Phil. He sat staring at Sean's face, seemingly oblivious to Gabbie's conversation.

With a sick feeling inside, Gabbie said, "Thank you, Doctor." She went to her father's side, leaning over to hug him.

Dr. Murphy watched her and for a moment considered what a stunning young woman she was. Then, putting aside a momentary flash of interest, he considered the presence of the attentive young man. To him he said, "She's something."

Jack said, "Well I know, Doctor," as he left to follow her.

In Sean's room, Gabbie sat oblivious to the discomfort of the chair arm she perched upon as she hugged her father tightly. Jack came up beside her and put his hand upon her shoulder. No words were spoken. All they could do was wait.

Two floors below, a nurse glanced through the glass partition at Patrick. As she looked away, she caught a glimpse of movement and quickly looked back. The boy lay exactly as he had since she had come on duty, but somehow she had thought, for a moment, that he had moved. Imperceptibly, perhaps, but she couldn't shake the feeling that he *had* moved. She glanced at the readouts from Patrick's monitors, but the chaotic displays were still unreadable. Shrugging off the feeling, she muttered to herself, "Too many years to be getting jumpy. I think I need a vacation."

In an alien land, Patrick struggled to hear a distant voice. His mother's? Then the voice faded and his attention returned to his surroundings. So strange, he thought. The black trees and the distant stars, the fragrances on the warm wind. Thoughts came like light fighting through a dim and heavy fog; Patrick knew something was wrong, but he didn't know what, and in an odd detached way, he really didn't care. He let his mind wander, and soon the voice was forgotten.

15

Dr. Theodore Wingate examined the printout from the computer with the data from the monitoring station at the ICU. Dr. Latham stood behind the neurosurgeon while he examined the fanfold paper. Dr. Murphy was with Patrick.

Phil sat with the doctors in Wingate's office. Gabbie and Jack were due to arrive soon to pick up Sean, who was going to be released today. Gloria was home, under sedation, being looked after by Aggie.

Wingate had a rough manner, all grumbles and complaints, but Phil had quickly seen through him: Teddy Wingate was a considerate, kind man, a competent neurosurgeon who put on a constant show of being beset and put upon by everyone he met. But behind the bluster was a warm person who had everyone on a first-name basis within a minute of introduction. He put down the readouts and pushed up the small Ben Franklin glasses that had migrated to the tip of his nose. He had a roundish face and his hair was prematurely white, which set off his ruddy complexion. He seemed to be constantly struggling inside his rumpled suit to find a comfortable position. In a soft voice he said, "Phil, I don't know what this all means."

Phil sighed. He found this uncertainty oppressive, and with each passing hour he found himself becoming increasingly impatient. "What do we do?"

"We wait," said Wingate softly. "Phil, Patrick underwent a severe fever, which damaged his brain in some way." He glanced at the read-outs. "Apparently, higher functions are scrambled. His brain activity is . . . unique. I can't even tell you what's making his heart pump and his lungs breathe. He's over that cardiac crisis, but why he's even alive . . . Phil, I don't know what the hell I'm talking about. It may be there was some sort of brain . . . short circuit that will sort itself out. It may be he's . . . gone for good. But I just don't know. I can't begin to guess what we're looking at with these readouts. I'm sorry."

"What am I to do?" Phil asked in a hoarse whisper.

"What the rest of us are doing: wait," said John Latham. "You'd better go home, Phil. You need the rest."

Phil nodded mutely. He knew he'd have to face Gloria. But what could he tell her? Phil had not known her father, who had died two years before Phil met Gloria, but conversations with Gloria and her mother had painted a pretty detailed picture of him, both before and after the cancer had been diagnosed. A powerful, larger-than-life man, one who took pleasure in vigorous pastimes—camping, riding, hunting, sailing, a man who had taken up long-distance running at the age of fifty —that man had been reduced to depending upon strangers to hold his bedpan while he cried in pain, and shame. It was more than Gloria could manage to talk about her father's death. And Phil knew the thought of Patrick's being helpless was a terror that far overshadowed death in her view of things. Steeling himself for the painful ordeal, Phil started to rise. "You're probably right. . . ." He was going to say good-bye, but suddenly the enormity of this not knowing struck him. He collapsed back into the seat with a wounded cry of pain, an agonized sob from the depth of his broken soul. "Oh my God! He's just a baby!" Dr. Latham reached out and held Phil's shoulder, trying vainly to add whatever comfort he could. Suddenly Phil's crying turned into a tormented question. "What am I going to say to Gloria?"

After a long, painful time, Wingate said, "Go on home, Phil. I'll call your wife if you like."

Phil shook his head, looking up with red eyes. He suddenly seemed self-conscious. Dr. Latham took a box of Kleenex from atop the desk and handed it to him. Phil blew his nose. "No, Teddy. Gabbie and Jack are coming. . . ." He glanced at a wall clock and said, "Shit. They're probably here by now, waiting outside." He rose, slightly wobbly.

Dr. Latham motioned him back to the chair. "I'll get them."

"No, I'd better be the one." As he moved toward the door, Phil said, "Thank you, both of you."

Dr. Wingate said, "Phil, I really wish there was something we could do. Truly I do."

Phil left and both doctors seemed to let go of something, to sag a little now that the grieving father was gone. Dr. Latham said, "Never gets any easier, does it?"

"No," Wingate answered quietly. "When I was a resident, we had a brilliant intern rotate through our service. The kid was so damn smart he made me feel stupid—no easy task, as you know. When he had finished rotation, I tried to sell him on joining our service the following year. I remember his answer. He said, 'Neurosurgery? I didn't become a doctor so I could watch my patients die.' "

Nodding in understanding, John Latham said, "Truth, Teddy. That's why I'm happy to be just a G.P. Well, I've rounds," and he moved toward the door. "I'll see you—"

Suddenly the door opened and Dr. Murphy stuck his head in. "You'd better come quick!"

Both doctors followed Murphy through the hall to the stairs. Even the stout Wingate ran up the stairs to the ICU. Pushing through the doors, they were greeted by a raucous, animal-like shriek. Patrick was sitting up in bed, an evil grin on his face, hooting and yowling. He had torn off his hospital gown and sat in bed, one hand clutching his groin. With the other he was rubbing a dark substance in his hair, while he laughed maniacally. The sensors from the various monitoring devices had been pulled off and cast aside; now they dangled from the machines.

One of the nurses stood by the door, while another furiously cleaned off the front of her white uniform. Wingate looked to the nurse with the towel and said, "Nancy, what happened?"

With a look close to murder, the young woman said, "I was checking the leads to the machine when he woke up. The screens were impossible to read, so I didn't have any warning."

As Wingate went in to examine Patrick, Murphy said, "What's that all over your uniform?"

The nurse said, "Shit. Can't you tell from the delightful odor?"

Dr. Latham said, "He did that?"

Fighting to retain some vestige of professional poise, she said, "I felt something grab my right breast and looked down. He was awake and had defecated in the bed. He was rubbing it on my breasts."

Latham's expression was open disbelief. The nurse's voice had modulated to something almost calm, but her expression was openly wrathful. Latham couldn't imagine what could have caused this strong a reaction. Nancy Roth was a trained, experienced nurse and had dealt repeatedly with the nastier side of nursing. She'd had to clean patients before, been vomited upon, had blood spattered on her. Nothing as mundane as excrement would cause a tenth part of the distress and anger she exhibited. "What else?" he asked.

The woman's eyes remained controlled storms of rage. "I pulled away and the . . . *patient,*" she said, "was masturbating." Her voice softened, and her tone turned from anger to confusion, and her expression turned to distress. "And he gave me a . . . look."

Murphy and Latham both glanced through the glass partition to where Wingate and another nurse were attempting to examine the shrieking child. The nurse continued her narration. "Doctors, I don't know if I can tell you . . . I've been looked at . . . Doctor, he had an expression on his face that . . . it's nothing you should ever see on a kid."

Both doctors turned to watch the nurse. Dr. Murphy said, "Nancy, what do you mean, a look?"

"He looked like a sailor at a topless bar. No, it was worse." Her manner became less angry, more confused. "It was an obscene look." She glanced at Patrick, then averted her eyes. Her voice dropped to a whisper, as if she was embarrassed. "I know he's just a kid, but . . . it's like he was ready to fuck." Both doctors exchanged questioning glances. Waving her hand in resignation, Nurse Roth said, "I know. It's impossible. But . . . something's not right. The patient . . . Doctors, I don't know what it was. But it was sick. And he tried to grab at me when I tried to restrain him." She blew out her cheeks as she sought to control herself. "I . . . he reached up right between my legs . . . like some filthy degenerate. Uh!" The last was a sound of pure revulsion. She tossed aside the towel. "I've got to change."

"Go on," agreed Latham. The nurse left as Wingate returned. To Murphy he said, "Find Phil Hastings before he goes home." As the young resident nearly ran from the room, Wingate shouted after, "And for Christ's sake, tell him to get ready for another shock." Wingate and Latham turned and watched Patrick through the glass of the ICU, as the shrieking, howling child struggled with the three nurses who were attempting to clean off the excrement he had rubbed all over his body.

16

Phil stood before the door in the psychiatric ward, waiting for Gloria and Aggie. With the news that Patrick was revived had come hope reborn, then dashed again. Through the small glass window, Phil could see Patrick sitting on his bed, again naked, since he tore off any clothing that was put upon him. He sat rocking back and forth, holding his penis, while he hooted and shrieked, all the time with eyes fixed on the television on the wall high up and across from his bed. The television was behind safety plastic, so all the food and excrement Patrick had thrown at it had only managed to coat the plastic with a multicolored mess that seemed to detract little from Patrick's enjoyment of the program.

Phil felt a hand on his shoulder and turned to Gabbie behind him, with Jack at her side.

Teddy Wingate and another doctor entered the ward and came up to Phil. "I've given the charts over to Dr. Webster, our head of service in psychiatry."

Phil shook hands. "What's happened to my son?" he asked.

Dr. Webster replied, "It's too early to tell, Mr. Hastings." Seeing Phil's dissatisfaction with that answer, he said, "I think Patrick's brain damage has left him with a . . . baby's mental function. A sixth-month-old or so."

Phil sagged against the door, ignoring the sounds coming through. "What can we do?"

Webster looked over the chart. "We'll do more testing and see what we can do about mitigating some of this violent behavior. Look, I'll talk to you later today, all right?"

Webster turned away without waiting for Phil's reply and moved through another door. Gabbie turned to her dad and said, "I don't like him."

Wingate said, "Peter can be abrupt, but he's good." Seeing the doubt on Gabbie's face, he repeated, "Really, he is good."

Gabbie said, "I want to call in a specialist."

"Who?" asked Wingate without embarrassment.

"Who's the best?"

Without hesitation, Wingate said, "Michael Bergman, down at Johns Hopkins in Baltimore. He's done more work in odd brain dysfunction than anyone. And he's got this prototype magnetic response imager, which will give you a lovely color picture of what's going on inside Patrick's head. This puppy's portable, or at least two strong men can carry it. It's the first one smaller than a room."

"He's the best?" said Gabbie.

"For this weirdness," said Wingate, "no doubt. I met him once at a conference. He's one very sharp customer."

"Then I'll get him."

Murphy smiled. "You can get him to come here?"

Gabbie nodded. "You just watch me. Can I use your phone?" Wingate nodded and led Phil, Jack, and Gabbie from psychiatry. Once inside Wingate's office, Gabbie sat behind the desk, reached over, and picked up the receiver, dialing the outside operator. She instructed her as to billing and waited as the phone at the other end rang several times. "Helen? Gabbie. I need to speak to John." After a moment Gabbie's features clouded, and she said, "Then interrupt the meeting. This is vital." The voice at the other end started to say something, and Gabbie said, "Don't fuck with me, Helen. My little brother is very sick and I want John on this line in sixty seconds, or you can start looking for a new job in sixty-one. Clear?" In less than a minute she said, "John? Gabbie Hastings. Listen, do we have a company plane anywhere near Baltimore? In Washington? Good, have someone tell the pilot to fly to Baltimore as soon as possible. I want—" After a moment she said in icy tones, "Now listen: my little brother is very ill and I want a plane to fly a specialist here as soon as I track him down." Again came a response. "Screw the stockholder. I own 51 percent of Larkercorp and if I want to use a company jet for personal reasons, then I damn well will. The corporation can bill me, if you think that will keep the board happy. Now, please have the pilot alerted, and as soon as the doctor is there, I want him flown to Buffalo. No, the airport here can't handle a jet. I'll have someone ready to pick him up. The man's name is Dr. Michael Bergman, at Johns Hopkins. Use someone at Larker Foundation to get to him. He's got some sort of a prototype machine . . ." Wingate spoke and she repeated, "a magnetic response imager. We need that here, too. Pay him anything, John, or get him a million-dollar grant or something. Just get him here." She gave him the particulars of where she was and Dr. Wingate's name. A short silence passed, and she said, "Thank you. Oh and, John, sorry about the meeting. And tell Helen I'm sorry about being such a bitch."

She hung up. "He said he'll take care of it. Now we need to wait for Dr. Bergman's call."

Jack said, "I'm impressed."

"It's just money, Jack. Nothing to be impressed with." She smiled faintly.

Dr. Wingate said, "Can you get him a grant just like that?"

"Grandfather and Grandmother established the Larker Foundation for all kinds of research. I'm sure I'll have no problems getting a grant." She sighed and returned to sit next to her father.

Wingate said, "I've some papers to push, so forgive me if I'm not social while we wait." Less than a half hour later, the call came.

Wingate answered at once. "Dr. Bergman? You don't remember me, but we spoke briefly once. . . ." He smiled. "Well, I'm flattered you do. Look, what we've got is one pretty sick little boy, and he's got the damnedest EEG's I've ever seen, and some very odd behaviors; it's just weird enough to be of interest to you. If what I've read is accurate, it might be just the thing for that new magnetic imager you're working on." He listened. "I know it's a prototype, Dr. Bergman. But don't worry about its breaking. The kid's got a rich sister." He winked at Gabbie. He listened, then said, "No, she wants you to fly here. He's too . . . violent to risk moving. She'll have a plane waiting for you and your equipment."

There was a long answer, then Wingate spoke again. "Now, how long? Good, see you then." He hung up. "I'll be go-to-hell. He'll be here tomorrow."

Phil looked at his daughter with an unreadable expression. Softly he said, "Thanks, honey. I don't know what—"

She cut him off. "It's okay, Dad." She fought against tears and barely held her own. "Patrick's my little brother."

Phil said with a faint smile, "You know, for a minute there you sounded just like your Grandmother Larker."

Considering Dr. Murphy's observation the day before, Jack said, "I bet she was something, too."

Phil said, "That she was. That she was."

Dr. Wingate said, "Well, Gabbie, you realize that should our Dr. Bergman break his toy along the way, you're buying him a new one?"

She said, "If you can help Patrick, I'll buy you both a new one."

Wingate grinned. "I'll remember that, pretty girl, I'll remember." Standing up, he said, "I'll run along. I've got patients to see to. Use the office as you like."

Gabbie turned to her father, reaching across the space between the two chairs to hug him. "It'll be all right, Dad."

With a soft near cry of pain, he said, "God, I hope so."

Gabbie nodded to Jack that she wanted a moment alone with her father. Jack nodded back and left the room. When they were alone, Gabbie said, "Dad, will you go home for a while? You're exhausted. And Gloria's been really stressed out. I don't know what's going on, but she's said some pretty weird things. She'd feel better if you were with her, I think. When she comes to get Sean, go home with her."

Phil said, "I'm afraid to, Gabbie. I . . . I don't know why, but somehow I feel like I'm needed here." He looked at his daughter through red-rimmed eyes and whispered, "He needs protecting."

Gabbie's eyes narrowed. She began to say something, but a faint echoing memory intruded, a hint of chimes and music and the almost recalled scent of flowers and spices. She felt herself grow flushed, and stood up. Saying nothing, she gripped her father's shoulder and squeezed. Then she leaned over and kissed his cheek, ignoring the stubble. Putting her face beside his, she could feel the warmth of a tear between her cheek and his. Whose it was she didn't know. "I love you, Dad," she said softly.

"I love you, too, kitten," he whispered. Without further words, she left her father alone, knowing that his feeling about Patrick's needing protection wasn't just an emotional reaction to the child's illness. Somehow there was danger, danger around them all, and it hadn't finished manifesting itself. Gabbie had felt it and Gloria knew it, and now her father sensed it as well. Jack stood waiting out in the corridor and she came to him, and without words he took her in his arms. For a moment she felt safe and she wished that feeling would endure.

Gloria and Aggie came into view and Gabbie hugged them both while Jack opened the door and informed Phil. He kissed his wife and said, "Sean seems fine. They can't find anything wrong with him and he can go home now."

Gloria, looking drawn but otherwise composed, seemed to pick up at that news. "Good. Patrick?"

Phil took his wife by the arm, leading her past the others, who followed a short distance behind. He took her up the stairs one flight, then down the long corridor to the psychiatric ward. Before he took her to the door of Patrick's room he said, "You've got to be strong, honey. Patrick's changed."

Gloria's eyes grew wide. "Changed?"

"He's had some . . . brain damage."

With an animal cry, Gloria turned to push past her husband, and thrust open the door. A nurse on duty a distance off began to protest the unauthorized entry as Gabbie shouted, "Get Dr. Latham!"

Phil, caught off guard, was slow in reacting and entered as his wife rushed to Patrick's side. The nurses had attempted to clean him up, but he had urinated in his bed and the room reeked with the ammonia odor. He sat holding himself, rocking back and forth, watching the television. He turned to face his parents and the look on his face froze both in their tracks. There was something so alien on his features that they could not bring themselves to cross that last few feet. Phil reached out and put his hands on Gloria's shoulders, and she cried out, "Patrick!"

Lying in the soft darkness, Patrick heard the distant voice again and for a moment felt a note of alarm. Then it fled as the dark servant returned. Patrick's thought became diffused again as he settled back into the dark flowers that surrounded the master's bed. A few of the others there stirred fitfully, slumbering through the day until night fell in the world of light and it would be time to go again and play. For the first time since coming here, Patrick felt a strange sense of pleasure at that prospect. Then a thought intruded. There was something about outside. . . . The thought vanished as the dark servant settled into the blooms next to Patrick. The boy considered the sick-sweet odor of the dark one and noticed it was not as repellent as he had once thought. As sleep returned, Patrick wondered at that, and at how quickly he had accepted the creature he had once called the Bad Thing as his companion. The dark creature reached around Patrick, its clawed hand resting lightly upon the boy's stomach, and for the first time Patrick felt an odd comfort in the touch of the leathery skin. And for the briefest instant he wondered at the familiar voice that had roused him.

17

Phil hovered outside the examining room. No one said anything as long as Phil stayed out of the way. Everyone knew the torment he felt as he watched through the small glass window. It was now noon. The doctors had been working over Patrick most of the morning and were finishing the last of the tests they had begun. Gloria was at home with Sean, who showed every indication he was recovered from his illness. The boy had insisted that his nightmare had been real, something about a shining man and a bad thing. The story seemed to unnerve Gloria, but Phil knew it was only the product of fever delirium. Now the nearly exhausted father waited to hear the latest on Patrick. Phil absently wondered what had happened to Gabbie and Jack, then recalled they had undertaken the shopping for Gloria, as well as mailing some bills Phil had left on his desk, and would return shortly to the hospital.

Patrick lay strapped down to an examining table, in the room set aside for Dr. Bergman's magnetic response imager. The four doctors, Wingate, Bergman, Latham, and Murphy, with a pair of male nurses and two technicians, watched lines dance across graphs on three large color screens and several smaller monitors. Patrick looked tiny in the midst of all the machinery around him, his face a contorted mask of anger barely seen for the sensor ring that looped around the head of the table. He shrieked and hooted like a demented monkey while the orderlies kept him from pulling at his restraints and injuring himself.

Phil felt his stomach knot each time he witnessed these displays. His baby looked like some alien thing in there, and there was nothing Phil could do to help him. For an instant Phil was revisited by the image of the first night, of Patrick caught in some distant, dark place. Phil took a deep breath, and for the first time in the nine years since he had quit— since Gloria's pregnancy—he wished for a cigarette.

Phil could see the doctors speaking but couldn't hear what they said. He looked at the back of Michael Bergman, who insisted everyone call him Mickey. Bergman was a dashing man in his fifties, wearing an expensively tailored Italian silk suit under his hospital coat. His hair was styled, a dapper steel-grey, and he sported a small mustache. He moved around the machine to examine a dozen sensors attached to a large metal ring that encircled the examination table and Patrick's head. He traced the lines back to the machine and made sure everything was plugged in properly. Before he moved away, he couldn't resist gently running his hand over the child's cheek, a grandfatherly impulse. He snatched it away, barely in time, as Patrick tried to bite it.

At last he came to the front of the console and studied the graphs. After a few moments he motioned the other doctors outside, while an pair of burly orderlies began to unhook Patrick from the restraints.

Bergman and Wingate, followed by Murphy and Latham, left the room. Phil said, "Well?" expectantly.

Wingate said, "Come along, Phil. We need to talk."

"I've got to check on some other patients," said Murphy to Phil. "We've had an unexpectedly hectic time in E.R. the last two nights. I've been playing hooky so I could watch the interesting stuff."

As he began to leave, Phil said, "Dr. Murphy? I . . . just thanks. And you didn't flunk bedside manner."

The tired resident managed a wan smile. "One can only try, Mr. Hastings." He looked past Phil to where the usually voluble Dr. Wingate stood patiently waiting with Drs. Bergman and Latham and gave Phil a reassuring squeeze on the arm. "Believe me, Bergman's the best there is. If anything can be done, he'll do it." Phil nodded in agreement as Murphy left.

Phil accompanied the doctors to Wingate's office. Teddy Wingate heaved himself into the chair behind the desk, and Phil and Bergman also sat. Dr. Latham stood near the door.

Bergman sighed. "Phil. I have had many hundreds of cases in the last twenty years. Now you've handed me the strangest case I've ever seen." He waved at the printouts. "These make anything else I've seen look downright normal."

"What is it?" Phil asked, reluctant to assume anything, lest he find hope again crushed.

"According to my brain response imager . . . your son doesn't have a brain."

Phil couldn't bring himself to speak. Bergman said, "I just ran a bunch of tests to make sure nothing got busted in transit, and the machine's fine. But according to my readings, nothing remotely normal is happening inside Patrick's skull."

"What do you mean?" asked Phil at last.

The doctors exchanged glances. "I don't even know my name today, Phil," said Wingate. "The EEG shows all the same garbage we've gotten all along. But Mickey's machine shows no electrochemical brain response to stimulation." He tapped his glasses upon the desk top. "Either one of the two machines is lying, or we've something here that begs all rational explanation."

Phil looked confused. "I . . . don't understand."

Wingate said, "Mickey?"

"My imager shows you what's happening in the brain, electrochemically. The field of nuclear medicine has been making strides in a lot of areas, and recently we've been working hard on magnetic resonance imaging. Most magnetic imagers are great for showing soft tissue, quite a bit better than X rays, in fact, with none of the risks. My particular machine is a variation that maps chemical shifts in those soft tissues. It's an analog computer image, a re-creation based on energy state changes being tracked through the brain. If you were to watch the screen while I clapped my hands loudly next to someone's ear, you'd see a color shift indicating the brain's response to the stimulus. We're presently mapping dozens of volunteers at Johns Hopkins, trying to develop a catalog of 'normal' responses. Someday we'll use this machine and others like it to identify trouble spots in the brain before they become life-threatening."

Teddy Wingate chimed in. "And to diagnose other things, like epilepsy, learning disorders, maybe even psychosis-inducing brain dysfunctions and autism."

"Maybe. But now we're just beginning," finished Bergman. He leaned back. "What we have so far is a general diagnostic tool. We can look at someone's brain responses and say, 'This guy falls into the range of normal responses,' or 'outside of the normal range.' We can't yet say, 'This fellow's developing Alzheimer's,' or 'This child's dyslexic.' At least, not for a long time.

"Now, EEGs measure electrochemical impulses, using sensors on the head. My machine actually tries to track what the chemical changes are. With Patrick, the EEG shows us that something's going on; at least, there's enough energy being picked up by the sensors to screw up all the graphs. But my imager says there's nothing chemical going on inside Patrick's head. One says the brain is working, in a unique, messed-up sort of way, and the other says there's nothing inside his skull. If my machine is right, either Patrick's got a vacuum tube full of electricity between his ears or he's dead." Almost bitterly he added, "And for a corpse he's certainly loud. I don't know if I can explain it any better."

Wingate said, "You've heard the expression, 'The light's on but nobody's home'?" Phil nodded. "Well, this is as close as I've seen to that being the case."

Bergman said, "Phil, it is impossible for Patrick to be breathing and have *no* brain chemistry. Even if his higher functions were totally burned out by the illness, leaving only the brain stem functioning—a Karen Anne Quinlan kind of thing—we'd still track a lot of brain chemistry. So we have to assume my machine is busted—despite all my diagnostics saying it's fine—and that Patrick has suffered some sort of gross brain damage, which explains all these unexplainable EEGs." He looked at some of the printouts left on Wingate's desk and said, "Though what the hell these mean is beyond me."

"That doesn't make sense," said Phil.

"Right," said Wingate. "It doesn't make sense. We've a patient who's given us nothing like normal reactions to what he's been through."

Phil said, "What can you do?"

"Watch him," said Wingate. "I'd like to keep him here a few more days, then we can talk about moving him to a fully equipped, long-term psychiatric facility."

Bergman nodded. "I'm going to stay here awhile. Maybe when I've watched him for a few days longer, we can begin to make sense of all this."

Wingate sighed, obviously fighting off a feeling of defeat. Phil said, "What are his chances of improving?"

Bergman was the one who spoke. "I can't even begin to hold out the prospect of any improvement, Phil." He looked thoughtfully down at the papers. "We don't even know what's wrong physiologically. And it's been a while since I've studied abnormal behavior pathologies."

Wingate nodded in agreement. "There are some things he's doing which would suggest autistic behavior. The constant masturbation is classic self-stimulating behavior, as is the rocking back and forth."

Phil shifted in his seat uncomfortably. "I was wondering about the sex thing."

Bergman said, "We don't know it's sex like you'd normally think of it. Though the way he grabs at the nurses makes me think it may be, despite his youth—that's why we turned his care over to the male nurses and the orderlies. Still, clutching the penis is a common enough behavior in male babies. But the hooting and the laughing and the rest, it's . . ." Bergman's eyes got a distant look.

"What?" asked Phil.

"For a moment, when Patrick tried to bite my hand . . . I could have sworn I saw intelligence in his eyes. Like the whole thing was some sort of big game." He closed his eyes and rubbed them. "I'm sorry, Phil. I shouldn't put my own fatigue delusions on you. You'll think Patrick was possessed by a dybbuk if I keep this up."

Phil shook his head in frustration. "I'd be thankful if he threw up pea soup and his head twisted around. I'd call an exorcist and we'd be done."

Latham said, "Phil, we can only imagine the torment this is for you and Gloria. Go home, and we'll keep an eye on him for a few more days. I'll arrange for a transfer to Tonawanda State Hospital, or a private institution if you like, but let's hold off until after"—he glanced at a calendar on the wall—"let's make it Monday the second of November, all right?"

Bergman rose. "I agree. We must fall back on the old and slow but tried and true—observation, different medications, therapy—and see what happens. It's either that or magic." Latham and Wingate also made as if to leave the office.

Phil rose and followed the three doctors out of the room. Gabbie and Jack were waiting just outside. Gabbie kissed her father on the cheek as he said, "Is . . . there really hope?"

Dr. Bergman said, "I'm tempted to spout the old saw 'Where there's life . . .' but . . . I'm afraid all I can say is we don't have the faintest idea. We just don't know."

"What now?" said Gabbie to her father.

"We go home, tell Gloria what's going on." He paused, looking at his daughter and future son-in-law. "And we make some plans." Jack nodded, knowing that he was talking about long-term care for Patrick. Phil forced himself to smile. "Come on. I think I could use a day off from here." Without further words they walked toward the outside door.

Latham turned to Wingate and said, "Teddy?"

The usually talkative Wingate had been unusually quiet since returning from the psych ward. "I didn't want to say anything in front of

Phil, but have either of you noticed one other odd thing about our little patient?"

"Just what I said," answered Bergman. "I thought I saw something in his eyes."

"That's it," said Latham. "Sometimes he's looking at things like he knows what's going on. Is that what you mean?"

Wingate shook his head as he began to walk off. "No, not that, though I get that feeling, too. It's just that being around the kid more than a few minutes gives me a most unprofessional case of the creeps."

Latham and Bergman exchanged glances, but neither commented on Teddy's remark.

18

Patrick stood in the center of the circle, his eyes unfocused and glazed. Around him moved figures of dark aspect, things that defied the eye's attempts at definition. Sounds were muffled by a dark fog, and, above, faint lights pierced the gloom. Then a presence manifested itself, something so terrible it could not be endured. Patrick turned slowly to look at the approaching horror, and his eyes remained blank. Then the terror was upon him, sweeping him up and carrying away.

"No!" shrieked Gloria, sitting up in bed. Her heart pounded and she swallowed a sob. She glanced around and saw Phil's side of the bed empty. She knew she'd find him asleep on the couch in his study, the television going as he slept through some cable news show or another.

Then the sound of Sean's voice intruded. "Mommy!"

Gloria ran to her son's room. He was sleeping in Patrick's bed, as he had since returning home. Gloria sat on the bed next to Sean, gathering him to her. He cried, a pitiful, aching sound. "I had a bad dream," he sobbed into her shoulder. "About Patrick."

With her tears mingling with his, she said, "I know, baby. I know."

Gloria held her child as Gabbie appeared in the door. "Is he okay?" she asked sleepily.

"Yes," said Gloria, her voice strained. "Go back to sleep, honey."

Gabbie hesitated an instant, then trundled back to her room. "Can I sleep with you?" asked Sean.

Gloria barely spoke agreement as she led Sean back to her bedroom. The boy climbed up into the bed shared by his mom and dad and snuggled into Phil's pillow. Gloria got back in, missing Phil terribly, but knowing that, once wakened, he'd be all night getting back to sleep.

Gloria watched Sean as his breathing turned deep and regular. They shared an understanding of something dark and beyond Phil's understanding, something felt, not known. They knew that all the science and doctors in the world wouldn't get Patrick back. Fighting off a despair so terrible it could hardly be borne, Gloria tried to return to sleep, letting the sound of Sean's breathing lull her. Sleep took a long time to arrive. And images of dark places and lost little boys took a long time to depart.

19

Gabbie peeked out the window at the sound of the car in the driveway. "It's Gary!" she shouted to the others. Jack and Phil were in Phil's study, quietly discussing long-term care for Patrick. Aggie was in the kitchen, helping Gloria with tea, while Sean watched television in the parlor.

They all met Gary at the door, and Gabbie gave him a hug. "You look bushed."

"Would you like a cup of tea?" asked Gloria.

"How about I bum a drink off of you, instead?" asked Gary.

"No sweat," answered Phil.

They entered the living room, where Aggie Grant deposited a tea service on the table before the couch. Gary removed his topcoat and glanced around the room. He saw the tension and said, "Is something wrong?"

Gloria's eyes began to tear and she inclined her head at her husband. Phil explained about Patrick's illness. Sitting down, Gary said, "That's terrible, Phil. I'm really sorry. Maybe I should—"

"No," interrupted Phil. "You sit tight. It won't help anything if you take off."

"So how are you?" asked Jack.

"Tired." He sipped the drink Phil handed him. "Thanks. I'm tired and I'm worried."

"Why?" asked Phil.

Gary said, "Mark's vanished."

"What are you talking about?" asked Gabbie.

"Mark's disappeared somewhere in Germany." Gary paused, then said, "It's tied in to that business about Fredrick Kessler being a member of some organization or another. I talked to Mark back when I was in Seattle and he was still in New York, and we compared notes. I sent him copies of the translations we got from the parchments. They're no more bizarre than a lot of other ancient religious stuff looks to us modern types. But Mark came across something in New York that sent him to Germany. He didn't say what. I know him well enough, however, to know he was truly disturbed. And," he said with a sigh, "sometime since I last talked to him, he's just vanished.

"He called me in Seattle from his hotel in Munich and asked me to investigate a friend of Kessler's who had settled in Canada. I went to Ottawa, then London, Ontario, then back to Ottawa. I called his hotel in Munich at the agreed-upon time, and he'd checked out. They gave me his destination, but he never got there. Now, Mark's jumped off the track before, side excursions that last a week or two, but he always gets word to me where he can be reached. This time . . . nothing."

Gary sipped his drink while the others exchanged glances. Phil asked, "Should we try to contact someone in Germany?"

Gary shrugged. "I don't know. Maybe the American embassy. They might know who to contact." He shook his head. "But I have a feeling that if Mark's in trouble, we might not see him again."

Those words had a chilling effect on everyone in the room. Gloria spoke in almost a whisper. "Gary, you're scaring me." She remembered the premonition she had had the night she had last seen Mark.

Gary said, "Sorry, folks. It's just things in Canada were pretty weird." He sipped his drink again. "What was the most . . . disturbing about Canada wasn't what I found but what I couldn't find."

"What do you mean?" asked Gabbie.

"In Canada I kept hitting walls. Kessler's buddy who had come to Canada was named Hans von Leer. In London he changed it to Hans Van der Leer."

"That sounds Dutch," said Jack.

"Right. He was reported in the local papers as a Dutchman. He showed up about five years after Kessler came to Pittsville. Where he was before that is tough to figure. Mr. Van der Leer, or von Leer if you will, went to a great deal of trouble to hide his origins. Everywhere I turned I found pages missing from documents, files misplaced, notations erased, a thousand things designed to make it impossible to get a hint as to who Van der Leer had been in Germany. I think that's some of what Mark went to Germany to discover: who was this Van der Leer, and how did he relate to Kessler and the others from southern Germany? How was it all tied in to that business at the turn of the century?

"So I looked hard and came up dry. What's got me jumpy is . . . it looks like Kessler's organization still exists, is still active."

Gabbie said, "That's scary."

Phil said, "Gary, Mark said something about this secret society business, but not much more. Do you have any idea of what this might all be about?"

Gary said, "If what Mark thinks is true, there's a someone, maybe a group, who can confuse your memory, even make you forget interactions with them." Gary paused, then said, "No one else answer. Gabbie, what do you remember about the barn?"

Gabbie looked at the others in the room, confused, then smiled. "The barn?" She laughed. "You mean like it needs painting, or the roof leaks?"

"No, I mean like the fellow you met there who tried to rape you."

Gabbie's expression was one of confusion. "Rape?" Then slowly her look of perplexity was changed to one of fright as her face drained of color. Softly, almost inaudibly, she said, "I'd forgotten."

Jack's expression was one of disbelief. "You'd forgotten? How's that possible?"

Gary held up his hand when questions came thick and fast. "Slowly, folks. I just wanted to demonstrate something Mark discovered the night we chased the assailant into the woods. Gabbie's forgotten because the fellow she met had . . . some ability to make her forget what happened that night. If I keep prodding, Gabbie will remember things, but as soon as I stop, she'll begin to forget it all. I'm not certain, but it may be that if we don't remind her for a long enough time, she'll completely forget it ever happened. Maybe"—he looked around the room—"even deny it happened."

Gabbie said, "If I concentrate, I can . . . It's weird, but it's like I can barely remember a movie I saw a long time ago, or . . . a dream I had when I was a kid."

Gary said, "It's more than weird. It's damn near impossible. From what little I know about assaults and rape, you should have everything that happened etched in your memory in vivid detail—or be in a classic denial, blanking it out." He sipped his drink. "Mark was subject to the same thing." He explained what happened the night Mark and Gary chased the assailant into the woods, and how Mark couldn't remember without listening to the tape recording he'd made, until Gary hypnotized him to remember. Looking at Jack he said, "How's your shoulder?"

Jack seemed surprised by the question. "Fine. . . . Which shoulder?"

"Your right, the one that was infected."

Jack whistled low. He looked at the others. "Damn, me too."

"Mark . . . palmed some sort of odd little dart. . . . The doctor thought it was a bone chip, he told me."

Gloria's agitation was obvious. "Gary, what are you saying? That we've got some sort of crazy people hiding in the woods out there? Who rape and shoot poisoned darts and . . . shit, what?"

Gary added, "I don't know if I should be telling you this . . . but . . . damn it, if Mark doesn't . . . come back, I don't want to deal with this by myself. Mark didn't just see a kid in the woods that night." He told them what he had heard on the tape, and what Mark had confided in him after hypnosis.

All sat stunned by the description of the riders in the woods. Aggie was the first to speak. In even tones she said, "Gary, it's impossible."

"If I hadn't been sitting there watching Mark when he heard the tape, saw his reaction, well, I'd agree the whole thing was impossible. I've given a lot of thought to this, Aggie; either Mark saw the impossible. Or"—he paused—"his mind was controlled."

Gabbie said, "Maybe riders did come through"—her voice trailed off—"in costume?"

Aggie said, "Girl, what Mark described is the Wild Hunt."

Phil said, "Aggie?"

"It's a legend. The riders of the Wild Hunt ride the woods at night, chasing those who . . . are evil, or who have offended the riders, or—depending on the version of the legend—just happen to be in the wrong place at the wrong time."

Phil said, "What is this?" His voice held a nervous laugh, as if all this was passing beyond his ability to understand. "Some sort of Irish Ku Klux Klan?"

Aggie's voice showed she was disturbed. "Philip, the riders are Daonie Sidhe—the Old People, fairies." Phil blinked. "Their leader is a creature with the head of a wild stag. They ride horses no mortal may mount. It's an Irish fairy legend."

"That's impossible," said Jack.

"Dad," said Gabbie softly, "remember the tapestry? It shows those riders and some of the . . . game hanging from poles is people."

Phil shook his head. "I'll buy some sort of nut group dressing up and pretending this stuff . . . maybe. Even that Kessler and his bunch were run out of Germany for being found out as a gang of religious terrorists—but what's this all got to do with Gabbie's assault and Mark's encounter?"

Gary looked defeated. "I just don't know. Mostly because I don't know what Mark's doing in Germany. He's been unusually close-mouthed about what he believes. I can sort of put two and two together because of what he's had me doing." He sighed. "All I can say is there is strong evidence that there are people around today who are still involved with what Kessler was involved with eighty years ago.

"Suppose this secret group Kessler and Van der Leer were members of was privy to some secret of mind control—just play along for a minute—which makes them cause people to forget . . . or gives them the power to cause people to see visions. Maybe someone else besides the Shadow has the power to cloud men's minds." Gary's voice rose at the last, frustration clearly evident. He forced himself back to calmness. "Sorry, I'm beat. Look, if such a group once did exist, and they did have some unusual power, it explains why they can still be around, still thrive even, without anyone else knowing they're active.

"Assume there's nothing supernatural about it at all. Suppose for a moment Phil's right, and it's a group of people dressed up and riding around and there's some rational explanation for the weird qualities Mark attributed to them. Maybe they used a drug on Mark and Gabbie —there was certainly some sort of fast-acting drug on the dart they shot Jack with, from what Mark told me. You're still left with the fact there's a bunch of pretty strange jokers getting dressed up and riding around the countryside at night, doing their best to imitate something out of Celtic myth. That's what Mark had me digging around in before you guys found the stuff in the basement, by the way. He's had me generate pages of notes on Celtic legends and later Irish and Scottish myth. Anyway, maybe we've run afoul of Kessler's group, and this stuff is just window dressing. But until we understand who they are, what they're doing, we don't have a clue about what we're dealing with. Mark knew more about this, but he's . . . gone. It's clear, though, that what happened in Germany at the turn of the century is happening again here, if to a lesser degree." He was silent for a minute. "And from what I experienced in Canada, I think someone's trying to prevent outsiders from discovering what they're up to."

Gabbie put her hand to her mouth. "Oh, Gary, you're really scaring me now."

"I'm scared too, Gabbie. This is so weird. Weirder than most of the stuff we usually mess with. And it's getting harder to understand what we're into as we dig deeper. The more I uncover, the less I know. I just wish I knew where Mark was." Gary closed his eyes and rubbed them. With a shake of his head, he said, "Well, now that I've made everybody's day, I could use some sleep. So I think I'll be off."

"Won't you stay and eat something?" asked Phil. "We've a ham in the oven."

"Thanks, but no. I'm not hungry and I really do need a nap. Besides, if I know Ellen, she'll want to come by and fix something, considering I've been gone all but three days the last month. Give me a day to get it together, then I'll drop by again. And let me know how things are with Patrick."

They all stood. Good-byes were made, and as Gary left, Sean appeared at the doorway, inquiring about dinner. Aggie herded him down the hall to the kitchen for a snack to hold him over, while Gabbie said, "That was some business. It's pretty scary stuff all right."

Jack nodded. "And there's still Kessler's gold. Maybe that's what they're after."

"Could be," said Gabbie. "Maybe they don't know we've already found it, and are trying to scare us off so they can look for it themselves."

Phil said, "Well, that's the first theory that makes some sense. If it is Kessler's old buddies looking for the gold, that would certainly explain away everything—a hallucinogenic dust, and costumes. 'Cause, until I see one of these fairies, Kessler's mysterious colleagues make a lot more sense. But I think I'll withhold judgment, because even that's a little too strange for me. As weird as all this conjecture is, I still think the truth will prove a whole lot simpler than ancient secret societies with mysterious mind powers."

Gloria came to Phil's side and put her arms around him. Softly she said, "No. It all fits together somehow. We're just not seeing how the pieces mesh. And it has something to do with Patrick—"

Phil cut her off, afraid of her becoming too emotional again. "Honey, this is the twentieth century, to coin a cliché. We're not sitting atop an ancient shrine to Cthulhu, after all. What we've got is some gold and strange stuff left over from an odd old immigrant from Germany, and"—his voice softened—"a tragic illness. That's plenty for now." He hugged her tight, then in lighter tone said, "Look, maybe you ought to take Sean out to the Coast and visit your mother?" The last two days had been pretty rugged for them all, but Gloria and Sean seemed to be getting the worst of it. The shock of seeing Patrick had made her hysterical for hours, and while she'd gotten a hold of herself, the strain showed. And Sean had become moody and withdrawn.

Gloria didn't hesitate as she said, "No. Thanks for the offer, but . . .

I want to stay close, and it wouldn't be good for Sean. Let's try to keep things as normal around here as possible."

"Okay, if you're sure. For now I think I'll go and catch a few minutes of the news on the tube. Join me?"

With a halfhearted smile, Gloria nodded and went with Phil to the parlor. At the door he paused and said, "Jack, in all this craziness, I've forgotten to ask. What about your orals?"

Jack winced. "Tomorrow afternoon at three. I was going to postpone—"

"But I wouldn't let him," said Gabbie.

Gloria smiled a half-sad smile. "Good for you, kid. Well, good luck, Jack."

Phil echoed the wish as they left the room.

Gabbie looked at Jack. "That thing about the assault was weird."

"You really forgot?"

"All of it. If Gary or you or someone hadn't mentioned it, I think I might never have remembered. And even now I've got to work at remembering."

"It's creepy. I have to work at remembering just how messed up my shoulder got."

"What do you think of all this?"

"I don't know. Gary was talking some pretty weird-sounding stuff. Maybe your dad's right. Maybe there's a rational explanation behind everything." He stood up. With a theatrical sigh he said, "Look, I'm going to have to do some last-minute cramming for my exams. I could use a little coaching, if you don't mind."

Gabbie took his hand. "Later—tonight." She stood and her expression brightened. "Right now I want a quiet walk with my fella. Let's stroll down the road. This is the first non-wet day I've seen in a week, and it's not too cold."

Jack smiled. "That sounds just about right."

Tugging on his hand, she led him through the kitchen. With a quick promise to Aggie they'd be back in time to help with dinner, they headed out toward the road for an evening walk. Aggie watched them leave while Sean silently ate half of a peanut butter sandwich. Behind the everyday tableau, she sensed something terrible was approaching and felt a chill rising in her chest.

For a moment Aggie stood silently, then sensed Sean's eyes upon her. She fought back the urge to shiver, pushing down the sense of impending trouble, and forced her mind back to the concerns of the moment. She had a family to feed.

Sean watched Jack and Gabbie leave and turned his attention to the sandwich. Absently he wondered what Patrick was having for dinner with the— He dropped his sandwich on the plate as his eyes widened. With the . . . For a moment he had understood something, then that knowledge had fled. He sat quietly for a long minute as his heart raced, trying in vain to recapture what he had grasped for only an instant. He waited a long minute, hoping for the thought to return. When it didn't, he sighed and picked up his sandwich, eating it halfheartedly as he considered that Patrick was being fed off a plastic plate at the hospital. But he couldn't shake the image of something dark yet shining in a corner. At last he put the half-eaten sandwich down and left the kitchen.

20

Phil stuck his head into the kitchen, informing his wife and son he was on his way back to the hospital. Gloria nodded as the door swung closed behind him. Phil maintained a degree of normalcy in his outward behavior, keeping everyone on an even keel.

Phil got in his car and turned the key. The engine rattled to life fitfully, despite having been run earlier in the day. Overdue for a tune-up, he thought absently. As he pulled out of the drive and turned onto the road, he considered the toll Patrick's illness was having on everyone. For the last two days Gabbie had taken to fixing Sean's breakfast and lunch and seeing the house stayed in order, as Gloria barely managed dinner with Aggie's help. Despite his preoccupation with Patrick, Phil was concerned over Gloria's mental state. He didn't know how to cope with it; the last week had left him too emotionally exhausted to make any rational judgment. He knew that under more normal circumstances, his wife would have been constantly at Patrick's side. But she couldn't deal with this odd creature who was once Patrick. And Phil knew she felt guilty over not going back to the hospital. Maybe when they got him moved, to a long-term care facility, or even if they could bring him home again someday . . . He let the last thought trail off.

Phil knew that somewhere down the line Gloria would need some sort of help. She moved like a zombie half the time, or she sat around staring off into the distance. If anyone spoke to her she seemed to snap out of the mood, but as soon as she was alone she withdrew into herself again. She fell asleep about eight-thirty and slept the clock round, unless she woke up screaming from dreams. Often her shouts awoke Sean, and he would be brought in to sleep with his parents. It was almost as if Sean awakened at the same instant. For a moment Phil considered that. He shrugged off the thought. But until something concrete occurred—until Patrick's fate was decided—Phil, like the others, simply held his breath and waited. As he increased the car's speed, he remembered he hadn't said good-bye to Sean. Pushing aside a twinge of guilt, Phil turned the car onto the highway toward the hospital.

21

Gloria absently washed the dishes, staring out the window, unaware of the quiet boy who sat at the table. Gloria was silently desperate. She couldn't talk of Patrick without tears, and the few visits to the hospital had been more than she could endure. Her near phobia about illness, joined with her pain for her son, was pushing her beyond her ability to cope. In her own private world there was a blank space once filled by a boy named Patrick. No one in the family said anything about her reluctance to go to the hospital. Had Patrick been physically sick she would have stayed at his side. But that unspeakable thing he had become, that miasma of . . . the unholy . . . about him caused her to feel more than grief. There was a darkness surrounding Patrick, an aura not of the normal world. Despite her emotional confusion, Gloria struggled to remember; there was something everyone else was missing, something she had seen. And if she could only remember it, Patrick would return to her. She was frustrated to the point of anger by her inability to remember, and her short temper was making everyone tiptoe around her. She vaguely heard Sean putting down his glass of breakfast milk and returned her attention to the dishes.

Sean was in a pout because his mother wouldn't let him go outside or to Saturday night's Halloween Party. He really didn't want to go to the party, he just didn't want to be sitting around alone—missing Patrick. He hadn't assimilated his experiences the night he and Patrick had been taken to the hospital; something clouded his memory, making things dim and hard to handle. Yet he was on the verge of understanding. Holding the fairy stone seemed to help. And each day it seemed he could recall the images faster, and they were more clear. He had given up trying to get anyone to understand about the images. They just wouldn't listen. They just didn't understand. Sean sighed silently.

He gripped the fairy stone in his fist and stared at it. There was something he could remember about the night Patrick got so sick. It was a vague shape in darkness, something that hovered at the edge of memory, something that had reached out and—

Sean's eyes opened wide as his heart leaped. He remembered! The Shining Man! And the thing that looked like Sean! The Shining Man and the Bad Thing had taken Patrick! Sean squirmed in his chair, his agitation unnoticed by his mother. He had to do something; he just wasn't sure what it was. And he couldn't do it cooped up at home. He had to get some help, and he knew where he might be able to find it. Sean pushed aside the half-eaten sandwich and said, "Mom, can I go outside?"

"No!"

Sean jumped at the vehemence of her answer. She looked at Sean through tired eyes and softened her tone. "No, honey. You've been sick." She thought it best not to say anything about what Gary had told them. But she wasn't going to let Sean anywhere near the woods.

"But, Mom . . ." Sean began, but then his mother turned to face him, and he saw a new Look, one that frightened him. She knew! Or at least she suspected. On some level, conscious or subconscious, she had decided that one son lost was enough. Sean knew any revelation to his mother of what he remembered would only increase her resistance to letting him out. He ceased his complaint and quit the kitchen, finding his way to the parlor, where he resigned himself to another round of Saturday cartoons or sports on TV while he puzzled out a means of getting away. Maybe he could go to bed early, then sneak out after Mom went to sleep. He sat back on the floor, his back against a chair, and used the remote control to turn on the TV. He used the satellite dish controls to lock in on a college football game. He didn't care who was playing.

Less than an hour later, Gabbie stuck her head in and asked, "What are you doing hanging around here, kiddo? It's a beautiful day outside, Indian summer."

Considering his reply, Sean said, "I was just watching this game." Casually he stood and turned off the TV. "Where's Mom?"

"Taking a nap. Why?"

He shrugged. "Nothing. I'm going to the park, okay? The guys are going to play touch."

Gabbie almost said no, thinking about Gary's conjecture, but she remembered he'd said all the odd goings-on took place after sundown. "Sure, just be back before it starts to get dark."

"Sure. I'll be back early." He waved a casual good-bye and exited through the kitchen, then out the back porch door. As soon as his sneakers hit the ground, he was off at a dead run. He sprinted through the woods, reaching the Troll Bridge in record time. He paused to catch his breath and felt the evil aura that signaled the presence of the Bad Thing under the bridge. He removed his fairy stone from beneath his shirt and clutched it tightly. With resolution he marched across the bridge. Once across the creek, he felt a giddy sense of accomplishment. As he looked back at the bridge, a clear remembrance and certainty descended upon him. It *was* his responsibility to help Patrick. Not his father's, or his mother's, or the doctor's. None of them knew what the boys had endured, and none were willing to listen. Whatever caused people to be the way they were when kids tried to explain things was working overtime now. Even Sean's dad, who normally took time to listen, seemed unable to consider for a moment his son's confused attempts to describe what happened that night. Now that Sean could tell him exactly, he knew his father still wouldn't allow for a moment that what the boy said might have some foundation in truth.

Sean now understood what he must do. He must face the Shining Man and the Bad Thing one more time. They still scared him, but he somehow knew that having reached the nadir of fear that night, he would never be that terrified of them again. He had confronted them and survived. And he knew he must do it once more, only this time it would be battle. Patrick's fate depended upon it.

Sean knew there was only one person who could possibly understand what the boys had faced. Sean raced through the woods. Running the entire way, he was soon pounding on the door of Barney Doyle's workshop.

The door opened and Barney looked down at Sean. "Here then, what's the ruckus?"

Sean blurted, "Barney, it was the Shining Man! Everyone thinks me and Patrick just got sick. But it was the Shining Man. He and the Bad Thing came into our room with these two things that looked like us and they took Patrick. They'd have taken me, but I had the stone—" Sean stopped when he saw another figure move in the darkness behind Barney. Aggie Grant came forward, a concerned expression on her face.

"What is this?" she said.

Sean backed away, but Barney put a hand on his shoulder and said, "It's all right, boy. Come in."

Sean allowed himself to be steered into the shack and saw that Aggie had been consulting a large notebook. He glanced at her, and Barney said, "Miss Grant's dropped by on her way to your home, to listen to some more tales, Sean."

"What did you say about a shining man, Sean?" asked Aggie patiently.

Sean looked at Barney, who never took his eyes from the boy. Quietly the old handyman said, "The *Amadán-na-Briona.*"

Aggie spoke softly. "The Fool?" Her eyes were wide with disbelief. "You can't be serious. Patrick is ill from a fever."

Barney ran his hand over his face, showing uncertainty, then he spoke, his voice low and controlled, but intense with an impatient, frustrated tone neither Aggie or Sean had heard before. "Aggie Grant, there are truths you'll never find in books, and that's a fact. God has a plan, and it's only those of us who are filled with pride who think we know what that plan is. You come around and ask to hear stories of the Good People. . . ." He paused, as if struggling for words. "But what you don't understand is that the stories aren't . . . made up. They're stories told and retold because they teach. They teach us how to live with the Good People. They're stories told first by people who met the Good People"—his voice lowered—"and lived through the meeting."

Aggie's expression was clearly one of disbelief. "Barney," she said softly, in wonder, "you don't honestly believe the old tales, do you?" The man's face was set in a resolute mask, showing he did believe, as he nodded his head once. Aggie looked at Sean and said, "I think I should take you home."

Sean made as if to bolt. "No! I've got to talk to Barney. Please." Sean pleaded, but Aggie heard an odd note in his voice: something else was there, a sense of final desperation.

Aggie again looked at Barney, unwilling to accept his statement or Sean's at face value. "Barney, what stories have you been telling the boys?"

"The more common ones," he answered frankly, "but nary a word about the Fool. I'd not scare the lads like that. And I still haven't puzzled out what in fact this Bad Thing might be."

Aggie sat back on Barney's stool, her eyes traveling from Sean to Barney and back. Years of teaching had made her sensitive to the frustration encountered by youngsters who feel they are not being listened to. She was thoughtful a long time, then said, "All right, go on."

Sean said, "The night we got sick, we didn't get sick. The Shining Man and the Bad Thing came into our room. . . ." Sean continued until he had finished the narrative of that night.

Aggie listened closely and, when Sean finished, said, "Sean, what did this Shining Man look like?" An intuition told her that whatever else was happening, before her stood not a boy who was simply repeating a tale once or twice heard, or story fabricated to mislead adults, but rather a boy who was revealing something he believed in with conviction. Sean believed he had seen what he said he saw, and Aggie wasn't about to dismiss something this important to him. Sean described as best he could how the man looked, and the more he spoke, the more she became convinced he had seen either a myth come to life or the most incredible hallucination on record. When he had answered all her questions, her manner was subdued, her voice barely above a whisper. "Barney, this is unbelievable. I don't for a moment believe the boy actually saw the Amadán-na-Briona. You can't possibly believe that either." Her tone was not one of disbelief, but rather a plea that sanity be returned, that this impossible description issuing from the lips of an eight-year-old be a cleverly rehearsed script, a strange, tasteless, and inexplicable joke. If not, the world was an alien place and man a blind creature passing through, ignorant of the dangers at every hand. Aggie's face was pale as she said, "Can you?"

Barney said, "I can. And I do, Aggie Grant. Your nose is too much in books and not enough in the real world." He stood and pointed at the window. "Out there is mystery after mystery and wonders hidden by magics so profound all your science can't describe it. Our history tells of when we came to Ireland: how we found the Firbolg and the Tuatha De Danann already living upon the island, and how we wrested the land from them. The British and their American children have wandered too far from their Celtic roots and the Old Knowledge, the lore before the Church came to save us all. The Britons are one with the Roman, Saxon, and Norman invaders, losing their vision of the past. Many of us Irish have not."

"But—" Aggie began.

"No buts, then, if you please, Miss Agatha Grant," interrupted Barney, his eyes distant as he stared out the dirty window of his shack. "You've heard the tales told by the old folks. You've written them down, counting them quaint and colorful. You've not for a moment asked one person you've interviewed if they believed. Have you?"

Aggie shook her head. Where she had thought lived a simple Irishman she discovered resided a man with a deep appreciation of his cultural heritage and more than just passing knowledge of simple folktales. He remembered all he had heard and he had been a good listener. And he passed that lore along. In his own way, Barney Doyle was a bard, keeping ancient tradition alive. "I simply assumed . . ." she said weakly.

"Yes, and that's the word, then, isn't it? Assumed. You think the old stories nothing but myth and legend. We know they are true," he whispered. He never took his eyes from the darkening sky outside. "We'll get some rain soon, I'm thinking." His voice softened. "What, then, would you say should I tell you I myself once saw the Daonie Sidhe, dancing upon a knoll in the moonlight? A boy I was, not much older than Sean. But I'll never forget the sight. Both beautiful and terrifying, joyous and sad, all at once, it was. The music so faint it's a breath on the wind, and the smell of flowers . . . flowers from another place. Longings and desires I felt, with fear in no small measure." He crossed himself. "And danger to my immortal soul.

"They are often gone from sight, the Old People, the Good People." He looked hard at Aggie. "But they are still here, with us. They live in the same world, and it's foolishness itself to deny the truth because it's not convenient to believe."

Aggie felt helpless before the certainty of Barney's words.

Sean said, "Please, Barney, we've got to get Patrick back. Where can I find him?"

Barney stared out the window as the afternoon sun turned the sky the color of yellow roses between the growing black clouds. "He's with the Fool, lad, and for all of that, he's as good as lost."

"Who's the Fool?" asked the boy, seemingly unwilling to accept Patrick as being irretrievable.

Barney looked out from under bushy brows, his eyes unreadable. But it was Aggie who spoke. "Your Shining Man, Sean. The Amadán-na-Briona, leader of the Dark Folk. He's the head of what the Scots call the Unseely Court, the evil ones among the Sidhe."

Sean, who'd been squirming, said, "But why'd he take Patrick?"

Aggie watched Barney's face as he looked at Sean, then herself again. "Because they're a wicked and perverse fellowship, Sean. 'Tis certain, the boy's been a-changelinged."

"A changeling?" said Aggie. "But he's in the hospital."

"That's not Patrick in that room," said Barney firmly.

Sean looked up at Barney and tears formed in the boy's eyes. Relief flooded through him. At last he had found somebody who understood. Barney knew that the thing in the hospital that looked like Patrick wasn't Sean's brother.

Aggie stood up. "This is all too much for me to take, Barney Doyle. I'll not sit and listen to this as if we were talking of a kidnapping." She was obviously disturbed by Barney's words, and she fought to regain her composure. "Come on, Sean, I think you should be at home. The weather's turning, so I'll drive you."

Sean stood up as if making to bolt to the door, but Barney put a restraining hand upon his shoulder. "Nay, lad, you'd do well to go." Barney's eyes seemed to shine, as if on the verge of tears. "There's nothing for it. Nothing you can do. There is no way to go after Patrick." He waited until Aggie had retrieved her purse and notebook, and opened the door for them. After they had gone through, Barney closed it softly. Then he said quietly, "We're past the age of heroes, Sean. 'Tis a sad thing to be admitting, but it is the truth."

Sean thought to run away, but Aggie had a lifetime of dealing with boys of all sizes and temperaments, and a light touch upon his shoulder stilled the impulse to rebel in the usually obedient boy. He quietly got into her car and allowed himself to be taken home.

22

Sean brooded in his room as the setting sun passed behind the old tree outside, throwing twisted shadows across the wall. He had been quietly desperate since coming back from Barney's the day before. Luckily his mother had still been napping when Aggie brought him home. Aggie had been quiet the entire way back. She had not said a word to Gabbie about what had taken place at Barney's, as if to speak of the conversation would give weight to Barney's words. But it was obvious even to someone as young as Sean that she was deeply disturbed by what Barney had said, and she did urge Gabbie to keep Sean home until he'd fully recovered. After she had left, Sean begged his sister not to tell on him. Gabbie agreed not to say anything in exchange for his promise not to leave the house until Gloria said it was all right.

His father was due home for dinner in a short while, after visiting the thing they thought was Patrick and checking some stuff with the doctors. Sean fumed as he rolled over. He had one last shot at getting out, and he knew that tonight was the night he had to act. He just wished for a chance to talk to Barney again, rather than having to wait until everyone was asleep. That would give him too little time, he was certain. He didn't understand it all, but he had figured out enough to know he had to act tonight, and the later he got started, the less time he had left to do something about Patrick.

The door downstairs shut and Sean jumped up. He hurried down the hall and the stairs to where his father stood. Phil looked at his son and smiled. "Hi, sport. How're things?"

Sean steeled himself against looking too anxious. He gave his dad a quick hug, then made his pitch. "Mom won't let me go to the Halloween party tonight." His tone made it seem the most unreasonable sort of confinement, and was just short of whiny.

Phil moved slowly toward the kitchen. "Look, there'll be other parties and . . . well, your mom's pretty upset these days." He stopped and studied the face of his son. With all Phil's worry about Patrick, he had all but ignored Sean. After a moment he said, "But then, it's been no picnic for you, has it?"

An odd expression crossed Phil's face and he pushed open the door to the kitchen. Gloria and Gabbie were both readying dinner. Greetings were exchanged, and Gabbie said, "Jack called. He's on his way down, hangover and all. He'll be here in an hour." Jack had passed his orals Friday afternoon, advancing him to candidacy for a doctorate. He had called to tell her and had wanted to come back at once, but Gabbie had overruled him, insisting he let some of his grad student friends take him out to celebrate, a party that had lasted until late. As a result, Jack didn't get started until Saturday afternoon on some paperwork that needed to be on his adviser's desk first thing Monday morning. That had made driving down to Pittsville on Saturday out of the question. Gabbie had wished she had been with him, but had refused to leave, with Gloria in such rugged shape.

Phil said, "Honey, I think it's all right if we let Sean go to the party tonight."

Gloria's head jerked up, a panic-stricken look in her eyes. Before she could object, he said, "He's been fine for a couple of days now, and it would do him good to get out." Sean threw Gabbie a pleading look, silently begging her not to speak of his encounter with Aggie the day before. Gabbie shook her head slightly and winked, then turned her attention back to the salad.

Gloria seemed on the verge of saying something, but instead turned back to the cooking, saying, "Well . . . he doesn't have a costume."

Sean jumped in. "I can go as a pirate! I can put a bandanna around my head and tuck my pants in my rain boots, and wear one of Dad's belts like this"—he made an over-the-shoulder motion—"and Gabbie can make me a scar with lipstick. Please, Mom."

Gloria seemed close to tears, and Phil calmly said, "It's at the school. They'll be supervised and he'll be home by nine. How about it?"

Gloria struggled within herself. Something was building around her and she couldn't understand what it was. Her intellect said there would be no real harm in letting Sean attend a supervised school function, but her gut, her instinct, said there was a terrible risk. Yet she couldn't articulate those terrible fears, so at the last she simply nodded, her face drawn and ashen. Sean leaped from the chair, yelling "Thanks, Mom!" and dashed through the door.

Phil went to his wife and hugged her. "We'll drop him off on our way to the hospital."

Gabbie said, "And Jack and I can pick him up."

Gloria put her head on Phil's shoulder a moment. She almost understood, recognition hung just beyond her grasp: something of awesome power moved in the night, something that had entrapped her family. They were overwhelmed by ancient mysteries, dark magics and lost gold, and creatures not of this earth. Those creatures had taken one of her sons. And with dread certainty she knew that tonight she would lose the other. But she also knew she was powerless to do anything, and those around her, those she loved most, could never understand. All this knowledge was tantalizingly close to being articulated, but something kept that knowledge from coalescing, from becoming concrete enough to be shared. She simply closed her eyes a moment, then with a sigh of resignation said, "Gabbie, will you take the chicken out when it's done? I think I'm going to lie down for a little while before dinner." She turned away from her husband, opened the door to the hall, and left.

23

Sean walked out of the house between his parents. He was pleased with the makeshift costume. One of Gabbie's old white blouses gave just the right effect, had the right collar and everything, and with the puffy sleeves rolled up looked just like a pirate shirt. His jeans were tucked into his rain boots and an old belt of his dad's hung over one shoulder in a fair imitation of a baldric. A red bandanna was tied around his head in pirate fashion. Gloria opened the car door, saying nothing as they got in the car, her eyes red-rimmed. She had slept through dinner, but had risen to join her husband and son. She said little, just repeatedly cautioning Sean to be careful. Sean didn't notice, as he was busy praying no one remarked on his funny walk, for concealed in his right boot was his father's silver letter opener.

Phil kept up a light banter, as if forcing normalcy on his family. Sean answered his father's questions as they drove to the school, making small talk. Phil attempted to reestablish some sense of normalcy with his son—his surviving son, he thought grimly. Rain began to fall again, and Phil said, "You should have brought a jacket, son."

"I'll be okay," Sean insisted. "It's only a little way from the street to the auditorium, and I'll wait inside till Jack an' Gabbie get me."

"Okay, buccaneer," said Phil, with forced joviality. He pulled up to the curbside before the elementary school and watched as Gloria got out, allowing Sean to leave. As he started past his mother, she reached out and grabbed him, and for one panic-stricken moment Sean was afraid she'd drag him back into the car. Instead all she did was hug him fiercely, all the while silent, then without a word she let him go and stood in the misting drizzle watching as Sean walked to the auditorium. With a sudden sense of melancholia, Phil felt a tear run down his cheek, and he was visited with the feeling that he was seeing Sean for the last time. He shrugged off the feeling as being due to too much stress and fatigue over the last week, and after Gloria was again in the car, he drove off.

Sean approached the auditorium. The other kids had already begun to gather. There would be some organized activities, a lot of booths set up with games of chance—pitch a dime to win a goldfish, darts and balloons, a wheel of fortune, beanbag toss, and other stuff—and free treats for everyone. They'd also have organized games and records, so kids could dance, though Sean thought that was something the girls would like more than the boys.

Sean heard his parents' car pull away and glanced back to watch as they drove off. The high clouds hid the last rays of the setting sun, reducing the landscape to black and grey as the mist turned to a more honest drizzle. Sean considered: the party was scheduled to run from six to nine, so he had to time everything perfectly. Sean looked about, joined a knot of kids by the door, and waited.

24

Aggie negotiated the turns in Highway 117, the main artery down to Pittsville from Interstate 90 out of Buffalo. She squinted against the dazzling lights of oncoming cars, reflected off the slick roadway. The rain had halted, for which she was thankful, for her old full-size Ford handled like a battleship on these slick roads. She made the transition from the state highway to the local road heading toward the Hastingses' place.

As she passed under the overpass, the classical music station faded and the rain resumed with a vengeance. Sheets of water poured down, obscuring everything but the yellow broken line that ran down the road. Aggie flipped the wipers to high speed and slowed the car. There were two bad turns before she reached the cutoff to the Hastings farm, and she wasn't exactly sure where she was. Familiar landmarks were nonexistent. With no roadside lamps, all she could see was the area covered by the glare of her car's high beams. She rode through a tunnel of night. Distant lightning flashes caused the radio to issue raucous noises, so Aggie turned it off.

She drove for a while until she began to wonder if she'd somehow taken a wrong turn. She was tired from lack of sleep—she had spent long hours at the Hastings home the last week. And she had also lived with a bone-deep weariness born of worry for Patrick. The conversation with Barney and Sean the day before had put her on edge, visiting her with an unfocused pensive anxiety. She had been troubled by a feeling with no name. Since Mark had called she had a name for the feeling: fear.

Aggie glanced at her passenger, who sat stoically with eyes forward, saying nothing. Less than six hours before, she had received a call from Mark Blackman. He had tried to call Gary, but the younger man was off someplace for a day with his girlfriend. Mark had tried the Hastings house, but the phone had been busy. In desperation, he had called Aggie and, with that strange and cryptic long-distance conversation, had plunged her into a frightening world, a world she had glimpsed for the first time when Sean had come to Barney Doyle's shack the day before.

Then another call had come, and with persuasion beyond Aggie's understanding, her passenger had convinced her to make the drive to Buffalo, to pick him up at the airport. And all Aggie knew about this man was he was German and said he was expected by Mark Blackman, when he showed up. Aggie had not be able to articulate her confusion as she agreed to come fetch this stranger. Some power was at play this night, and that power was beyond her ability to know fully, but she could discern part of the whole; she could see how alien that power was. And recognizing that alien quality added to her understanding.

What she had at last come to understand, even if only a part of a larger whole, frightened her, frightened her more than she would have thought anything could. She was so concerned over her passenger's presence that she had to force herself to keep her mind on her driving. Mark and Gary's speculation about some secret organization to which Kessler belonged being in existence in this era was no longer a theory. For a member of that organization sat in the passenger seat, after a long flight from Germany. And they were riding down to the Hastings place in this terrible storm because somehow this man must get there before Mark.

Mark had not told Aggie where he was. He might have called from New York City, or from Buffalo, or from Toronto. He might have flown in an hour before this man, rented a car and be just a few miles ahead, or he could be speeding to overtake them. But however he was coming, Mark had said it was imperative he reach Erl King Hill before midnight, yet no one should know he was coming. And without Mark's saying anything, Aggie had understood his life was at risk.

And despite her promise to say nothing about Mark's return, this stranger had overcome her will, had made her come for him, tell him what she knew, and bring him to find Mark. Now every shadow held menace, every dark place a threat of destruction.

Aggie considered what knowledge meant and the never before understood wisdom inherent in the old saw "Ignorance is bliss." The threat of a mugger was unreal to a farm boy, while it inspired terror in a city dweller. Such was the price of knowledge. Now threats Aggie would have dismissed as fantastic and impossible days ago were a tangible danger, terribly real. She felt the same as that farm boy would have to find himself suddenly in an alley with a gun pointed at his head by a drug-crazed junkie.

Aggie wished she could have tracked down Gary before driving to Buffalo and told him to meet her at the Hastings house. But some force of this man's will had prevented that. She decided that she'd call Gary as soon as she got there—assuming her passenger would let her. She glanced over at him. He had barely spoken a dozen words, all with a heavy German accent, to her since she found him at the airport. He looked nothing so much as a small-town businessman, portly, balding, and wearing an inexpensive, rumpled suit. All she knew was his name, August . . . something. She gripped the wheel tighter. She was scared, for despite the man's harmless appearance, he radiated that alien strength she had sensed all night.

Aggie blinked several times, wondering where she was. Then she saw the first landmark, Lonny Boggs's mailbox. The Hastings place would be two farms up. They made the first turn in the road carefully, but as she approached the second, she picked up speed. She spoke softly to her passenger, saying they were almost at their destination. All the man said was a half-grunt, which might have been *"Gut."* As Aggie came out of the turn, a lighting flash illuminated the road.

Something sprang across the road from out of the woods. For a scant moment Aggie thought it a deer, for she saw a rack of antlers. An instant later, she was turning the wheel furiously, for the thing in the middle of the road had stopped, preventing her passing. The car swerved and Aggie reflexively hit the brakes as her passenger swore an oath of astonishment in German. Suddenly the car was spinning out of control, and Aggie vainly attempted to turn back into the drift of the automobile.

To Aggie it was as if everything was instantly moving sideways. For a second, whatever was in the road was illuminated by the sweep of the car's headlights, and Aggie saw a figure sitting atop a horse. As the car spun, Aggie had a brief thought that somehow Jack or Gabbie was out riding in the rain, then, as the car completed a circle, the figure was again visible in the lights. It wasn't Jack or Gabbie. The horse was impossibly white, nearly glowing in the rain, the mane and tail almost aflame with golden highlights. And the rider wasn't human. Squarely atop the shoulders rested a golden helm, topped by ivory antlers. And in the open face of the helm, a visage of inhuman features regarded the out-of-control car. Eyes glowing with their own inner light followed its spinning path. Aggie's mouth opened in a scream of terror, more for certain knowledge of what she faced in that instant than for fear of the crash. Through her own fear she was dimly aware that her companion was shouting, but not so much in fear as in anger and warning. Aggie's mind rebelled at the truth seen, even though she had known what it was, and she closed her eyes and braced herself against the steering wheel as the car began to turn over.

As Aggie's car left the road, slamming into a tree, the rider threw back his head and howled an inhuman laugh. The noise of the crash was muted by the driving rain.

Aggie sat motionless, in shock for a long minute, then she shook her head to clear it. Her eyes burned and she wiped them. Her hand encountered warmth, and she knew she was bleeding. She glanced toward her passenger and saw the man's head had smashed the side window, spider-webbing the glass. Blood was flowing copiously across his forehead, but the blank, slack-jawed expression and vacant eyes told Aggie the man was dead.

Somehow the car had landed mostly upright, pointing up toward the road as it sat on the embankment. Aggie vainly tried to unfasten her safety belt, her fingers unable to coordinate to push the simple button. Through the window, the rain beating down upon it, she could see movement. As she tried to free herself, waves of nausea swept over her and she collapsed as her head swam, leaning against the side window, her vision blurring.

Aggie closed her eyes and that made the dizziness worse, so she forced herself alert and opened them. She felt an odd detachment and wondered if she was dying. Upon the road she could make out the rider, a dim figure in the dark, and she could feel the creature's malevolent gaze on her.

As the creature spurred his mount toward the wreckage, Aggie felt her strength ebb and knew that soon she would be dead. The rider knew of their coming, and knew that Aggie's passenger was an enemy. Old tales remembered, tales now known to be, as Barney had said, true stories, those old tales made her understand that destruction rode toward her at leisurely pace. Aggie found her fear had fled with the certainty of death, but she felt a deep regret at the price others would soon be forced to pay.

Then the night was lit by flashing red and blue lights as another car rounded the corner, a county sheriff's car. Aggie saw the rider turn his

steed and spur it back into the woods. As darkness began to enfold
Aggie, she was dimly aware of the squawking sound made by the car's
police radio. She thought that someone at Lonny Boggs's farm must
have heard the crash and called in. Aggie cried out and her voice
sounded weak and distant in her own ear. She fought to stay conscious,
since there was so little time left, only hours.

As darkness closed around her, she thought she could hear another
car approaching, pulling over, then a door slam. From a great distance
away she could hear a voice, Mark's voice, calling her name. Her last
thoughts were *Poor, poor Patrick.* Then she sank into a black void.

25

At seven-thirty Sean walked to the auditorium door and asked Mr.
Hanes, the third-grade teacher, if he could go to the boys' room. The
instructor nodded absently, for kids had been going in and out all
evening. Several boys were using the rest room, and Sean made a show
of entering one of the stalls. He sat with his pants around his ankles for
what he judged the proper amount of time, then left. Instead of returning to the auditorium, he ducked into a side hall, then ran in the
opposite direction from the auditorium, toward the library. He remembered a piece of trivia he had overheard: during any school activity, all
doors in the building were set so the crash bars would let people out,
even if they couldn't be opened from the outside. Sean reached the
outside door next to the school library, he pushed down quietly on the
crash bar, and the door opened with a loud click. Sean made good his
escape. Within minutes he was running across the park, heading for
Barney's shack.

It was raining again, heavy and cold. Sean was wet and chilled
when he reached the shack. He hit the door with his fist, yelling Barney's name.

After what seemed an eternity, the door opened and Barney stood
before him, holding a bottle of Jameson's whiskey, obviously halfway to
being drunk. The handyman said, "Ah! Have you come for some treats,
Sean Hastings? I've none, as you no doubt know. Come in, then, for

you're certain to catch your death if you stand there gawking." The boy entered and Barney sought out a fairly clean towel and tossed it to the boy, who dried himself as best he could. " 'Tis a foolish thing for you to be doing, dashing about in the rain without a coat, Sean, and you just being over a high fever."

"Barney, I've got to find Patrick. You said the Good People were leaving tonight!"

"True. At the first stroke of midnight, they'll pack up, kit and kaboodle, and off they'll go. And by the twelfth stroke they'll be gone from sight, finding some other plot of woodlands—God knows where— and some other poor community to terrorize. God grant that it's the English." He lifted the bottle of whiskey in salute to that and drank. Fixing the boy with a still-steady eye, he said, "Then have you brought a silver arrow and a bow, or a silver sword, as I told your brother?"

Sean reached down into his boot and pulled out the silver letter opener. "I got this."

Slowly Barney went down on his knees before the boy. He took the letter opener and turned it in his hand. It was silver. He looked at it for what seemed a long time, then looked at Sean. He let out a soft sigh. Tears welled up in his eyes as he reached out a shaking hand to touch the boy's shoulder. "You're bound to do this thing, then?"

"I've got to, Barney. Patrick will go with them tonight, won't he?"

Almost whispering, Barney answered. "Aye, and he'll be lost for eternity, for the chances of finding the Good People again are scant. I've seen them once and then once again in my life, and it was a good fifty years between. And most see them not at all during their mortal span. But it's a fearful and dangerous thing you're proposing, Sean Hastings. Your parents may mourn two sons this night. Have you wrestled with that?"

Sean nodded his head curtly, then said, "Where is Patrick?"

Barney got up, taking the letter opener. He turned and took up a sharpener he used on scissors, shears, and knives, and put a sharp edge to the blade, paying special attention to giving it a wicked point. Satisfied the ersatz dagger was as keen as possible, he returned it to Sean. Barney fetched a coat from a hook, placing the half-empty bottle of whiskey in one large pocket and a long waterproof flashlight in the other. He took down a small jar and emptied all the screws from it. He searched and found a lid, then fit it into place. "Then if you're committed, you'd best go armed with whatever you can find. Come with me quickly, for there's scant time, in truth." He started to move, then thought of something. He pulled open a drawer and rifled through it until at last he pulled out a string of rosary beads and a cross. " 'Tis an age since I've had the good sense to pray, Sean, but this night I'll make up for those lost days."

Barney led the boy out of the shack, slamming the door behind but not bothering to lock it. He half ran, half walked, as fast as his old legs could manage, while Sean trotted beside him. "First," said Barney, "we must go to St. Catherine's."

He hurried Sean along to the large church on Third Street, four blocks from the park. Pushing open the large doors, he whispered, " 'Tis All Saints' Day on the morrow, and there'll be those at prayer, so walk softly." He led the boy through the narthex of the church to where a font of holy water awaited the congregation. Barney unscrewed the cap and filled the jar, quickly screwing the cap back on.

With a motion for silence, Barney led the boy into the nave. They passed a pair of silent worshippers who didn't bother to look up as Barney and Sean moved toward the front of the church. In the transept stood a statue of the Virgin, before which were burning dozens of candles. Barney reached the point before the altar and knelt, crossing himself, and Sean imitated him. Then he moved to the altar of the Virgin and rummaged through his pocket for coins. Depositing some quarters in a box, he took a candle and gave it to Sean. "Light this, and while you do, pray to Our Lady to watch over you, Sean. This sort of undertaking must have holy sanctification, or 'tis doomed to failure. Do you understand?"

Sean nodded. His parents had never practiced, but he had been to church with his Grandmother O'Brien. He lit the candle and placed it before the statue of the Virgin. He closed his eyes and softly said, "Please, Lady, help me find Patrick and get him back safe."

Barney studied the small boy for a long moment, his eyes showing approval. "That's as honest as a prayer can be, in truth. Now we must hurry."

He led the boy down one aisle, past the confessionals. Outside the church the rain pelted them as they hurried along the streets, passed Barney's shack, then into the woods. Barney took out the flashlight and turned it on. "From here you must listen carefully, for the way is perilous. Should you become lost, you'll be lost forever. Do you understand?"

Sean swallowed his fear and nodded. Barney sighed in resignation. "Then listen: the way to the land of the Good People lies under the hill on your property."

"Erl King Hill," said Sean.

"So the German called it. A proper fairy mound it is, no doubt." They walked slowly through the trees, along the path the boys used to travel to and from the park. Sean knew the way and had little trouble following Barney's lead. The half-drunk Irishman continued his instructions. "Facing the setting sun, you walk nine times widdershins—that's anticlockwise, lad—until you find the entrance to the land of the Good People." He rubbed his face, forcing back to the surface long-forgotten lore. "Once through the cave, you'll find a path."

"Like the Yellow Brick Road?"

"You can think of it that way, lad. But it won't be yellow. But if you say this: 'By the blessed St. Patrick, Our Lady, and in the name of our Lord, guide my way,' you'll find a guide."

"A guide? Who?"

"I don't know, lad, for the stories are confused. It may be a raven, who you must be leery of, for he is a wily and treacherous guide who'll try to lead you astray unless you keep an eye on him and command him to truth. It may be a man or woman, who'll speak in a foreign language and may seek to beguile you. Or it may be a child. But most likely it will be a golden ball of light. Or so the legends say. Follow it. You must not leave the roadway save to follow the guide. You must not stop longer than it takes to catch a breath, or you'll lose your guide. And you may not trust anyone you meet, no matter how fair they seem." He thought, then said, "Save one. There may be a man, called True Tom, so the stories say. He cannot lie, so if you meet him, you can trust his answers to be without falsehood. You'll know him by his speech, for he's a Scotsman, which means he's almost Irish." Then with a shrug, he added, "At least he's not an Englishman."

Sean nodded, but he was beginning to feel overwhelmed with the enormity of what he was undertaking. He just kept in mind what Barney had said, and found that concentrating on the long list of things to do and not to do was a convenient way to ignore his fear.

"Now, along the way you may see sights of wonder and beauty, but never, never leave the path, save at your guide's bidding. There'll be a house of light and music, and one whose cornerposts are mighty trees, larger than redwoods. You'll be tempted to enter, but do not. You may not return." Barney turned his head away as if seeking to see something in the night, and his red-rimmed eyes ran with tears. "There are so many stories, lad, and I can't recall but a tenth part of them. Ah, where have my wits fled? I can't remember." With emphasis he said, "Sean, whatever else, remember this one thing. Don't leave the path, save when you're bid to by whatever guide God sends you."

They approached the backside of the hill, and Barney led Sean up the side, shining the light on the wet ground. He reached down and plucked up a handful of grass.

"What are you doing?" asked Sean.

"Making it possible for you to see what is real," answered Barney, holding out his hand for Sean to see. "Shamrocks."

"That's clover," said Sean.

"And what do you think a shamrock is, Sean Hastings? A bloody California cactus?" He unscrewed the cap of the jar of holy water. He crushed the shamrocks in the lid, holding the open jar under his coat. Adding some holy water, he used his thumb to mix the mess together. "I don't think any of God's clean rain will dilute this too much," he whispered, a half prayer. He motioned Sean close and dipped his thumb in the greenish mess. "Close your eyes," he instructed. He rubbed his damp thumb lightly over Sean's eyelids. "Use your hand to cover your eyes, so the rain doesn't wash the stain off."

Sean did as he was told. Quickly Barney intoned, "Blessed St. Patrick, watch over this boy and let his eyes see what is true and what is not. Amen." He said to Sean, "Without the juice of the shamrock mixed with holy water, you'd not be able to resist their guiles. The fairy stone will keep their hands off your person, lad, and this will keep your mind free of their glamours and spells, but only so long as you don't wash it off. Remember, there is much that is beautiful but false in the land of the Good People. Be cautious." He emptied out the lid and, still protecting the holy water, used the falling rain to cleanse the lid of stains. When he was satisfied he had purged the lid of foreign matter, he screwed the cap back on the jar.

He handed the jar to Sean and led him toward the Troll Bridge. "When you reach the end of your journey, you'll meet the Fool." Barney stopped before the burned-out oak stump under which Jack had found the gold. Barney knelt, ignoring the mud, and gripped Sean's shoulders. "Listen close if you would have any hope for your brother or yourself. They call him the Fool, for in the old tongue that is his name, but you can't be thinking him a silly or clownish fellow. In the old language 'fool' means one who is unmindful of risk: a wanton, reckless sort of a rogue with no mind for danger, one who will dare things no sane man would. And this Fool is dangerous beyond contemplation. Do you understand what I'm saying to you, Sean Hastings?"

Sean nodded, but it was evident much of what Barney was saying was confusing him. At last Barney said, "Well then, just be mindful he's as dangerous as anyone this side of the devil can be, and you'll have the right of it. Now here's what you must do, lad. You must call him by his true name. Amadán-na-Briona. Say that name." Sean repeated the name, and Barney said, "No, that will never do." He drilled Sean a dozen times until he was satisfied with the boy's pronunciation.

Barney glanced toward the hill, a black shadow rising against a

broken gloom of trees. "When you say his true name, you'll have power
over him. Not much, but enough. Command him by our blessed Lord
Jesus to give back your brother to you and let you go free. You must
instruct him, and his followers, to let you go unmolested. He must do
this thing. But be cautious of how you say it, lad, for you may only
command him once." Barney told Sean exactly what to say, then his
face clouded. "I wish we knew what sort of beastie this Bad Thing of
yours may be, but we don't, so there's no use dwelling on it. If he comes,
he comes. The fairy stone will keep him leery of you, but you must
protect Patrick. Use your dagger and perhaps some holy water. These
creatures were those who stood aside when Satan led his host in rebel-
lion against our Heavenly Father. Not so righteous they could remain in
God's heaven but not so evil they deserved hell with the devil, they
were placed in this land between. Still, they are given to avoiding things
holy, so use the water if you must, but save some. This is most important." Barney gripped the boy's shoulders tightly, as if to impress upon
him what he was saying. "Once you've found your brother, you must
pour some of the holy water on his head and make the sign of the cross
upon his forehead and say, 'In the name of our Lord, you are free.'
Repeat it." Sean did so and got it right.

"Do not overlook this in the excitement of the moment. For until
you do this thing, Patrick'll be the servant of the Fool, and he may fight
to stay. Then you must leave quickly, for should there be any way the
Fool can devise to follow after you, any way he can get around your
order to let you go free, he will. And should he follow you outside the
hill, he may take you again. And that would be for once and for all. No
one outside can best him, save a true bard or some other manner of
sorcerer, and neither you nor I've the knack of magic. So bid him stay
behind when he frees your brother, for after midnight he must leave.
Now, the last: *do not stop to rest*, even should your guide permit it. Time
is not there as 'tis here. Stop to nap and you'll awaken years from now,
no older but for a night, but hopelessly lost to return, and too faraway
for finding. So keep awake and keep moving."

Tears filled Barney's eyes and he said, "Ah, 'tis a perilous path
you've chosen, Sean. Keep moving, remember what I've told you, and
trust no one save True Tom if you should chance to meet him. When
you've returned, come out the cave, and move deasil—clockwise—
round the hill nine times and you'll be back. You must be gone from the
hill by midnight, or who knows where you'll come out." His voice
softened, and he hugged the boy tightly. "If I were a man instead of a
drunken old sod I would be doing this brave thing instead of standing
fearfully aside while a boy goes to do it. You're a fine and courageous lad,

Sean O'Brien Hastings, even if you're only half Irish. Go now and be quickly back, and may blessed St. Patrick and the Holy Mother protect you."

With the sign of the cross, and a shove, he sent Sean off. The boy spun and faced the hill. He moved off to the right, making a complete circle of the hill. After the eighth pass, he disappeared from Barney's sight. The old handyman continued to kneel in the mud, and he took out the rosary beads and shouted into the night. "I'll pray for you, Sean Hastings. I'll pray to St. Jude, who watches over impossible undertakings, and Our Lady, and St. Patrick . . . and even to that Englishman, St. George, so he might guide your dagger should there be need." His voice softened, and he added, "And I'll not leave until the twelfth stroke of midnight, you dear brave lad." Ignoring the rain that beat down upon him, and the mud in which he knelt, Barney Doyle prayed. And he prayed with a fervency he hadn't felt since a boy.

26

Sean moved away from Barney, shielding his eyes against the heavy rain. He was conscious of everything around him, the tattoo of the rain in the trees and the odd echoes that sound made around him. There was a pungent and wet piny odor in the air, a damp wood smell so intense it made Sean heady as he breathed it in. He felt and heard the plopping of sticky mud reluctant to let go of his rubber rain boots. Gabbie's blouse stuck to his body, and he felt the chill caress of the wind. He pushed these concerns from his mind and tried to recall everything Barney had told him as he moved around the hill, passing from Barney's sight.

On his third pass, the rain halted, and he lowered his hand from where it had shaded the grass stains around his eyes. He saw that Barney looked odd, as if they were separated by some strange sheet of amber glass.

On his fourth, it got warmer.

On his sixth, there seemed to be more light.

On his seventh trip, the hill was definitely brighter, while the surrounding woods were plunged into jet blackness, so that he could no longer see the kneeling Barney. The wind was a distant whisper and the odor of pine and wet earth a faint memory.

On his eighth pass, the hill was an island in space, with no hint of surrounding countryside. No light or sound existed beyond the hill.

On his ninth pass about the hill, he came to a cave mouth. Through it he could see light a great distance off.

Sean paused, took a deep breath, and entered the hill.

27

Sean stepped into the cave in the side of Erl King Hill. Cautiously at first, he crept down a long tunnel, feeling his way in the blackness. Suddenly he fell forward, as if stepping into a huge hole. For an instant he screamed in terror as his stomach twisted. Then abruptly he was standing on firm ground. He cried out again as he experienced the jolting change in orientation. It was as if the world had swung up ninety degrees; he was falling, then suddenly standing upright as gravity caught up with him.

Sean knew he was someplace else.

He could see nothing save a faint illumination at the far end of the tunnel. Forcing himself to stop crying, he felt around in the gloom until he recovered his dagger. He checked the holy water and was relieved to find the jar still safely in his shirt. Sean took a deep breath, then told himself, "Shut up, crybaby." Feeling better for that admonition, he resumed his travels.

He walked for what seemed a long time through the darkened tunnel, surrounded by the rich, musty odors of damp earth. After a subjective eternity, he saw the distant golden light begin to grow larger. He made his way to it and emerged from a cave in a hillside.

Sean exhaled as his eyes drank in the alien landscape before him. Trees too perfect to exist on earth swayed in a gentle breeze under a sky halfway between blue and black. It was daylight, but eerily so, as if the light came from all directions rather than any single source, and at a quarter normal illumination. It was a hazy beach day without the glare. And there was something golden in the light, a shade of champagne color that gently skewed the eye's perception. Everything within Sean's view looked dark, yet he could perceive detail.

The boy shuddered a moment and fought off his first real attack of panic. This was like nothing he had expected. He had thought of some sort of Walt Disney place, painted in bright colors of intense hue. Instead he looked out across a land of halftones, of golden hazes and soft smokes, every color cut and muted as if he looked through grey lenses. It was a place of fog, yet that fog was unseen. Light came gently, as if the rules for light were different here. No sunlight, Sean thought; ever.

A path, or rather a road, ran from under his feet off into the distance. It was fashioned of stone, light, almost white in color. He stood unable to move. He looked off into the distance and saw some people issuing from the darker places between trees near the edge of the meadow. He hadn't seen them a moment before. They moved toward him, as if in frolic, pointing at him and speaking in an unknown language. Sean's eyes nearly boggled as they came close enough for him to see detail. They wore all manner of clothing, from being almost entirely naked to being covered from head to foot in richly embroidered period clothing of fine weave and complex fashion. But all of them had green skin. The wind carried the faint sounds of laughter, and Sean shivered. It was not the mad laugh of the Fool, but there was nothing human in its sound either.

Sean swallowed a giddy fear and reached up to touch the stain on his right eyelid. He felt the gunk still there, so if what Barney had said was true, there were green people running toward him. He swallowed the urge to cry and spoke the words Barney had forced him to remember. "By the blessed St. Patrick, Our Lady, and in the name of our Lord, guide my way." His voice was high-pitched, strained by fear, but somehow he managed to say the words loudly.

Instantly a humming sound filled the air, and the green people halted their movement toward him. From the far end of the path an object appeared, speeding along toward him. A miniature sun hurled toward Sean, but as it neared he saw it was only bright in comparison to the muted landscape in which he found himself. It was a globe of golden light, spinning rapidly, so that no feature or detail of its surface was apparent. The green people spoke softly among themselves, gesturing to the boy and the golden sphere. It raced toward him with a low hum, until at last it hovered before the boy. Sean said, "Are you my guide?"

The globe bobbed, as if affirming its nature, and Sean said, "Help me. I want to find my brother, Patrick. The Fool's got him."

The globe seemed to spin erratically for a moment, as if struck by fear, but after an instant of odd movement it circled around Sean and began moving down the road. Sean sucked in a deep breath, realized he had tears on his cheeks, and wiped them away. With a show of resolution he didn't feel, he marched after the slowly moving globe, determined to follow it to quest's end. The green people were silent as the boy moved past them. They seemed undisturbed by what they had witnessed, but they had lost their gay demeanor at the mention of the Fool's name, and they stepped out of Sean's way, letting him follow his guide unhindered.

28

There seemed no time. Barney had mentioned something about this, but Sean couldn't recall what he'd said. Sean felt the faint stirrings of hunger and wished he had brought something to eat, maybe a peanut butter sandwich. But he couldn't be expected to think of everything. He clutched his dagger of silver in his right hand and followed after the golden ball of light. He had tried talking to the light, but it had remained mute. The landscape through which they moved was an eerie delight to the senses, woodlands of dark and alien beauty. Streams of crystal water flowed nearby, and Sean wondered if the water was safe to drink. Barney hadn't said anything, but Sean thought it best to wait until he absolutely had to have a drink.

The ball moved in an odd rhythm, swaying from side to side above the road, almost as if dancing or skipping. Sean plodded silently along the center of the off-white stones.

After some long and uncounted time, Sean saw a castle in the distance. He thought it took the longest time to reach it, for it was very large and grew slowly as he marched along. Rounding a curve in the road, Sean saw a man sitting near the roadside. He was perched upon a large rock that sat at an intersection of the white road and a smaller path that led to the drawbridge of the castle.

The boy squinted to get a better view of the castle in the haze, and for all his efforts, he could only tell it was an immense place, with walls

that seemed more like glass than stone. Upon the distant towers brave
pennants flew in the odd breeze and people moved, though Sean
couldn't tell if they were really people. The light in this place made
anything distant look funny. The castle rose up above a beach, upon the
shore of a large lake or bay. Sean wondered how he could not see such a
large body of water until now. He glanced off to the other side of the
castle and saw the shore quickly enshrouded in mists, which faded to
silver and gold light. A tremble passed through Sean as he tried to
understand what he was seeing. To him it seemed like a TV picture
where the screen changed from one image to another, but somehow got
stuck in the middle of the dissolve. Putting aside his disquiet, the boy
keep moving along the road, bringing him to where the man sat.

Sean slowed to study the man as he passed him. The man's dark hair
hung to his shoulders and his beard was thick and unkempt. He wore a
shirt of iron rings sewn to leather, with a simple pair of woolen trousers
tucked into boots of soft leather, sheepskin surrounding the top. Sean
thought he looked sort of like a Viking, but he had no helm with horns.
Sean approached cautiously to the edge of the road, bringing him to
within twenty feet of the silent warrior, but the man showed no sign of
being aware of the boy's presence. He seemed in a trance, or so deep in
thought he was oblivious to anything else. Along his scalp ran a deep
scar, pink and puckered, with only a short growth of hair around it,
looking only recently healed. Sean noted he held an empty scabbard
across his knees. The boy slowed his progress even more, so he could
watch as four women accompanied by a cortege of servants emerged
from the barbican of the castle and crossed the bridge. Each seemed
human, if not without an otherworldly quality to their beauty. One was
dressed in regal raiments of crimson and gold, while the second was
equally splendid and commanding in a gown of deep green. The third
wore white and silver, while the fourth was dressed in black. As they
approached, Sean halted, unable to take his eyes from the wondrous
procession. The woman in black was the only one who seemed to notice
Sean, but she merely looked at him a brief moment, a sad and resigned
expression in her blue eyes, as she gifted him with a hint of a smile, then
turned to face the man upon the rock. She spoke so softly that Sean
could not hear her words, and the man seemed to come out of some
trance.

The four women waited while the warrior slowly stood. He paused
a moment as he caught sight of Sean, then spoke. His words were in a
language unknown to the boy, and faint, as if some agency were
preventing Sean from clearly hearing what was said, and his manner
was hesitant and uncertain. The woman in black spoke, casting a brief

glance at the boy. The man nodded and offered his arm to the woman. She took it and the pair turned toward the castle, the other three women following, their servants bringing up the rear.

Sean was fascinated by the display, wondering who these fabulous people could be, but his attention was pulled away by the sight of his golden guide vanishing over the horizon. Then Sean remembered Barney's warning about not stopping lest he lose his guide. Feeling panic strike, he saw the guide was gone. He sprinted after the ball of light.

He crested a hill and saw he had gained ground on the orb, but still he ran, fearing to lose his only hope of finding his brother. By the time he had overtaken the ball of golden light, he noticed the trees had closed in on both sides of the road and everything had grown darker. These woods were more oppressive, more somber, than those that stretched back from the castle to the hill with the green people. Sean gripped his dagger tighter. Forcing himself to calmness, the boy followed doggedly on behind the shimmering guide.

29

Phil glanced through the glass to where Mickey Bergman was examining Patrick one last time before leaving for Baltimore in the morning.

The doctor left Patrick's bedside and came out of the room. Bergman took Phil by the arm, steering him to where Gloria sat in the waiting area. She had left Phil's side, unable to watch the shrieking creature that had once been her son struggling to bite and scratch the attendants as they held him down so Mickey Bergman could examine him. "Philip, I was going to call you if you hadn't come in. There's something I need tell you."

"About Patrick?" said Gloria.

"Yes. I'm sorry, but his behavior is becoming more . . . extreme. He's also . . . stronger, as if . . . I don't know, a kind of hysterical strength, maybe. It's getting more difficult to work with him. He . . . attacked a candy striper today."

"What?" said Phil in astonishment.

Bergman sat down opposite Phil and Gloria. "The girl meant well, but she was being pretty stupid entering that room—she's new. She said she saw Patrick through the window and he *seemed* so upset and frightened. It took two orderlies and a nurse to pull him off of her."

"What did he do?" asked Gloria.

Mickey shook his head. "If he wasn't only eight years old, I'd say he tried to rape her."

Gloria's expression was eloquent, even if she couldn't find words. Bergman continued, "He had the girl's blouse torn half off and was holding her down on the bed." Mickey's face showed uncertainty. "He bit her on the left breast, a nasty wound. The girl's going to have a scar.

"Look, if this continues, I don't know if that state hospital Wingate's suggested is the best place for Patrick. I can get him into one of the psych research units at Johns Hopkins. I think I'd like to follow this case a while longer."

Phil said, "Thanks, Mickey. But why the sudden interest?"

Bergman sat back, arms crossed. "I can't tell you really. There's just something about this one that bugs the hell out of me." He looked at Gloria, finding her more collected than he had seen her so far, so he ventured an opinion. "I don't know what's with Patrick, but it's unique. And . . . if we can find out what it is . . . maybe we can . . ."

"Help him?" said Gloria with little hope evidenced in her tone or manner.

Mickey shook his head. "I can't say that. I just think we might discover something important. I really can't tell you why. Call it a hunch."

Phil said, "We'll talk it over. How long before we can see Patrick?"

"A while, I'm afraid. You'll have to wait a bit. It's taking more drugs to calm him, and longer for them to take effect. I'm thinking of changing what we give him so he doesn't develop drug problems along with everything else. And . . . it'll be a while before he's cleaned up." Looking hard at them, he said, "You realize he'll be under restraints when you see him?"

Both nodded, and Mickey rose. "Very well. I'll call you tomorrow when I get to Baltimore." Phil rose and stuck out his hand. They shook and Bergman said, "I'm glad I came. Not just for that outrageous bribe offer, either. This one's unique. I just wish I could have done more."

Phil watched him leave and sat down next to his wife. Gloria seemed numb, off in her own world, while they waited for the nurse to tell them they could visit Patrick. Phil wished the sharp churning feeling in his stomach would go away. He'd been eating antacids almost hourly since all this had begun. And things seemed to be getting worse. Mark's vanishing act had a strangely unsettling effect on everyone. And Sean seemed so moody and disturbed. Running a hand over a tired face, Phil said to himself, "Don't make too much of this, old son."

Gloria turned slightly. "Huh?"

He shook his head. "Just talking to myself." Gloria returned to her own lonely world.

Phil chided himself: of course everyone was on edge and there was some general fallout from that anxiety. Mark was probably off poking around and somehow had managed to miscommunicate with Gary. And Sean . . . well, he'd had a brother—more than a brother—a twin taken from him. Of course he'd be moody and disturbed. Phil hoped the party tonight would make things a little easier for Sean.

Phil felt exhaustion pull at him. Nervous fatigue, with its strangely electric numbing quality, caused him to drift into a twitchy half doze, one in which he was aware of his surroundings but also not quite awake.

He thought of Patrick and could see his son just a dozen feet away, as if the walls between the waiting room and his bed had vanished. Then something odd occurred and somehow he also could see Patrick lying on . . . clover? The boy seemed to doze in some other place, asleep upon a bed of flowers and grasses. And near him rested something . . . black. Something . . . evil. Phil tried to warn Patrick, to shout to him to get up and run to Daddy, but his body wouldn't obey him. He felt himself strain, but his arms and legs wouldn't budge and his voice stayed mute. In his mind he screamed Patrick's name. The boy sat up. Phil's heart leaped as he saw his son look around, blinking in confusion. Then the boy saw his father. With a smile he stood and took a slow step toward his father. But the evil black thing rose up behind. Phil screamed to the boy to run and tried to go to him, but his body wouldn't answer his demands. Patrick sensed the presence of the evil thing behind and turned to look over his shoulder. The boy's eyes widened in terror at the vague black shape and he turned to face his father. He took an agonizingly slow step toward his father as the black horror reached out and encompassed the boy with long, sooty black arms. Opening his mouth, Patrick cried out.

"Phil!"

Phil jerked awake, drenched in sweat, his heart pounding. It took him a few seconds to gain his bearings and discover he had fallen asleep in the chair. Mark was kneeling before his chair. He said, "Are you all right?"

"Ya," said Phil huskily. "Just dozed for a second. A nightmare." He wiped his face and took a deep breath, collecting himself.

Then Mark's presence hit Phil and Gloria and both started to speak. "Don't ask anything," Mark interrupted. His face showed he had been without sleep for some time. The area above his normally trimmed beard showed several day's growth and his eyes were red-rimmed, set in deep, dark sockets, and his skin looked chalky. He was wet, as if he had been outside in the rain for a while.

"You okay?" asked Gloria.

"Never mind me," said Mark. "Tell me exactly what's happened since I left. I went to your place and Gabbie said you were here with Patrick."

Phil began and Gloria joined in, and after a few minutes Mark had a fairly accurate narrative of all that had occurred since his departure. He still knelt before Phil and Gloria, his hand held before his mouth as he thought. Then he said, "Christ, you were taken for a ride."

"What?" asked Phil.

Mark's expression showed something else wasn't right and Phil said, "What's wrong?"

"Aggie's been in an accident. She's downstairs. Dr. Murphy said he thought you'd be up here with Dr. Bergman, Phil, so I came up to tell you."

Phil said, "What happened?"

Mark said, "After I left your place, I passed the accident. I recognized Aggie's car." He spoke without emotion. "She spun out on the road between your place and Lonny Boggs's."

"Is she going to be all right?" asked Gloria, rising.

Phil stood and made to move toward the elevator, but Mark held him back. "She didn't make it."

"How did you know?" asked Phil.

"I saw the cops pull her from the wreckage and put a tarp over her and her passenger. And she's downstairs in pathology, not E.R."

"Goddamnitall," whispered Gloria. Her eyes began to tear and she softly repeated, "Goddamnitall." Phil stood silently, too numb to take in Aggie's death. She had been like a member of his family and his closest professional mentor. Mechanically he asked, "How did it happen?"

Mark spoke. "I can only guess. But details aren't important now." He glanced at the clock on the wall. "Time is."

"What do you mean?" asked Gloria.

Mark pushed by Phil and stood right in front of Gloria. "On the night Patrick was taken ill, do you remember anything unusual, besides Sean's screaming?"

Gloria shook her head, then remembered faintly a dim image of a shadow in the corner. "Well, there was something."

"What?" Mark's dark eyes seemed to bore through her.

She explained what she had seen in the corner as best as she could, and Mark said, "How much has Gary told you?"

"A lot of weird shit," Phil answered. "He couldn't seem to believe half of what he said himself, but he told me what you let him in on just before he left for Seattle. But he was holding something back."

All Mark said was "It's worse than he told you. I'm going to have to leave again, for two reasons. The first is that man with Aggie tonight.

He'll have friends, and they'll be coming after him quickly. Some may be on their way here even now. If they find me, they might kill me."

Gloria appeared on the edge of hysteria as she sat wide-eyed, holding a hard ball of crumpled Kleenex in her fist, pressed against her lips.

Mark said, "We're going underground for a while, Gary and I. Running will only delay the inevitable. They'll find us sooner or later. But when they do, I hope we'll be able to bargain with them."

"Who's 'them'?" demanded Phil.

Mark ignored the question. "The other reason I'm leaving is to go someplace, Phil, and you have to come with me."

"Where?"

"To a place where few men have ever gone, to prevent a great deal of harm to a great many people. I need help, but Gary's got to do some things that prevent him from coming with me. I have no one else to ask, but I don't ask you to come to help me. You have a very personal stake in coming."

"What reason?" asked Phil.

"I'm going to the place your sons have gone. I'm the only one who can help you go after Patrick and Sean."

"What do you mean?" asked Gloria, her voice barely a whisper.

"I went to your house and Gabbie said Sean wasn't at the school when she and Jack went to get him. They've called the police, but they won't find him. I know where he is. He's gone to get Patrick back."

"What the fuck are you talking about, Mark! You come in here telling us Aggie's dead and somebody's after you and all sorts of mysterious bullshit, and then you're on about Sean going off into the night after Patrick!" Phil's voice rose as frustration and anger sought to fight their way out of that place he had bottled them up. "Now, it may have escaped your notice, but Patrick is over there in that ward, brain-damaged but otherwise intact!"

Mark put his hand on Phil's arm. His voice remained steady, but there was a hard edge in it as he said, "That's not Patrick in there, Phil."

Phil pulled away from Mark's grasp. "What are you saying? I know my own son."

Mark glanced at Gloria and suddenly pushed past Phil toward the ward door. Phil stood motionless a moment before springing after him.

Mark walked in and glanced through one glass window and the next until he saw Patrick. He walked straight to the nurses' station. Keys lay on the desk while the woman read a magazine. Most of the patients were quiet this time of night, asleep or watching television.

Mark just took the keys, and before the woman could react, he was trying them in the lock to Patrick's room. "Sir!" shouted the nurse.

"What are you doing!" Before she was halfway to him he had the door open and was through.

The nurse was rudely shoved aside as Phil and Gloria entered. "You can't go in there!" she shouted.

Phil entered to see Mark standing at the foot of Patrick's bed. The boy lay tied by heavy leather restraints. He glared up at Mark, hissing like an enraged snake.

Mark pointed at the boy, saying something to him in a foreign language. Patrick flinched and cowered, trying to pull away from Mark, as if terrified by the man's presence. The boy's restraints were stretched taut. Phil reached Mark's side, but before he could grab him, something caused his heart to freeze. For the first time since the night of Patrick's illness, there was a shrewd intelligence in the boy's eyes. A keening sound issued from the boy's mouth and he pulled at the straps, then he looked at Phil and spoke. "Daddy, he's hurting me."

Gloria gasped and shrank back, clutching the doorjamb. Mark continued his chanting, and Phil recognized the language as something Gaelic, ancient Scottish or Irish. Then Patrick pulled and one of the restraints ripped. Three more yanks and the boy was free of the leather restraints. He crouched before Mark's accusing finger, bending his head as if the words were somehow hurting him. He backed away until he reached the head of the bed, then he continued his movement and began to crawl backward up the wall.

Mark continued to point at Patrick and began to shout at him in the strange language. Gloria screamed, and the nurse went ashen at the sight of Patrick climbing the wall. Two burly orderlies pushed past Gloria and the nurse, and stopped at the sight of the boy climbing backward up the wall.

One of the two orderlies, a huge black man, said, "Holy shit! Fuckin' Spiderman!"

Then Mark's voice rang out. "In the name of God give us back the bairn!"

"Never!" hissed Patrick and his form began to shimmer.

"Bring back the bairn!" commanded Mark.

"The Compact is broken!" cried the thing that hugged the wall. "You may not compel me!"

Mark turned and found a pitcher of water and threw it at the child. "Water cleanse thee! The glamour be banished! The spell be broken! Changeling begone!"

The water spattered over the boy and suddenly Patrick was no more. Hugging the wall was a creature about the same size as the boy, a squat, fat thing with spindly arms and legs, huge belly, and enormous penis. But its head was twice the size of the boy's and its face a frog mask of hate and rage, its wide mouth split in a hideous grimace. A long tongue lolled out between sharp teeth that could be seen even across the room. Frog eyes with yellows around red irises darted about the room. The creature's skin was a dull grey, and ears like small fans or seashells rose up on each side of its head. Both feet and hands were tipped with black-taloned fingers and toes. It was a nightmare made real.

The creature threw back its head, opening wide its mouth, and howled, a terrible sound like a claxon, echoing with a deep rumble. A stench of rotten eggs filled the room and the creature's voice shot up in register, from bass to tenor, until it shrilled, "My master is great. You are his meat." With a peal of laughter that raised gooseflesh like the sound of nails on a blackboard, the creature sprang from the wall, upon the bed, and bounced as if it were a trampoline. It hurled impossibly through the air, smashing through the window, sending glass flying outward as the thing fled into the night.

Mark hurried over to the window; honking and screeching sounded from the road as motorists swerved to avoid the creature racing across the highway. The sound of several cars crashing into one another filled the night. One of the stunned orderlies looked across the room at the shattered window and said, "That's impossible! That's safety glass. You couldn't break it with a sledgehammer!"

Mark took Phil by the arm and half led, half dragged him past the man. Gloria was crying, hysterical with shock, and the nurse was trying to control her. Another nurse had arrived at the door and had fainted, and the black orderly was trying to revive her.

As they made their departure amid the bedlam erupting in the psych ward, Mark took Phil by the arm and led him calmly through the visitors' area. He ducked into the stairwell and continued to hold Phil's arm as they descended the stone steps.

Phil seemed to lose his stunned confusion and asked, "Where are we going?"

"Erl King Hill."

30

Mark herded Phil out the stairwell and through the relative calm of the main waiting room of the hospital. He motioned for Phil to move calmly toward the main door. "This won't keep for long. As soon as someone up in psych starts yelling, this place is going to be crawling with nurses, orderlies, security types, and a couple of doctors. And they're all going to be looking for the madman who broke into the kid's room."

"What do we do?" asked Phil. He glanced over his shoulder. "Gloria . . ."

Mark kept his voice low, but his tone was intense. "Phil, someone'll take care of her. All hell's about to break loose. You and I have to do a lot in the"—he glanced at the clock on the wall as they crossed the room; it read eleven—"the next hour."

"Mark, what's going on?"

"We're going to use magic to save the world. And get Sean and Patrick back."

Phil blinked. "Magic? Sure, why not. After what I've just seen . . ."

Mark said, "My rental car is out in the parking lot. There're records of me having it. Gary has my car. We'll take yours."

They left the lobby and crossed the parking lot to Phil's car. Phil started up the engine and asked, "What's Gary doing?"

"Being my insurance, I hope." Mark looked at Phil and there was sadness in his eyes. "The people we're dealing with might think nothing of snuffing us all out." Phil backed the car out and turned it toward the road. When another car turned into the lot, its lights playing across the two men, Mark glanced away, turning his shoulder so the other driver couldn't see his face. As Phil pulled out into traffic, Mark said, "Over the centuries, thousands of people have died to protect some incredible secrets, Phil. Gary and I know those secrets now. We may have something to bargain with."

"Jesus, Mark, what the hell are you talking about? What secrets?"

Mark seemed to sink down into the car seat as Phil accelerated down the road. "It's a long and complex story. And anyone who has even the slightest involvement is . . . well, they're all potentially in danger. I don't know." He glanced out the window as if collecting his thoughts and pointed at an approaching crossroad that would take them through town. "Head over toward Barney Doyle's. I want to get to Erl King Hill, but I don't want to use the path at your house, in case . . . they're already waiting for me."

Phil turned. "Just who are these people you are so afraid of? And what would they be doing at my house?"

Mark looked out into the rainy night. "I was in Friedrichshafen—on the border of Switzerland. For a week I was held prisoner. They got a little sloppy one night and I escaped. It took me three days to get to Paris—I had some problems at the border and had to pull strings. I think they almost found me twice."

"Mark, I know you're stressed out, man; we all are. But you're not making sense. They who?"

"The Magi."

Phil said, "Magi? Like in 'We Three Kings' . . . ?"

Mark's face was illuminated briefly as they passed under a lamp at an intersection. "Gary sent me some translations of what he'd taken to Seattle, while I was still in New York, and they gave me the leads I needed. Along with what I'd gotten translated in New York, it all fit together with what I'd come to believe. I knew that Kessler's group was still around." He paused. "Well, they found me.

"The guy in the car with Aggie was named August Erhardt. Erhardt was a Magus."

Phil glanced at Mark. "Like in the John Fowles novel?"

Mark said, "There's a lot of history here, and we don't have a great deal of time, so I'm going to just skip across the high points.

"About 550 B.C. the Persians conquered Media, what is now Azarbaijan in Iran and Azerbajdzh in the Soviet Union. There was a secret priesthood in Media called the Magi which was quickly assimilated into Persian society, becoming a political power. Historians don't know a lot about them." A car passing in the other direction shot a shower of water at Phil's Pontiac that drenched the window in a curtain of wavering fluid. Then the wipers swept it aside. "When Persia fell to Alexander the Great, they survived. They also survived Rome, Genghis Khan, and Tamerlane. By the third century they'd become one of the dominant religions in the East. It was thought they were finally destroyed by the Shiites during the seventh century, when Islam conquered Persia. But it turns out they weren't."

Phil shook his head, unsure of what he was hearing. "You're saying that this man with Aggie was a member of some supersecret Persian cult that's been around twenty-five hundred years?"

Mark nodded. *"As was Fredrick Kessler.* Kessler, Erhardt, and Gary's friend up in Canada, Van der Leer, all were inheritors of some tradition that came down over the years from that ancient Magian priesthood. And that Persian tradition is directly linked to a primitive spirit worship that has evolved into legends of fairies and other races which lived on Earth alongside mankind."

Phil said, "That thing in Patrick's room? That's some sort of fairy changeling?"

"Something like that, though there's a lot more here than fairy tales can explain away. I'll know better after we get where we're going."

"Then tell me, how could these Magi be around all these years and no one knows about them? Couldn't it just be some sort of group that . . . claims to have gone back all those years?"

"You still don't believe, truly believe, in the magic. You've seen it, that thing in the hospital, but you still don't believe it." Mark thought a moment as Phil drove. "The Masons claim a history back to the founding of Solomon's temple. And other groups claim ancient roots as well. Who can say not? All I know is there was a lot about Fredrick Kessler that made no sense, until you understand he was backed by a powerful organization that provided him with the way out of Germany, smoothed over things with the German and American governments, gave him his capital for investment, his introduction to local bankers, everything. It was the same for Van der Leer in Canada. He had a lot of the same advantages.

"What happened in Germany at the turn of the century was a completely unnecessary conflict between this secret priesthood and the traditional religions. One of the Magi went insane and tried to go public. He turned some of the peasants around, returning to ancient rites, until the local religious leaders opened up on him and his followers. It was open warfare for a time. And it was the *other Magi* behind the efforts of the churches to hush things up. They arranged for anyone who was known to have connections with the crazy Magus to leave Germany. Other Magi took their places."

Phil pulled over to pass a slow pickup truck and was reentering the right lane when another car came speeding around a curve in the road. Lightning tore the sky as headlights briefly illuminated the passing vehicle.

"Damn," said Mark, almost a whisper.

"What?" said Phil, glancing over at his passenger.

"The men in the car that just passed by. I recognized the one in back, I think. It's a man named Wycheck. He's one of them."

"Them? The Magi?"

Mark only nodded. "They're heading for the hospital. That means we've only got about fifteen minutes on them."

Phil turned the car down county road 451, heading toward Barney's workshop. "This is all too much for me. What does this have to do with your being held prisoner? And what about magic and that thing that took Patrick's place?"

Mark said, "The Magian priesthood is not just another cult. They are a real *power*, a supersecret worldwide organization: a delusional paranoid's worst conspiracy fantasy come to life. The Illuminati was just an inaccurate reference to the Magi. They are men and women who have taken positions of importance in governments, churches, businesses, all through history. They ran the sisterhood of Vesta in Rome—they had the power to pardon prisoners condemned to death by the imperial Senate, on a whim! They were the Druid class of the ancient Celtic races—the scholars, the priests, the rulers—and, for all I know, the obliteration of the Druids by the Romans may have been a sham, the consolidation of their position in various governments, or it may have been a power struggle between factions. We'll never know. And they probably had shamans and medicine men all over the New World long before Columbus got here, from what I can tell.

"Anyway, I'm not positive of all the details, but what I think is going on is that a faction within the Magi are trying to seize power. I'm not sure, but I think the world situation is getting too complex for even them to ensure we don't blow ourselves up in a nuclear holocaust, so some of them want to take over openly, and to do that they have to have an edge." He shook his head. "I think they plan to unleash these fairies on humanity, let us knock each other around a bit, then take over. It's a mad plan.

"Everybody's lives are on the line, but even if I somehow prevent that from happening, both factions of Magi might still be trying to kill me—one because I balked their plans, the other simply because I know too much. And then they'll come after me, and you"—he nodded at Phil —"and Gloria, and Jack and Gabbie, the kids if we get them back, Ellen, the doctors and nurses at the hospital, and anyone else who might have a clue they exist."

"Oh fuck," whispered Phil. "I think I'm going to be sick." He looked nearly green with nausea.

"You don't have time," said Mark.

Phil's voice was a whisper. "What do we have to do?"

Mark said, "This is the part Gary couldn't bring himself to tell you. Hell, he didn't believe it all himself. That thing in the hospital was a creature of another race, a race that we've called over the centuries gnomes, elves, pixies, and other names; I've come to think of them as fairies. I've had evidence of their existence before, maddening bits and scraps of nothing more than hints, never enough to make me undertake serious research, nothing like this year on this property. Gabbie's attack, Jack's wound, your problems around the house, all were part of what these creatures are.

"This race has a name in their own language, but whatever they are called, they are a race of . . . the irrational, the unreal. They're spirit beings. But these fairy creatures have corporeal qualities just as humans have spiritual qualities. Their world is separate from ours, but it over-laps. You get there using . . . we call it magic."

Phil said, "That's imposs . . ." but stilled his voice before he fin-ished. It would have been a plea, not an objection. "Oh shit!" he said as he passed the cutoff to Williams Avenue. He had lost his concentration. He made an illegal U-turn and then pulled around the corner. The mundane consideration of driving seemed to restore some of his calm. He said, "So what have the Magi to do with the fairies?"

Mark said, "The oldest-known legend of the fairy people is the Peri wife. Persian, which hints that the oldest stories about them are coinci-dental to the rise of the Magi. The old lore was real stories, a . . . guide of how to deal with the Old People, not a collection of legends.

"Now, there's a treaty, something called the Compact. It's what keeps the fairies from waging war on us. There's more to it than that, but I can't tell you much more, because that's about all I know. There is among the fairies a being, and he's the one who's trying to mess up this treaty. That's what these Magi do. They keep him from breaking the rules, from ending the peace between the two races. It's this being who has Patrick."

Phil began to speak, then paused, helpless before these words. At last he said, "What are we going to do?"

Mark looked over his shoulder at Phil. "We must repair damage. By taking the gold you voided the Compact."

"The gold?"

Mark nodded. "It's theirs, part of the . . . treaty. I've got to go where these creatures are and talk to them. These scrolls tell how to get there . . . and survive. I've memorized what I need. I told Gary to grab them as he and Ellen left town. I want them out of your place for insurance."

"Against the Magi?" asked Phil. Mark nodded.

"I'm confused," said Phil. "You want to keep the treaty intact, and the Magi want the treaty kept, so what's the problem?"

Mark laughed a bitter laugh, its sound softened by the falling rain. "Because of some mess-ups on my part and because of our adversary's being especially clever, the Magi think I'm in league with the creature who took Patrick. They sent Erhardt to fix the damage, but this elf, this creature who started all the trouble, ran Aggie off the road, killing the only man close enough to keep the Compact intact. I'm certain this cinches in the Magi's minds that I'm in league with this creature. The only possible hope I—we—have is if I can somehow take his place and fix things before midnight. Otherwise . . ."

"Who?" said Phil. "Who has our Patrick?"

"The same guy who engineered the breaking of the Compact, by leading you to the gold. He's likely the one to have grabbed Patrick. The Erl King."

Phil said, "I don't know if I can handle this, Mark."

Nearing Barney's shack, Phil slowed, as if reluctant to reach his objective. Mark spoke. "You don't have much choice, Phil. We've the Magi on one side, fairies on the other, and if we don't do the right things before midnight, we're all going to find ourselves in the middle of the next world war, and it won't be the Russians we're fighting." He laughed bitterly. "And even if we do, the Magi might still come after us all."

They pulled up outside Barney's shack. Mark said, "Have you got a flashlight?"

Phil reached back under the seat and pulled out a large three-way light, flood, fluorescent, and emergency blinker. He flicked it on, testing that the battery was up, and it produced a satisfactory light.

Phil seemed reluctant to leave the car. "What you've just told me sounds crazy, Mark. If I hadn't seen that thing in the hospital, I'd be calling for the wire bus to come get you. But a lot of this is speculation. What do you *know*?"

"Not much." Mark switched the light back on and glanced at his watch. "We don't have much time, but I'll tell you what little I know and what I've surmised as we head over to your place. We've only got a little time left."

Both men got out of the car and looked at each other. The rain had lessened to a drizzle again, but both were getting wet. They ignored the discomfort.

Mark flicked on the light and led Phil into the woods.

31

Moving through the wet woodlands, Mark said, "These Magi have always been a thorny problem for historians: few documented facts. We
know they ran things in Persia for a long time. They headed Zoroastri-
anism after Zoroaster, and the most famous of them was a man named
Saena. We know some things from the Zend Avesta, the Zoroastrians'
sacred book, but we can only guess at what beliefs were common to
both religions. Everything else is only inference." He thought a moment, then added, "Now, maybe as sort of protective covering, the
terms 'magi' and 'magus' came to be applied to the priests of most any
hereditary religion in that part of the world. Some remnants of the
Zoroastrian faith exist today. The Parsis in India are still hereditary: you
have to be born into the faith; no converts allowed. But we know now
that, behind the public sects, this secret organization of Magi continued
to function."

They maintained a steady pace along the path, but the trail was
slippery and, despite the light, the footing treacherous in the dark. "The
Magi were monotheists. The Zoroastrians speak of two demigods created by the Supreme Being, a good force called Ormuzd who remained
loyal to God, and an evil force called Ahriman who, like Satan, rebelled.
The Magi had no temples, conducting their rites in the woods and on
mountaintops—the room in your basement was a storeroom, and a
library of sorts, not a secret temple. They worshipped fire or light, and

the sun, in a manner of speaking. Not the forms of fire and light, but rather some spiritual energy or essence demonstrated by fire and light. They were astrologers and, reputedly, enchanters." Dryly he added, "Which seems to be fact more than legend. They were conversant with spirits and could control them. Before the discovery in your cellar, the origins of the sect had been attributed to everything from their being the lost tribes of Israel to the last priesthood of Atlantis. But those were only legends."

Mark lapsed into silence as they moved down a gully running fast with water. Phil found himself in water up to his ankles and felt his socks soak through.

Mark seemed unmindful of the discomfort and continued his narration. "I don't know how many of them still exist. But they can't be under every rock. You shouldn't have been allowed to buy Kessler's place, Phil. Had it stayed on the market for a while, the priesthood would have sent someone to buy it. That you did proves there wasn't another Magus close by. But even without great numbers, they have great influence.

"They have contacts at every level of business and government, I'm certain, a network of people that makes the wildest conspiracy theory look reasonable. The priesthood must have some impressive connections to be able to keep all this under wraps for this long. We're speaking of centuries."

"Even if somebody stumbles on the truth, who's going to believe him?" Phil pointed out. "Christ, I've seen some of this shit, and *I* don't believe it." After a moment he said, "No, I believe it." Then he asked, "So, then, why are the . . . fairies on my land?"

Mark said, "They've got to be somewhere." He pushed a low-hanging branch aside, his breathing a little heavy, and said, "This is all guesswork on my part, but . . . Have you ever considered man's social development? *Homo sapiens* has been around for something like a million years, yet civilization been around only, say, nine thousand— giving the broadest definition to civilization as we accept the term. What was going on for the previous nine hundred ninety-one thousand years? Maybe constant warfare between the two races, neither quite able to finish off the other. Dozens of attempts to rise above the level of barbarism lost as the fairies knocked mankind back down to the level of simple hunter-gatherer. And we wreaked as much havoc upon the fairies, capturing and enslaving them, stealing their powers by . . . er, magic, destroying them as they destroyed us.

"Then something happened. If we get through all this, maybe we can someday learn what that was. But a peace was established, and both races were allowed to exist. A truce, or armistice"—he thought—"a compact. That's what the Magi who found me called it. The Compact.

"Perhaps a battle was fought that was too bloody for either side to withstand another onslaught. Perhaps some cooler heads on both sides agitated for treaty, I don't know. I can't even begin to guess how these creatures might think.

"But if all I surmised is true, then it would be likely that when this treaty between men and fairies was first made, part of the agreement was the priesthood would set aside places where the fairies could spend their six months unmolested, and in turn have a free shot at whoever trespassed as long as they left everyone outside alone."

"Sort of like a reservation?" asked Phil. "You mean these priests are sort of like Indian agents for fairies?"

"More like jailers," said Mark, "if mankind had the upper hand when the Compact was agreed to. That's a guess," he admitted.

"Anyway, it's clear Herman Kessler was the last Magus around here. And the thing with Gabbie, and with me in the woods, satisfies me that things are happening that wouldn't have if a priest were still close by."

"What do you mean?" said Phil.

"The line of priests stopped here with Herman. He had no children. He never married, which is—if the hereditary thing still works—strange for a Magus. Even so, someone should have been ready to take over. But Herman died unexpectedly on his trip to Germany, and that news was slow in reaching the other Magi, maybe. Something kept them from finding out until about the time I showed up, and they were a little suspicious of me nosing around—they thought I had something to do with Herman's death.

"Normally, with Herman gone, there would be no problem with Erl King Hill's being unattended unless the fairies showed up—which they did. I think they come and go without pattern, so there was a good chance the priesthood might be tending 'reservations' like this one without the fairies showing up for a lifetime. But they did show and there's no priest, so things start getting out of hand. And it's no accident. There's something about all this I couldn't discover. They kept me locked in a hotel room for almost two weeks." He grew reflective. "When Erhardt was dispatched to come here and repair the damage, they made a mistake—forgot to move me or have anyone with me when a maid showed up. I just smiled at her, tipped her a hundred German marks, and walked out of the room. I spend three days on buses getting to the French border—I knew they'd think I'd gone to Austria or toward Stuttgart. But while I was with them, I got the feeling they're suspicious that someone human might be in league with some faction among the fairies, probably with the Erl King himself."

"Okay," Phil said, now almost normally calm again; "now what has this to do with my son?"

"Something's gone wrong," answered Mark. "I still don't know what it was or is, but somehow the rules have been changed. If I read things right, you never should have been troubled, other than maybe a little prank or two, like souring milk, things getting misplaced around the house, or weird noises at night." He had to raise his voice as the rain picked up again, the hammering intensity causing their eyes to sting. The sound of it in the branches was like the rolling of breakers against the beach. "But things aren't the way they're supposed to be. At the heart of everything that's happened is someone, or some group, who wants a return to the open warfare of ages past. That's why they led you to the gold."

"You mentioned that before. What about the gold?" said Phil.

"That gold wasn't Kessler's. It's human gold, but it belonged to the fairies, a pledge made for ages by humans to keep the pact. Every year a rite was conducted, and a little more gold added to the treasure, as a sign of good faith. Every 'reservation' has its pledge hoard. That may be where the legend of getting gold from leprechauns began. Anyway, you broke the treaty, Phil, when you removed that gold." He held up his hand. "My college class ring is gold. We are going to hope that if I do the ritual and give them this ring, we can keep the lid on until another Magus shows up. If not . . ."

"What happened in Germany at the turn of the century?" asked Phil.

Mark nodded. "Worse, I'm afraid. A thousand times worse. That was a minor conflict when the locals started worshipping the fairies because of that crazy Magus. It would have passed quickly if some of the locals hadn't gotten into some very bizarre rites. I've some files that show some of the peasants were practicing human sacrifice. Anyway, if the government hadn't jumped in and started a witch-hunt, the Magi would have hushed things up. What we'd have here would be a complete breakdown of the treaty, and I can't begin to guess what that would mean. But even if we don't know if some humans are involved in our world, at least we know who is responsible in this realm."

"The Erl King?" said Phil.

"The Erl King. And he's a thoroughly bad actor. The Irish call him the Fool and he's known by other names, but he's the one. He's the best candidate to resent the confinement to the lands ceded by the pact." After a moment of silence he said, "I don't know how he did it, but I *know* he's responsible for the accident that killed Aggie. And the fact he knew Erhardt was coming shows he has some means of communication with someone who knows what the Magi are doing."

Phil felt despair threatening to overwhelm him. He said, "How the hell are we going to do anything in, what, fifteen minutes?"

"We've just got to be outside that hill at midnight. If what I think is going to happen happens, then we don't need to get there any earlier. But heaven help the world if we're a moment late."

Phil silently followed Mark. Suddenly the world had become an impossibly alien and frightening place.

32

Sean felt fatigue dogging his heels as he followed after the ball of light. He was still alert, but the steady, uneventful trek through the woodlands had diminished his anxiety. Around him the alien, murky woods were somehow not frightening, just strange. The trees were . . . weird was the only word Sean could think of. The trees were slender, delicate things, swaying gently in the light breeze, their murky colors giving the branches the illusion of transparency. No, this place was weird, but not really scary. He knew he would be tested when he reached Patrick's place of confinement, and that prospect frightened him, but he still was only eight and a half years old and it was past his bedtime and he was too tired for worry.

Sean halted. In harmony to the humming of the breeze through the branches, he heard music. He resumed walking, and as he followed the globe of light he heard the music grow louder. It was pipes and harps and bells and tinny-sounding drums. The road entered a clearing and Sean's eyes widened in astonishment as he saw what at first he took to be Erl King Hill before him. A quick glance about told him the resemblance was only that, for the trees on all sides were unlike any seen in New York State.

But the crest of the hill was alive with moving figures, where men and women of alien beauty danced before a throne. The woman upon the throne was a striking figure, erect and proud as well as lithe and beautiful. All around her glowed a light, crowning the hilltop with a blue-white nimbus that illuminated all around her. In the halflight of this land, the hilltop was an isle of lights. The golden ball of light moved down the road past the merrymakers, but the woman upon the throne waved her hand and the light veered toward her.

Sean hesitated, then followed the light up the hill. The dancing halted and the music faded away as Sean passed between the revelers. Atop the hill it was still twilight, but much brighter than it had been upon the road.

The woman upon the throne was stunning. Her red-gold hair was swept back from a high forehead, held in place by a golden circlet. Her gown was filmy, revealing a full bosom. Her neck and arms were graceful and without blemish. Sean couldn't be sure, but either she had some weird things on the back of her dress or she had translucent wings! She smiled and Sean felt no hint of fear. Pale blue eyes regarded him as a musical contralto said, "A little mortal boy! What brings you upon the heels of the Quest Guide, small, pretty one? Have you come to brighten our court with your sweet smile?" She bent forward and reached to cup Sean's chin with her hand. Her fingers recoiled as they touched his skin. "You wear a ward! You must remove it."

Sean looked about. Near the base of the throne were tiny beings, all whispering and pointing at Sean. Several diminutive creatures flew in circles around the throne area, though it seemed they were cautious not to fly directly above the stunning woman. Near her stood several alien men, all beautiful, slender creatures. A short distance away, many lovely women also waited silently. Both sexes were dressed in all manner of fashions, as had been the green people, from near nudity to ornate, ponderous costumes. These people had skin tones that were more human, however. Sean wondered why this lady had only men near her, but shrugged off the thought as he considered doing what the woman said.

Behind the throne stood a man of middle years, clearly human while the others were not. He wore a splendid tunic of fine weave, silver threads bedecking a green cloth. Gems and pearls were sewn into the collar, giving him a regal look, though he was but a shadow to the light of the woman. Barely, so the others wouldn't notice, he shook his head no.

Sean glanced about, while the beautiful woman said, "Come, little one. Stay with us and dance and sing. We shall regale you with food and drink, and you shall be a pretty page in our service." With a sensual smile she said, "You will learn pleasures undreamed of by your race, pretty human boy . . ." She measured his size, then added, ". . . when you are a little older."

Sean took a deep breath. There was some quality about the woman that made him uneasy. Not that she wasn't pretty or nice. There was none of the feeling of danger or terror that had accompanied his encounters with the Bad Thing and the Shining Man. But in the spice and wildflower scent in the air and the intoxicating music and the powerful allure of the woman there was a quality that made Sean uncomfortable, causing his pulse to race. He vaguely recognized it as something he had felt in a milder way once when a girl at his old school had kissed him at a birthday party. He had made a display of displeasure, but he had secretly wanted to try it again, yet he hadn't said anything lest the other boys pick on him. He had also felt the same discomfort another time when he had barged into the bathroom and caught sight of Gabbie drying herself off after a shower. He had been haunted by the memory of her naked body still damp and pink from the hot water for days after, and had wished he could have stayed there, just to watch her. He didn't know why. With her clothes on, Gabbie was just another dumb girl, except when she was teaching the boys to ride. It had been as if he had seen a hint of something he would understand when he was older, something that now only confused him. It was a powerful, distressing, yet compelling urge, which disturbed Sean greatly and made him feel guilty, though of what he couldn't say. Putting aside the churning sensation of discomfort in his stomach, Sean said, "I've come to find my brother."

The woman's smile faded to a look of true regret. "You refuse our offer of hospitality?" She almost pouted.

"I've got to find my brother," Sean repeated.

With a sigh of resignation, the woman said, "How then did you come to our land, pretty mortal boy?"

"Barney told me to walk around the hill nine times, and through the cave. He told me how to get the light to take me to Patrick."

"And how did your brother, Patrick, come here?"

"The Shining Man took him."

The woman's face lost its warmth, and her eyes became electric, and suddenly the feeling Sean had of wanting to climb into her lap and nestle his head on her bosom vanished. The woman's voice had an angry edge to it, a harsh quality like a shrieking trumpet that made Sean shiver as she said, "Tell me of this Shining Man!"

Sean described the encounter with the Shining Man and the Bad Thing and the false Patrick and Sean, and when he was done, the woman said, "That one has tried our patience long enough. Listen well, boy on a quest. When you find your brother, your path back will lie along two routes; which, you must choose. Bring him back by the white path, so that I may have an accounting of this business and your brother and yourself may return home. Avoid the black path."

Sean recalled Barney's warning. Softly, so as not to offend the great lady, he said, "I just want my brother back." Sean considered, then said, "Can't you get him for me?"

"Here in the Bright Lands we rule, mortal boy. But know that in the mortal world and in the Shadow Lands he and we are equals, and in the Dark Lands the one you call the Shining Man is supreme, and there must we fear him. You must bring him to us," the woman said, "here into the Bright Lands, so that we may deal with him. In any other place, the issue would be in doubt. Do this and we shall return you and your brother safely home. That is our word on the subject."

Sean watched the glowing ball, which seemed to wiggle impatiently. He didn't want to lie to the woman, but Barney said not to trust anyone. Then he glanced at the man. He seemed sad, but he smiled slightly and nodded yes.

Making himself bold, Sean said, "Are you True Tom?"

The man said, "So I am called by some." His accent was thick and made his words hard to understand, but Sean remembered Barney saying Tom was a Scotsman.

The woman said, "He is of your race, though long have we kept him with us"—she smiled warmly up at him—"occasionally against our better judgment." To Sean she said, "But he is loved here and is loyal to us."

Sean said, "I'll come back with Patrick. You'll let us go home?"

The woman laughed, and again her voice was soft, like a singing harp, as she said, "Yes, brave boy, we shall let you and your brother go home. But first you must find the one you call the Shining Man and retrieve your brother. Then you must return to us, but be wary: to reach that one's court you must pass through the Hall of Ancient Seasons. Avoid all doors save those at the ends and you will be safe. And you must guard against trickery. Then must you be quickly back, for our court and that one's will be moved this night upon your world, and you will be a long way from your home. Go, then."

With a wave of her hand, she released the Quest Guide, as she had called the globe of light, and it shot down the hill toward the white path. Sean scrambled after, afraid the thing would leave him far behind, but once upon the path, the light resumed its lazy dance from side to side as it moved down the path. Sean took a deep breath to steel himself and followed after. Within a few minutes, Sean noticed that the path beneath his feet had turned from off-white to a neutral grey. And the sky above him was getting darker. Pushing back encroaching fear, he trudged on.

33

The woods were getting darker, but had none of the foreboding aspect Sean would have expected from the deepening shadows. There was simply less light. They followed a path by a bubbling brook, and Sean cast an eye toward the Quest Guide. It was still doing its mindless weaving dance from side to side on the road, so he could easily catch up with it if he didn't let it get too far ahead. He hurried to the brook and knelt down to drink.

Sean's lips touched the water and he drank quickly. Abruptly an image manifested itself before him. His head jerked away from the face in the water. He glanced about and was certain there could be no one swimming in the stream. It was only a few feet across and certainly only inches deep. He peered over the edge and again was struck by the certainty this place was not like home. The surface of the water was only a plane between where he was and another realm, a turquoise and green world of oceans and lakes. He moved a little closer to the water and regarded the face below the surface. It was a woman's face, or so Sean thought, and it seemed to hover scant inches below the surface. Her skin was pale blue, and, dimly below, he could see a fish's tail, covered with bluish scales, where legs should be. He could see she was nude and from the waist up normally formed; in fact—if Sean could judge such things—she was beautiful, with large breasts, a lovely line to her neck, and slender arms that moved gracefully in counterpoint to the lazy movement of her tail. Her black hair spread out around her head like a nimbus of dark and feathery silk threads, and her lips, more purple than red, were set in a smile. Her face was humanlike, save her eyes, which were entirely black, showing neither iris nor sclera. She seemed to wave at Sean, beckoning him to come into the water. Below her, Sean could see into the depths. The view was like the time his parents took Patrick and him to Catalina and they went on the glass-bottomed boat. From the blue murk of the ocean floor mighty spires of coral rose, and Sean suddenly understood they weren't natural spikes, but rather hugh spires of some city rearing high above the ocean floor.

The boy backed away from the bank, feeling discomfited rather than frightened, visited by the same odd feeling in his stomach as when he looked at the Queen. His boyish body wasn't ready to deal with the drives of adults, and the only effect her seductive beauty had upon him was disquiet and confusion. The boy noticed the progress of the Quest Guide and ran after the light, feeling relief to be away from the beautiful fish-woman. Even the water here was alien. He shivered slightly as he remembered Barney's warnings not to leave the road.

The light was a hundred yards down the path and it took Sean only a minute to catch up with the meandering globe. Forcing himself to calmness, the little boy fell into step behind his guide and continued on.

34

Sean saw the woods opening up around him. Since leaving the stream's bank, he had entered thickening woods, of dark aspect. Unlike the other woods he had passed through, these held a note of menace, and he had clutched his silver dagger tightly. The path moved straight through the trees and intersected another path, one of dark stone. Sean paused a moment, for the dark path emerged from a cave. Through the cave he could see rain. It was another way home! He remembered the lady had said he had two paths to choose, and he should take the white one. But this one would quickly take him back to his own home, without the seemingly interminable walk back to the sunny hill through which he had emerged into this place.

He sighed and followed after the Quest Guide. The ball was nearly out of sight between the trees as he began to move again, and for an instant the boy was fearful he had let it escape, but after a short sprint he found the ball ambling along at steady pace. The woods seemed to be growing more dense as they moved deeper into them, more menacing in appearance. The trees seemed taller and the boles more tightly packed. Soon it felt as if he were walking in another tunnel. Fighting off the urge to turn and run to the cave back to home, he walked resolutely after the glowing light.

The boy and his guide rounded another curve and Sean discovered that the road passed before as strange a house as he had seen. It stood between four huge trees, of what kind Sean didn't know, maybe giant oaks. As he got closer he saw the trees stood as corners of the house, the walls stretching between them. Inviting yellow light shone through the windows, merry and warm against the gloom of the woods. The Quest Guide hesitated before the entrance, bobbing and weaving in a circle. Sean came up beside it and then looked at the door of the house. After a minute he said, "Is Patrick in there?"

The guide bobbed from side to side, and Sean wished the thing could speak or somehow communicate with him. Then a thought struck the boy, as he remembered how it had answered his first question back on the sunlit hill. "Are you asking me if I want to go in?"

The ball bounced up and down vigorously. The thing could answer yes or no! Sean said, "Should I go in?" The ball wobbled a little. "You don't know?"

The ball bounced up and down again. "Will it help me find Patrick if I go there?" Again the indecisive wobble. Sean was then struck by something Barney had told him. "Is it dangerous in there?"

The ball bobbed up and down again. Sean said, "Let's go. Take me to Patrick."

The ball hesitated, moving in circles. Sean understood then. "It's a shortcut!" The ball bounced up and down. "Will it save a lot of time?" Again the up-and-down motion. Sean swallowed hard and said, "Then we'll go this way."

The ball of light moved toward the door of the great wooden house and the door opened without being touched. Sean gripped his dagger and followed after.

35

Sean stood a moment in awe. The house was a single room. But such a room! The floors were polished wood of grains so deep and rich they seemed a flowing river of dark and light lines. The boles of the mighty trees that formed the corners of the room had been carved, the columns describing people, and other creatures, in every conceivable undertaking. Sean let his eyes follow the bas-relief and saw every event in life: birth, death, lovemaking, warfare, discovery, healing, acts heroic and craven, pastimes mundane and extraordinary. He didn't know how he understood what the carvings represented, he just knew what each signified and he was sure of that knowledge. The ball moved slowly through the vast room, as if fearful of making noise.

The walls of the building were white, golden-veined marble, which struck Sean as odd considering that, outside, the building had looked like nothing so much as some giant wooden cabin. His eyes were enormous in silent wonder as he moved after the ball. There were six doors in the room, the one through which he had entered, another opposite at the far end of the hall, and two on each side. The side doors were of even size, but each had its own unique design. He reached the first pair and halted in fear as they both suddenly swung open.

Sean halted, his heart pounding, as he glanced from right to left, taking in what he saw through the portals. He knew that if that door opened through the wall, a forest of vast size would be revealed. But instead he saw a light woodland, greeting his eyes with a riot of every hue as trees splendid in their magnificent autumn colors stretched off into the distance. A crisp, nutty woods scent greeted the boy's nostrils as he looked into the beautiful vista, while a tiny red squirrel chattered a scolding at a thieving jaybird over a purloined hickory nut. Into Sean's view came a man and woman, each with grey hair but otherwise erect in their bearing. They wore fashionable clothing, the woman a tweed skirt and jacket and walking shoes, and the man a corduroy coat over a turtleneck sweater. Both carried walking sticks, which seemed more for effect than infirmity. The man halted and tipped a jaunty little cap at Sean, while the woman smiled and motioned for the boy to approach.

Sean knew he should move on, but the desire to go see what these two nice people wanted was overwhelming. He began to take a step when a bird's chirp caused him to spin and look behind. Through the opposite door he saw a lovely meadow, mantled in deep, almost emerald, green. Flowers speckled the hillsides and fruit trees were in full bloom, their white blossoms playing host to a thousand nectar-gathering honeybees. A robin in a branch near the door was in full song. Sean sighed. He didn't know what this place was, and he was frightened of it. He moved toward the far door where the Quest Guide patiently waited. A red ball bounced into Sean's field of vision and two children, a boy and girl, scampered after it. Both wore simple tunics, straight white cloth cut above the knees, and sandals. They each grabbed the ball at once, and a struggle ensued. As the tugging began to approach conflict, the girl, almost perfect in her childish beauty, saw Sean through the door. She let go of the ball and pointed at him. The boy was dark of hair and eyes, but as fair in features as the girl. He regarded Sean with something akin to distrust, but the girl smiled and waved and beckoned for Sean to come play with them. Sean felt a sudden desire to abandon his journey and go play. The two children seemed to be having such a wonderful time.

A step toward the door and suddenly Sean felt another tugging. He glanced back and saw that the man and woman had come to the edge of the door and were waving vigorously at Sean to come to them. The boy felt pulled in that direction, and his heartbeat increased. Something magic was happening, he thought. He knew that he must not give in to these odd urges to visit with these people, but must go find Patrick. The thought of his brother seemed to aid him in turning toward the far door and moving away from the four figures waving for him to join them.

Moving slowly along, he passed between the next pair of doors, and they opened. Sean regarded the right door. Through it he saw an impossibly lovely winterscape. Through the cold air pouring out of the door he heard the sound of laughter. A very old man and woman entered the scene, obviously enjoying something funny one of them had just said. Hair as white as the surrounding snow peeked out from under heavy fur hats, like ones Sean had seen on Russians in the news on TV. They spoke in a language Sean couldn't understand. They moved past his vantage point without hesitation, Sean's presence unacknowledged, until, just as they were leaving his view, the man caught sight of him. At once he began motioning for Sean to come to them, speaking quickly in the odd language.

Sean backed away, fighting the urge to join the elderly couple. He turned and regarded the opposite portal. Through it he could see a beach scene, and his heart ached. It looked like where his folks used to take him and Patrick back in California, up near Point Dume and Zuma Beach. Then a young man and woman dashed through the surf. The woman was as bare-chested as the man; each wore an identical skimpy black thong loincloth that barely covered anything. As they playfully splashed each other, their cries of delight were carried away over the sound of the breakers by a warm summer's breeze. The scent of salt spray and the feel of summer heat washed over Sean and he cried silent tears of longing as a sea gull's squawk came faintly through the portal. He wanted to be back in California with his friends, not lost in some terrible place looking for Patrick. Then the young couple were embracing, and again laughing, as the young man pulled the woman to the sand. He kissed her as he rolled over on top of her, and then he looked up, seeing Sean. With a dazzling smile of white teeth against his tan face, the young man shouted out in friendly greeting. The girl rolled over as the young man pushed up, coming to his feet. She stayed on the ground, smiling and waving. Sean felt a hot rush of panic at his urge to go to this place, the most familiar of all four views. Swallowing hard, and focusing his mind on Patrick, he turned toward the far door and made himself take a step. Slowly he made his way to the far door, and when he had a hand upon the handle, he said to the guide, "Is this the Hall of Ancient Seasons?"

The guide bounced up and down and Sean looked back at the scenes visible through the doors. "I'd be in trouble if I went through those doors, huh?"

The guide's agreement was vigorous, as it spun faster on its axis and bobbed up and down. Sean wondered what would happen if he chanced through those side doors. Probably he'd be trapped somewhere, unable to get home. He pushed aside his curiosity and considered the door. Unlike the front door, this one hadn't opened at their approach. Sean opened it by depressing the large latch and it swung open toward them, ponderously.

Sean stood motionless for a moment, and even the Quest Guide seemed to hesitate before it plunged into the dark and foreboding woods behind the building. Sean took a deep breath and gingerly stepped out upon a black path, and followed the golden light into despair.

36

The woods were now something fashioned from hopeless dreams, vaulted dark trees so close together their twisted branches seemed woven brown lines inscribed on a black tent, a batik canopy of woeful aspect raised high overhead. There was a sense of ages here; Sean glanced fearfully from side to side, as if something might leap out at him at any turn. The trees' bark was deeply etched, ravaged by time, looking like the leathery faces of ancient men, men who had been tormented for aeons. An echoing wind blew, and the swaying branches seemed to reach toward him, as if threatening . . . or pleading.

Sean walked on, remembering the terror of the night Patrick was taken and his own fear. He knew that had it not been for Barney's fairy stone, he would be a captive along with Patrick. And when the Shining Man had come for them, Sean had been reduced to something less than human, an animal, a thing cringing in fear. Nothing he saw now could match that hopelessness, that surrender of all sense of survival. His youthful mind wrestled with the reality of injured pride and a thirst for revenge and, finding them far different from what he had watched on Saturday morning television, failed to recognize them. But he felt those drives nevertheless, and he knew that once he faced the Shining Man he would act, despite his terror at the prospect. He didn't reflect on this; he accepted it. Without Patrick, a piece was missing within himself, as that special bond between them—the one that allowed them to share the odd thought, sense how the other felt, know where the other was—that bond had been severed. Without Patrick, Sean was less than before. Fate had given him a chance to redeem his brother, and nothing short of death would stop him.

The fluting, haunting sound of the wind was torn by the sound of hoofbeats rapidly approaching. The sky darkened ominously, as if night advanced before the nearing horseman. Sean stood, uncertain of his best course of action, to hide, to flee, or to stand. He chose the first alternative and raced to overtake the light. He reached for it and found it solid at the core, an orb the size of a baseball. He snatched it and scampered into the thicket by the roadside, crouching behind a fallen log, and peeked through the tall wild grass, while he hid the light of the Quest Guide beneath his body.

A horseman raced along the road, a figure of nightmare. A glowing white horse stretched out, seeming to fly as long legs moved in fluid rhythm. A fiery mane and tail blew behind as the rider spurred his mount along. The rider was dressed all in black and silver, armor and helm, cape and tunic. His ebon cloak trailed behind like some giant sail blown out and flapping in a gale. His head was held high, as if he was seeking, for black eye slits in the antler-bedecked silver helmet seemed to peer into the woods as he raced along.

Perched upon his stirrup, clutching his master's boot, was the Bad Thing, his evil, shrill laughter cutting through the drumming of the horse's hooves. It seemed to be enjoying its precarious ride. In the space between two terror-stricken heartbeats, the rider was past.

Sean paused a long minute to allow his heart to slow, then he remembered the guide. He moved off it and saw a dull grey orb of metal, now heavy and motionless. He looked at it in despair, for how was he to find Patrick without the guide? He felt tears coming to his eyes as he whispered, "Please. Don't die. Help me find Patrick!"

He repeated the words Barney had taught him, but the orb lay still. At last he had resigned himself to wandering, when a faint, friendly laugh sounded from above. Sean rolled over, scrambling backward as he brandished his silver dagger.

A boy of fourteen or fifteen dropped casually from the trees, his pale blue eyes fastened on Sean. He seemed unmindful of the dagger, but Sean kept its point leveled at the youth. Then he recognized the boy from his description. "You're the guy who hurt Gabbie!"

The youth shook his head with a grin, and like a cat was suddenly moving. Faster than Sean could react the boy knelt before him, reached out, and seized his wrist, immobilizing Sean's arm. "If I intended you harm, Sean Hastings, 'twould be easy enough a feat. But the fact I can

touch you, despite your ward, proves more than words my good inten-
tions." Releasing the boy's hand, the youth continued. "I am not the one
who troubled your sister."

Sean scooted back fearfully. The fact the stranger could have hurt
him but didn't wasn't all that reassuring. "You look like him," he said,
mustering his bravery.

With a sigh, the youth said, "With our race, looks are an issue of
whim." He shimmered an instant, with a blue-white light much like the
nimbus that had shrouded the Shining Man the night he had come for
the boys, then he shifted in form, a dark outline in brilliance, and the
glow vanished. The transformation had been only a second or so in
duration. Where the youth had been knelt a man, older than the youth,
but still young. He wore a funny hat with a broad brim, a beard, and
simple trousers, shirt, and sturdy work boots. With a voice now deep
and mature, he seized Sean under the arms before the boy could protest
and lifted him. "You see what we wish you t'see, you of mortal blood.
'Tis our will that lends us shape. And in this guise could I have taken
your sister had I wished." He smiled in remembrance and said, "That
one is among the fairest of your race I've beheld in years, but though she
would have opened her legs t'me willingly and with joy, I'd not be the
one to break the Compact." He released Sean and again the glow
surrounded him, and suddenly a little boy, no more than six or seven
years from his appearance stood before Sean.

> "Come you near or go you far,
> light from candle or flick'ring star?
> See what you will, or so you think,
> but is water sweet before you drink?
> Who can know of truth and lies?
> When can a man believe his eyes?
> Suspect what's known to mortal senses,
> for our nature vaults all mystic fences,
> that stand between that which is and seems,
> and back we are to truth . . . or dreams."

He spoke in an impish, childish, singsong voice. He glowed, and
once again the youth stood there. "That is the secret of our power, for
what you see you believe, and arms and armor, food and drink, all are
real to those who accept them as such. Illusion is powerful when viewed
as truth. Why, had you the will to believe, you could live forever from
the very life abounding in the air! You wear the green stain upon your
eyes and can therefore see through the illusion, not because the stain

has power, but because you believe it does." He laughed, and Sean felt something hot run down his back at the sound. "And you will remember.

"No, I troubled your fair sister not, lad. Another sought to cause harm, as he has before and will again if allowed, and upon me cast the blame. It was a small revenge upon me for a past deed, a harmless prank that still nettles him."

Sean got up, wanting to be away from this disturbing boy. "I've got to find my brother." He said it as a challenge, as if defying the youth to stop him.

The youth laughed, a ringing, lighthearted peal. "And I'll not halt your search, Sean." Looking down the road, as if expecting the rider to reappear, he said, "That one has caused much trouble over the ages, despite the Compact, but this time more than the Queen will tolerate. . . ." He laughed, as if finding that prospect amusing. Then his tone turned serious. "But beyond the boundaries of the Bright Lands, he is as powerful as she. Find your brother, while the Fool is abroad, then run to the Queen's court by way of the white path. Should that one overtake you, fight as best you can. Some will aid you, though none of us—not even myself—can match the Fool in power. Only the Queen is his equal." The youth laughed again, as if all this were but a game. "Still, some of us who are less than the Fool are still more than most." He reached out and took up the lifeless orb and blew upon it. At once a hot spot appeared upon the side where he blew and blossomed into a glow. With a flick of his hand and spin of the wrist, he tossed the ball, twirling, high into the air and the glow burst into brilliance around the orb. "Revive, little spirit of light, guide on this one's quest; take him where his heart desires. Find he who is as this one in body with a spirit of another, two from the same womb. Go!"

The Quest Guide spun around a point above Sean's head, then shot back to the road, where it commenced its wandering from side to side as it danced down the road, but faster than before, as if the youth's instructions had given it impetus. Sean ran after, catching up as the orb spun around a bend in the roadway. He looked back over his shoulder to shout thanks to the youth, but no sign that anyone had been by the road remained. Sean shivered, again forcing aside fear as he resumed his search for Patrick.

37

The twisted, barren landscape seemed to last for miles. Sean had long since lost track of time on the path, simply resigning himself to plodding along behind the glowing Quest Guide. He felt as if he had been moving through this desolate place for ages.

Then they crested a rise, and through the twisted trees they saw another strange house. It faced against a mound, or rather it was part of the mound, for only one wall could be seen. It appeared someone had fashioned a wall over a cave or excavation in the side of the hillock, and voices could be heard coming through the open door. Sean couldn't understand the language, for it consisted mostly of grunts and bellows, shrieks and mad laughs—accompanied by the sounds of crockery breaking and objects of some weight slamming into walls—and he had no wish to meet the authors of that riotous conversation, so he hurried past.

Sean moved rapidly enough that he passed the Quest Guide slightly and had to wait until it caught up with him. While he stood waiting, he noticed a strange property of the roadway. By turning his head, he saw it shift back and forth between white and black, reminding him of the illusion given by those "moving" charms given away in breakfast cereal boxes from time to time. To Sean it was clear that both the black path and the white path ran along here.

Sean followed the road down into a dell and up the other side and was abruptly confronted by a change in the landscape. Before him rose a massive forest of dark trees, and the sky above shifted rapidly from grey to black. He knew without being told that he was leaving what the Queen had called the Shadow Lands and was entering the Dark Lands.

Sean halted, daunted by what he saw. While the Shadow Lands had seemed a haunted, sad country, these Dark Lands were a place of magnificent unworldly beauty. Delicate and alien trees swayed in a soft summer night's breeze, and in their branches night birds trilled haunting, poignant songs. Each tree had leaves of deep green and some sprouted blooms, but there was no light in the sky. Instead, the light came from the boles, the leaves, the blooms, the grasses, even the bare ground. It was a landscape of impossible phosphorescent glows, no single source of illumination providing shadows. The scent of night-blooming flowers hung in the air and crickets chirped in counterpoint to the birds' songs. This was no brooding, evil place where mad spirits harbored their black hates against mankind. These were magic woods, fairy woods, woods of enchantment and wonder. Their beauty was nearly overpowering, yet there was nothing to fear in these soft, dark woodlands. Rather, Sean felt as if he moved through the world's most perfect and excellent woods at night. And there were colors, but alien and unexpected. Everything looked like a faint black-light painting, with subtle hues on the flowers and leaves, but everything was alive, everything was in harmony, not twisted and corrupted as in the Shadow Lands. This was the fairy land he had expected in his heart!

Sean noticed the Quest Guide seemed to be glowing fainter; as if needing less light to be seen, it produced less light than in the Bright Lands or Shadow Lands. But otherwise the object seemed content to move along in its merry side-to-side pattern, seemingly unconcerned by its location. Given its agitated response to Sean's request to find the Fool, the boy found this a reassuring sign. Sean silently hoped the Shining Man and the Bad Thing were still riding through the Shadow Lands and not coming back this way soon. More than anything, the boy prayed he could find Patrick and make good his escape without having to confront the Shining Man. He felt somehow that that would prove unlikely, but the thought gave him a more optimistic frame of mind.

The Quest Guide seemed to pick up speed, and Sean matched the quickening pace. He took it as a sign they were nearing their destination, or some danger was overtaking them, so his heart rate increased and he became again alert, all fatigue washed away.

Through the thick boles they passed, the pathway narrowing so much in places the boy wondered how the Shining Man's horse managed to get through. Then suddenly they were before another fairy hill, except this one seemed bigger than the Queen's hill, with the low-hanging branches nearly forming a black canopy above the summit. It appeared deserted, or at least Sean couldn't see anyone.

The guide swung off the path and moved up the hillside and Sean followed, his short legs pumping as he climbed. At the crest he found a pavilion, all black silks and cushions, and within the pavilion he found Patrick.

Patrick lay amid the pile of cushions, in a deep sleep. Sean looked down upon his brother and felt his heart leap. In just the few days he had been held captive, Patrick had begun to change. He wore no clothing, save a small loincloth fashioned of leaves, and black-blossom garlands and leaves of the darkest green had been woven into his hair. His lips had been rouged to a deep red, and his eyelids painted with something that gave them a pearly sheen, as had his nails. About him tiny creatures lay sleeping and none seemed disturbed by Sean's approach. Sean stared at them, for he was confronted for the first time with fairies who matched his boyhood expectation. Tiny sprites and pixies nestled against Patrick; each was human in appearance and nude, with delicate wings gracing their backs. But also slumbering around Patrick were creatures of less wholesome appearance, toadlike creatures and furry things of deformed aspect. Sean averted his eyes from these, as if to stare might wake them from their deep slumber.

Around the pavilion night insects buzzed, softly glowing fireflies that graced the black canopy with tiny spots of warm blue-green illumination. Haunting songs came through the evernight, as alien birds warbled their secrets. The night breeze was soft, even sensuous, in its caress and Sean felt like crying from the beauty of the place. Then upon the breeze he smelled the soft scent of wildflowers and spices, but from blooms and seasonings never seen on earth. Their musky odor set Sean's heart to beating, and he knew that whatever was done in this bed, under this bower, if continued, would twist and change Patrick. He must get his brother away at once.

He tiptoed into the pavilion and reached down to wake Patrick. Patrick stirred heavily, as if drugged, and Sean had to shake him several times. At last his eyes opened, then widened as he perceived his twin above him. Sean made a motion for silence, and Patrick nodded, though his movement was sluggish. He had to gently move a tiny woman-creature who lay nestled against his chest to stand. The boys waited a long moment, but the pixielike creatures were deep in slumber, oblivious to Sean and Patrick's movements. Sean took Patrick's hand and pulled him away from the pavilion. Patrick moved sluggishly, but managed not to step on any of the sleeping sprites.

Outside, Sean took a deep breath and looked at his brother. Patrick kept blinking, as if trying to clear his vision, and he shook his head. His eyelids appeared heavy and his jaw slightly slack, as if he had to fight to keep awake.

Sean half dragged, half led Patrick down to the base of the hill. "Come on," he whispered at the bottom, "we've got to get away."

Patrick nodded, still disoriented, and Sean remembered what Barney had said about being asleep in this place. Patrick might have been asleep the entire time since the Shining Man had taken him! Even now, he was half-asleep; perhaps he thought this was a dream. He might not have any idea of where they were or what their predicament was. Sean would have to take charge and simply trust his brother to follow without question until they were safe.

The Quest Guide followed the twins down the hill. Sean had half expected it to vanish or go away once Patrick was found, but now he said, "Will you show us the way back?"

The Quest Guide bounced up and down and began to take them back the way Sean had come. The glowing orb's presence somehow buoyed Sean's spirits, and for the first time he actually hoped he could get his brother away from this place without encountering the Shining Man. He knew that if they could get out of the hill and stay free of the Shining Man until after midnight, the Good People would go away and they'd all be safe. Sean said softly, "Please, God, let us get home all right."

Patrick stumbled along behind his brother, allowing himself to be pulled along by the hand, his eyes still unfocused and his expression a dreamy, faraway one. He said nothing as Sean led him back down the path to home.

38

Sean and Patrick waited. Something had caused the Quest Guide to halt its carefree movement back and forth across the road. It hung poised in midair, rotating upon its axis, as if considering which way to move. They had been back in the Shadow Lands for some time—to Sean it seemed hours, though it could have been but minutes. The woods were dark and forlorn, a place of desperation, the perfect environs for things fashioned of evil dreams and dark purposes. Trees with grey leaves and twisted black branches that never bore fruit nor bloom, ebony wood boles that lived forever in the greyest autumn, seemed trapped by the roadside, silently pleading for rescue. A bitter wind blew across Sean's face, stinging his nostrils with the faint memory of smoke and decay. He turned to Patrick and found his brother's eyes distant, as if his mind were far away. Patrick had been unusually quiet since being rescued. Sean had to repeat himself to get any sort of answer, and then it tended to the short and distracted, Patrick's manner preoccupied. Sean counted it the result of Patrick's captivity and after a while gave up on conversation, fatigue and fear making silence the easier. Sean began to walk, taking his brother by the hand. Patrick hesitated, then followed a step behind.

A noise came from the trees to the right, answered a moment later from the left. Sean stopped and had to yank on Patrick's hand to get him to halt. The noise increased on all sides, the rustle of branches being moved and the clopping of horses' hooves and the rattle of armor. As certainty about what he faced came to Sean, riders emerged from the trees on either side, positioning themselves so that they could easily encircle the boys.

Then from the woods poured forth a host of creatures, all twisted and misshapen, in soul if not in form. Ladies of astonishing beauty, wearing translucent white gowns that flowed to the ground, half floated, half walked from between the gnarled trees. The small creatures who had been with Patrick, little bigger than hummingbirds, sped through the air to greet Sean. The riders and horses, all magnificent in splendid armor and bardings, moved slowly to surround the twins. Squat creatures of ill aspect, their hideous features set in mocking grins of evil delight, darted between the legs of the horses. Sean wondered how so many people, even the little ones, could have hidden from him only a moment before. He felt afraid but held his ground, keeping Patrick's hand in his own and clutching tightly to the dagger.

"This is our heritage," said a voice from behind.

Sean jumped and spun, his heart racing as the Fool looked down upon him. The horseman had silently approached him from the rear. Sean knew why the Quest Guide had stopped: the Shining Man had used magic to halt it, as had the Queen.

The Fool stood resplendent in his black and silver armor, holding his helm under one arm. His white stallion silently regarded Sean with glowing golden eyes. The armored figure moved his head slightly as he studied the small boy who stood before him, dagger held poised for battle. "You are a brave one, small warrior," said the Fool, laughing. He called out, "Attend me, my children! Come! We have a guest." He held out his helm and a boyish fairy ran forward and took it from his master.

As the approaching fairies circled him, Sean glanced around for any sign of escape. The Fool rode forward and halted his mount before the boys. He leaned down, his face hovering above Sean's. "This was once as were the other lands through which you have passed," said the Fool. He turned and with a wide sweep of his hand indicated the barren woods. "Between the Bright Lands and the Dark Lands, these were the Twilight Lands, where the children of the People played as we who were their masters looked on. All was in balance and all was in harmony, and the one court was at peace. I ruled, my Queen at my side. And it was good. Then came the Magi with their spells and conjurations, and a great battle was fought." He sat upright in the saddle, pulling himself to the limit of his majestic height, and his voice was proud. "The struggle was heroic." Then his voice quieted. "But we were vanquished, and forced to swear to the Compact." Again leaning forward to face Sean, he said, "This is our heritage. This is the handiwork of your race, the Shadow Lands. The balance was destroyed, the harmony ended, and the powers rent asunder, so that now where the one court reigned, two are pitted in strife. My Queen no longer stands at my side. And naught is good." Narrowing his gaze as he studied Sean, he said, "So tell me, small and brave boy, what do you think of your race's gifts to the People?"

Sean glanced over at Patrick, who still seemed dazed. Sean swallowed hard. The Fool leaned down again and his hand moved toward Sean tentatively. A scant half inch from his shoulder, it was snatched back. "You still wear the ward, boy." He reached out, a seemingly impossible reach, and grabbed Patrick. "But this one does not! He will remain, boy, and so shall you." With a laugh of madness, he added, "I shall have my brace." Patrick hung from the Shining Man's hand, like a kitten held by the scruff of the neck, without protest or movement.

Sean swallowed fear. Slowly, so as not to get it wrong, he said, "Amadán-na-Briona. In the name of our Lord Jesus, I command you and your court to let go my brother and don't you follow us." Through fear and doubt he knew he hadn't gotten it exactly like Barney had told him to say, but he prayed to the Lady in the church that it was good enough.

The Fool threw back his head and screamed as if in pain, and the surrounding fairies stepped back, breath indrawn like some sudden gust of wind. The Fool's stallion reared and spun about, his forelegs pawing the air and his hind legs stamping the ground, as if the animal shared his master's rage. The Fool maintained his seat yet kept both arms outstretched, holding Patrick in one hand as if he weighed nothing. Light burned brightly about him, an aura of angry, fierce illumination. The sound of the Fool's shriek terrified Sean and he also stepped back with a shudder, and a sob escaped his lips. Tears ran down his face at the terrible sound, but he stood fast, rejecting the urge to run. The scream filled the air, evoking memories of that tormented sound Sean had made the night the Shining Man had come and stolen Patrick. On and on it went, an impossible raw noise of rage and hate. Then it trailed off and the armored figure turned a mask of pure insanity toward Sean. The illumination around the Fool lessened as he dropped Patrick, and the boy fell heavily to the ground, where he shook his head slightly, as if trying to gather his wits, and slowly got to his feet. The black form of the Bad Thing appeared from within the press and scampered over to Patrick, holding him by the arm, awaiting his master's bidding. The Shining Man's expression turned from pain to rage. He reached down and grabbed the front of Sean's loose blouse and with a powerful lift pulled Sean toward him, despite the fact the contact with one wearing a fairy stone was clearly causing him pain. Sean emitted a tiny yelp of startled fear and lashed out with his dagger, slicing the back of the Shining Man's hand, shouting, "Let go!"

The Fool screamed in pain and released the boy. Sean fell into the roadway, where he sat for a moment, watching the Fool. He grabbed his hand, as if struck by agony, and writhed in the saddle, the light around him again increasing. The horse pranced nervously while his master screamed. The sound continued, and the other fairies drew back another step. Then the sound diminished and the light diminished, and the Fool sat motionless atop his horse in front of Sean. Through clenched teeth, with blue eyes flashing as if with mad lightning, the Fool said, "You have my name, mortal child. I must do what you've willed, for the *geas* is upon me. But you've not yet won free. The way back is long. And you may only command me once, and that you've done. I'll do as you've bidden, but no more!" He sat holding his wounded hand as red blood flowed freely across the back of it. He waved it three times in the air, and the wound vanished. With a mad laugh, he spun his mount around to regard his minions. "Let them go, for they've my word 'pon it!" The crowd of dark fairies ceased to move menacingly toward Sean, save the Bad Thing, who reached out and began pulling Patrick away by the hand.

The Fool shrieked again, in glee rather than rage and pain. He sat astride his horse, his face alight with a madness equal to that shown the night he had come to the boys' room. His animal pawed the ground, snorting and showing the whites of his eyes. Sean hurried over to his brother's side. The Bad Thing crouched down, backing away from Patrick, its simple intelligence in turmoil at its master's change of orders. Sean regarded this fearsome creature, finding it smaller in stature than he had thought. Its almost glowing brown and yellow eyes blinked as they followed Sean's movement, then it turned to regard the Shining Man, awaiting orders. A terrible anger struck Sean—he was tired of being frightened and bossed around by these creatures. Sean shouted, "Leave us alone!" He slashed wildly at the Bad Thing and it fell away, hissing in anger and fearful of the silver dagger. The creature bared fangs, but Sean menaced it again with the dagger and the creature scampered back to crouch at the rear of his master's horse.

Patrick seemed still in a daze, his eyes unfocused, and he showed no sign of recognition. Uncertain what to do next, Sean pulled on Patrick's hand, as if to lead him back down the road.

Patrick followed a few feet; then the Fool's voice sounded. "Patrick, take him!"

Sean felt his arm jerked and he spun around as Patrick planted his feet. Patrick yanked again and Sean fell. Then Patrick was atop his brother. Sean had never been able to best Patrick in a scrap. All their young lives, there had always been something holding him back, some limit on how much anger he could focus on his brother, as if to visit pain on Patrick were to visit it upon himself. Patrick had never seemed to share that inhibition, freely punishing Sean when their sibling conflicts had come to a head. Now Sean knew that to lose this struggle would be to lose more than another brotherly tussle.

With a fury new to him, he heaved Patrick aside and rolled away. Then another figure leaped into the fray, and Sean smelled decay in his face. Powerful arms grappled with him, and the sounds of shrieking told him that the owner of those hands paid the price for touching him, as the magic of the fairy stone caused the Bad Thing torment. Sean didn't hesitate. Blindly, wildly, he lashed out with his dagger and felt the point dig in. The Bad Thing howled in pain and fled, leaving the half-dazed Sean sitting on the white road.

Sean could hear the roar of the Fool's anger echoing through the murky woods and the shrieking of the Bad Thing as it fled through the trees, but he could see only Patrick as his brother again hurled himself atop Sean. Sean felt the jar in his shirt shatter and felt water drench his side. The holy water! He had forgotten to release Patrick from the Fool's control and now the water was spilled.

Frantic, his terror at losing Patrick giving him a near-hysterical strength, Sean shoved his brother aside and gripped the side of his shirt with his left hand, drenching it with water. He let Patrick leap at him again, and reached out with his wet hand. Smearing Patrick's face with the water, he clumsily made the sign of the cross and half grunted, "In the name of our Lord, you are free!"

Patrick rocked forward, as if struck from behind by a brick. His eyes blinked and seemed to focus for the first time. He looked at his brother and then around. His eyes widened as if he couldn't believe what he saw, but before he could speak, Sean was up and yanking Patrick to his feet. Shaking in terror, Sean gulped back his fear and shouted at the Shining Man, "You broke your word!" He half expected something bad to happen, but the Fool only sat regarding the boys with a baleful gaze.

"That simple one," he said, pointing after the fleeing Bad Thing, "defied my order. And he"—he pointed at Patrick—"was no member yet of my court. I have done as you have bidden."

Sean knew somehow he had not done as well as he could have, but he was unable to contain himself any longer. Patrick stood beside him, his eyes boggling at what he saw, and he appeared on the edge of fainting. Sean grabbed his brother's hand, yanking him around. "Come on!"

Patrick let himself be turned and pulled, but he couldn't take his eyes from the assembled host of fairies. Sean turned to face the fairies, who sat motionless, watching the twins.

Suddenly the Fool shrieked, a high, almost feminine, ear-shattering screech. Pain took voice and he spun his mount in a full circle and raised his fist toward the heavens. Again he spun his horse, with hand out-stretched as he waved in anger, shrieking, "Go! Begone! All of you!"

The dark fairies fled back to the woods, retreating in the face of their master's anger. As quickly as they had come they had gone, and the boys stood alone on the road with the Fool. He moved a menacing step toward them, and Sean and Patrick bolted.

Young feet pounded the stones as the twins raced along the path through the trees, the Quest Guide speeding along with them. Each step they flew carried them closer to safe haven, away from terrors so overpowering they had been given form and substance: the Fool.

Patrick shouted, "What's going on! Where are we?" He seemed to be waking from a dream.

"Just keep running!" answered Sean. Both continued silent in their flight, and kept eyes fixed forward, as if to look back would be to surrender what had been so difficult to win. Each moment was another test, another risk, another trap to prevent their escape.

Then, after a timeless flight, they could see the back of the strange house that seemed to mark the boundary between the land of the Queen and the land where Sean had met the Fool. Only a few gnarled trees stood between the boys and that boundary.

A few yards from the rear door of the house, the boys slowed. Patrick said, "What's going on?"

Sean pointed backward. "That guy, the Shining Man, he took you from home. You've been here for more than a week."

"I don't remember!" said Patrick, obviously disturbed. "Where are we?"

"Barney said it's the Good People's land. I don't know what it's called. I didn't ask."

"How do we get back?"

Sean pointed. "Through this place, then down a white road, to where this Queen lady is going to help us. Then out a cave to where Barney's waiting."

"Why does that guy want to hurt us?" asked Patrick.

"I don't know. Maybe Barney can tell us." Then he considered. "He said humans made that sad place, you know, where all the trees are ugly. Maybe he's just mad at all of us."

Patrick was usually the leader in any undertaking the boys embarked upon, but under these bizarre circumstances he was more than willing to follow Sean's lead. Waking up in the middle of a fight with his brother, with all those weird things standing around, was too much even for his sense of adventure. He reached up and felt the garlands in his hair. "What's this junk?" Patrick asked, pulling the leaves and black blooms from his curls.

Then a figure dropped from the trees, landing with shocking force upon Sean's back. Patrick yelled in surprise and leaped away.

Sean rolled over on his back, the thing holding tight to him. He didn't need to see his assailant to know the Bad Thing had moved through the trees ahead of him, attempting to intercept him before leaving the Shadow Lands. The Bad Thing hooted in pain as it struggled to restrain Sean, obviously tormented by contact with one wearing a ward. Taloned black hands tore at Sean's blouse as the creature attempted to rip the fairy stone from around Sean's neck.

Sean lashed out backward with the dagger, but only dug the tip into moist ground. He yelled, half in anger, half in fear, and rolled again, but the Bad Thing held tight to his back.

Sean then felt powerful claws grip his throat, and in a spasm of panic he managed to roll onto his chest. He made a crawling motion while the Bad Thing cried, almost a human sound. It was in torment from the fairy stone but it continued to do its master's bidding: rid the boy of the stone and return them both.

Then the Bad Thing rocked, and Sean felt the weight roll off him. Sean turned and saw that Patrick had struck the creature, knocking it away, and now the other twin was struggling. Patrick flailed out with the rock he used as a weapon, but Sean knew that without the ward and silver dagger, Patrick was no opponent for the Bad Thing.

Without hesitation Sean leaped atop the struggling pair, adding his weight to Patrick's, to press the creature to the earth. He cut downward with his dagger and felt the point dig in. The creature screamed, a sound to linger forever in the boys' nightmares.

Sean cried in fear, his vision blurred by tears, but he held his position and let his weight fall upon the handle of the dagger, using his mass where he lacked strength of arm. The hilt dug into Sean's stomach as the blade bit deep into the stomach of the Bad Thing, and to Sean it was as if their pain were shared. The Bad Thing screamed. And the boys' shrieks of fear made a counterpoint to the thing's cry of pain. It was a gurgling, strangled sound, then a hissing and scratchy sound. Patrick threw himself across Sean's back, and the dagger was driven deeper into the Bad Thing. The heartrending scream of pain changed, trailing off to a warble, a hiss of steam leaking from a boiler, a shrill, final sound. It was the sound of death.

Patrick rolled off his brother. Sean scrambled back, as if repelled by the most noxious thing ever seen. Neither boy spoke as they watched the black creature writhe upon the ground, the dagger protruding from its stomach. It flopped like a freshly landed fish, crimson blood spraying from its nose and mouth, then lay still, only to twitch and shiver, then lie still again.

Sean looked at Patrick, who sat silently with tears flowing from eyes wide with panic. Sean rubbed his own runny nose on the back of his sleeve, then wiped his eyes and left his brother. He went to where the Bad Thing lay, slowly circling it to ensure it was dead.

At last he was satisfied, and he bent over to get the dagger. As his fingers touched the hilt, a black hand swung up and gripped his shirt front. Sean yelled. The Bad Thing pulled the boy toward him, the yellow and brown eyes now open and alive. Scant inches from the thing's face, the pulling stopped. Then the Bad Thing spoke, its bloody lips barely moving. In a gurgling whisper, soft and tiny, like a little child's voice, it said, "I . . . was once . . . like you." Then in a hissing whisper, almost inaudible, it said, "Free . . . thank . . . you."

For an instant Sean saw the hate leave the creature's face. Sean looked into its eyes, and in that instant they were not mad with inhuman lights, but large, brown, and soft. And hidden deep in those moist eyes, far in the shadow of hate and rage, was a hint of something more. Then Sean understood: once, long ago, this Bad Thing had been as human as Sean. From wherever the Bad Thing had come, it had had parents and a home, a life of promise and hope, and the expectation of youth. But all that had been taken from it by the black, glowing figure. Like Patrick, the Bad Thing had been a child stolen from his parents by fairies, taken to this alien place. That forgotten child had been twisted and warped over the years, his once child's flesh distorted by inhuman passions into this creature of horror. And Sean understood more: to be taken by the Shining Man was to become such as this. Then the light extinguished in those eyes as the creature's head fell back, its hand still clinging to Sean's blouse. Sean gently pried apart the thing's fingers, and the grip on Sean's blouse was released.

Sean stood away from the thing, knowing now what his and Patrick's fate would be should the Shining Man somehow recapture them. As objects of perverted lust and desire, they would be used, warped, and twisted, their bodies and spirits reshaped until they were like the Bad Thing, creatures so blackened of soul that even the memory of humanity was a dim, nearly forgotten thing.

Sean stared down at the twisted thing that had once been a child much like himself, feeling a mixture of relief and sorrow. Perhaps it had been that almost lost humanity that had given the creature the ability to resist the ward. And perhaps it had been that almost lost humanity that had let the boys drive home the dagger, giving the creature final rest.

Then, at the sound of approaching hoofbeats, he knew danger once again raced after them. He turned away from the Bad Thing, the dagger forgotten. Patrick stood mute, as if the spoken words were some sort of narcotic, rendering him without volition. Sean seized his hand and pulled him toward the rear door of the strange house, where the Quest Guide waited, moving rapidly from side to side, as if impatient—or frightened. They reached the back door and Sean tugged on the handle, but the door would not open. Panic struck, for they seemed to be balked by the reluctant door. Again and again Sean tugged, until at last the latch moved. The door swung open ponderously, and Sean pushed it wide to reveal the interior of the Hall of Ancient Seasons. The boys took a single step toward the interior and halted as a tall figure stepped into view, coming out of the gloom deep within the building. No longer dressed in armor, but now wearing a barbaric hat topped with antelope horns, and a jerkin sewn with gems and the skulls of seabirds on each shoulder, the Fool blocked their path through the house. He studied the motionless boys a long moment, then threw back his head and howled his pleasure.

39

Phil and Mark found Barney kneeling in the rain, clutching his rosary as he prayed. Phil approached from the side. So he could be heard over the driving rain, he shouted, "Sean?"

"In there," said Doyle, pointing at the hill.

"What?" said Phil, astonished. "Where's the entrance?"

Mark gripped Phil's shoulder. "Nine times around the hill to the right. Like the old legends."

"Well, let's get them!" shouted Phil.

Mark held Phil's shoulder, while Barney said, "Wait!" Phil quit moving toward the hill, as Barney motioned for a hand. Slowly, letting Mark help him, Barney got to his feet. "If you go barging in after, you may lose all you hope to save. Time and distance are canted in the land of the Good People, so the tales say."

"I don't know what the hell's going on," shouted Phil, "but if my sons are wandering around in there, I'm going to get them out."

Barney sighed. "Said like a man, Philip Hastings. But it is almost midnight, and if they're not out within minutes, there's nothing to say you'll survive as well. You've a wife and daughter in this world you must also think about."

Mark said, "We stay."

Phil was about to object, but Mark said, "If what I think is going to happen happens, then we'll get the boys back, Phil. If I mess up . . . it won't matter."

Atop the crest of the hill, the night was suddenly rent by brilliance as a white glow erupted. Phil saw a magnificent woman—if she was human—surrounded by what seemed a royal court take form atop the hill, dim figures stepping out of the brilliance to walk down the hill. Mark came up to stand beside Phil.

The three men watched the Queen of Faerie. She seemed to float above the mud as she descended farther down the hillside. How she had moved between the realms was not apparent. Behind her came the members of her court, including one who was obviously human, a man who alone in the Queen's company had to plod over muddy sod. All the others glided above the surface of the earth.

Barney stood weaving—whether from being still slightly drunk or from fright, it couldn't be said—his mouth open in disbelief at the sight of the Queen of the Fairies standing nearby. The Queen looked at Mark, as if expecting him to speak. When he remained silent, she said, "You are not of the Magi."

Mark spoke softly, yet his words carried in the now still air. "The Erl King, who is called the Fool, was responsible for a breach of the Compact; he was in league with traitors within the Magi—men who would share power over the rest of humanity with him. He set it up for this man"—he pointed at Phil—"to find the gold. And not knowing it to be a pledge of faith, this man took it. There was no intent to break the law."

"We know the truth when we hear it. We mourn for that which once was. If the Compact is broken, it is because of no mortal doing. One wished for the old ways and thought to revenge himself upon those who vanquished us so long ago." Almost sadly she added, "Rightly has he named himself the Fool, he who is King no longer." She heaved a sigh that would have been called theatrical coming from any mortal woman, but looked only appropriate to her more than human nature. "We shall finally have to call him to account when he comes." She glanced about. "The hour to move is almost here. He is overlong in coming. Fool or King, yet must we wait upon him, for it is by his will as much as our own that we travel again."

"Titania and Oberon," said Mark quietly.

"So they have been called," agreed the Queen's human companion. "Those are but mortal names and not their own, any more than he is Elberich or she Gloriana. Nor are they truly Ahriman and Ormuzd. They are only they who once ruled the *Faie*."

"Faie," said Phil. "It that what they call themselves?"

The man shook his head. "It is a Norman word. They call them-selves the Race, or People—much as any people do—but their words cannot be spoken by mortals, for only angels or demons have voices like theirs. To us they are the *Fee, Peri,* or *Sidhe.* Or a dozen other names. But, simply, they are what they are—as we are but what we are. And each race and nation of man sees them in a form that is like to its own."

Mark shook his head wearily. "What will happen now?"

The man said, "That is as it has been for ages, in the long and the short. There will be a change. But for good or ill, I cannot say."

Mark said, "I don't understand."

The man pointed. "Ariel comes. And behind him close should come his master."

A glowing dust devil spun past the silent members of the Queen's court who dotted the clearing, and came up the hillside. Behind it came those creatures who had served the Fool. They halted at sight of the Queen, but the glowing column of spinning wind moved boldly past her to halt before Phil and the others. The spinning form quickly resolved itself into the shape of the young boy who had rescued Sean and Patrick.

"Hail, Thomas," said the youth, obviously weary.

"Welcome, Ariel," replied the man. "Come and rest. You appear bested."

With resignation, Ariel said, "True. My master again took my mea-sure and made me cry out in pleasure. It was a great and wonderful defeat." Grinning, he said, "But though I must again count him my master, still did I task him greatly. And he did fall prey to fate's whims and now finds himself within the Hall of Ancient Seasons. And should he not quit that hall before the twelfth chime strikes, even his powers will serve him not. So then I would have a master, but then I would not. It would be, in short, a matter of some perplexity."

"And what were you to do with Dark Lands? Went you with the Queen's consent?" asked Thomas.

"Not entirely," said the youth. "But she knew what I was about. It is not the first time she has lost me to the dark court and the Fool's bidding. And if the Fool has not lost himself in time's dream, she will win me again, and it will not be the last I change the King's court for hers." With a wicked smile he said, "Neither counts me a particularly reliable servant." He frowned almost petulantly. "I think now I must be about a different calling, for I deem it time to change my lot. Ah, now to be master instead of servant." He sighed. "To serve the Fool has its benefits. The last time he sent me to dwell among mortals was to establish contact with the Magi in the woods of Greece. Ah! What joys I had traveling with university students on tour! And the nights were filled with revels fit to put old Dionysus to shame. Before that it was to watch the Magus Kessler for a span."

Mark looked to Phil. "I think we've just found Wayland Smith."

The boy grinned and nodded. He shimmered and turned to the shape of the blacksmith. "It is a talent we have." His voice was now deep and resonant. "It is a shape pleasing to mortal women. In my more common form they find me childish and wish to mother me. This shape seems to excite more notice. I have also discovered that in this guise it is not necessary to use arts to gain women. As I look now, they come to me. A fair word, a quiet touch, a promise of love, and they are more than willing to spread their legs and make the beast with two backs." He laughed. "When I wore this form while watching the Magus Kessler, I had many a pleasurable hour with a mortal wench, and those whose society I enjoyed were a high-spirited and jolly company, ruffians all. Though, I think, to serve the Fool after this struggle will be less a joy than that occasion. Should he win, it will be war. Should he not, he will be wroth and unleash his vexation upon me." His voice rose in pitch as he shifted back to his boyish appearance.

Phil looked confused. "Who's Wayland Smith?"

Mark said, "I'll tell you later. If there's a later."

Phil studied the youth for a moment, then said, "My daughter! Are you . . . ?"

With a stretch, the youth said, "Nay, proud father. I am not the one who troubled your children. She saw me but once in my more manly guise, and I did but do her a small service. She is a fair one and gladly would I have taken her pleasures." He shivered and grinned. "My flesh hardens to think of her." His smile vanished and he added, "But she did not offer and I did not wish to be the one to break oath by using arts. The one I call master did take my most common form and think to place the blame for the breach of peace upon me, should word of the deed reach the Queen. Causing her to cast me out would seem a splendid jest to him. It was a cruel thing to do. It was a long feud we had, for among the People have I alone risen to be near his match, I who was once his knavish jester. And as he sought to dishonor me," said the youth with an evil grin, "I think I shall repay him most bitterly, by taking his place." With a shimmer of light, the boy changed his form, and suddenly, in all his towering splendor, the Fool stood again before the stunned humans.

40

The Fool laughed, and Phil felt the hair on his neck and arms rise at the sheer alien quality of the sound.

From where she had stood, the Queen called out, "At once put away that mask! You mock one who is your better!"

Instantly the youth reappeared. He made a courtly bow toward the Queen, who motioned for her attendants to come to her. Tiny glowing sprites flew up the hill while she sought to regain her poise. With a sly wink to the humans, the youth called Ariel said, "It is not quite time, though it shall be soon."

Almost absently, Ariel said to the Queen, "The Indian king's boy is dead."

The Queen nodded. "We sensed his death."

Thomas sighed. "It is good he rests at last. His nature had become foul *in extremis* since the Fool won him from the Queen. And long has he been a cause of contention between the two courts. How did he pass?"

Ariel said, "That one's son called Sean slew him with a dagger of silver." He grinned. "He's a brave tad. The Indian king's boy thanked him for the deed. That faint gratitude sang on the wind for all to hear. His soul is now free to find God's rest."

Phil said, "Sean? What . . ."

Mark said, "Ten thousand questions. And I don't know where to start."

Barney nodded as he sat down heavily upon the muddy ground. "And scant good would answers gain you, Mark Blackman. What sober man would believe you?"

Mark looked at the youth. "What do you mean, it's not quite time?"

Ariel glanced at the Queen, who stood surrounded by her court. He barely hid his laugh as he spoke. "For ages have I served her, and the other, tossed from court to court as fate's whim directed. Soon, I think, I shall rule, for if my master does not best the mortal boys in the Hall of Ancient Seasons, I shall take his place. And to the Queen's bed go without suffering the consequence."

"Consequence?" said Mark, obviously confused.

Ariel glanced at Thomas. "The Queen's needs are savage in appetite. Twice have I had the pleasure to be her passing fancy. Greatly was I vanquished. None can withstand the Queen's embrace without being bested, save"—he inclined his head toward Thomas—"that one."

Mark raised an eyebrow. Thomas shrugged. "The Queen finds me . . . pleasurable. I can bring her things . . . of the body. With me she needs no issues of dominance resolved. She can take from me without surrender and fear, and I survive her gifts."

Ariel chortled, a high-pitched gleeful sound. "So wonderful a lover she found him that when he sought to leave, she cursed him." Now the boy fell to the ground, and rolled over to lie on his back, hands behind his head, obviously delighted at the chance to tell the story. "And such a curse! Never could he speak without telling the truth—only the truth, no more, no less. No embellishments, no liberties, no coloring or lightening, no kind dissembling, no charitable allusions. Just truth. A poet under such a curse could find but little favor in the company of other mortals. Lords who are willing patrons need fawning praise, not unvarnished truth." He glanced at Thomas. "And I would think rhyming would become much more difficult with so many words denied you, poet." Looking back to Mark, the youth said, "He returned to us, lore keeper, as the Queen knew he would."

Mark's eyes widened. "Of course! You're Thomas Learmont!"

"I am he," answered the man.

Phil glanced at the man and said, "Who?"

Mark said, "Thomas of Erceldoune. Thomas the Rhymer."

Barney, who had recovered his wits, laughed a weak, hoarse-sounding laugh, cut through by fear, but he boldly said, "A Scotsman, which is nearly as bad as an Englishman, but a poet, which makes him almost Irish."

Thomas ignored the barb. "Please," said Mark, "there's so little time. What are these creatures?"

Thomas shrugged. "Beings of the spirit. They have no true mortal form; they take shape as pleases them." He looked at Mark. "They cause terror or lust, love and fear, those strongest of emotions, to rise up within mortal hearts, fanning them like a flame into a blaze; then they feed upon those passions, devouring them like food or drink. When they take mortal lovers, their spirit and the spirits of their lovers burn like a fire. If they are kind, they cause only a little fear or a little passion, taking sparingly, and leaving the mortal to recover. But if they are without kindness, they take all until they've devoured the mind and spirit of the human whom they use in this fashion, leaving only ashes behind. It is a difficult thing to understand. It is their way. They are denied flesh, and long for it. They mimic us and our bodies, since they have none of their own. They envy us. For all their frolic, they are an ofttimes sad race."

Phil said, "But you're human; you stay with them?"

"I abide," agreed Thomas. "The Queen and I have come to know each other. It is a satisfactory arrangement." His voice trailed off. "Though now and again I long for the sight of fog on the moors and sun on the hills of Scotland."

"Perhaps this year," said Ariel. "One never knows where she will choose. Now the courts are reunited, and she free of his sour orders, it may prove she'll choose a place where a great celebration can be undertaken."

To Mark and the others Thomas said, "Before this night, since the time of the Compact, the Queen and the Fool had been in all ways equal. Each had their court, and both needed to agree on where we would troop next. The Seely and Unseely courts are separate in their realm, but in this mortal world they must move as one."

Ariel's grin widened and his voice took on a conspiratorial tone. "Once, ages past, there was but one court. It was after the Destruction, when the Compact was forced upon us, that we were split as a people." His eyes seemed alive with delight. "Though it may be, should my master fall, we shall again be as one!" Then his eyes betrayed a dark side. "Or should she not wish to share her rule and those below be agreed, we might see another in control of the Dark Lands. No courser can withstand me."

Ariel giggled, and Phil shivered at the madness in the sound. "Is it not a grand and fitting irony, humans? Has there ever been a more dolorous race than we? For to take pleasure is to become a slave, and to give it without return is hollow victory. So we seek humans to prey upon, that we not destroy ourselves." He laughed again, but this time it was a bitter laugh. "Yet our perversity is nothing compared to mankind's. Someday I must come to understand what makes you humans so wasteful of the gifts God has given you. To feel so strongly . . . to know pleasure and pain . . . joy and wonder . . . even death!"

Mark's tone was one of disbelief. "You don't die?"

Thomas said, "They are of the spirit, and to die is utter obliteration. They have no souls, or they are only souls, however you choose to understand such things. But if they fall, they fall for eternity, while man's light passes to another and better world."

Mark and Phil exchanged glances. Mark was about to ask another question, but in the distance the sound of a church bell cut the night. Thomas said, "It is time."

With the chiming of the bell, the fairies began to glow brightly. Many shifted shape. The knights of the Queen's court and the Fool's coursers were all surrounded by a white-blue glow. The horses vanished, as did all the armor. Only small beings with sheer wings, hovering above the ground, remained.

"What . . . ?" said Phil.

The Queen quickly surrounded herself with light as the second chime struck. She resolved herself into a different form, even more stunning and beautiful than before. Her wings were golden, but with faint shimmering stripes of colors, and her hair hung to her shoulders like the finest spun gold. She wore a fabulous robe of stunning fashion, yet it was transparent, revealing her naked body as she rose into the air. Her breasts, hips, buttocks, and long tapering legs were perfect in proportion and form, but she was of heroic size, easily a full head taller than Mark. Her skin was without blemish and her muscles impossibly smooth and fluid in every movement. Her legs and arms were almost golden in this light, and her body was devoid of hair save her groin, which was covered in soft-looking, feathery golden down. Her face was now even more perfect than before, each line more finely drawn, each curve more subtle, each angle more graceful. Yet now, more than before, her alien nature was revealed.

Mark glanced about, but it was Phil who shouted, "Where are my sons!"

With a savage laugh, Ariel answered, "In a place of timelessness and despair, and should they not win free of my master, and quickly, there shall they abide for eternity."

The sound of his voice sent a chill of dread through Phil's soul, plunging him into a darkness of the heart beyond any despair he had known thus far. He turned to watch the hillside for any sign of his boys, knowing he had but ten more chimes before they were lost to him forever.

41

Sean and Patrick stood motionless. The sound of hoofbeats reverberated through the dark woodlands, now closer. Sean willed himself to speak, saying, "You didn't do like I told you!" He was suddenly conscious of having left the dagger behind in the body of the Bad Thing. "You broke your word!"

With evil amusement the Fool placed hands on hips, saying, "Indeed I did not! I was told not to follow after." With a mock graciousness that terrified Sean as much as any demonstration of anger, the Fool continued. "But you said nothing about me riding ahead of you. And you said nothing about *them* following after!"

He pointed to the woods behind the boys, past the still figure of the Bad Thing, where a veritable army of dark fairies was emerging into sight. Those upon horse rode slowly and those on foot crouched, in anticipation of the boys' bolting away from the Fool. "Now you are mine!"

To the advancing fairies he said, "Take them!"

Sean and Patrick exchanged glances and one of those silent communications they had known since birth. Both boys broke toward the door and the Fool, away from his minions. The spinning golden globe of the Quest Guide moved to follow.

As soon as the three passed the threshold, the door slammed behind them, freeing them momentarily from pursuit. The Fool hesitated an instant at the unexpected charge, as Patrick ran to the right and Sean the left.

Patrick dodged, and as he passed the door that held summer in check, it slammed open. The noise caused him to falter, and he instinctively moved away, which brought him within reach of the Fool.

A powerful hand reached out and gripped the boy's flesh, but he squirmed and pulled away, feeling scorching heat, as if touched by a live electric wire. He fell forward, rolling and turning, to rise in a crouch.

But instead of the expected sight of the Fool advancing upon him, Patrick saw that the dread creature had spun to face Sean, who had not quite gotten past him. And this time there was a handful of clothing to grip as the Fool's now gloved fist seized hold of Gabbie's blouse. With a shout of triumph, the Fool lifted Sean. "You will torment me no longer, boy!" And with a searing laugh, he said, "Now you will know pain!"

Lifting Sean toward him, he reached out with his free hand, and Patrick could see that the leather glove had clawed tips, poised to tear his brother's flesh.

42

Patrick screamed, "Sean! Get away!"

Sean twisted and squirmed, and the clawed glove descended.

Sean cried out as the shirt tore and his child's flesh was cut. Patrick stood motionless, helpless to aid his brother in this moment of his torment, as crimson stained his sister's tattered blouse. The Fool giggled, a sound to freeze the mind. Patrick could see that the cuts upon Sean's chest were light, for the Fool was only toying with his victim.

Then Sean jerked at the front of his shirt with his free hand. The buttons tore and suddenly he was sliding downward. The Fool's eyes went wide with astonishment as the boy wriggled free and he was left holding limp cloth. The now bare-chested boy dodged away, and the Fool turned to cut off his escape.

Sean moved away, and the door leading to winter flew open. The boy backed toward it, sensing the opening behind him. The Fool's face came alight with evil glee. "There's no escape there, boy. There lies Forever's Winter, and to enter that realm is to lose all hope."

Sean crouched, as if to make a leap for freedom past the Fool, and the Fool answered his movements with a move to his right. Sean feigned a move in the other direction, and the Fool answered that. The boy was helpless.

Sean crouched, seeming consumed at last by panic. Seeing him immobilized by terror caused a stiffening of Patrick's resolve. He wouldn't let this shiny guy take Sean. Patrick spun about, looking for anything that might help. There was only one other object in the room. Patrick reached out and grabbed the Quest Guide, as Sean had before. The baseball-sized orb brightened as if angry or fearful. "Sorry," was all Patrick said as he reared back.

Patrick shouted, "Sean! Pitchout!"

At this the Shining Man turned toward Patrick, while Sean hunkered down even lower. Patrick took aim at the Shining Man's head and threw the Quest Guide. He didn't have Sean's finesse as a pitcher, but his throw to second base was the strongest of any boy his age he had met, and he knew this was the most important throw of his young life. Straight and true went the Quest Guide, speeding at the head of the Fool. The Quest Guide struck the Shining Man full in the face, and with a shriek—of pain or anger, the twins couldn't judge—the Fool stumbled back.

Sean braced himself, in the age-old position of the boy who creeps behind another, waiting for a companion to push the unsuspecting dupe backward. The Fool's leather boot struck Sean and he toppled backward and with a mind-numbing scream fell through the door into winter.

Sean rolled forward, scrambling around on all fours in a crablike motion. But instead of a figure of towering rage emerging from the door to claim them, they saw the Fool sitting in the snow. The old man and woman were rushing to him, one on each side, helping him to his feet. Then the boys saw that the man and woman weren't just helping him, they were holding him. What had been smiling faces, set in warm expressions, were now masks of madness beyond that seen upon the Shining Man. The Fool struggled against the pair, but even his magical strength could not budge them.

Patrick came up behind where Sean crouched and said, "Look at that!"

As they watched, the Fool's face seemed to grow pale, and to wither, until his apparent age matched that of the pair who held him motionless. He cried out, and his scream was only the faintest whisper of agony.

Then Patrick gripped Sean's shoulder, and Sean turned. In the opposite doorway, another Fool, young and vigorous, was held in identical pose to his older doppelgänger, his motion restricted by the young pair of summer lovers.

Sean rose unsteadily to his feet. With a voice choked with fatigue and emotion, he said, "Let's go."

Patrick gave him a steadying arm and then let him go. Sean walked slowly toward the far door. As they passed out of sight of the first pair of doors, they swung shut and the second pair opened. Within the door to autumn a mature-looking version of the Fool was being pulled back from the door by the man and woman Sean had seen on his previous way through the hall. The boys turned.

Beyond the last door, the door into spring, a child Fool, in the same raiment as the others but diminished in size to a boy of seven, was being dragged away by the boy and girl. In those three faces both twins saw something unholy. And his faintly heard child's screams were of unalloyed terror.

Sean turned away and saw his own tears mirrored upon Patrick's cheeks. "Let's go home."

Patrick nodded and knew that no words would ever convey to another what they had just witnessed. Then the distant sound of a chime could be heard, and Sean said, "It's midnight! We've got to hurry!" Forcing legs weary beyond belief to move, they ran for the far door.

43

The night was rent by a boy's cry: Sean screaming, "Barney!"

Seemingly out of nowhere, the twins hurried on leaden legs toward the three men. Phil dashed forward, sweeping up both his boys in his arms, his voice breaking with emotion as he repeated their names over and over. Barney came hurrying through the mud as fast as his cramped and ancient legs could carry him. He reached the boys with tears in his eyes and prayers on his lips, saying, "Blessed St. Patrick be praised! You did it, Sean! You brought him back!"

Sean began to speak, but couldn't, fear and fatigue finally overwhelming him. All he could do was let his father hold him. The exhausted boys allowed Phil to support them, letting themselves go limp. Almost breathless, Patrick said, "The Shining Man tried to get us, but we tricked him and now he's stuck in the house with the doors."

The Queen's voice sang out. "Within the Hall of Ancient Seasons?"

Patrick nodded. "He grabbed Sean, and I threw the shining ball at him. He fell through the door."

The Queen covered her face with her hands and openly sobbed.

Mark glanced at the human who stood beside the Queen. "I don't understand," he said. The bell at St. Catherine's struck the third chime of midnight.

"She did love him greatly," answered Thomas.

Hugging his sons and considering what he had heard about the Fool, Phil said, "She loves that maniac?"

With a sad note, Thomas said, "The Queen loves many, and many love her. But that one who is lost in ancient seasons was first among her lovers and foes."

"Once," she said in a voice almost plaintive in quality, "we stood as masters of this mortal world; then as contestants with man for our place upon it." Her hand inscribed a circle, indicating the land inside the hill, in which they lived. "We discovered that world, and unraveled its secrets, its place in time and the how and why of traveling between the realms of spirit and substance." She sighed. "But when humans learned to use arts, then we suffered. It is the age of man, and we exist at his sufferance. His numbers grow daily while ours are as always, and his arts are powerful beyond belief. He has unlocked the secrets of metal and the hated electricity which robs us of our strength. And, beyond, he knows the secrets of the universe, or will soon, the very heart of mystery." She looked up at Mark. "We are no longer your match. We must now depend upon your kindness."

Mark nodded in understanding. Phil came to his side and said, "What does she mean? Are we safe?" He looked upon his sons with concern.

Mark nodded. "From the fairies? Yes. They're energy beings. Knowing that, we could find a way to defeat them, even without magic. The Queen just said 'hated electricity.' I think we could build weapons." His frustration showed. "So we find ourselves forced to cooperate with those who've kept them hidden from most of humanity over the ages."

"The Magi?" said Phil, keeping his boys close at his side.

Mark took a breath, calming his ire. "Yes, and it's a good bet that while we're doing their work for them, they'll be trying to make sure we don't betray their existence. The Magi already have enough clout within the governments of the world to hush things up. We could all have 'accidents.' It's a no-win situation if we talk. So we don't talk." Then he shook his head. "Not that anyone would ever believe this."

The Queen spoke to the two men. "I do not know of everything you say, but I sense you understand our plight. The Fool and his coursers might chase a lone man in the woods with their Wild Hunt, but you have armies without limit and machines that bring terrible destruction. What the Magi did ages past to the Shadow Lands would be nothing compared to what you are capable of now. All, the Bright Lands, the Dark Lands, all would become like that. The People would end."

"So," said Mark, "we must ensure no one learns the truth." He shook his head. "I'll never write my book." Then he said, "Majesty, there are so many things I would know, even if I might never tell another. So many things that concern the days so long ago. Thomas has spoken of angels and demons, and God placing you above the People—"

Softly the Queen said, "Mortal friend, we of the People know our history less well than you know your own. The People have no lore keepers such as yourself, and we are not the first to rule, nor shall we be the last. We are but the most recent of those who guide the People in this guise. Our days do not number endless, though to your kind it must seem so. We do not remember back before the time of the Compact."

Mark looked confused. "But Thomas said—"

"He brings his mortal understanding to what he sees, as do all of your people save the Magi. We are not as you. When she who first wore this form faded, another took it, the same form, yet a different essence, as I took it in my turn, and as another will from me someday. And she who went before is again as these little fliers." She indicated the simple, tiny sprites who darted around their Queen. "Or the Quest Guide. They are all young beings, with little understanding, just beginning to grow. I may not make you understand. I am she who was first given to rule at my Lord's side, yet I am not. It is all part of the cycle of things."

Mark considered. "When your energy state runs down, another comes and assumes the role, one whose energy is rising." He glanced at Ariel. "As his is. And the predecessors' energy runs down to where they begin again, as if they were children!" Mark's eyes widened. He said to Ariel, "You'll be the Fool!"

Ariel shrugged. "It is not our fate to read the future." With an insouciant grin he said, "And unlike you we have no wish to do so." Then he winked as the fourth chime sounded at St. Catherine's. "Though I think soon."

"We think you already know more of our truth than does our beloved Thomas," observed the Queen. Nodding toward the youth called Ariel, she added, "I expect that one day it will be as you say, and I will discover that he has changed and become the one now lost in the Hall of Ancient Seasons. That one had remained unchanged much longer than I." Her eyes became distant, as if remembering. "I think hatred for your race had fueled his existence." She looked at Mark, eyes seeming to glow with emotion. "No, you will not learn more, human. And remember this above all, in every thing there is always Mystery, what you mortals call God."

The Queen looked around as the sky seemed to change hue, losing some of the alien blue under the black that had come into existence with the Queen's appearance upon the scene. "It now comes that we must begin to move, so this world and our own will stay in harmony. The People must troop to a new hill on this earth. We must choose our destination." To Ariel she said, "Let us away. We must decide where our courts shall be for the next six turns of the moon."

Mark touched Phil's arm and pointed, and Phil saw what Mark indicated. While the humans were filthy from all the muck and rain, none of the fairies showed any trace of mud upon their bodies or clothing. Mark said, "They are illusions, in all their forms. They *are* energy beings. I wish I could know more!" He felt a deep sadness at all the unanswered questions. Then he remembered the problems still unresolved, and said, "And we must hurry, as well. I don't know how much time we have before the Magi catch up with us, and I have no doubt of what they'll do to us."

"I'm afraid you're given to an overblown sense of the dramatic, Mr. Blackman."

All eyes turned to the author of those words, a man who stepped out of the shadows on the path from the Troll Bridge. The man who emerged was attired in an expensive vicuña topcoat, trimmed with mink. He was neither young nor old, possibly thirty-nine or possibly fifty-nine, it was hard to tell. His beard was closely trimmed, in a natty fashion not widely seen since the thirties, and his hands were manicured. He wore a homburg and carried a gold-tipped walking stick in one hand. In the other he held an efficient-looking gun, pointed at Mark and Phil.

The man executed a slight bow. "Mr. Hastings?" Phil nodded. "My name is Anton Wycheck, Mr. Hastings." His accent was slightly Middle European. "I've come after your friend Mr. Blackman to settle a few matters."

Phil said, "Somehow, Mr. Wycheck, that doesn't surprise me in the least."

Mark said, "Hello, Anton." He said to Phil, "It was Anton I spotted in the car. Anton was one of my hosts in Germany."

"A regrettable misunderstanding, Mr. Blackman. We have since divined the truth of things. And we would have no need of that proof, in light of what I have just witnessed." To the Queen he bowed and spoke in a language completely unrecognizable to Phil. He then spoke with equal deference to Ariel.

Phil felt his boys both trembling and said, "I'd feel a whole lot easier if you'd point that thing somewhere else, Mr. Wycheck."

The man regarded the gun and put it in his pocket. "I apologize. I was uncertain what I would find here, and felt the need. I forgot I was carrying it." He then spoke in a different language, something Eastern

European, over his shoulder, and three men appeared, all dressed in black turtleneck sweaters and Levi's. Two carried the gold chest Jack had uncovered, and the third some of the robes from the secret room and a shovel. The chest was put down and the robes handed around to the four men, who changed. "We must be quick, my brothers," said Wycheck. "Midnight is upon us."

Phil glanced at the Queen, who along with her court stood silently observing the four newcomers.

"The Compact is honored," said Wycheck, turning to face the Queen. He bowed, produced a gold coin, and held it forth to be seen. It was placed in the chest, and at once one of the other men began digging, while the others stood on each side of the chest.

"The Compact is honored," she answered. "The gifts of the Magi are tokens of good faith. There was never a breach of that faith on your part. It was only a misguided one's dreams of ages long dead. We thank you for your good faith."

It was Tom who spoke next. "Stand you there, and come no closer, for all here shall go in one instant to that new place where faerie and mortal realms meet. I stand near and travel with my Queen, but you have no such wish. By yon stump is safe. Fare you well; it is close to All Saints' Morn, and we must depart."

Mark hesitated, as if the thought of so many unanswered questions was more than he could endure, but at last he simply nodded and waited.

Sean hung close to his father and looked at Patrick. His twin seemed to be more relaxed, more himself, as he also watched the spectacle of the fairy court departing.

Then Sean looked to where the adults looked. All eyes were fixed upon the Queen, who rose up, followed an instant later by Ariel. All became light, and in an instant two shimmering columns of energy pulsed in silent rhythm. All the fairies upon the hill rose into the air, and from out of the woods came others, scampering, leaping, flying, dozens and dozens to join with those upon the hill. All glowed brightly and in an instant were small pillars of energy, the tiny winged ones becoming little more than firefly lights, while the youth called Ariel was a pillar almost equal to the Queen. Then the distant bell of St. Catherine's chimed again, the tenth or eleventh—Phil had lost count. The fairies began to move in a strange ritual-like pattern around the two who were brightest. They picked up tempo, moving faster. Thomas the Rhymer stood beside the twin columns of light, unfazed by the display. Again came the chime and again the pace increased. Just before the last stroke a voice was heard. "Take not this victory for granted, mortals. Who can know what fate may allow another day?" Sean gripped his father's hand, for the voice might have been Ariel's, or it might have been the Shining Man's.

Then came the last stroke, and the light and the fairies were gone. Yet sounds filled the glade, and the Queen's aura, preventing the rain from falling, was still surrounding them all. For a long moment the humans stood in a quiet island, then it was dark.

Suddenly only Barney's flashlight illuminated the clearing as rain again fell upon them and cold wind bit at them.

Then the voice of Ariel sang out, "Your debt to me is discharged, lore keeper. May God watch over you."

With a hint of regret, mixed with humor, Mark shouted, "Farewell, merry wanderer of the night; indeed thou art a shrewd and knavish sprite!"

From thin air Ariel's shrieking laughter pealed like a small bell, then faded into silence.

Wycheck said, "Gentlemen, it is a poor night to be out in the woods. May I suggest we retire to Mr. Hastings' home? From all appearance, you have had a night of it."

They discovered Wycheck and his companions had removed their robes. "I don't suppose you'd care to fill us in on some things, Mr. Wycheck?" asked Phil.

"Only this," said the dapper stranger, his tone warm and friendly, but his eyes like nothing so much as blue flint. "The universe is a vast place, and few have an opportunity to even glimpse a portion of its true scope and nature. Of those who do, even fewer survive the experience. Simply count yourself and your family as among those very few and fortunate souls, Mr. Hastings. Put all this behind you and let it fade from memory. Should we—my associates and myself—ever discover you involved in our affairs again . . . we shall be forced to take measures." The last was said without any hostility or threat. He was simply stating facts as he saw them. "Now I suggest we return to Mrs. Hastings and your daughter and her fiancé, Mr. Hastings. I am sure they are anxious to know you are well, and your sons look in need of a hot bath and warm beds. We shall speak more when we reach your home; we have much to discuss." To Mark he said, "By the way, your associate Mr. Thieus and his lovely lady friend are also waiting there for you, Mr. Blackman."

Watching one of Wycheck's companions cover the chest with shovelfuls of dirt, Phil said, "How did you get that out of the police station?"

Mr. Wycheck motioned with his hand in a courtly gesture for Phil to precede him on the path. "As Mr. Blackman has no doubt told you, Mr. Hastings, we are well connected."

"The Magi?"

The man only smiled as he said, "We prefer to keep our identity to ourselves. Now, if you would be so kind, I think we'd best get your two tired boys home."

Phil couldn't argue with that, for both boys were almost asleep on their feet. He put a hand on each of them, relieved he could again do so, and, as Barney recovered his flashlight, took them home.

44

Gabbie nearly flew through the screen door when she heard her father's voice in the night, and Gloria was a step behind her. Sean and Patrick trudged alongside their dad, obviously exhausted. Phil and Mark spoke in quiet tones, discussing what they had encountered.

"Dad!" cried the girl. "There's these strange men with guns. . . ." Her voice trailed off as she saw Patrick. Gloria hurried and grabbed both her sons, hugging them fiercely. She couldn't stop herself from crying as she rocked back and forth, holding them tight. After a minute Patrick said, "Mom, you're squeezing the breath out of me!"

Phil felt something inside break and tears ran down his face. Nothing else could have told him that things were back to normal with his son as well as that complaint did. He realized how much he had held down his feelings over the last few weeks, and how much more he had forced his mind to accept on this wild and improbable night. Now he felt his knees go wobbly. To Barney and Mark he said, "Gentlemen, let me buy you a drink—if you'll take scotch, Barney, for I've no Irish."

"Whiskey's whiskey, when it comes down to it, and a guest has no right to complain over his host's hospitality. Thank you, I'll stay. But it'll be the last, for tomorrow I'm back to A.A. and once more the pledge . . . unless they come again." He glanced at Wycheck and his companions. "Assumin' there's no objections?"

Mark shook his head. He knew how Barney felt. "Come on, Phil.

Pour us all a round." Looking at the dapper man, he said, "Care to join us, Anton?"

The man only smiled and said, "No, my associates and I will only stay a short time." But he followed them into the house. The other three men went around the outside of the house, toward the front porch. Phil noticed they were chanting softly, some odd ritualistic thing, and for an instant something in the words seemed to pull at his mind. He shrugged off the odd sensation and led the others into the house.

As Phil entered the living room, he found Jack, Gary, and his girlfriend Ellen sitting on the couch, with two men, like the others in black turtleneck shirts and blue jeans, standing nearby. They appeared relaxed, but it was clear that up to a few minutes before they had been standing guard. Gary rose and crossed to Mark's side, quickly speaking to him. Phil poured a round of drinks and began passing them around. Gabbie went to sit next to Jack, who looked grim-faced.

Taking a swig, Phil watched Gloria turn to Mr. Wycheck. "The boys are exhausted. Can they get baths and go to bed?"

With a smile, the man said, "By all means, Mrs. Hastings. Please, we wish to be as accommodating as possible."

Both Sean and Patrick came over and hugged their dad good night, and Gloria took them upstairs. With his wife and sons out of the room, Phil said, "So, then, Mr. Wycheck. What's in store for us?"

"Why, I wish to buy this house." Seeing Phil's face set in a grim mask, he took a check from within a coat pocket and said, "I think you'll find this a more than fair offer, Mr. Hastings."

Phil read the amount on the check and nodded. "This is twice what I paid."

"We have no desire to take advantage of your need to sell. I know you and your family need to move quickly, before the first of the year. Is there any problem?"

"No," answered Phil. "That will be ample time."

Wycheck said, "A lawyer will contact you with papers to sign, but you may cash the check now, if you like."

Phil shook his head. " 'Need to sell.' I like that. It's a nice euphemism for extortion."

"Hardly extortion, Mr. Hastings. You need to sell this house. Why, only this morning you heard from your agent that your studio wants another *Star Pirates* film. He strongly urged you to accept, since the money's too good to say no. And as Henderson Crawley has declined to direct another, they want you to direct as well." As he spoke, Phil's mind seemed filled with odd echoes, as if each word heard was instantly repeated by another voice, somewhere inside Phil's head, as if his agent's voice were saying those words. He found the sensation disconcerting, but it ended the instant Wycheck stopped speaking.

Mark said, "I thought we'd just all disappear."

"Mr. Blackman, the days where violence is required to solve problems is, alas, not yet behind us, but we do find any other means to resolve difficulties whenever possible. People of some celebrity vanishing causes too many concerns. Besides your own notoriety and that of Mr. Hastings, can you imagine the stir should the sole heir to the Larker fortune vanish without a trace? No, we try to be reasonable if at all possible. Those among our brotherhood who took a part in this unfortunate attempt to change the nature of our 'agreements' have been identified, isolated, and dealt with. Mr. Blackman, had you but stayed another day with us, you would have been given transport back here, rather than having to ride all those uncomfortable buses. You see, it was August Erhardt who was the last spy in our midst. Some of our brothers thought resuming conflict might offer opportunities for us to consolidate our already not inconsequential positions in the world, leading even, perhaps, to a unified world order. A utopian dream, not unknown in our ranks from time to time, and more appealing in the light of present world tensions. Misplaced idealism, I'm afraid. We sent word—how, you do not need to know—identifying him as one sent to rectify the situation. His death was just reward for his activities."

Mark spoke bitterly. "And what about Aggie Grant?"

"That is most regrettable," answered Wycheck, and his manner seemed sincere. "But as in all wars, the innocent perish."

Gary spoke up. "Well, how are you going to cover that up? And the business at the hospital?"

"Mrs. Grant died in an accident; that is public record. John Wilson, a transient hitchhiker from Selma, Alabama, to whom she was kind enough to offer a ride, perished with her. Mr. Wilson had no next of kin. He will be buried at public expense."

Again as he listened, Phil found himself hearing strange echoes, but this time the voice seemed to be Dr. John Latham's.

Wycheck nodded to one of the silent, black-clad men, who handed over a thick sheaf of documents in a folder. A fire had been built in the fireplace and Mr. Wycheck began tossing papers into the fire. "These records never existed. Dr. Michael Bergman of Johns Hopkins graciously came to Pittsville to try his experimental machine on a very ill young boy from a local orphanage. Unfortunately, the child died, and Dr. Bergman was unable to help. In a lovely gesture, Dr. Bergman paid for the child's cremation, and the ashes will be spread in these very woods. Also, a transient police suspect—the very man thought to have assaulted Miss Hastings two months ago—was being held under psychiatric observation by the police. He escaped tonight by attacking a nurse and two orderlies, tossing a chair through a defective safety window, and fleeing into the night. The police are now looking for him, but they will be unsuccessful in recapturing him."

Phil shook his head, as this time the echoing voice sounded like Detective Mathews. With a sigh he said, "You've made your point."

Wycheck threw the last of the papers into the fire.

He indicated a suitcase on the floor. "Those documents found in the basement will return here with whoever we send to occupy these premises, Mr. Hastings. We shall keep them until that time. I'm sure you understand."

Phil nodded. With a smile, and a salute with his cane, Wycheck said, "Our business is finished. So I will bid you all a good night."

He signaled to the men in black, one of whom picked up the suitcase, and they left. Wycheck saw himself out, while Phil looked at Mark. After a while Mark said, "It would have been a hell of a book, Phil."

"That it would have been, Mark." Phil started to laugh. "But who in the name of sanity would have believed a single word?"

Mark's expression turned less somber; after a moment he began to laugh as well. "You're probably right."

Phil heard an odd buzzing and strained to hear it. It was as if someone outside was chanting not quite audibly. He shook his head and the sound was gone.

Gloria entered. "I thought I heard someone come in!" She came and kissed Mark on the cheek. "God, I'm glad you made it back all right. You've been gone such a long time. It's almost two months!" Her expression was relaxed, though there was an air of sadness about her, but none of the frantic qualities that had lived in Gloria's face for the last few weeks were visible.

Mark and Phil exchanged glances as Gloria said, "You know, I could use a drink, too. Such terrible news about Aggie." She glanced upward. "It hit the twins harder than I thought it would. They're both simply exhausted."

Phil looked at Mark, and they both glanced at Ellen and Gary, Jack and Gabbie. Gary seemed himself, but Gabbie, Jack, and Ellen were all glassy-eyed.

Then Ellen shook her head, as if waking up, and said, "It's . . . so sad. You know, we came by to tell you we're getting married, and now that seems so inappropriate."

Gloria said, "I think Aggie would have been happy for you."

Gary, Mark, and Phil all stood still, each sharing the same thought: they're beginning to forget. Barney sat rubbing his head, as if suffering a headache. He said, "Well, thank you, Mr. Hastings, for the drink." He stood, rubbing his head again. "I think it's back to the pledge. It's taking its toll, the drink. My head's pounding like a trip-hammer." He reached down by the chair and picked up the big flashlight and said, "Sorry about the car. But we'll have another look in the morning."

Phil nodded, feeling as if something was slipping away from him. He put his thumb to his head, above the bridge of his nose, and said, "Okay, Barney, but . . . whew! Have you ever drunk something cold too fast and it shoots a pain right up here?" Gloria nodded. "Oww!"

"Well then, and it's a good night to you all, as much as it can be with such sad news about Mrs. Grant. And that poor fellow she gave a ride to. Pity such a fate."

Gloria looked at Phil, covered in grass and mud from his tussle with the Fool. "I wish you'd just left the car alone instead of crawling under it."

Phil said, "I should have, but I limped along from the kids' school to Barney's and"—he squinted, again holding his thumb to his forehead—"and we thought we'd take a look. Hell, we were going to get wet walking home anyway."

Gloria's tone was disapproving. "You should have called." She looked at Mark. "Sean wore one of Gabbie's blouses, which was bad enough in this weather. But then he got caught in a thicket and had to leave it somewhere out there. And Patrick went dressed as Puck, if you can believe it. Green leaves sewn to his underwear! Why I ever agreed to that idea I'll never know."

Jack sat on the couch, his arms tightly around him, looking pale and drawn. Phil said, "Jack, you okay?"

Jack nodded. "Yes, it's just . . . Aggie's death's hitting kind of hard." Gabbie held him close.

As Barney could be heard leaving by the back door, Mark motioned Gary to come closer. "They're all forgetting. I think we should compare notes. We might not be able to tell anyone else about any of this, but there's no law says we can't . . ."

He saw a strange expression come over Gary's face. "Any of what, Mark?"

Mark said, "Why . . . the . . ." He groped for words as thoughts seemed to leave his mind of their own volition.

Outside, a car door slammed, and Gloria said, "Who is that?" She crossed to freshen drinks for Phil and Mark.

Phil said, "Mr. Wycheck, the man who's buying the house. He

insisted on coming by and dropping off the check tonight. I told him on the phone . . ." Phil's brow contracted, as if he had a sudden headache, then he continued, ". . . it wasn't necessary, but he insisted."

Mark turned, about to say something, but his mind seemed a riot of images. He took a deep breath, feeling an instant of vertigo, then it passed. He shook it off and said, "I . . . I forgot what I was going to say." He blinked. "What's this about selling your house?"

Phil shrugged. "It's all happened pretty fast. I got a call this morning from my agent. The studio wants another *Star Pirates* film, and they want me to direct."

Gloria handed the refilled drinks to the men. "And within ten minutes, this Wycheck character calls out of the blue, saying he's interested in property around here and would we care to sell. The man's a nut. You wouldn't believe the profit we're making from the sale." She sat down on the chair Barney had vacated. "So tell us about Germany. Did you find anything?"

Mark took a drink as his headache lessened. For a moment he felt a strange itch, as if trying to remember something, then, frustrated at his inability to remember, he shoved aside the irritation. "No, still a lot of blind alleys. I think I may just have to give up on finding out anything about what the hell was going on in Germany when Kessler's dad left." His face split into a grin. "I did come across a really strange little document in"—his face clouded as he fought to remember something, then it was gone again—"Köln. I know this is going to sound too wild for belief, but it looks like the genuine article. I think I may be able to prove Atlantis *was* Crete during the Mycenaean era. So as soon as Gary and I close down our house—assuming Ellen doesn't keep him from coming with me—we're off to the Mediterranean."

Ellen, who had been sitting silently, said, "No, a working honeymoon's fine, as long as it's on a Mediterranean island!"

Gloria said, "Tell us about it!"

Outside, the man called Wycheck sat motionless as he listened to the faint words carried through the open window. In his car and the other occupied by his brethren, low chanting could be heard as ancient arts were used. Satisfied everything was as it should be, he signaled the other car to move out. Then he motioned for his driver to follow, while he rolled up the window. Slowly, almost silently, the car edged up the driveway and turned out onto the road.

EPILOGUE:
December

Patrick and Sean trudged through the woods on their way home from school as a light snow fell to melt upon the ground. It was their last day. The Christmas break was beginning, but they wouldn't be coming back. Their father had sold the house to a strange man and they were moving back to California. Their parents had flown west for two weeks in November, then returned with the news they had found a wonderful house in some town called Carpinteria. It was near Santa Barbara, Gabbie had said. Their dad would stay in L.A. during the week while he worked on his new movie, but would drive home for the weekends.

Jack had to do something about selling Aggie's house, which would take time, the boys' parents had told them. Gabbie and Jack would stay at Aggie's until Jack finished something called a defense, then they would sell the house and come to California, where they'd get married. The boys were delighted to learn that Gabbie's horse, Bumper, would be stabled at the new house until Gabbie and Jack found a home, for the Hastingses' new place had a barn, and Gabbie said they could ride him if they didn't try anything fancy, like jumping fences. Besides, their mother had hinted they might get horses of their own for Christmas.

The boys crossed the Troll Bridge without an instant's hesitation. All dread was gone, all illusion vanished. In seven months' time they had gone from having normal childhood fears to having survived a terrifying reality. Now they found no menace in the dark and felt no discomfort at confronting the unknown. They had lived through an experience that had changed their children's expectations of what the world held, and were both wiser and sadder for that change. Their school friends seemed somehow less worthy of their time, as if they were preoccupied with trivialities. Still, they found much to divert their thoughts from the events of the last seven months.

Sean took the lead as they approached their home. Since their ordeal on Halloween, Patrick no longer dominated his brother. They now treated each other as equals. Patrick knew his survival had depended on Sean, but Sean never made a point of that fact. They were closer than ever before.

Bad Luck knew it was time for school to be out and ran to meet them, while their mother stood patiently on the stoop waiting for the boys, the smell of hot cookies carried on the cold winter air. They both glanced at the top of the steps for a moment, almost expecting to see Ernie lying there in a sunny spot, exhibiting a tomcat's certainty that all is well. Had he lived, he would be oblivious to the organized confusion around him. The movers would arrive the next day, and the family was off to New York for a long weekend. Gloria and the boys would see the sights while Phil talked to his publisher on Monday, before the Christmas dead time in publishing. Then they'd be heading to their new home, in time to have Christmas with Grandma O'Brien in Glendale. The boys looked forward to that.

Sean lingered near the sunny spot and Patrick nodded understanding. A local farmer had shot a raccoon the morning after Halloween, and the destruction of dogs and cats, ducks and chickens, had halted. But both boys knew how Ernie had died. They wondered why everyone else seemed to have forgotten what had happened. Sean fingered his fairy stone, the one Barney had given him, and thought perhaps that was the reason the twins could still remember. Patrick fingered the one he wore, found after days of searching the creek bed. In silence, he nodded: *Yes, I think that's why.*

From the steps of their home—home for so short a time—they both looked back as one. The barn, the shed, the trees, all had become known to them, the alien quality they had first experienced upon arrival gone, replaced by a comfortable, familiar feeling. Now they would be leaving this place behind to move to a new one, to begin again adjusting to new surroundings, new friends, new experiences. Regarding the woods beyond the barn, they silently remembered their encounter with another race in another world. They exchange an unspoken question.

Will we ever see them again?

Then they remembered those last words, uttered by Ariel or, some-how, by the Fool: *Who can know what fate may allow another day?*

Without an answer, the boys mounted the steps. Sean followed Patrick, but glanced back, feeling a sudden chill. For a moment he couldn't tell if he felt eyes watching from the woods or if it was simply his imagination. And he couldn't be certain if it was simply the wind rustling the branches, or if the sounds of faint, boyish laughter hung for an instant on the air. Pushing aside the momentary disquiet, he turned and entered the warm kitchen.

> *If we shadows have offended,*
> *Think but this, and all is mended,*
> *That you have but slumber'd here,*
> *While these visions did appear.*
>
> Shakespeare, *A Midsummer Night's Dream*
> Act V, Scene i

ABOUT THE AUTHOR

Raymond E. Feist, who resides in San Diego, California, was born and raised in Southern California. He has worked in and around the film industry, sold cars, built and refurbished swimming pools, designed games, and served as project coordinator for a community health service and as an assistant resident dean at a California college. He is the author of a three-book fantasy series, the Riftwar Saga, comprising *Magician, Silverthorn,* and *A Darkness at Sethanon.* His most recent novel is a collaboration with Janny Wurts called *Daughter of the Empire.*